Doris Lessing

# Five
# short novels

Panther

Granada Publishing Limited
Published in 1969 by Panther Books Ltd
Frogmore, St Albans, Herts, AL2 2NF
Reprinted 1974

First published in Great Britain by
Michael Joseph Ltd 1953
Copyright © Doris Lessing 1953
Made and printed in Great Britain by
Cox & Wyman Ltd, London, Reading and Fakenham
Set in Intertype Times

To Mrs. Toni Sussman with my love

# Contents

# A Home for the Highland Cattle

# A Home for the Highland Cattle

THESE days, when people emigrate, it is not so much in search of sunshine, or food, or even servants. It is fairly safe to say that the family bound for Australia, or wherever it may be, has in its mind a vision of a nice house, or a flat, with maybe a bit of garden. I don't know how things were a hundred or fifty years ago. It seems, from books, that the colonizers and adventurers went sailing off to a new fine life, a new country, opportunities and so forth. Now all they want is a roof over their heads.

An interesting thing, this: how is it that otherwise reasonable people come to believe that this same roof, that practically vanishing commodity, is freely obtainable just by packing up and going to another country? After all, headlines like: World Housing Shortage, are common to the point of tedium; and there is not a brochure or pamphlet issued by immigration departments that does not say (though probably in small print, throwing it away, as it were) that it is undesirable to leave home, without first making sure of a place to live.

Marina Giles left England with her husband in just this frame of mind. They had been living where they could, sharing flats and baths and kitchens, for some years. If someone remarked enviously: 'They say that in Africa the sky is always blue,' she was likely to reply absentmindedly: 'Yes, and won't it be nice to have a proper house after all these years.'

They arrived in Southern Rhodesia, and there was a choice of an immigrants' camp, consisting of mud huts with a communal water supply, or a hotel; and they chose the hotel, being what are known as people of means. That is to say, they had a few hundred pounds, with which they had intended to buy a house as soon as they arrived. It was quite possible to buy a house, just as it is in England, provided one gives up all idea of buying a home one likes, and at a reasonable price. For years Marina had been inspecting houses. They fell into two groups, those she liked, and those she could afford. Now Marina was a romantic, she had not yet fallen into that passive state of mind which accepts (as nine-tenths of the population do) that one should find a corner to live, anywhere, and then arrange one's whole life around it, schooling for one's children, one's place of work, and so on. And since she refused to accept it, she had been living in extreme discomfort, exclaiming: 'Why should we spend all the capital we are ever likely to have, tying ourselves down to a place we detest!' Nothing could be more reasonable, on the face of it.

But she had not expected to cross an ocean, enter a new and indubitably romantic-sounding country, and find herself in exactly the same position.

The city, seen from the air, is half-buried in trees. Sixty years ago, this was all bare veld; and even now it appears not as if the veld encloses an area of buildings and streets, but rather as if the houses have forced themselves up, under and among the trees. Flying low over it, one sees greenness, growth, then the white flash of a high building, the fragment of a street that has no beginning nor end, for it emerges from trees, and is at once reabsorbed by them. And yet it is a large town, spreading wide and scattered, for here there is no problem of space: pressure scatters people outwards, it does not force them perpendicularly. Driving through it from suburb to suburb, is perhaps fifteen miles – some of the important cities of the world are not much less; but if one asks a person who lives there what the population is, he will say ten thousand, which is very little. Why do so small a number of people need so large a space? The inhabitant will probably shrug, for he has never wondered. The truth is that there are not ten thousand, but more likely 150,000, but the others are black, which means that they are not considered. The blacks do not so much *live* here, as squeeze themselves in as they can – all this is very confusing for the newcomer, and it takes quite a time to adjust oneself.

Perhaps every city has one particular thing by which it is known, something which sums it up, both for the people who live in it, and those who have never known it, save in books or legend. Three hundred miles South, for instance, old Lobengula's kraal had the Big Tree. Under its branches sat the betrayed, sorrowful, magnificent King in his rolls of black fat and beads and gauds, watching his doom approach in the white people's advance from the South, and dispensing life and death according to known and honoured customs. That was only sixty years ago. ...

This town has The Kopje. When the Pioneers were sent North, they were told to trek on till they reached a large and noble mountain they could not possibly mistake; and there they must stop and build their city. Twenty miles too soon, due to some confusion of mind, or perhaps to understandable exhaustion, they stopped near a small and less shapely hill. This has rankled ever since. Each year, when the ceremonies are held to honour those pioneers, and the vision of Rhodes who sent them forth, the thought creeps in that this is not really what the Founder intended. ... Standing there, at the foot of that kopje, the speech-makers say: Sixty years, look what we have accomplished in sixty years. And in the minds of the listeners springs a vision of that city we all dream of, that planned and shapely city without stain or slum – the city that could in fact have been created in those sixty years.

The town spread from the foot of this hill. Around it are the slums, the narrow and crooked streets where the coloured people eke out their short swarming lives among decaying brick and tin. Five minutes walk to one side, and the street peters out in long, soiled grass, above which a power chimney pours black smoke, and where an old petrol tin lies in a gulley, so that a diving hawk swerves away and up, squawking, scared out of his nature by a flash of sunlight. Ten minutes the other way is the business centre, the dazzling white blocks of concrete, modern buildings like modern buildings the world over. Here are the imported clothes, the glass windows full of cars from America, the neon lights, the counters full of pamphlets advertising flights Home – wherever one's home might be. A few blocks further on, and the business part of the town is left behind. This was once the smart area. People who have grown with the city will drive through here on a Sunday afternoon, and, looking at the bungalows raised on their foundations and ornamented with iron scrollwork will say: In 1910 there was nothing beyond this house but bare veld.

Now, however, there are more houses, small and ugly houses, until all at once we are in the 'thirties, with tall houses eight to a block, like very big soldiers standing to attention in a small space. The verandahs have gone. Tiny balconies project like eyelids, the roofs are like bowler hats, rimless. Exposed to the blistering sun, these houses crowd together without invitation to shade or coolness, for they were not planned for this climate, and until the trees grow, and the creepers spread, they are extremely uncomfortable. (Though, of course, very smart.) Beyond these? The veld again, wastes of grass clotted with the dung of humans and animals, a vlei that is crossed and criss-crossed by innumerable footpaths where the natives walk in the afternoons from suburb to suburb, stopping to snatch a mouthful of water in cupped palms from potholes filmed with irridescent oil, for safety against mosquitoes.

Over the vlei (which is rapidly being invaded by building, so that soon there will be no open spaces left) is a new suburb. Now, this is something really quite different. Where the houses, only twenty minutes walk away, stood eight to a block, now there are twenty, tiny, flimsy little houses, and the men who planned them had in mind the cheap houses along the ribbon roads of England. Small patches of roofed cement, with room, perhaps, for a couple of chairs, call themselves verandahs. There is a hall a couple of yards square – for otherwise where should one hang one's hat? Each little house is divided into rooms so small that there is no space to move from one wall to the other without circling a table or stumbling over a chair. And white walls, glaring white walls, so that one's eyes turn in relief to the trees.

The trees – these houses are intolerable unless foliage softens and hides them. Any new owner, moving in, says wistfully: It won't be so bad when the shrubs grow up. And they grow very quickly. It is an extraordinary thing that this town, which must be one of the most graceless and inconvenient in existence, considered simply as an association of streets and buildings, is so beautiful that no one fails to fall in love with it at first sight. Every street is lined and double-lined with trees, every house screened with brilliant growth. It is a city of gardens.

Marina was at first enchanted. Then her mood changed. For the only houses they could afford were in those mass-produced suburbs, that were spreading like measles as fast as materials could be imported to build them. She said to Philip: 'In England, we did not buy a house because we did not want to live in a suburb. We uproot ourselves, come to a reputedly exotic and wild country, and the only place we can afford to live is another suburb. I'd rather be dead.'

Philip listened. He was not as upset as she was. They were rather different. Marina was that liberally-minded person produced so plentifully in England during the 'thirties, while Philip was a scientist, and put his faith in techniques, rather than in the inherent decency of human beings. He was, it is true, in his own way an idealist, for he had come to this continent in a mood of fine optimism. England, it seemed to him, did not offer opportunities to young men equipped, as he was, with enthusiasm and so much training. Things would be different overseas. All that was necessary was a go-ahead Government prepared to vote sufficient money to Science – this was just common sense. (Clearly, a new country was likely to have more common sense than an old one.) He was prepared to make gardens flourish where deserts had been. Africa appeared to him eminently suitable for this treatment; and the more he saw of it, those first few weeks, the more enthusiastic he became.

But he soon came to understand that in the evenings, when he propounded these ideas to Marina, her mind was elsewhere. It seemed to him bad luck that they should be in this hotel, which was uncomfortable, with bad food, and packed by fellow-immigrants all desperately searching for the legendary roof. But a house would turn up sooner or later – he had been convinced of this for years. He would not have objected to buying one of those suburban houses. He did not like them, certainly, but he knew quite well that it was not the house, as such, that Marina revolted against. Ah, this feeling we all have about the suburbs! How we dislike the thought of being just like the fellow next door! Bad luck, when the whole world rapidly fills with suburbs, for what is a British Colony but a sort of highly-flavoured suburb to England itself? Somewhere in the back of Marina's mind had been a vision of herself and Philip living in a group of amiable people, pleasantly interested in the arts, who read the *New Statesman* week by week, and held that discreditable phenomena like the colour bar, and the black-white struggle could be solved by sufficient good-will . . . a delightful picture.

Temporarily Philip turned his mind from thoughts of blossoming deserts, and so on, and tried another approach. Perhaps they could buy a house through one of the Schemes for Immigrants? He would return from this Housing Board or that, and say in a worried voice: 'There isn't a hope unless one has three children.' At this, Marina was likely to become depressed; for she still held the old-fashioned view that before one has children, one should have a house to put them in.

'It's all very well for you,' said Marina. 'As far as I can see, you'll be spending half your time gallivanting in your lorry from one end of the country to the other, visiting native reserves and having a lovely time. I don't *mind*, but I have to make some sort of life for myself while you do it.' Philip looked rather guilty; for in fact he was away three or four days a week, on trips with fellow experts, and Marina would be very often left alone.

'Perhaps we could find somewhere temporary, while we wait for a house to turn up?' he suggested.

This offered itself quite soon. Philip heard from a man he met casually that there was a flat available for three months, but he wouldn't swear to it, because it was only an overheard remark at a sundowner party – Philip followed the trail, clinched the deal and returned to Marina. 'It's only for three months,' he comforted her.

138 Cecil John Rhodes Vista was in that part of the town built before the sudden expansion in the 'thirties. These were all old houses, unfashionable, built to no imported recipe, but according to the whims of the first owners. On one side of 138 was a house whose roof curved down, Chinese fashion, built on a platform for protection against ants, with wooden steps. Its walls were of wood, and it was possible to hear feet tramping over the wooden floors even in the street outside. The other neighbour was a house whose walls were invisible under a mass of golden shower – thick yellow clusters, like smoky honey, dripped from roof to ground. The houses opposite were hidden by massed shrubs.

From the street, all but the roof of 138 was screened by a tall and straggling hedge. The sidewalks were of dusty grass, scattered with faggots of dogs' dirt, so that one had to walk carefully. Outside the gate was a great clump of bamboo reaching high into the sky, and all the year round weaver-birds' nests, like woven-grass cricket balls, dangled there bouncing and swaying in the wind. Near it reached the angled brown sticks of the frangipani, breaking into white and creamy pink, as if a young coloured girl held armfuls of blossom. The street itself was double-lined with trees, first jacarandah, fine green lace against the blue sky, and behind heavy dark masses of the cedrilatoona. All the way down the street were bursts of colour, a drape of purple bougain-villaea, the sparse scarlet flowers of the hibiscus. It was very beautiful, very peaceful.

Once inside the unkempt hedge, 138 was exposed as a shallow brick building, tin-roofed, like an elongated barn, that occupied the centre of two building stands, leaving plenty of space for front and back yards. It had a history. Some twenty years back, some enterprising businessman had built the place, ignoring every known rule of hygiene, in the interests of economy. By the time the local authorities had come to notice its unfitness to exist, the roof was on. There followed a series of court cases. An exhausted judge had finally remarked that there was a housing shortage; and on this basis the place was allowed to remain.

It was really eight semi-detached houses, stuck together in such a way that standing before the front door of any one, it was possible to see clear through the two rooms which composed each, to the back yard, where washing flapped over the woodpile. A verandah enclosed the front of the building: eight short flights of steps, eight front doors, eight windows – but these windows illuminated the front rooms only. The back room opened into a porch that was screened in by dull green mosquito gauze; and in this way the archi-tect had achieved the really remarkable feat of producing, in a country continually drenched by sunlight, rooms in which it was necessary to have the lights burning all day.

The back yard, a space of bare dust enclosed by parallel hibiscus hedges, was a triumph of individualism over com-munal living. Eight separate wood piles, eight clothes-lines, eight short paths edged with brick leading to the eight lavatories that were built side by side like segments of chocolate, behind an enclosing tin screen: the locks (and therefore the keys) were identical, for the sake of cheapness, a system which guaranteed strife among the inhabitants. On either side of the lavatories were two rooms, built as a unit. In these four rooms lived eight native servants. At least, officially there were eight, in practice far more.

When Marina, a woman who took her responsibilities seriously, as has been indicated, looked inside the room which her servant shared with the servant from next door, she exclaimed helplessly: 'Dear me, how awful!' The room was very small. The brick walls were unplastered, the tin of the roof bare, focusing the sun's intensity inwards all day, so that even while she stood on the threshold, she began to feel a little faint, because of the enclosed heat. The floor was cement, and the blankets that served as beds lay directly on it. No cupboards or shelves: these were substituted by a string stretching from corner to corner. Two small, high windows, whose glass was cracked and pasted with paper. On the walls were pictures of the English royal family, torn out of illustrated magazines, and of various female film stars, mostly unclothed.

'Dear me,' said Marina again, vaguely. She was feeling very guilty, because of this squalor. She came out of the room with relief, wiping the sweat from her face, and looked around the yard. Seen from the back, 138 Cecil John Rhodes Vista was undeniably picturesque. The yard, enclosed by low, scarlet-flowering hibiscus hedges, was of dull red earth; the piles of grey wood were each surrounded by a patch of scattered chips, yellow, orange, white. The colourful washing lines swung and danced. The servants, in their crisp white, leaned on their axes, or gossiped. There was a little black nurse-girl seated on one of the logs, under a big tree, with a white child in her arms. A delightful scene; it would have done as it was for the opening number of a musical comedy. Marina turned her back on it; and with her stern reformer's eye looked again at the end of the yard. In the spaces between the lavatories and the servants' rooms stood eight rubbish cans, each covered by its cloud of flies, and exuding a stale, sour smell. She walked through them into the sanitary lane. Now, if one drives down the streets of such a city, one sees the trees, the gardens, the flowering hedges; the streets form neat squares. Squares (one might suppose) filled with blossoms and greenness, in which the houses are charmingly arranged. But each block is divided down the middle by a sanitary lane, a dust lane, which is lined by rubbish cans, and in this the servants have their social life. Here they go for a quick smoke, in the middle of the day's work; here they meet their friends, or flirt with the women who sell vegetables. It is as if, between each of the streets of the white man's city, there is a hidden street, ignored, forgotten. Marina, emerging into it, found it swarming with gossiping and laughing natives. They froze, gave her a long suspicious stare, and all at once seemed to vanish, escaping into their respective back yards. In a moment she was alone.

She walked slowly back across the yard to her back door, picking her way among the soft litter from the wood piles, ducking her head under the flapping clothes. She was watched, cautiously, by the servants, who were suspicious of this sudden curiosity about their way of life – experience had taught them to be suspicious. She was watched, also, by several of the women, through their kitchen windows. They saw a small Englishwoman, with a neat and composed body, pretty fair hair, and a pink and white face under a large straw hat, which she balanced in position with a hand clothed in a white glove. She moved delicately and with obvious distaste through the dust, as if at any moment she might take wings and fly away altogether.

When she reached her back steps, she stopped and called: 'Charlie! Come here a moment, please.' It was a high voice, a little querulous. When they heard the accents of that voice, saw the white glove, and noted that *please* the watching women found all their worst fears confirmed.

A young African emerged from the sanitary lane where he had been gossiping (until interrupted by Marina's appearance) with some passing friends. He ran to his new mistress. He wore white shorts, a scarlet American-style shirt, tartan socks which were secured by mauve suspenders, and white tennis shoes. He stopped before her with a polite smile, which almost at once spread into a grin of pure friendliness. He was an amiable and cheerful young man by temperament. This was Marina's first morning in her new home, and she was already conscious of the disproportion between her strong pity for her servant, and that inveterately cheerful face.

She did not, of course, speak any native language, but Charlie spoke English.

'Charlie, how long have you been working here?'

'Two years, madam.'

'Where do you come from?'

'Madam?'

'Where is your home?'

'Nyasaland.'

'Oh.' For this was hundreds of miles North.

'Do you go home to visit your family?'

'Perhaps this year, madam.'

'I see. Do you like it here?'

'Madam?' A pause; and he involuntarily glanced back over the rubbish cans at the sanitary lane. He hoped that his friends, who worked on the other side of the town, and whom he did not often see, would not get tired of waiting for him. He hoped, too, that this new mistress (whose politeness to him he did not trust) was not going to choose this moment to order him to clean the silver or do the washing. He continued to grin, but his face was a little anxious, and his eyes rolled continually backwards at the sanitary lane.

'I hope you will be happy working for me,' said Marina.

'Oh, yes, madam,' he said at once, disappointedly; for clearly she was going to tell him to work.

'If there is anything you want, you must ask me. I am new to the country, and I may make mistakes.'

He hesitated, handling the words in his mind. But they were difficult, and he let them slip. He did not think in terms of countries, of continents. He knew the white man's town – this town. He knew the veld. He knew the village from which he came. He knew, from his educated friends, that there was 'a big water' across which the white men came in ships: he had seen pictures of ships in old magazines, but this 'big water' was confused in his mind with the great lake in his own country. He understood that these white people came from places called England, Germany, Europe, but these were names to him. Once, a friend of his who had been three years to a mission school, had said that Africa was one of several continents, and had shown him a tattered sheet of paper – one half of the map of the world – saying: Here is Africa, here is England, here is India. He pointed out Nyasaland, a tiny strip of country, and Charlie felt confused and diminished, for Nyasaland was what he knew, and it seemed to him so vast. Now, when Marina used the phrase 'this country' Charlie saw, for a moment, this flat piece of paper, tinted pink and green and blue – the world. But from the sanitary lane came shouts of laughter – again he glanced anxiously over his shoulder; and Marina was conscious of a feeling remarkably like irritation. 'Well, you may go,' she said formally; and saw his smile flash white right across his face. He turned, and ran back across the yard like an athlete, clearing the woodpile, then the rubbish cans, in a series of great bounds, and vanished behind the lavatories. Marina went inside her 'flat' with what was, had she known it, an angry frown. 'Disgraceful,' she muttered, including in this condemnation the bare room in which this man was expected to fit his life, the dirty sanitary lane bordered with stinking rubbish cans, and also his unreasonable cheerfulness.

Inside, she forgot him in her own discomfort. It was a truly shocking place. The two small rooms were so made that the interleading door was in the centre of the wall. They were more like passages than rooms. She switched on the light in what would be the bedroom, and put her hands to her cheek, for it stung where the sun had caught her unaccustomed skin through the chinks of the straw of her hat. The furniture was really beyond description! Two iron bedsteads, on either side of the door, a vast chocolate-brown wardrobe, whose door would not properly shut, one dingy straw mat that slid this way and that over the slippery boards as one walked on it. And the front room! If possible, it was even worse. An enormous cretonne-covered sofa, like a solidified flower bed, a hard and shiny table stuck in the middle of the floor, so that one must walk carefully around it, and four straight, hard chairs, ranged like soldiers against the wall. And the pictures – she did not know such pictures still existed. There was a desert scene, done in coloured cloth, behind glass; a motto in woven straw, also framed in glass, saying: '*Welcome all who come in here, Good luck to you and all good cheer.*'

There was also a very large picture of highland cattle. Half a dozen of these shaggy and ferocious creatures glared down at her from where they stood knee-deep in sunset-tinted pools. One might imagine that pictures of highland cattle no longer existed outside of Victorian novels, or remote suburban boarding-houses – but no, here they were. Really, why bother to emigrate?

She almost marched over and wrenched that picture from the wall. A curious inhibition prevented her. It was, though she did not know it, the spirit of the building. Some time later she heard Mrs. Black, who had been living for years in the next flat with her husband and three children, remark grimly: 'My front door handle has been stuck for weeks, but I'm not going to mend it. If I start doing the place up, it means I'm here for ever.' Marina recognized her own feeling when she heard these words. It accounted for the fact that while the families here were all respectable, in the sense that they owned cars, and could expect a regular monthly income, if one looked through the neglected hedge it was impossible not to conclude that every person in the building was born sloven or slut. No one really lived here. They might have been here for years, without prospect of anything better, but they did not live here.

There was one exception, Mrs. Pond, who painted her walls and mended what broke. It was felt she let everyone else down. In front of *her* steps a narrow path edged with brick led to her segment of yard, which was perhaps two feet across, in which lilies and roses were held upright by trellis work, like a tall, green sandwich standing at random in the dusty yard.

Marina thought: Well what's the point? I'm not going to *live* here. The picture could stay. Similarly, she decided there was no sense in unpacking her nice curtains or her books. And the furniture might remain as it was, for it was too awful to waste effort on it. Her thoughts returned to the servants' rooms at the back: it was a disgrace. The whole system was disgraceful. . . .

At this point, Mrs. Pond knocked perfunctorily and entered. She was a short, solid woman, tied in at the waist, like a tight sausage, by the string of her apron. She had hard red cheeks, a full, hard bosom, and energetic red hands. Her eyes were small and inquisitive. Her face was ill-tempered, perhaps because she could not help knowing she was disliked. She was used to the disapproving eyes of her fellow tenants, watching her attend to her strip of 'garden'; or while she swept the narrow strip across the back yard that was her path from the back door to her lavatory. There she stood, every morning, among the washing and the wood-piles, wearing a pink satin dressing-gown trimmed with swansdown, among the clouds of dust stirred up by her yard broom, returning defiant glances for the disapproving ones; and later she would say: 'Two rooms is quite enough for a woman by herself. I'm quite satisfied.'

She had no right to be satisfied, or at any rate, to say so. . . .

But for a woman contented with her lot, there was a look in those sharp eyes which could too easily be diagnosed as envy; and when she said, much too sweetly: 'You are an old friend of Mrs. Skinner, maybe?' Marina recognized, with the exhaustion that comes to everyone who has lived too long in overfull buildings, the existence of conspiracy. 'I have never met Mrs. Skinner,' she said briefly. 'She said she was coming here this morning, to make arrangements.'

Now, arrangements had been made already, with Philip; and Marina knew Mrs. Skinner was coming to inspect herself; and this thought irritated her.

'She is a nice lady,' said Mrs. Pond. 'She's my friend. We two have been living here longer than anyone else.' Her voice was sour. Marina followed the direction of her eyes, and saw a large white door set into the wall. A built-in cupboard, in fact. She had already noted that cupboard as the only sensible amenity the 'flat' possessed.

'That's a nice cupboard,' said Mrs. Pond.

'Have all the flats got built-in cupboards?'

'Oh, no. Mrs. Skinner had this put in special last year. She paid for it. Not the landlord. You don't catch the landlord paying for anything.'

'I see,' said Marina.

'Mrs. Skinner promised me this flat,' said Mrs. Pond.

Martha made no reply. She looked at her wrist-watch. It was a beautiful gesture; she even felt a little guilty because of the pointedness of it; but Mrs. Pond promptly said :'It's eleven o'clock. The clock just struck.'

'I must finish the unpacking,' said Marina.

Mrs. Pond seated herself on the flowery sofa, and remarked: 'There's always plenty to do when you move in. That cupboard will save you plenty of space. Mrs. Skinner kept her linen in it. I was going to put all my clothes in. You're Civil Service, so I hear?'

'Yes,' said Marina. She could not account for the grudging tone of that last, apparently irrelevant question. She did not know that in this country the privileged class was the Civil Service, or considered to be. No aristocracy, no class distinctions – but alas, one must have something to hate, and the Civil Service does as well as anything. She added: 'My husband chose this country rather than the Gold Coast, because it seems the climate is better, even though the pay is bad.'

This remark was received with the same sceptical smile that she would have earned in England had she been tactless enough to say to her charwoman: Death duties spell the doom of the middle classes.

'You have to be in the Service to get what's going,' said Mrs. Pond, with what she imagined to be a friendly smile. 'The Service gets all the plums.' And she glanced at the cupboard.

'I think,' said Marina icily, 'that you are under some misapprehension. My husband happened to hear of this flat by chance.'

'There were plenty of people waiting for this flat,' said Mrs. Pond reprovingly. 'The lady next door, Mrs. Black, would have been glad of it. And she's got three children, too. You have no children, perhaps?'

'Mrs. Pond, I have no idea at all why Mrs. Skinner gave us this flat when she had promised it to Mrs. Black. . . .'

'Oh, no, she had promised it to me. It was a faithful promise.'

At this moment another lady entered the room without knocking. She was an ample, middle-aged person, in tight corsets, with rigidly-waved hair, and a sharp, efficient face that was now scarlet from heat. She said peremptorily: 'Excuse me for coming in without knocking, but I can't get used to a stranger being here when I've lived here so long.' Suddenly she saw Mrs. Pond, and at once stiffened into aggression. 'I see you have already made friends with Mrs. Pond,' she said, giving that lady a glare.

Mrs. Pond was standing, hands on hips, in the traditional attitude of combat; but she squeezed a smile on to her face and said: 'I'm making acquaintance.'

'Well,' said Mrs. Skinner, dismissing her, 'I'm going to discuss business with my tenant.'

Mrs. Pond hesitated. Mrs. Skinner gave her a long, quelling stare. Mrs. Pond slowly deflated, and went to the door. From the verandah floated back the words: 'When people make promises, they should keep them, that's what I say, instead of giving it to people new to the country, and civil servants. . . .'

Mrs. Skinner waited until the loud and angry voice faded, and then said briskly: 'If you take my advice, you'll have nothing to do with Mrs. Pond, she's more trouble than she's worth.'

Marina now understood that she owed this flat to the fact that this highly-coloured lady decided to let it to a stranger simply in order to spite all her friends in the building who hoped to inherit that beautiful cupboard, if only for three months. Mrs. Skinner was looking suspiciously around her; she said at last: 'I wouldn't like to think my things weren't looked after.'

'Naturally not,' said Marina politely.

'When I spoke to your husband we were rather in a hurry, I hope you will make yourself comfortable, but I don't want to have anything altered.'

Marina maintained a polite silence.

Mrs. Skinner marched to the inbuilt cupboard, opened it, and found it empty. 'I paid a lot of money to have this fitted,' she said in an aggrieved voice.

'We only came in yesterday,' said Marina. 'I haven't unpacked yet.'

'You'll find it very useful,' said Mrs. Skinner. 'I paid for it myself. Some people would have made allowances in the rent.'

'I think the rent is quite high enough,' said Marina, joining battle at last.

Clearly, this note of defiance was what Mrs. Skinner had been waiting for. She made use of the familiar weapon: 'There are plenty of people who would have been glad of it, I can tell you.'

'So I gather.'

'I could let it tomorrow.'

'But,' said Marina, in that high formal voice, 'you have in fact let it to us, and the lease has been signed, so there is no more to be said, is there?'

Mrs. Skinner hesitated, and finally contented herself by repeating: 'I hope my furniture will be looked after. I said in the lease nothing must be altered.'

Suddenly Marina found herself saying: 'Well, I shall of course move the furniture to suit myself, and hang my own pictures.'

'This flat is let furnished, and I'm very fond of my pictures.'

'But you will be away, won't you?' This, a sufficiently crude way of saying: 'But it is we who will be looking at the pictures, and not you,' misfired completely, for Mrs. Skinner merely said: 'Yes, I like my pictures, and I don't like to think of them being packed.'

Marina looked at the highland cattle and, though not half an hour before she had decided to leave it, said now: 'I should like to take that one down.'

Mrs. Skinner clasped her hands together before her, in a pose of simple devotion, compressed her lips, and stood staring mournfully up at the picture. 'That picture means a lot to me. It used to hang in the parlour when I was a child, back Home. It was my granny's picture first. When I married Mr. Skinner, my mother packed it and sent it especial over the sea, knowing how I was fond of it. It's moved with me everywhere I've been. I wouldn't like to think of it being treated bad, I wouldn't really.'

'Oh, very well,' said Marina, suddenly exhausted. What, after all, did it matter?

Mrs. Skinner gave her a doubtful look: was it possible she had won her point so easily? 'You must keep an eye on Charlie,' she went on. 'The number of times I've told him he'd poke his broom-handle through that picture. . . .'

Hope flared in Marina. There was an extraordinary amount of glass. It seemed that the entire wall was surfaced by angry, shaggy cattle. Accidents did happen. . . .

'You must keep an eye on Charlie, anyway. He never does a stroke more than he has to. He's bred bone lazy. You'd better keep an eye on the food too. He steals. I had to have the police to him only last month, when I lost my garnet brooch. Of course he swore he hadn't taken it, but I've never laid my hands on it since. My husband gave him a good hiding, but Master Charlie came up smiling, as usual.'

Marina, revolted by this tale, raised her eyebrows disapprovingly. 'Indeed?' she said, in her coolest voice.

Mrs. Skinner looked at her, as if to say: 'What are you making that funny face for?' She remarked: 'They're all born thieves and liars. You shouldn't trust them further than you can kick them. I'm warning you. Of course, you're new here. Only last week a friend was saying, I'm surprised at you letting to people just from England, they always spoil the servants, with their ideas, and I said: 'Oh, Mr. Giles is a sensible man, I trust him.' This last was said pointedly.

'I don't think,' remarked Marina coldly, 'that you would be well-advised to trust my husband to give people "hidings".' She delicately isolated this word. 'I rather feel, in similar circumstances, that even if he did, he would first make sure whether the man had, in fact, stolen the brooch.'

Mrs. Skinner disentangled this sentence and in due course gave Marina a distrustful stare. 'Well,' she said, 'it's too late now, and everyone has his way, but of course this is my furniture, and if it is stolen or damaged, you are responsible.'

'That, I should have thought, went without saying,' said Marina.

They shook hands, with formality, and Mrs. Skinner went out. She returned from the verandah twice, first to say that Marina must not forget to fumigate the native quarters once a month if she didn't want livestock brought into her own flat . . . ('Not that I care if they want to live with lice, dirty creatures, but you have to protect yourself . . .') and the second time to say that after you've lived in a place for years, it was hard to leave it, even for a holiday, and she was really regretting the day she let it at all. She gave Marina a final accusing and sorrowful look, as if the flat had been stolen from her, and this time finally departed. Marina was left, in a mood of defiant anger, looking at the highland cattle picture, which had assumed, during this exchange, the look of a battleground. 'Really,' she said aloud to herself, 'Really! One might have thought that one would be entitled to pack away a picture, if one rents a place. . . .'

Two days later she got a note from Mrs. Skinner, saying that she hoped Marina would be happy in the flat, she must remember to keep an eye on Mrs. Pond, who was a real trouble-maker, and she must remember to look after the picture – Mrs. Skinner positively could not sleep for worrying about it.

Since Marina had decided she was not living here, there was comparatively little unpacking to be done. Things were stored. She had more than ever the appearance of a migrating bird who dislikes the twig it has chosen to alight on, but is rather too exhausted to move to another.

But she did read the advertisement columns every day, which were exactly like those in the papers back home. The *accommodation wanted* occupied a full column, while the *accommodation offered* usually did not figure at all. When houses were advertised they usually cost between five and twelve thousand – Marina saw some of them. They were very beautiful; if one had five thousand pounds, what a happy life one might lead – but the same might be said of any country. She also paid another visit to one of the new suburbs, and returned shuddering. 'What!' she exclaimed to Philip. 'Have we emigrated in order that I may spend the rest of life gossiping and taking tea with women like Mrs. Black and Mrs. Skinner?'

'Perhaps they aren't all like that,' he suggested absent-mindedly. For he was quite absorbed in his work. This country was fascinating! He was spending his days in his Government lorry, rushing over hundreds of miles of veld, visiting native reserves and settlements. Never had soil been so misused! Thousands of acres of it, denuded, robbed, fit for nothing, cattle and human beings crowded together – the solution, of course, was perfectly obvious. All one had to do was – and if the Government had any sense—

Marina understood that Philip was acclimatized. One does not speak of the 'Government' with that particular mixture of affection and exasperation unless one feels at home. But she was not at all at home. She found herself playing with the idea of buying one of those revolting little houses. After all, one has to live somewhere. . . .

Almost every morning, in 138, one might see a group of women standing outside one or other of the flats, debating how to rearrange the rooms. The plan of the building being so eccentric, no solution could possibly be satisfactory, and as soon as everything had been moved around, it was bound to be just as uncomfortable as before. 'If I move the bookcase behind the door, then perhaps . . .' Or: 'It might be better if I put it into the bathroom. . . .'

The problem was: Where should one eat? If the dining-table was in the front room, then the servant had to come through the bedroom with the food. On the other hand, if one had the front room as bedroom, then visitors had to walk through it to the living-room. Marina kept Mrs. Skinner's arrangement. On the back porch, which was the width of a passage, stood a collapsible card-table. When it was set up, Philip sat crouched under the window that opened inwards over his head, while Marina shrank sideways into the bathroom door as Charlie came past with the vegetables. To serve food, Charlie put on a starched white coat, red fez, and white cotton gloves. In between courses he stood just behind them, in the kitchen door, while Marina and Philip ate in state, if discomfort.

Marina found herself becoming increasingly sensitive to what she imagined was his attitude of tolerance. It seemed ridiculous that the ritual of soup, fish and sweet, silver and glass and fish-knives, should continue under such circumstances. She began to wonder how it all appeared to this young man, who, as soon as their meal was finished, took an enormous pot of mealie porridge off the stove and retired with it to his room, where he shared it (eating with his fingers and squatting on the floor) with the servant from next door, and any of his friends or relatives who happened to be out of work at the time.

That no such thoughts entered the heads of the other inhabitants was clear; and Marina could understand how necessary it was to banish them as quickly as possible. On the other hand . . .

There was something absurd in a system which allowed a healthy young man to spend his life in her kitchen, so that she might do nothing. Besides, it was more trouble than it was worth. Before she and Philip rose, Charlie walked around the outside of the building, and into the front room, and cleaned it. But as the wall was thin and he energetic, they were awakened every morning by the violent banging of his broom and the scraping of furniture. On the other hand, if it were left till they woke up, where should Marina sit while he cleaned it? On the bed, presumably, in the dark bedroom, till he had finished? It seemed to her that she spent half her time arranging her actions so that she might not get in Charlie's way while he cleaned or cooked. But she had learned better than to suggest doing her own work. On one of Mrs. Pond's visits, she had spoken with disgust of certain immigrants from England, who had so far forgotten what was due to their position as white people, as to dispense with servants. Marina felt it was hardly worth while upsetting Mrs. Pond for such a small matter. Particularly, of course, as it was only for three months. . . .

But upset Mrs. Pond she did, and almost immediately.

When it came to the end of the month, when Charlie's wages were due, and she laid out the twenty shillings he earned, she was filled with guilt. She really could not pay him such an idiotic sum for a whole month's work. But were twenty-five shillings, or thirty, any less ridiculous? She paid him twenty-five, and saw him beam with amazed surprise. He had been planning to ask for a rise, since this woman was easy-going, and he naturally optimistic; but to get a rise without asking for it, and then a full five shillings! Why, it had taken him three months of hard bargaining with Mrs. Skinner to get raised from seventeen and sixpence to nineteen shillings. 'Thank you, madam,' he said hastily; grabbing the money as if at any moment she might change her mind and take it back. Later that same day, she saw that he was wearing a new pair of crimson satin garters, and felt rather annoyed. Surely those five shillings might have been more sensibly spent? What these unfortunate people needed was an education in civilized values – but before she could pursue the thought, Mrs. Pond entered, looking aggrieved.

It appeared that Mrs. Pond's servant had also demanded a rise, from his nineteen shillings. If Charlie could earn twenty-five shillings, why not he? Marina understood that Mrs. Pond was speaking for all the women in the building.

'You shouldn't spoil them,' she said. 'I know you are from England, and all that, but . . .'

'It seems to me they are absurdly underpaid,' said Marina.

'Before the war they were lucky to get ten bob. They're never satisfied.'

'Well, according to the cost-of-living index, the value of money has halved,' said Marina. But as even the Government had not come to terms with this official and indisputable fact, Mrs. Pond could not be expected to, and she said crossly: 'All you people are the same, you come here with your fancy ideas.'

Marina was conscious that every time she left her rooms, she was followed by resentful eyes. Besides, she was feeling a little ridiculous. Crimson satin garters, really!

She discussed the thing with Philip, and decided that payment in kind was more practical. She arranged that Charlie should be supplied, in addition to a pound of meat twice a week, with vegetables. Once again Mrs. Pond came on a deputation of protest. All the natives in the building were demanding vegetables. 'They aren't used to it,' she complained. 'Their stomachs aren't like ours. They don't need vegetables. You're just putting ideas into their heads.'

'According to the regulations,' Marina pointed out in that high clear voice, 'natives should be supplied with vegetables.'

'Where did you get that from?' said Mrs. Pond suspiciously.

Marina produced the regulations, which Mrs. Pond read in grim silence. 'The Government doesn't have to pay for it,' she pointed out, very aggrieved. And then, 'They're getting out of hand, that's what it is. There'll be trouble, you mark my words. . . .'

Marina completed her disgrace on the day when she bought a second-hand iron bedstead and installed it in Charlie's room. That her servant should have to sleep on the bare cement floor, wrapped in a blanket, this she could no longer tolerate. As for Charlie, he accepted his good fortune fatalistically. He could not understand Marina. She appeared to feel guilty about telling him to do the simplest thing, such as clearing away cobwebs he had forgotten. Mrs. Skinner would have docked his wages, and Mr. Skinner cuffed him. This woman presented him with a new bed on the day that he broke her best cut-glass bowl.

He bought himself some new ties, and began swaggering around the back yard among the other servants, whose attitude towards him was as one might expect: one did not expect justice from the white man, whose ways were incomprehensible, but there should be a certain proportion: why should Charlie be the one to chance on an employer who presented him with a fine bed, extra meat, vegetables, and gave him two afternoons off a week instead of one? They looked unkindly at Charlie, as he swanked across the yard in his fine new clothes; they might even shout sarcastic remarks after him. But Charlie was too good-natured and friendly a person to relish such a situation. He made a joke of it, in self-defence, as Marina soon learned.

She had discovered that there was no need to share the complicated social life of the building in order to find out what went on. If, for instance, Mrs. Pond had quarrelled with a neighbour over some sugar that had not been returned, so that all the women were taking sides, there was no need to listen to Mrs. Pond herself to find the truth. Instead, one went to the kitchen window overlooking the back yard, hid oneself behind the curtain, and peered out at the servants.

There they stood, leaning on their axes, or in the intervals of pegging the washing, a group of laughing and gesticulating men, who were creating the new chapter in that perpetually unrolling saga, the extraordinary life of the white people, their masters, in 138 Cecil John Rhodes Vista. . . .

February, Mrs. Pond's servant, stepped forward, while the others fell back in a circle around him, already grinning appreciatively. He thrust out his chest, stuck out his chin, and over a bad-tempered face he stretched his mouth in a smile so poisonously ingratiating that his audience roared and slapped their knees with delight. He was Mrs. Pond, one could not mistake it. He minced over to an invisible person, put on an attitude of supplication, held out his hand, received something in it. He returned to the centre of the circle, and looked at what he held with a triumphant smile. In one hand he held an invisible cup, with the other he spooned in invisible sugar. He was Mrs. Pond, drinking her tea, with immense satisfaction, in small and dainty sips. Then he belched, rubbed his belly, smacked his lips. Entering into the game another servant came forward, and acted a falsely amiable woman: hands on hips, the jutting elbows, the whole angry body showing indignation, but the face was smiling. February drew himself up, nodded and smiled, turned himself about, lifted something from the air behind him, and began pouring it out: sugar, one could positively hear it trickling. He took the container, and handed it proudly to the waiting visitor. But just as it was taken from him, he changed his mind. A look of agonized greed came over his face, and he withdrew the sugar. Hastily turning himself back, throwing furtive glances over his shoulder, he poured back some of the sugar, then, slowly, as if it hurt to do it, he forced himself round, held out the sugar, and again – just as it left his hand, he grabbed it and poured back just a little more. The other servants were rolling with laughter, as the two men faced each other in the centre of the yard, one indignant, but still polite, screwing up his eyes at the returned sugar, as if there were too small a quantity to be seen, while February held it out at arm's length, his face contorted with the agony it caused him to return it at all. Suddenly the two sprang together, faced each other like a pair of angry hens, and began screeching and flailing their arms.

'February!' came a shout from Mrs. Pond's flat, in her loud, shrill voice. 'February, I told you to do the ironing!'

'Madam!' said February, in his politest voice. He walked backwards to the steps, his face screwed up in a grimace of martyred suffering; as he reached the steps, his body fell into the pose of a willing servant, and he walked hastily into the kitchen, where Mrs. Pond was waiting for him.

But the other servants remained, unwilling to drop the game. There was a moment of indecision. They glanced guiltily at the back of the building: perhaps some of the other women were watching? No, complete silence. It was mid-morning, the sun poured down, the shadows lay deep under the big tree, the sap crystallized into little rivulets like burnt toffee on the wood chips, and sent a warm fragrance mingling into the odours of dust and warmed foliage. For the moment, they could not think of anything to do, they might as well go on with the wood-chopping. One yawned, another lifted his axe and let it fall into a log of wood, where it was held, vibrating. He plucked the handle, and it thrummed like a deep guitar note. At once, delightedly, the men gathered around the embedded axe. One twanged it, and the others began to sing. At first Marina was unable to make out the words. Then she heard:

> There's *man* who comes to *our* house,
> When poppa goes away,
> Poppa comes back, and ...

The men were laughing, and looking at No. 4 of the flats, where a certain lady was housed whose husband worked on the railways. They sang it again:

> There's a man who comes to this house,
> Every single day,
> The baas comes back, and
> The man goes away....

Marina found that she was angry. Really! The thing had turned into another drama. Charlie, her own servant, was driving an imaginary engine across the yard, chuff chuff, like a child, while two of the others, seated on a log of wood were – really, it was positively obscene!

Marina came away from the window, and reasoned with herself. She was using, in her mind, one of the formulae of the country: *What can one expect?*

At this moment, while she was standing beside the kitchen table, arguing with her anger, she heard the shrill cry: 'Peas! Nice potatoes! Cabbage! Ver' chip!'

Yes, she needed vegetables. She went to the back door. There stood a native woman, with a baby on her back, carefully unslinging the sacks of vegetables which she had supported over her shoulder. She opened the mouth of one, displaying the soft mass of green pea-pods.

'How much?'

'Only one sheeling,' said the woman hopefully.

'What!' began Marina, in protest; for this was twice what the shops charged. Then she stopped. Poor woman. No woman should have to carry a heavy child on her back, and great sacks of vegetables from house to house, street to street, all day – 'Give me a pound,' she said. Using a tin cup, the woman ladled out a small quantity of peas. Marina nearly insisted on weighing them; then she remembered how Mrs. Pond brought her scales out to the back door, on these occasions, shouting abuse at the vendor, if there was short weight. She took in the peas, and brought out a shilling. The woman, who had not expected this, gave Marina a considering look and fell into the pose of a suppliant. She held out her hands, palms upwards, her head bowed, and murmured: 'Present, missus, present for my baby.'

Again Marina hesitated. She looked at the woman, with her whining face and shifty eyes, and disliked her intensely. The phrase: What can one expect? came to the surface of her mind; and she went indoors and returned with sweets. The woman received them in open, humble palms, and promptly popped half into her own mouth. Then she said: 'Dress, missus?'

'No,' said Marina, with energy. Why should she?

Without a sign of disappointment, the woman twisted the necks of the sacks around her hand, and dragged them after her over the dust of the yard, and joined the group of servants who were watching this scene with interest. They exchanged greetings. The woman sat down on a log, easing her strained back, and moved the baby around under her armpit, still in its sling, so it could reach her breast. Charlie, the dandy, bent over her, and they began a flirtation. The others fell back. Who, indeed, could compete with that rainbow tie, the satin garters? Charlie was persuasive and assured, the woman bridling and laughing. It went on for some minutes until the baby let the nipple fall from its mouth. Then the woman got up, still laughing, shrugged the baby back into position in the small of her back, pulled the great sacks over one shoulder, and walked off, calling shrilly back to Charlie, so that all the men laughed. Suddenly they all became silent. The nurse-girl emerged from Mrs. Black's flat, and sauntered slowly past them. She was a little creature, a child, in a tight pink cotton dress, her hair braided into a dozen tiny plaits that stuck out all over her head, with a childish face that was usually vivacious and mischievous. But now she looked mournful. She dragged her feet as she walked past Charlie, and gave him a long reproachful look. Jealousy, thought Marina, there was no doubt of that! And Charlie was looking uncomfortable – one could not mistake that either. But surely not! Why, she wasn't old enough for this sort of thing. The phrase, *this sort of thing*, struck Marina herself as a shameful evasion, and she examined it. Then she shrugged and said to herself: All the same, where did the girl sleep? Presumably in one of these rooms, with the men of the place?

Theresa (she had been named after Saint Theresa at the mission school where she had been educated) tossed her head in the direction of the departing seller of vegetables, gave Charlie a final supplicating glance, and disappeared into the sanitary lane.

The men began laughing again, and this time the laughter was directed at Charlie, who received it grinning self-consciously.

Now February, who had finished the ironing, came from Mrs. Pond's flat and began hanging clothes over the line to air. The white things dazzled in the sun and made sharp, black shadows across the red dust. He called out to the others – what interesting events had happened since he went indoors? They laughed, shouted back. He finished pegging the clothes and went over to the others. The group stood under the big tree, talking; Marina, still watching, suddenly felt her cheeks grow hot. Charlie had separated himself off and, with a condensing, bowed movement of his body, had become the native woman, the seller of vegetables. Bent sideways with the weight of sacks, his belly thrust out to balance the heavy baby, he approached a log of wood – her own back step. Then he straightened, sprang back, stretched upwards, and pulled from the tree a frond of leaves. These he balanced on his head, and suddenly Marina saw herself. Very straight, precise, finicky, with a prim little face peering this way and that under the broad hat, hands clasped in front of her, she advanced to the log of wood and stood looking downwards.

'Peas, cabbage, potatoes,' said Charlie, in a shrill female voice.

'How much?' he answered himself, in Marina's precise, nervous voice.

'Ten sheelings a pound, missus, only ten sheelings a pound!' said Charlie, suddenly writhing on the log in an ecstasy of humility.

'How ridiculous!' said Marina, in that high, alas, absurdly high voice. Marina watched herself hesitate, her face showing mixed indignation and guilt and, finally, indecision. Charlie nodded twice, said nervously: 'Of course, but certainly.' Then, in a hurried, embarrassed way, he retreated, and came back, his arms full. He opened them and stood aside to avoid a falling shower of money. For a moment he mimed the native woman and, squatting on the ground, hastily raked in the money and stuffed it into his shirt. Then he stood up – Marina again. He bent uncertainly, with a cross, uncomfortable face, looking down. Then he bent stiffly and picked up a leaf – a single pea-pod, Marina realized – and marched off, looking at the leaf, saying: 'Cheap, very cheap!' one hand balancing the leaves on his head, his two feet set prim and precise in front of him.

As the laughter broke out from all the servants, Marina, who was not far from tears, stood by the window and said to herself: Serve you right for eavesdropping.

A clock struck. Various female voices shouted from their respective kitchens:

'February!' 'Noah!' 'Thursday!' 'Sixpence!' 'Blackbird!'

The morning lull was over. Time to prepare the midday meal for the white people. The yard was deserted, save for Theresa the nurse-girl, returning disconsolately from the sanitary lane, dragging her feet through the dust. Among the stiff quills of hair on her head she had perched a half-faded yellow flower that she had found in one of the rubbish-cans. She looked hopefully at Marina's flat for a glimpse of Charlie; then slowly entered Mrs. Black's.

It happened that Philip was away on one of his trips. Marina ate her lunch by herself, while Charlie, attired in his waiter's outfit, served her food. Not a trace of the cheerful clown remained in his manner. He appeared friendly, though nervous; at any moment, he seemed to be thinking, this strange white woman might revert to type and start scolding and shouting.

As Marina rose from the card-table, being careful not to bump her head on the window, she happened to glance out at the yard and saw Theresa, who was standing under the tree with the youngest of her charges in her arms. The baby was reaching up to play with the leaves. Theresa's eyes were fixed on Charlie's kitchen.

'Charlie,' said Marina, 'where does Theresa sleep?'

Charlie was startled. He avoided her eyes and muttered: 'I don't know, madam.'

'But you must know, surely,' said Marina, and heard her own voice climb to that high, insistent tone which Charlie had so successfully imitated.

He did not answer.

'How old is Theresa?'

'I don't know.' This was true, for he did not even know his own age. As for Theresa, he saw the spindly, little-girl body, with the sharp young breasts pushing out the pink stuff of the dress she wore; he saw the new languor of her walk as she passed him. 'She is nurse for Mrs. Black,' he said sullenly, meaning: 'Ask Mrs. Black. What's it got to do with me?'

Marina said: 'Very well,' and went out. As she did so she saw Charlie wave to Theresa through the gauze of the porch. Theresa pretended not to see. She was punishing him, because of the vegetable woman.

In the front room the light was falling full on the highland cattle, so that the glass was a square, blinding glitter. Marina shifted her seat, so that her eyes were no longer troubled by it, and contemplated those odious cattle. Why was it that Charlie, who broke a quite fantastic number of cups, saucers and vases, never – as Mrs. Skinner said he might – put that vigorously-jerking broom-handle through the glass? But it seemed he liked the picture. Marina had seen him standing in front of it, admiring it. Cattle, Marina knew from Philip, played a part in native tribal life that could only be described as religious – might it be that . . .

Some letters slapped on to the cement of the verandah, slid over its polished surface, and came to rest in the doorway. Two letters. Marina watched the uniformed postboy cycle slowly down the front of the building, flinging in the letters, eight times, slap, slap, slap, grinning with pleasure at his own skill. There was a shout of rage. One of the women yelled after him: 'You lazy black bastard, can't you even get off your bicycle to deliver the letters?' The postman, without taking any notice, cycled slowly off to the next house.

This was the hour of heat, when all activity faded into somnolence. The servants were away at the back, eating their midday meal. In the eight flats, separated by the flimsy walls which allowed every sound to be heard, the women reclined, sleeping, or lazily gossiping. Marina could hear Mrs. Pond, three rooms away, saying: 'The fuss she made over half a pound of sugar, you would think . . .'

Marina yawned. What a lazy life this was! She decided, at that moment, that she would put an end to this nonsense of hoping, year after year, for some miracle that would provide her, Marina Giles, with a nice house, a garden, and the other vanishing amenities of life. They would buy one of those suburban houses and she would have a baby. She would have several babies. Why not? Nursemaids cost practically nothing. She would become a domestic creature and learn to discuss servants and children with women like Mrs. Black and Mrs. Skinner. Why not? What had she expected? Ah, what had she not expected! For a moment she allowed herself to dream of that large house, that fine exotic garden, the free and amiable life released from the tensions and pressures of modern existence. She dreamed quite absurdly – but then, if no one dreamed these dreams, no one would emigrate, continents would remain undeveloped, and then what would happen to Charlie, whose salvation was (so the statesmen and newspapers continually proclaimed) contact with Mrs. Pond and Mrs. Skinner – white civilization, in short.

But that phrase 'white civilization' was already coming to affect Marina as violently as it affects everyone else in that violent continent. It is a phrase like 'white man's burden', 'way of life' or 'colour bar' – all of which are certain to touch off emotions better not classified. Marina was alarmed to find that these phrases were beginning to produce in her a feeling of fatigued distaste. For the liberal, so vociferously disapproving in the first six months, is quite certain to turn his back on the whole affair before the end of a year. Marina would soon be finding herself profoundly bored by politics.

But at this moment, having taken the momentous decision, she was quite light hearted. After all, the house next door to this building was an eyesore, with its corrugated iron and brick and wood flung hastily together; and yet it was beautiful, covered with the yellow and purple and crimson creepers. Yes, they would buy a house in the suburbs, shroud it with greenery, and have four children; and Philip would be perfectly happy rushing violently around the country in a permanent state of moral indignation, and thus they would both be usefully occupied.

Marina reached for the two letters, which still lay just inside the door, where they had been so expertly flung, and opened the first. It was from Mrs. Skinner, written from Cape Town, where she was, rather uneasily, it seemed, on holiday.

'I can't help worrying if everything is all right, and the furniture. Perhaps I ought to have packed away the things, because no stranger understands. I hope Charlie is not getting cheeky, he needs a firm hand, and I forgot to tell you you must deduct one shilling from his wages because he came back late one afternoon, instead of five o'clock as I said, and I had to teach him a lesson.

Yours truly,

Emily Skinner

P.S. I hope the picture is continuing all right.'

The second was from Philip.

'I'm afraid I shan't be back tomorrow as Smith suggests while we are here we might as well run over to the Nwenze reserve. It's only just across the river, about seventy miles as the crow flies, but the roads are anybody's guess, after the wet season. Spent this morning as planned, trying to persuade these blacks it is better to have one fat ox than ten all skin and bone, never seen such erosion in my life, gullies twenty feet deep, and the whole tribe will starve next dry season, but you can talk till you are blue, they won't kill a beast till they're forced, and that's what it will come to, and then imagine the outcry from the people back home. . . .'

At this point Martha remarked to herself: Well, well; and continued:

'You can imagine Screech-Jones or one of them shouting in the House: Compulsion of the poor natives. My eye. It's for their own good. Until all this mystical nonsense about cattle is driven out of their fat heads, we might as well save our breath. You should have seen where I was this morning! To get that reserve back in use, alone, would take the entire Vote this year for the whole country, otherwise the whole place will be a desert, it's all perfectly obvious, but you'll never get this damned Government to see that in a hundred years, and it'll be too late in five.

In haste,

*Phil.*

P.S. I do hope everything is all right, dear, I'll try not to be late.'

That night Marina took her evening meal early so that Charlie might finish the washing-up and get off. She was reading in the front room when she understood that her ear was straining through the noise from the wirelesses all around her for a quite different sort of music. Yes, it was a banjo, and loud singing, coming from the servant's rooms, and there was a quality in it that was not to be heard from any wireless set. Marina went through the rooms to the kitchen window. The deserted yard, roofed high with moon and stars, was slatted and barred with light from the eight back doors. The windows of the four servants' rooms gleamed dully; and from the room Charlie shared with February came laughter and singing and the thrumming of the banjo.

There's a man who comes to our house,
When poppa goes away. . . .

Marina smiled. It was a maternal smile. (As Mrs. Pond might remark, in a good mood: They are nothing but children.) She liked to think that these men were having a party. And women too: she could hear shrill female voices. How on earth did they all fit into that tiny room? As she returned through the back porch, she heard a man's voice shouting: 'Shut up there! Shut up, I say!' Mr. Black from his back porch: 'Don't make so much noise.'

Complete silence. Marina could see Mr. Black's long, black shadow poised motionless: he was listening. Marina heard him grumble: 'Can't hear yourself think with these bastards. . . .' He went back into his front room, and the sound of his heavy feet on the wood floor was absorbed by their wireless playing: I love you, Yes I do, I love you. . . . Slam! Mr. Black was in a rage.

Marina continued to read. It was not long before once more her distracted ear warned her that riotous music had begun again. They were singing: Congo Conga Conga, we do it in the Congo. . . .

Steps on the verandah, a loud knock, and Mr. Black entered.

'Mrs. Giles, your boy's gone haywire. Listen to the din.'

Marina said politely: 'Do sit down Mr. Black.'

Mr. Black who in England (from whence he had come as a child) would have been a lanky, pallid, genteel clerk, was in this country an assistant in a haberdasher's; but because of his sunfilled and energetic week-ends, he gave the impression, at first glance, of being that burly young Colonial one sees on advertisements for Empire tobacco. He was thin, bony, muscular, sunburnt; he had the free and easy Colonial manner, the back-slapping air that is always just a little too conscious. 'Look,' it seems to say, 'in this country we are all equal (among the whites, that is – that goes without saying) and I'll fight the first person who suggests anything to the contrary.' Democracy, as it were, with one eye on the audience. But alas, he was still a clerk, and felt it; and if there was one class of person he detested it was the civil servant; and if there was another, it was the person new from 'Home'.

Here they were, united in one person, Marina Giles, wife of Philip Giles, soil expert for the Department of Lands and

Afforestation, Marina, whose mere appearance acutely irritated him, every time he saw her moving delicately through the red dust, in her straw hat, white gloves and touch-me-not manner.

'I say!' he said aggressively, his face flushed, his eyes hot. 'I say, what are you going to do about it, because if you don't, I shall.'

'I don't doubt it,' said Marina precisely; 'but I really fail to see why these people should not have a party, if they choose, particularly as it is not yet nine o'clock, and as far as I know there is no law to forbid them.'

'Law!' said Mr. Black violently. 'Party! They're on our premises, aren't they? It's for us to say. Anyway, if I know anything they're visiting without passes.'

'I feel you are being unreasonable,' said Marina, with the intention of sounding mildly persuasive; but in fact her voice had lifted to that fatally querulous high note, and her face was as angry and flushed as his.

'Unreasonable! My kids can't sleep with that din.'

'It might help if you turned down your own wireless,' said Marina sarcastically.

He lifted his fists, clenching them unconsciously. 'You people . . .' he began inarticulately. 'If you were a man, Mrs. Giles, I tell you straight . . .' He dropped his fists and looked around wildly as Mrs. Pond entered, her face animated with delight in the scene.

'I see Mr. Black is talking to you about your boy,' she began, sugarily.

'And your boy too,' said Mr. Black.

'Oh, if I had a husband,' said Mrs. Pond, putting on an appearance of helpless womanhood, 'February would have got what's coming to him long ago.'

'For that matter,' said Marina, speaking with difficulty because of her loathing for the whole thing, 'I don't think you really find a husband necessary for this purpose, since it was only yesterday I saw you hitting February yourself. . . .'

'He was cheeky,' began Mrs. Pond indignantly.

Marina found words had failed her; but none were necessary for Mr. Black had gone striding out through her own bedroom, followed by Mrs. Pond, and she saw the pair of them cross the shadowy yard to Charlie's room, which was still in darkness, though the music was at a crescendo. As Mr. Black shouted: 'Come out of there, you black bastards!' the noise stopped, the door swung in, and half a dozen dark forms ducked under Mr. Black's extended arm and vanished into the sanitary lane. There was a scuffle, and Mr. Black found himself grasping, at arm's length, two people – Charlie and his own nursemaid, Theresa. He let the girl go and she ran after the others. He pushed Charlie against the wall. 'What do you mean by making all that noise when I told you not to?' he shouted.

'That's right, that's right,' gasped Mrs. Pond from behind him, running this way and that around the pair so as to get a good view.

Charlie, keeping his elbow lifted to shield his head, said: 'I'm sorry, baas, I'm sorry, I'm sorry. . . .'

'Sorry!' Mr. Black, keeping firm grasp of Charlie's shoulder, lifted his other hand to hit him; Charlie jerked his arm up over his face. Mr. Black's fist, expecting to encounter a cheek, met instead the rising arm and he was thrown off balance and staggered back. 'How dare you hit me,' he shouted furiously, rushing at Charlie; but Charlie had escaped in a bound over the rubbish-cans and away into the lane.

Mr. Black sent angry shouts after him; then turned and said indignantly to Mrs. Pond: 'Did you see that? He hit me!'

'He's out of hand,' said Mrs. Pond in a melancholy voice. 'What can you expect? He's been spoilt.'

They both turned to look accusingly at Marina.

'As a matter of accuracy,' said Marina breathlessly, 'he did not hit you.'

'What, are you taking that nigger's side?' demanded Mr. Black. He was completely taken aback. He looked, amazed, at Mrs. Pond, and said: 'She's taking his side!'

'It's not a question of sides,' said Marina in that high, precise voice. 'I was standing here and saw what happened. You know quite well he did not hit you. He wouldn't dare.'

'Yes,' said Mr. Black, 'that's what a state things have come to, with the Government spoiling them, they can hit us and get away with it, and if we touch them we get fined.'

'I don't know how many times I've seen the servants hit

since I've been here,' said Marina angrily. 'If it is the law, it is a remarkably ineffective one.'

'Well, I'm going to get the police,' shouted Mr. Black, running back to his own flat. 'No black bastard is going to hit me and get away with it. Besides, they can all be fined for visiting without passes after nine at night. . . .'

'Don't be childish,' said Marina, and went inside her rooms. She was crying with rage. Happening to catch a glimpse of herself in the mirror as she passed it, she hastily went to splash cold water on her face, for she looked – there was no getting away from it – rather like a particularly genteel school-marm in a temper. When she reached the front room, she found Charlie there throwing terrified glances out into the verandah for fear of Mr. Black or Mrs. Pond.

'Madam,' he said. 'Madam, I didn't hit him.'

'No, of course not,' said Marina; and she was astonished to find that she was feeling irritated with him, Charlie. 'Really,' she said, 'must you make such a noise and cause all this fuss.'

'But madam . . .'

'Oh, all right,' she said crossly. 'All right. But you aren't supposed to . . . who were all those people?'

'My friends.'

'Where from?' He was silent. 'Did they have passes to be out visiting?' He shifted his eyes uncomfortably. 'Well, really,' she said irritably, 'if the law is that you must have passes, for heaven's sake . . .' Charlie's whole appearance had changed; a moment before he had been a helpless small boy; he had become a sullen young man: this white woman was like all the rest.

Marina controlled her irritation and said gently: 'Listen Charlie, I don't agree with the law and all this nonsense about passes, but I can't change it, and it does seem to me . . .' Once again her irritation rose, once again she suppressed it, and found herself without words. Which was just as well, for Charlie was gazing at her with puzzled suspicion since he saw all white people as a sort of homogenous mass, a white layer, as it were, spread over the mass of blacks, all concerned in making life as difficult as possible for him and his kind; the idea that a white person might not agree with passes, curfew, and so on, was so outrageously new that he could not admit it to his mind at once. Marina said: 'Oh, well, Charlie, I know you didn't mean it, and I think you'd better go quietly to bed and keep out of Mr. Black's way, if you can.'

'Yes, madam,' he said submissively. As he went, she asked: 'Does Theresa sleep in the same room as Mr. Black's boy?'

He was silent. 'Does she sleep in your room perhaps?' And, as the silence persisted: 'Do you mean to tell me she sleeps with you and February?' No reply. 'But Charlie ...' She was about to protest again: But Theresa's nothing but a child; but this did not appear to be an argument which appealed to him.

There were loud voices outside, and Charlie shrank back: 'The police!' he said, terrified.

'Ridiculous nonsense,' said Marina. But looking out she saw a white policeman; and Charlie fled out through her bedroom and she heard the back door slam. It appeared he had no real confidence in her sympathy.

The policeman entered, alone. 'I understand there's been a spot of trouble,' he said.

'Over nothing,' said Marina.

'A tenant in this building claims he was hit by your servant.'

'It's not true. I saw the whole thing.'

The policeman looked at her doubtfully and said: 'Well, that makes things difficult, doesn't it?' After a moment he said: 'Excuse me a moment,' and went out. Marina saw him talking to Mr. Black outside her front steps. Soon the policeman came back. 'In view of your attitude the charge has been dropped,' he said.

'So I should think. I've never heard of anything so silly.'

'Well, Mrs. Giles, there was a row going on, and they all ran away, so they must have had guilty consciences about something, probably no passes. And you know they can't have women in their rooms.'

'The woman was Mr. Black's own nursemaid.'

'He says the girl is supposed to sleep in the location with her father.'

'It's a pity Mr. Black takes so little interest in his servants not to know. She sleeps here. How can a child that age be expected to walk five miles here every morning, to be here at seven, and walk five miles back at seven in the evening?'

The policeman gave her a look: 'Plenty do it,' he said. 'It's not the same for them as it is for us. Besides, it's the law.'

'The law!' said Marina bitterly.

Again the policeman looked uncertain. He was a pleasant young man, he dealt continually with cases of this kind, he always tried to smooth things over, if he could. He decided on his usual course, despite Marina's hostile manner. 'I think the best thing to do,' he said, 'is if we leave the whole thing. We'll never catch them now, anyway – miles away by this time. And Mr. Black has dropped the charge. You have a talk to your boy and tell him to be careful. Otherwise he'll be getting himself into trouble.'

'And what are you going to do about the nurse? It amounts to this: It's convenient for the Blacks to have her here, so they can go out at night, and so on, so they ask no questions. It's a damned disgrace, a girl of that age expected to share a room with the men.'

'It's not right, not right at all,' said the policeman. 'I'll have a word with Mr. Black.' And he took his leave, politely.

That night Marina relieved her feelings by writing a long letter about the incident to a friend of hers in England, full of phrases such as 'police state', 'despotism' and 'fascism'; which caused that friend to reply, rather tolerantly, to the effect that she understood these hot climates were rather upsetting and she did so hope Marina was looking after herself, one must have a sense of proportion, after all.

And, in fact, by the morning Marina was wondering why she had allowed herself to be so angry about such an absurd incident. What a country this was! Unless she was very careful she would find herself flying off into hysterical states as easily, for instance, as Mr. Black. If one was going to make a life here, one should adjust oneself. . . .

Charlie was grateful and apologetic. He repeated: 'Thank you, madam. Thank you.' He brought her a present of some vegetables and said: 'You are my father and my mother.' Marina was deeply touched. He rolled up his eyes and made a half-rueful joke: 'The police are no good, madam.' She discovered that he had spent the night in a friend's room some streets away for fear the police might come and take him to prison. For, in Charlie's mind, the police meant only one thing. Marina tried to explain that one wasn't put in prison without a trial of some sort; but he merely looked at her doubtfully, as if she were making fun of him. So she left it.

And Theresa? She was still working for the Blacks. A few evenings later, when Marina went to turn off the lights before going to bed, she saw Theresa gliding into Charlie's room. She said nothing about it: what could one expect?

Charlie had accepted her as an ally. One day, as he served vegetables, reaching behind her ducked head so that they might be presented, correctly, from the left, he remarked: 'That Theresa, she very nice, madam.'

'Very nice,' said Marina, uncomfortably helping herself to peas from an acute angle, sideways.

'Theresa says, perhaps madam give her a dress?'

'I'll see what I can find,' said Marina, after a pause.

'Thank you very much, thank you madam,' he said. He was grateful; but certainly he had expected just that reply: his thanks were not perfunctory, but he thanked her as one might thank one's parents, for instance, from whom one expects such goodness, even takes it a little for granted.

Next morning, when Marina and Philip lay as usual, trying to sleep through the cheerful din of cleaning from the next room, which included a shrill and sprightly whistling, there was a loud crash.

'Oh, damn the man,' said Philip, turning over and pulling the clothes over his ears.

'With a bit of luck he's broken that picture,' said Marina. She put a dressing-gown on, and went next door. On the floor lay fragments of white porcelain – her favourite vase, which she had brought all the way from England. Charlie was standing over it. 'Sorry, madam,' he said, cheerfully contrite.

Now that vase had stood on a shelf high above Charlie's head – to break it at all was something of an acrobatic feat. ... Marina pulled herself together. After all, it was only a vase. But her favourite vase, she had had it ten years: she stood there, tightening her lips over all the angry things she would have liked to say, looking at Charlie, who was carelessly sweeping the pieces together. He glanced up, saw her face, and said hastily, really apologetic: 'Sorry madam, very, very sorry, madam.' Then he added reassuringly: 'But the picture is all right.' He gazed admiringly up at the highland cattle which he clearly considered the main treasure of the room.

'So it is,' said Marina, suppressing the impulse to say: Charlie, if you break that picture I'll give you a present. 'Oh, well,' she said, 'I suppose it doesn't matter. Just sweep the pieces up.'

'Yes, missus, thank you,' said Charlie cheerfully; and she left, wondering how she had put herself in a position where it became impossible to be legitimately cross with her own servant. Coming back into that room some time later to ask Charlie why the breakfast was so late, she found him still standing under the picture. 'Very nice picture,' he said, reluctantly leaving the room. 'Six oxes. Six fine big oxes, in one picture!'

The work in the flat was finished by mid-morning. Marina told Charlie she wanted to bake; he filled the old-fashioned stove with wood for her, heated the oven and went off into the yard, whistling. She stood at the window, mixing her cake, looking out into the yard.

Charlie came out of his room, sat down on a big log under the tree, stretched his legs before him and propped a small mirror between his knees. He took a large metal comb and began to work on his thick hair, which he endeavoured to make lie flat, white man's fashion. He was sitting with his back to the yard.

Soon Theresa came out with a big enamel basin filled with washing. She wore the dress Marina had given her. It was an old black cocktail dress which hung loosely around her calves, and she had tied it at the waist with a big sash of printed cotton. The sophisticated dress, treated thus, hanging full and shapeless, looked grandmotherly and old-fashioned; she looked like an impish child in a matron's garb. She stood beside the washing-line gazing at Charlie's back; then slowly she began pegging the clothes, with long intervals to watch him.

It seemed Charlie did not know she was there. Then his pose of concentrated self-worship froze into a long, close inspection in the mirror, which he began to rock gently between his knees so that the sunlight flashed up from it, first into the branches over his head, then over the dust of the yard to the girl's feet, up her body: the ray of light hovered like a butterfly around her, then settled on her face. She remained still, her eyes shut, with the teasing light flickering on her lids. Then she opened them and exclaimed, indignantly: 'Hau!'

Charlie did not move. He held the mirror sideways on his knees, where he could see Theresa, and pretended to be hard at work on his parting. For a few seconds they remained thus, Charlie staring into the mirror, Theresa watching him reproachfully. Then he put the mirror back into his pocket, stretched his arms back in a magnificent slow yawn, and remained there, rocking back and forth on his log.

Theresa looked at him thoughtfully; and – since now he could not see her – darted over to the hedge, plucked a scarlet hibiscus flower and returned to the washing-line, where she continued to hang the washing, the flower held lightly between her lips.

Charlie got up, his arms still locked behind his head, and began a sort of shuffle dance in the sunny dust, among the fallen leaves and chips of wood. It was a crisp, bright morning, the sky was as blue and fresh as the sea: this idyllic scene moved Marina deeply, it must be confessed.

Still dancing, Charlie let his arms fall, turned himself round, and his hands began to move in time with his feet. Jerking, lolling, posing, he slowly approached the centre of the yard, apparently oblivious of Theresa's existence.

There was a shout from the back of the building: 'Theresa!' Charlie glanced around, then dived hastily into his room. The girl, left alone, gazed at the dark door into which Charlie had vanished, sighed, and blinked gently at the sunlight. A second shout: 'Theresa, are you going to be all day with that washing?'

She tucked the flower among the stiff quills of hair on her head and bent to the basin that stood in the dust. The washing flapped and billowed all around her, so that the small, wiry form appeared to be wrestling with the big, ungainly sheets. Charlie ducked out of his door and ran quickly up the hedge, out of sight of Mrs. Black. He stopped, watching:

Theresa, who was still fighting with the washing. He whistled, she ignored him. He whistled again, changing key: the long note dissolved into a dance tune, and he sauntered deliberately up the hedge, weight shifting from hip to hip with each step. It was almost a dance: the buttocks sharply protruding and then withdrawn inwards after the prancing, lifting knees. The girl stood motionless, gazing at him, tantalized. She glanced quickly over her shoulder at the building, then ran across the yard to Charlie. The two of them, safe for the moment beside the hedge, looked guiltily for possible spies. They saw Marina behind her curtain – an earnest English face, apparently wrestling with some severe moral problem. But she was a friend. Had she not saved Charlie from the police? Besides, she immediately vanished.

Hidden behind the curtain, Marina saw the couple face each other, smiling. Then the girl tossed her head and turned away. She picked a second flower from the hedge, held it to her lips, and began swinging lightly from the waist, sending Charlie provocative glances over her shoulder that were half disdain and half invitation. To Marina it was as if a mischievous black urchin was playing the part of a coquette; but Charlie was watching with a broad and appreciative smile. He followed her, strolling in an assured and masterful way, as she went before him into his room. The door closed.

Marina discovered herself to be furious. Really, the whole thing was preposterous!

'Philip,' she said energetically that night, 'we should do something.'

'What?' asked Philip, practically. Marina could not think of a sensible answer. Philip gave a short lecture on the problems of the indigenous African peoples who were halfway between the tribal society and modern industrialization. The thing, of course, should be tackled at its root. Since he was a soil expert, the root, to him, was a sensible organization of the land. (If he had been a churchman, the root would have been a correct attitude to whichever God he happened to represent; if an authority on money, a mere adjustment of currency would have provided the solution – there is very little comfort from experts these days.)

To Philip, it was all as clear as daylight. These people had no idea at all how to farm. They must give up this old attitude of theirs, based on the days when a tribe worked out one piece of ground and moved on to the next; they must learn to conserve their soil and, above all, to regard cattle, not as a sort of spiritual currency, but as an organic part of farm-work. (The word *organic* occurred very frequently in these lectures by Philip.) Once these things were done, everything else would follow. . . .

'But in the meantime, Philip, it is quite possible that something may *happen* to Theresa, and she can't be more than fifteen, if that. . . .'

Philip looked a little dazed as he adjusted himself from the level on which he had been thinking to the level of Theresa: women always think so personally! He said, rather stiffly: 'Well, old girl, in periods of transition, what can one expect?'

What one might expect did in fact occur, and quite soon. One of those long ripples of gossip and delighted indignation passed from one end to the other of 138 Cecil John Rhodes Vista. Mrs. Black's Theresa had got herself into trouble; these girls had no morals; no better than savages; besides, she was a thief. She was wearing clothes that had not been given to her by Mrs. Black. Marina paid a formal visit to Mrs. Black in order to say that she had given Theresa various dresses. The air was not at all cleared. No one cared to what degree Theresa had been corrupted, or by whom. The feeling was: if not Theresa, then someone else. Acts of theft, adultery, and so on, were necessary to preserve the proper balance between black and white; the balance was upset, not by Theresa, who played her allotted part, but by Marina, who insisted on introducing these Fabian scruples into a clear-cut situation.

Mrs. Black was polite, grudging, distrustful. She said: 'Well, if you've given her the dresses, then it's all right.' She added: 'But it doesn't alter what she'd done, does it now?' Marina could make no reply. The white women of the building continued to gossip and pass judgment for some days: one must, after all, talk about something. It was odd, however, that Mrs. Black made no move at all to sack Theresa, that immoral person, who continued to look after the children with her usual good-natured efficiency, in order that Mrs. Black might have time to gossip and drink tea.

So Marina, who had already made plans to rescue Theresa when she was flung out of her job, found that no rescue was necessary. From time to time Mrs. Black overflowed into reproaches, and lectures about sin. Theresa wept like the child she was, her fists stuck into her eyes. Five minutes afterwards she was helping Mrs. Black bath the baby, or flirting with Charlie in the yard.

For the principals of this scandal seemed the least concerned about it. The days passed, and at last Marina said to Charlie: 'Well, and what are you going to do now?'

'Madam?' said Charlie. He really did not know what she meant.

'About Theresa,' said Marina sternly.

'Theresa she going to have a baby,' said Charlie, trying to look penitent, but succeeding only in looking proud.

'It's all very well,' said Marina. Charlie continued to sweep the verandah, smiling to himself. 'But Charlie ...' began Marina again.

'Madam?' said Charlie, resting on his broom and waiting for her to go on.

'You can't just let things go on, and what will happen to the child when it is born?'

His face puckered, he sighed, and finally he went on sweeping, rather slower than before.

Suddenly Marina stamped her foot and said: 'Charlie, this really won't do!' She was really furious.

'Madam!' said Charlie reproachfully.

'Everybody has a good time,' said Marina. 'You and Theresa enjoy yourselves, all these females have a lovely time, gossiping, and the only thing no one ever thinks about is the baby.' After a pause, when he did not reply, she went on: 'I suppose you and Theresa think it's quite all right for the baby to be born here, and then you two, and the baby, and February, and all the rest of your friends who have nowhere to go, will all live together in that room. It really is shocking, Charlie.'

Charlie shrugged as if to say: 'Well, what do you suggest?'

'Can't Theresa go and live with her father?'

Charlie's face tightened into a scowl. 'Theresa's father, he no good. Theresa must work, earn money for father.'

'I see.' Charlie waited; he seemed to be waiting for Marina to solve this problem for him; his attitude said: I have unbounded trust and confidence in you.

'Are any of the other men working here married?'

'Yes, madam.'

'Where are their wives?'

'At home.' This meant, in their kraals, in the native reserves. But Marina had not meant the properly married wives, who usually stayed with the clan, and were visited by their men perhaps one month in a year, or in two years. She meant women like Theresa, who lived in town.

'Now listen, Charlie. Do be sensible. What happens to girls like Theresa when they have babies. Where do they live?'

He shrugged again, meaning: They live as they can, and is it my fault the white people don't let us have our families with us when they work? Suddenly he said grudgingly: 'The nannie next door, she had her baby, she works.'

'Where is her baby?'

Charlie jerked his head over at the servant's quarters of the next house.

'Does the baas know she has her baby there?'

He looked away, uncomfortably. 'Well, and what happens when the police find out?'

He gave her a look which she understood. 'Who is the father of the baby?'

He looked away; there was an uncomfortable silence; and then he quickly began sweeping the verandah again.

'Charlie!' said Marina, outraged. His whole body had become defensive, sullen; his face was angry. She said energetically: 'You should marry Theresa. You can't go on doing this sort of thing.'

'I have a wife in my kraal,' he said.

'Well, there's nothing to stop you having two wives, is there?'

Charlie pointed out that he had not yet finished paying for his first wife.

Marina thought for a moment. 'Theresa's a Christian, isn't

she? She was educated at the mission.' Charlie shrugged. 'If you marry Theresa Christian-fashion, you needn't pay lobola, need you?'

Charlie said: 'The Christians only like one wife. And Theresa's father, he wants lobola.'

Marina found herself delighted. At any rate he had tried to marry Theresa, and this was evidence of proper feeling. The fact that whether the position was legalized or not the baby's future was still uncertain, did not at once strike her. She was carried away by moral approval. 'Well, Charlie, that's much better,' she said warmly.

He gave her a rather puzzled look and shrugged again.

'How much lobola does Theresa's father want for her?'

'Plenty. He wants ten cattle.'

'What nonsense!' exclaimed Marina energetically. 'Where does he suppose you are going to find cattle, working in town, and where's he going to keep them?'

This seemed to annoy Charlie. 'In my kraal, I have fine cattle,' he pointed out. 'I have six fine oxes.' He swept, for a while, in silence. 'Theresa's father, he mad, he mad old man. I tell him I must give three oxes this year for my own wife. Where do I find ten oxes for Theresa?'

It appeared that Charlie, no more than Theresa's father, found nothing absurd about this desire for cattle on the part of an old man living in the town location. Involuntarily she looked over her shoulder as if Philip might be listening: this conversation would have plunged him into irritated despair. Luckily he was away on one of his trips, and was at this moment almost certain to be exhorting the natives, in some distant reserve, to abandon this irrational attitude to 'fine oxes' which in fact were bound to be nothing but skin and bone, and churning whole tracts of country to dust.

'Why don't you offer Theresa's father some money?' she suggested, glancing down at Charlie's garters which were, this morning, of cherry-coloured silk.

'He wants cattle, not money. He wants Theresa not to marry, he wants her to work for him.' Charlie rapidly finished sweeping the verandah and moved off, with relief, tucking the broom under his arm, with an apologetic smile which said: I know you mean well, but I'm glad to end this conversation.

But Marina was not at all inclined to drop the thing. She interviewed Theresa who, amid floods of tears, said Yes, she wanted to marry Charlie, but her father wanted to much lobola. The problem was quite simple to her, merely a question of lobola; Charlie's other wife did not concern her; nor did she, apparently, share Charlie's view that a proper wife in the kraal was one thing, while the women of the town were another.

Marina said: 'Shall I come down to the location and talk to your father?'

Theresa hung her head shyly, allowed the last big tears to roll glistening down her cheeks and go splashing to the dust. 'Yes, madam ' she said gratefully.

Marina returned to Charlie and said she would interview the old man. He appeared restive at this suggestion. 'I'll advance you some of your wages and you can pay for Theresa in instalments,' she said. He glanced down at his fine shirt, his gay socks, and sighed. If he were going to spend years of life paying five shillings a month, which was all he could afford, for Theresa, then his life as a dandy was over.

Marina said, crossly: 'Yes, it's all very well, but you can't have it both ways.'

He said hastily: 'I'll go down and see the father of Theresa, madam. I go soon.'

'I think you'd better,' she said sternly.

When she told Philip this story he became vigorously indignant. It presented in little, he said, the whole problem of this society. The Government couldn't see an inch in front of its nose. In the first place, by allowing the lobola system to continue, this emotional attitude towards cattle was perpetuated. In the second, by making no proper arrangements for these men to have their families in the towns it made the existence of prostitutes like Theresa inevitable.

'Theresa isn't a prostitute,' said Marina indignantly. 'It isn't her fault.'

'Of course it isn't her fault, that's what I'm saying. But she will be a prostitute, it's inevitable. When Charlie's fed up with her she'll find herself another man and have a child or two by him, and so on . . .'

'You talk about Theresa as if she were a vital statistic,'

said Marina, and Philip shrugged. That shrug expressed an attitude of mind which Marina would very soon find herself sharing, but she did not yet know that. She was still very worried about Theresa, and after some days she asked Charlie: 'Well, and did you see Theresa's father? What did he say?'

'He wants cattle.'

'Well, he can't have cattle.'

'No,' said Charlie brightening. 'My own wife, she cost six cattles. I paid three last year. I pay three more this year, when I go home.'

'When are you going home?'

'When Mrs. Skinner comes back. She no good. Not like you, madam, you are my father and mother,' he said, giving her that touching, grateful smile.

'And what will happen to Theresa?'

'She stay here.' After a long, troubled silence, he said: 'She my town wife. I come back to Theresa.' This idea seemed to cheer him up.

And it seemed he was genuinely fond of the girl. Looking out of the kitchen window, Marina could see the pair of them, during lulls in the work, seated side by side on the big log under the tree – charming! A charming picture! 'It's all very well . . .' said Marina to herself, uneasily.

Some mornings later she found Charlie in the front room, under the picture, and looking at it this time, not with reverent admiration, but rather nervously. As she came in he quickly returned to his work, but Marina could see he wanted to say something to her.

'Madam . . .'

'Well, what is it?'

'This picture costs plenty money?'

'I suppose it did, once.'

'Cattles cost plenty money, madam.'

'Yes, so they do, Charlie.'

'If you sell this picture, how much?'

'But it is Mrs. Skinner's picture.'

His body dropped with disappointment. 'Yes, madam,' he said politely, turning away.

'But wait, Charlie – what do you want the picture for?'

'It's all right, madam.' He was going out of the room.

'Stop a moment – why do you want it? You do want it, don't you?'

'Oh yes,' he said, his face lit with pleasure. He clasped his hands tight, looking at it. 'Oh yes, yes, madam!'

'What would you do with it? Keep it in your room?'

'I give it to Theresa's father.'

'Wha-a-a-t?' said Marina. Slowly she absorbed this idea. 'I see,' she said. And then, after a pause: 'I see . . .' She looked at his hopeful face, thought of Mrs. Skinner and said suddenly, filled with an undeniably spiteful delight: 'I'll give it to you Charlie.'

'Madam!' exclaimed Charlie. He even gave a couple of involuntary little steps, like a dance. 'Madam, thank you, thank you.'

She was as pleased as he. For a moment they stood smiling delightedly at each other. 'I'll tell Mrs. Skinner that I broke it,' she said. He went to the picture and lifted his hands gently to the great carved frame. 'You must be careful not to break it before you get it to her father.' He was staggering as he lifted it down. 'Wait!' said Marina suddenly. Checking himself, he stood politely: she saw he expected her to change her mind and take back the gift. 'You can't carry that great thing all the way to the location. I'll take it for you in the car!'

'Madam,' he said. 'Madam . . .' Then, looking helplessly around him for something, someone he could share his joy with, he said: 'I'll tell Theresa now . . .' And he ran from the room like a schoolboy.

Marina went to Mrs. Black and asked that Theresa might have the afternoon off. 'She had her afternoon off yesterday,' said that lady sharply.

'She's going to marry Charlie,' said Marina.

'She can marry him next Thursday, can't she?'

'No, because I'm taking them both down in the car to the location, to her father, and . . .'

Mrs Black said resentfully: 'She should have asked me herself.'

'It seems to me,' said Marina in that high, acid voice, replying not to the words Mrs. Black had used, but to what she had meant: 'It seems to me that if one employs a child of fifteen, and under such conditions, the very least one can

58

do is to assume the responsibility for her and it seems to me quite extraordinary that you never have the slightest idea what she does, where she lives, or even that she is going to get married.'

'You swallowed the dictionary?' said Mrs. Black, with an ingratiating smile. 'I'm not saying she shouldn't get married; she should have got married before, that's what I'm saying.'

Marina returned to her flat, feeling Mrs. Black's resentful eyes on her back: *Who the hell does she think she is, anyway*.

When Marina and Philip reached the lorry that afternoon that was waiting outside the gate, Theresa and Charlie were already sitting in the back, carefully balancing the picture on their knees. The two white people got in the front and Marina glanced anxiously through the window and said to Philip: 'Do drive carefully, dear, Theresa shouldn't be bumped around.'

'I'd be doing her a favour if I did bump her,' said Philip grimly. He was accompanying Marina unwillingly. 'Well, I don't know what you think you're going to achieve by it . . .' he had said. However, here he was, looking rather cross.

They drove down the tree-lined, shady streets, through the business area that was all concrete and modernity, past the slums where the half-caste people lived, past the factory sites, where smoke poured and hung, past the cemetery where angels and crosses gleamed white through the trees – they drove five miles, which was the distance Theresa had been expected to walk every morning and evening to her work. They turned off the main road into the location, and at once everything was quite different. No tarmac road, no avenues of beautiful trees here. Dust roads, dust paths, led from all directions inwards to the centre, where the housing area was. Dust lay thick and brown on the veld trees, the great blue sky was seen through a rust-coloured haze, dust gritted on the lips and tongue, and at once the lorry began to jolt and bounce. Marina looked back and saw Charlie and Theresa jerking and sliding with the lorry, under the great picture, clinging to each other for support, and laughing because of the joy-ride. It was the first time Theresa had ridden in a white man's car; and she was waving and calling shrill greetings to the groups of black children who ran after them.

They drove fast, bumping, so as to escape from the rivers of dust that spurted up from the wheels, making a whirling red cloud behind them, from which crowds of loitering natives ran, cursing and angry. Soon they were in an area that was like a cheap copy of the white man's town; small houses stood in blocks, intersected by dust streets. They were two-roomed shacks with tin roofs, the sun blistering off them; and Marina said angrily: 'Isn't it awful, isn't it terrible?'

Had she known that these same houses represented years of campaigning by the liberals of the city, against white public opinion, which obstinately held that houses for natives were merely another manifestation of that *Fabian* spirit from England which was spoiling the fine and uncorrupted savage, she might have been more respectful. Soon they left this new area and were among the sheds and barns that housed dozens of workers each, a state of affairs which caused Marina the acutest indignation. Another glance over her shoulder showed Theresa and Charlie giggling together like a couple of children as they tried to hold that picture still on their knees, for it slid this way and that as if it had a spiteful life of its own. 'Ask Charlie where we must go?' said Philip; and Marina tapped on the glass till Charlie turned his head and watched her gestures till he understood and pointed onwards with his thumb. More of these brick shacks, with throngs of natives at their doors, who watched the car indifferently until they saw it was a Government car, and then their eyes grew wary, suspicious. And now, blocking their way, was a wire fence, and Martha looked back at Charlie for instructions, and he indicated they should stop. Philip pulled the lorry up against the fence and Charlie and Theresa jumped down from the back, came forwards, and Charlie said apologetically: 'Now we must walk, madam.' The four went through a gap in the fence and saw a slope of soiled and matted grass that ended in a huddle of buildings on the banks of a small river.

Charlie pointed at it, and went ahead with Theresa. He held the picture on his shoulders, walking bent under it.

They passed through the grass, which smelled unpleasant and was covered by a haze of flies, and came to another expanse of dust, in which were scattered buildings – no, not buildings, shacks, extraordinary huts thrown together out of every conceivable substance, with walls perhaps of sacking, or of petrol boxes, roofs of beaten tin, or bits of scrap iron.

'And what happens when it rains?' said Marina, as they wound in and out of these dwellings, among scratching chickens and snarling native mongrels. She found herself profoundly dispirited, as if something inside her said: What's the use? For this area, officially, did not exist. The law was that all the workers, the servants, should live inside the location, or in one of the similar townships. But there was never enough room. People overflowed into such makeshift villages everywhere, but as they were not supposed to be there the police might at any moment swoop down and arrest them. Admittedly the police did not often swoop, as the white man must have servants, the servants must live somewhere – and so it all went on, year after year. The Government, from time to time, planned a new housing estate. On paper, all around the white man's city, were fine new townships for the blacks. One had even been built, and to this critical visitors (usually those *Fabians* from overseas) were taken, and came away impressed. They never saw these slums. And so all the time, every day, the black people came from their reserves, their kraals, drawn to the white man's city, to the glitter of money, cinemas, fine clothes; they came in their thousands, no one knew how many, making their own life, as they could, in such hovels. It was all hopeless, as long as Mrs. Black, Mr. Black, Mrs. Pond were the voters with the power; as long as the experts and administrators such as Philip had to work behind Mrs. Pond's back – for nothing is more remarkable than that democratic phenomenon, so clearly shown in this continent, where members of Parliament, civil servants (experts, in short) spend half their time and energy earnestly exhorting Mrs. Pond: For heaven's sake have some sense before it is too late; if you don't let us use enough money to house and feed these people, they'll rise and cut your throats. To which reasonable plea for self-preservation, Mrs. Pond merely turns a sullen and angry stare, muttering: They're getting out of hand, that's what it is, they're getting spoilt.

In a mood of grim despair, Marina found herself standing with Philip in front of a small shack that consisted of sheets of corrugated iron laid loosely together, resting in the dust, like a child's card castle. It was bound at the corners with string, and big stones held the sheet of iron that served as roof from flying away in the first gust of wind.

'Here, madam,' said Charlie. He thrust Theresa forward. She went shyly to the dark oblong that was the door, leaned inwards, and spoke some words in her own language. After a moment an old man stooped his way out. He was perhaps not so old – impossible to say. He was lean and tall, with a lined and angry face, and eyes that lifted under heavy lids to peer at Marina and Philip. Towards Charlie he directed a long, deadly stare, then turned away. He wore a pair of old khaki trousers, an old, filthy singlet that left his long, sinewed arms bare: all the bones and muscles of his neck and shoulders showed taut and knotted under the skin.

Theresa, smiling bashfully, indicated Philip and Marina; the old man offered some words of greeting; but he was angry, he did not want to see them, so the two white people fell back a little.

Charlie now came forward with the picture and leaned it gently against the iron of the shack in a way which said: 'Here you are, and that's all you are going to get from me.' In these surroundings those fierce Scottish cattle seemed to shrink a little. The picture that had dominated a room with its expanse of shining glass, its heavy carved frame, seemed not so enormous now. The cattle seemed even rather absurd, shaggy creatures standing in their wet sunset, glaring with a false challenge at the group of people. The old man looked at the picture, and then said something angry to Theresa. She seemed afraid, and came forward, unknotting a piece of cloth that had lain in the folds at her waist. She handed over some small change – about three shillings in all. The old man took the money, shaking it contemptuously in his hand before he slid it into his pocket. Then he spat, showing contempt. Again he spoke to Theresa, in short, angry sentences, and at the end he flung out his arm, as if throwing something away; and she began to cry and shrank back to Charlie. Charlie laid his hand on her shoulder and pressed it; then left her standing alone and went forward to his father-in-law. He smiled, spoke persuasively, indicated Philip and Marina. The old man listened without speaking, his eyes lowered. Those eyes slid sideways to the big picture, a gleam came into them; Charlie fell silent and they all looked at the picture.

The old man began to speak, in a different voice, sad and hopeless. He was telling how he had wooed his second wife, Theresa's mother. He spoke of the long courting, according to the old customs, how, with many gifts and courtesies between the clans, the marriage had been agreed on, how the cattle had been chosen, ten great cattle, heavy with good grazing; he told how he had driven them to Theresa's mother's family, carefully across the country, so that they might not be tired and thinned by the journey. As he spoke to the two young people he was reminding them, and himself, of that time when every action had its ritual, its meaning; he was asking them to contrast their graceless behaviour with the dignity of his own marriages, symbolized by the cattle, which were not to be thought of in terms of money, of simply buying a woman – not at all. They meant so much: a sign of good feeling, a token of union between the clans, an earnest that the woman would be looked after, an acknowledgment that she was someone very precious, whose departure would impoverish her family – the cattle were all these things, and many more. The old man looked at Charlie and Theresa and seemed to say: 'And what about you? What are you in comparison to what we were then?' Finally he spat again, lifted the picture and went into the dark of his hut. They could see him looking at the picture. He liked it: yes, he was pleased, in his way. But soon he left it leaning against the iron and returned to his former pose – he drew a blanket over his head and shoulders and squatted down inside the door, looking out, but not as if he still saw them or intended to make any further sign towards them.

The four were left standing there, in the dust, looking at each other.

Marina was feeling very foolish. Was that all? And Philip answered by saying brusquely, but uncomfortably: 'Well, there's your wedding for you.'

Theresa and Charlie had linked fingers and were together looking rather awkwardly at the white people. It was an awkward moment indeed – this was the end of it, the two were married, and it was Marina who had arranged the thing. What now?

But there was a more immediate problem. It was still early in the afternoon, the sun slanted overhead, with hours of light in it still, and presumably the newly-married couple would want to be together? Marina said: 'Do you want to come back with us in the lorry, or would you rather come later?'

Charlie and Theresa spoke together in their own language, then Charlie said apologetically: 'Thank you, madam, we stay.'

'With Theresa's father?'

Charlie said: 'He won't have Theresa now. He says Theresa can go away. He not want Theresa.'

Philip said: 'Don't worry, Marina, he'll take her back, he'll take her money all right.' He laughed, and Marina was angry with him for laughing.

'He very cross, madam,' said Charlie. He even laughed himself, but in a rather anxious way.

The old man still sat quite motionless, looking past them. There were flies at the corners of his eyes; he did not lift his hand to brush them off.

'Well . . .' said Marina. 'We can give you a lift back if you like.' But it was clear that Theresa was afraid of going back now; Mrs. Black might assume her afternoon off was over and make her work.

Charlie and Theresa smiled again and said 'Good-bye. Thank you, madam. Thank you, baas.' They went slowly off across the dusty earth, between the hovels, towards the river, where a group of tall brick huts stood like outsize sentry-boxes. There, though neither Marina nor Philip knew it, was sold illicit liquor; there they would find a tinny gramophone playing dance music from America, there would be singing, dancing, a good time. This was the place the police came first if they were in search of criminals. Marina thought the couple were going down to the river, and she said sentimentally: 'Well, they have this afternoon together, that's something.'

'Yes,' said Philip drily; The two were angry with each other, they did not know why. They walked in silence back to the lorry and drove home, making polite, clear sentences about indifferent topics.

Next day everything was as usual, Theresa back at work with Mrs. Black, Charlie whistling cheerfully in their own flat.

Almost immediately Marina bought a house that seemed passable, about seven miles from the centre of town, in a new suburb. Mrs. Skinner would not be returning for two weeks yet, but it was more convenient for them to move into the new home at once. The problem was Charlie. What would he do during that time? He said he was going home to visit his family. He had heard that his first wife had a new baby and he wanted to see it.

'Then I'll pay you your wages now,' said Marina. She paid him, with ten shillings over. It was an uncomfortable moment. This man had been working for them for over two months, intimately, in their home; they had influenced each other's lives – and now he was off, he disappeared, the thing was finished. 'Perhaps you'll come and work for me when you come back from your family?' said Marina.

Charlie was very pleased. 'Oh, yes, madam,' he said. 'Mrs. Skinner very bad, she no good, not like you.' He gave a comical grimace, and laughed.

'I'll give you our address.' Marina wrote it out and saw Charlie fold the piece of paper and place it carefully in an envelope which also held his official pass, a letter from her saying he was travelling to his family, and a further letter, for which he had asked, listing various bits of clothing that Philip had given him, for otherwise, as he explained, the police would catch him and say he had stolen them.

'Well, good-bye, Charlie,' said Marina. 'I do so hope your wife and your new baby are all right.' She thought of Theresa, but did not mention her; she found herself suffering from a curious disinclination to offer further advice or help. What would happen to Theresa? Would she simply move in with the first man who offered her shelter? Almost Marina shrugged.

'Good-bye, madam,' said Charlie. He went off to buy himself a new shirt with the ten shillings, and some sweets for Theresa. He was sad to be leaving Theresa. On the other hand, he was looking forward to seeing his new child and his wife; he expected to be home after about a week's walking, perhaps sooner if he could get a lift.

But things did not turn out like this.

Mrs. Skinner returned before she was expected. She found the flat locked and the key with Mrs. Black. Everything was very clean and tidy, but – where was her favourite picture? At first she saw only the lightish square patch on the dimming paint – then she thought of Charlie. Where was he? No sign of him. She came back into the flat and found the letter Marina had left, enclosing eight pounds for the picture 'which she had unfortunately broken'. The thought came to Mrs. Skinner that she would not have got ten shillings for that picture if she had tried to sell it; then the phrase 'sentimental value' came to her rescue, and she was furious. Where was Charlie? For, looking about her, she saw various other articles were missing. Where was her yellow earthen vase? Where was the wooden door-knocker that said *Welcome Friend*? Where was ... she went off to talk to Mrs. Black, and quite soon all the women dropped in, and she was told many things about Marina. At last she said: 'It serves me right for letting to an immigrant. I should have let it to you, dear.' The dear in question was Mrs. Pond. The ladies were again emotionally united; the long hostilities that had led to the flat being let to Marina were forgotten; that they were certain to break out again within a week was not to be admitted in this moment of pure friendship.

Mrs. Pond told Mrs. Skinner that she had seen the famous picture being loaded on to the lorry. Probably Mrs. Giles had sold it – but this thought was checked, for both ladies knew what the picture was worth. No, Marina must have disposed of it in some way connected with her *Fabian* outlook – what could one expect from these white kaffirs?

Fuming, Mrs. Skinner went to find Theresa. She saw Charlie, dressed to kill in his new clothes, who had come to say good-bye to Theresa before setting off on his long walk. She flew out, grabbed him by the arm and dragged him into the flat. 'Where's my picture?' she demanded.

At first Charlie denied all knowledge of the picture. Then

he said Marina had given it to him. Mrs. Skinner dropped his arm and stared: 'But it was my picture . . .' She reflected rapidly: that eight pounds was going to be very useful; she had returned from her holiday, as people do, rather short of money. She exclaimed instead: 'What have you done with my yellow vase? Where's my knocker?'

Charlie said he had not seen them. Finally Mrs. Skinner fetched the police. The police found the missing articles in Charlie's bundle. Normally Mrs. Skinner would have cuffed him and fined him five shillings. But there was this business of the picture – she told the police to take him off.

Now, in this city in the heart of what used to be known as the Dark Continent, at any hour of the day, women shopping, typists glancing up from their work out of the window, or the business men passing in their cars, may see (if they choose to look) a file of handcuffed natives, with two policemen in front and two behind, followed by a straggling group of native women who are accompanying their men to the courts. These are the natives who have been arrested for visiting without passes, or owning bicycles without lights, or being in possession of clothes or articles without being able to say how they came to own them. These natives are being marched off to explain themselves to the magistrates. They are given a small fine with the option of prison. They usually choose prison. After all, to pay a ten shilling fine when one earns perhaps twenty or thirty a month, is no joke, and it is something to be fed and housed, free, for a fortnight. This is an arrangement satisfactory to everyone concerned, for these prisoners mend roads, cut down grass, plant trees: it is as good as having a pool of free labour.

Marina happened to be turning into a shop one morning, where she hoped to buy a table for her new house, and saw, without really seeing them, a file of such handcuffed natives passing her. They were talking and laughing among themselves, and with the black policemen who herded them, and called back loud and jocular remarks at their women. In Marina's mind the vision of that ideal table (for which she had been searching for some days, without success) was rather stronger than what she actually saw; and it was not until the prisoners had passed that she suddenly said to

herself: 'Good heavens, that man looks rather like Charlie –
and that girl behind there, the plump girl with the spindly
legs, there was something about the back view of the girl
that was very like Theresa. . . .' The file had in the meantime
turned a corner and was out of sight. For a moment Marina
thought: Perhaps I should follow and see? Then she
thought: Nonsense, I'm seeing things, of course it can't be
Charlie, he must have reached home by now. . . . And she
went into the shop to buy her table.

*Second Novel*

# The Other Woman

ROSE'S mother was killed one morning crossing the street to do her shopping. Rose was fetched from work, and a young policeman, awkward with sympathy, asked questions and finally said: 'You ought to tell your Dad, Miss, he ought to know.' It had struck him as strange that she had not suggested it, but behaved as if the responsibility for everything must of course be hers. He thought Rose was too composed to be natural. Her mouth was set and there was a strained look in her eyes. He insisted; Rose sent a message to her father; but when he came she put him straight into bed with a cup of tea. Mr. Johnson was a plump, fair little man, with wisps of light hair lying over a rosy scalp, and blue, candid, trustful eyes. Then she came back to the kitchen and her manner told the policeman that she expected him to leave. From the door he said diffidently: 'Well, I'm sorry, Miss, I'm real sorry. A terrible thing – you can't rightly blame the lorry-driver, and your mum – it wasn't her fault, either.' Rose turned her white, shaken face, her cold and glittering eyes towards him and said tartly: 'Being sorry doesn't mend broken bones.' That last phrase seemed to take her by surprise, for she winced, her face worked in a rush of tears, and then she clenched her jaw again. 'Them lorries,' she said heavily, 'them machines, they ought to be stopped, that's what I think.' This irrational remark encouraged the policeman: it was nearer to the tears, the emotion that he thought would be good for her. He remarked encouragingly: 'I daresay, miss, but we couldn't do without them, could we now?' Rose's face did not change. She said politely: 'Yes?' It was sceptical and dismissing; that monosyllable said finally: 'You keep your opinions, I'll keep mine.' It examined and dismissed the whole machine age. The young policeman, still lingering over his duty, suggested: 'Isn't there anybody to come and sit with you? You don't look too good Miss, and that's a fact.'

'There isn't anybody,' said Rose briefly, and added: 'I'm all right.' She sounded irritated, and so he left. She sat down at the table and was shocked at herself for what she had said. She thought: I ought to tell George. ... But she did not move. She stared vaguely around the kitchen, her mind dimly churning around several ideas. One was that her father had taken it hard, she would have her hands full with him. Another, that policemen, officials – they were all nosey parkers, knowing what was best for everybody. She found herself staring at a certain picture at the wall, and thinking: 'Now I can take that picture down. Now she's gone I can do what I like.' She felt a little guilty, but almost at once she briskly rose and took the picture down. It was of a battleship in a stormy sea, and she hated it. She put it away in a cupboard. Then the white, empty square on the wall troubled her, and she replaced it by a calendar with yellow roses on it. Then she made herself a cup of tea and began cooking her father's supper, thinking: I'll wake him up and make him eat, do him good to have a bite of something hot.

At supper her father asked: 'Where's George?' Her face closed against him in irritation and she said: 'I don't know.' He was surprised and shocked, and he protested: 'But Rosie, you ought to tell him, it's only right.' Now, it was against this knowledge that she had been arming herself all day; but she knew that sooner or later she must tell George, and when she had finished the washing-up she took a sheet of writing-paper from the drawer of the dresser and sat down to write. She was as surprised at herself as her father was: Why didn't she want to tell George? Her father said, with the characteristic gentle protest: 'But Rosie, why don't you give him a ring at the factory? They'd give him the message.' Rose made as if she had not heard. She finished the letter, found some coppers in her bag for a stamp, and went out to post it. Afterwards she found herself thinking of George's arrival with the reluctance that deserved the name of fear. She could not understand herself, and soon went to bed in order to lose herself in sleep. She dreamed of the lorry that had killed her mother; she dreamed, too, of an enormous black machine, relentlessly moving its great arms back and forth, back and forth, in a way that was menacing to Rose.

George found the letter when he returned from work the following evening. His first thought was: Why couldn't she have got killed next week, after we were married, instead of now?' He was shocked at the cruel and selfish idea. But he and Rose had been going together now for three years, and he could not help feeling that it was cruel of fate to cloud their wedding with this terrible, senseless death. He had not liked Rose's mother: he thought her a fussy and domineering woman; but to be killed like that, all of a sudden, in her vigorous fifties— He thought suddenly: 'Poor little Rosie, she'll be upset bad, and there's her Dad, he's just like a big baby; I'd better get to her quick.' He was putting the letter in his pocket when it struck him: 'Why did she write? Why didn't she telephone to the works?' He looked at the letter and saw that Mrs. Johnson had been killed as long ago as yesterday morning. At first he was too astonished to be angry; then he was extraordinarily angry. 'What!' he muttered, 'why the hell – what's she doing?' He was a member of the family, wasn't he? – or as good as. And she wrote him stiff little letters, beginning *Dear George*, and ending, *Rose* – no love, not even a sincerely. But underneath the anger he was deeply dismayed. He was remembering that there had been a listlessness, an apathy about her recently that could almost be taken as indifference. For instance, when he took her to see the two rooms that would be their home, she had made all kinds of objections instead of being as delighted as he was. 'Look at all those stairs,' she had said, 'it's so high up,' and so on. You might almost think she wasn't keen on marrying him – but this idea was insupportable, and he abandoned it quickly. He remembered that at the beginning, three years ago, she had pleaded for them to marry at once; she didn't mind taking a chance, she had said; lots of people got married on less money than they had. But he was a cautious man and had talked her into waiting for some kind of security. That's where he made his mistake, he decided now; he should have taken her at a word and married her straight off, and then ... He hastened across London to comfort Rose; and all the time his thoughts of her were uneasy and aggrieved; and he felt as anxious as a lost child.

When he entered the kitchen it was with no clear idea of what to expect; but he was surprised to find her seated at her usual place at the table, her hands folded idly before her, pale, heavy-lidded, but quite composed. The kitchen was spotless and there was a smell of soapsuds and clean warmth. Evidently the place had just been given a good scrub.

Rose turned heavy eyes on him and said: 'It was good of you to come over, George.'

He had been going to give her a comforting kiss, but this took him by surprise. His feeling of outrage deepened. 'Hey,' he said, accusingly, 'what's all this, Rosie, why didn't you let me know?'

She looked upset, but said, evasively: 'It was all over so quick, and they took her away – there didn't seem no point in getting you disturbed too.'

George pulled out a chair and sat opposite her. He had thought that there was nothing new to learn about Rose, after three years. But now he was giving her troubled and apprehensive glances; she seemed a stranger. In appearance she was small and dark, rather too thin. She had a sharp, pale face, with an irregular prettiness about it. She usually wore a dark skirt and a white blouse. She would sit up at night to wash and iron the blouse so that it would always be fresh. This freshness, the neatness, was her strongest characteristic. 'You look as if you could be pulled through a hedge backwards and come out with every hair in order,' he used to tease her. To which she might reply: 'Don't make me laugh. How could I?' She would be quite serious; and at such moments he might sigh, humourously, admitting that she had no sense of humour. But really he liked her seriousness, her calm practicality: he relied on it. Now he said, rather helplessly: 'Don't take on Rosie, everything's all right.'

'I'm not taking on,' she replied unnecessarily, looking quietly at him, or rather, through him, with an air of patient waiting. He was now more apprehensive than angry. 'How's your Dad?' he asked.

'I've put him to bed with a nice cup of tea.'

'How's he taking it?'

She seemed to shrug. 'Well, he's upset, but he's getting over it now.'

And now, for the life of him, he could think of nothing to say. The clock's ticking seemed very loud, and he shifted his feet noisily. After a long silence he said aggressively:

'This won't make any difference to us, it'll be all right next week, Rosie?'

He knew that it wasn't all right when, after a further pause, she turned her eyes towards him with a full, dark, vague stare: 'Oh, well, I don't know. . . .'

'What do you mean?' he challenged quickly, leaning across at her, forcibly, so that she might be made to respond: 'What do you mean, Rosie, let us have it now.'

'Well – there's Dad,' she replied, with that maddening vagueness.

'You mean we shan't get married?' he shouted angrily. 'Three years, Rosie . . .' As her silence persisted: 'Your Dad can live with us. Or – he might be getting married again – or something.'

Suddenly she laughed, and he winced: her moments of rough humour always disconcerted him. At the same time they pained him because they seemed brutal. 'You mean to say,' she said, clumsily jeering, 'you mean you hope he gets married again, even if no one else'd ever think of it.' But her eyes were filled with tears. They were lonely and self-sufficing tears. He slowly fell back into his chair, letting his hands drop loosely. He simply could not understand it. He could not understand her. It flashed into his mind that she intended not to marry him at all, but this was too monstrous a thought, and he comforted himself: 'She'll be all right by tomorrow, it's the shock, that's all. She liked her ma, really, even though they scrapped like two cats.' He was just going to say: 'Well, if I can't do anything I'll be getting along; I'll come and see you tomorrow,' when she asked him carefully, as if it were an immense effort for her to force her attention on to him: 'Would you like a cuppa tea?'

'Rose!' he shouted miserably.

'What?' She sounded unhappy but stubborn; and she was unreachable, shut off from him behind a barrier of – what? He did not know. 'Oh, go to hell then,' he muttered, and got up and stamped out of the kitchen. At the door he gave her an appealing glance, but she was not looking at him. He slammed the door hard. Afterwards he thought guiltily: She's upset, and then I treat her bad.

But Rose did not think of him when he had gone. She

remained where she was, for some time, looking vaguely at the calendar with the yellow roses. Then she got up, washed her hands, hung her apron on the hook behind the door, as usual, and went to bed. 'That's over,' she said to herself, meaning George. She began to cry. She knew she would not marry him – rather, *could* not marry him. She did not know why this was impossible or why she was crying: she could not understand her own behaviour. Up till so few hours before she had been going to marry George, live with him in the little flat: everything was settled. Yet, from the moment she had heard the shocked voices saying outside in the street: Mrs. Johnson's dead, she's been killed – from that moment, or so it seemed now, it had become impossible to marry George. One day he had meant everything to her, he represented her future, and the next, he meant nothing. The knowledge was shocking to her; above all she prided herself on being a sensible person; the greatest praise she could offer was: 'You've got sense,' or 'I like people to behave proper, no messing about.' And what she felt was not sensible, therefore, she could not think too closely about. She cried for a long time, stifling her sobs so that her father could not hear them where he lay through the wall. Then she lay awake and stared at the square of light that showed chimney-pots and the dissolving yellowish clouds of a rainy London dawn, scolding herself scornfully: What's the good of crying? while she mopped up the tears that rose steadily under her lids and soaked down her cheeks to the already damp pillow.

Next morning when her father asked over breakfast cups: 'Rosie, what are you going to do about George?' she replied calmly, 'It's all right, he came last night and I told him.'

'You told him what?' He spoke cautiously. His round, fresh face looked troubled, the clear, rather childlike blue eyes were not altogether approving. His workmates knew him as a jaunty, humorous man with a warm, quick laugh and ingrained opinions about life and politics. In his home he was easy and uncritical. He had been married for twenty-five years to a woman who had outwardly let him do as he pleased while taking all the responsibility on herself. He knew this. He used to say of his wife: 'Once she's got an idea into her head you might as well whistle at a wall!' And now he was looking at his daughter as he had at the mother. He did not know what she had planned, but he knew nothing he said would make any difference.

'Everything's all right, Dad,' Rose said quietly.

I daresay, he thought; but what's it all about? He asked: 'You don't have to get ideas into your head about not getting married. I'm easy.' Without looking at him she filled his cup with the strong, brown, sweet tea he loved, and said again: It's all right.' He persisted: 'You don't want to make any mistakes now, Rosie, you're upset, and you want to give yourself time to have a good think about things.'

To this there was no reply at all. He sighed and took his newspaper to the fire. It was Sunday. Rose was cooking the dinner when George came in. Jem, the father, turned his back on the couple, having nodded at George, thus indicating that as far as he was concerned they were alone. He was thinking: George's a good bloke, she's a fool if she gives him up.

'Well, Rosie?' said George, challengingly, the misery of the sleepless night bursting out of him.

'Well what?' temporized Rose, wiping dishes. She kept her head lowered and her face was pale and set hard. Confronted thus, with George's unhappiness, her decision did not seem so secure. She wanted to cry. She could not afford to cry now, in front of him. She went to the window so that her back might be turned to him. It was a deep basement, and she looked up at the rubbish-can and railings showing dirty black against the damp, grey houses opposite. This had been her view of the world since she could remember. She heard George saying, uncertainly: 'You marry me on Wednesday, the way we fixed it, and your Dad'll be all right, he can stay here or live with us, just as you like.'

'I'm sorry,' said Rose after a pause.

'But why, Rosie, why?'

Silence. 'Don't know,' she muttered. She sounded obstinate but unhappy. Grasping this moment of weakness in her, he laid his hand on her shoulder and appealed: 'Rosie girl, you're upset, that's all it is.' But she tensed her shoulder against him and then, since his hand remained there, jerked herself away and said angrily: 'I'm sorry. It's no good. I keep telling you.'

'Three years,' he said slowly, looking at her in amazed anger. 'Three years! And now you throw me over.'

She did not reply at once. She could see the monstrousness of what she was doing and could not help herself. She had loved him then. Now he exasperated her. 'I'm not throwing you over,' she said defensively.

'So you're not!' he shouted in derision, his face clenched in pain and rage. 'What are you doing then?'

'I don't know,' she said helplessly.

He stared at her, suddenly swore under his breath and went to the door: 'I'm not coming back,' he said, 'you're just playing the fool with me, Rosie. You shouldn't 've treated me like this. No one'd stand for it, and I'm not going to.' There was no sound from Rose, and so he went out.

Jem slowly let down the paper and remarked: 'You want to think what you're doing, Rosie.'

She did not reply. The tears were pouring down her face, but she wiped them impatiently away and bent to the oven. Later that day Jem watched her secretly over the top of the paper. There was a towel-rail beside the dresser. She was unscrewing it and moving it to a different position. She rolled the dresser itself into the opposite corner and then shifted various ornaments on the mantelpiece. Jem remembered that over each of these things she had bickered with her mother: the women could not agree about where the dresser would stand best, or the height of the towel-rail. So now Rose was having her own way, thought Jem, amazed at the sight of his daughter's quiet but determined face. The moment her mother was dead she moved everything to suit herself. . . . Later she made tea and sat down opposite him, in her mother's chair. Women, thought Jem, half humorous, half shocked at the persistence of the thing. And she was throwing over a nice, decent chap just because of – what? At last he shrugged and accepted it; he knew she would have her way. Also, at the bottom of his heart, he was pleased. He would never have put any pressure on her to give up marriage, but he was glad that he did not have to move, that he could stay in his old ways without disturbance. She's still young, he comforted himself; there's plenty of time for her to marry.

A month later they heard George had married someone else. Rose had a pang of regret, but it was the kind of regret one feels for something inevitable, that could not have been otherwise. When they met in the street, she said 'Hullo George,' and he gave her a curt, stiff nod. She even felt a little hurt because he would not let bygones be; that he felt he had to store resentment. If she could greet him nicely, as a friend, then it was unkind of him to treat her coldly. ... She glanced with covert interest at the girl who was his wife, and waited for a greeting; but the girl averted her face and stared coldly away. She knew about Rose; she knew she had got George on the rebound.

This was in 1938. The rumours and the fear of war were still more an undercurrent in people's minds than a part of their thinking. Vaguely, Rose and her father expected that everything would continue as they were. About four months after the mother's death, Jem said one day: 'Why don't you give up your work now. We can manage without what you earn, if we're careful.'

'Yes?' said Rose, in the sceptical way which already told him his pleading was wasted. 'You've got too much,' he persisted. 'Cleaning and cooking, and then out all day at work.'

'Men,' she said simply, with a good-natured but dismissing sniff.

'There's no sense in it,' he protested, knowing he was wasting his breath. His wife had insisted on working until Rose was sixteen and could take her place. 'Women should be independent,' she had said. And now Rose was saying: 'I like to be independent.'

Jem said: 'Women. They say all women want is a man to keep them, but you and your mother, you go on as if I'm trying to do you out of something when I say you mustn't work.'

'Women here and women there,' said Rose. 'I don't know about *women*. All I know is what I think.'

Jem was that old type of Labour man who has been brought up in the trade union movement. He went to meetings once or twice a week, and sometimes his friends came in for a cup of tea and an argument. For years he had been saying to his wife: 'If they paid you proper, it'd be different. You work ten hours a day, and it's all for the bosses.' Now he used the argument on Rose, and she said: 'Oh, politics, I'm not interested.' Her father said: 'You're as stubborn as a mule, like your mother.'

'Then I am,' said Rose, good-humouredly. She would have said she had not 'got on' with her mother; she had had to fight to become independent of that efficient and possessive woman. But in this she agreed with her: it had been instilled into her ever since she could remember, that women must look after themselves. Like her mother, she was indulgent about the trade union meetings, as if they were a childish amusement that men should be allowed; and she voted Labour to please him, as her mother had done. And every time her father pleaded with her to give up her job at the bakery she inexorably replied: 'Who knows what might happen? It's silly not to be careful.' And so she continued to get up early in order to clean the basement kitchen and the two little rooms over it that was their home; then she made the breakfast and went out to shop. Then she went to the bakery, and at six o'clock came back to cook supper for her father. At week-ends she had a grand clean-up of the whole place, and cooked puddings and cakes. They were in bed most nights by nine. They never went out. They listened to the radio while they ate, and they read the newspapers. It was a hard life, but Rose did not think of it as hard. If she had ever used words like happiness she would have said she was happy. Sometimes she thought wistfully, not of George, but of the baby his wife was going to have. Perhaps, after all, she had made a terrible mistake? Then she squashed the thought and comforted herself: There's plenty of time, there's no hurry, I couldn't leave Dad now.

When the war started she accepted it fatalistically, while her father was deeply upset. His vision of the future had been the old socialist one: everything would slowly get better and better; and one day the working man would get into power by the automatic persuasion of common sense, and then – but his picture of that time was not so clear. Vaguely he thought of a house with a little garden and a holiday by the sea once a year. The family had never been able to afford a proper holiday. But the war cut right across this vision.

'Well, what did you expect?' asked Rose satirically.

'What do you mean?' he demanded aggressively. 'If Labour'd been in, it wouldn't have happened.'

'Maybe, maybe not.'

'You're just like your mother,' he complained again. 'You haven't got any logic.'

'Well, you've been going to meetings for years and years, and you make resolutions, and you talk, but there's a war just the same.' She felt as if this ended the argument. She felt, though she could never have put it into words, that there was a deep basic insecurity, that life itself was an enemy to be placated and humoured, liable at any moment to confront her, or people like her, with death or destitution. The only sensible thing to do was to gather together every penny that came along and keep it safe. When her mother had been alive, she paid thirty shillings of the two pounds a week she earned towards the housekeeping. Now that thirty shillings went straight into the post-office. When the newspapers and the wireless blared war and horror at her, she thought of that money, and it comforted her. It didn't amount to much, but if something happened. ... What that *something* might be, she did not clearly know. But life was terrible, there was no justice – had not her own mother been killed by a silly lorry crossing the street she had crossed every day of her life for twenty-five years ... that just proved it. And now there was a war, and all sorts of people were going to be hurt, all for nothing – that proved it too, if it needed any proof. Life was frightening and dangerous – therefore, put money into the post-office; hold on to your job, work, and – put money into the post-office.

Her father sat over the wireless set, bought newspapers, argued with his cronies, trying to make sense of the complicated, cynical movements of power politics, while the familiar pattern of life dissolved into the slogans and noise of war, and the streets filled with uniforms and rumours. 'It's all Hitler,' he would say aggressively to Rose.

'Maybe, maybe not.'

'Well, he started it, didn't he?'

'I'm not interested who started it. All I know is, ordinary

people don't want war. And there's war all the time. They make me sick if you want to know – and you men make me sick, too. If you were young enough, you'd be off like the rest of them,' she said accusingly.

'But Rosie,' he said, really shocked, 'Hitler's got to be stopped, hasn't he?'

'Hitler,' she said scornfully. 'Hitler and Churchill and Stalin and Roosevelt – they all make me sick, if you want to know. And that goes for your Attlee too.'

'Women haven't got any logic,' he said, in despair.

So they came not to discuss the war at all, they merely suffered it. Slowly, Rose came to use the same words and slogans as everyone else; and like everyone else, with the deep, sad knowledge that it was all talk, and what was really happening in the world was something vast and terrible, beyond her comprehension; and perhaps it was wonderful, too, if she only knew – but she could never hope to understand. Better get on with the job, live as best she could, try not to be afraid and – put money in the post office.

Soon she switched to a job in a munitions factory. She felt she ought to do something for the war, and also, she was paid much better than in the bakery. She did fire-watching, too. Often she was up till three or four and then woke at six to clean and cook. Her father continued as a bricklayer and did fire-watching three or four nights a week. They were both permanently tired and sad. The war went on, month after month, year after year, food was short, it was hard to keep warm, the searchlights wheeled over the dark wilderness of London, the bombs fell screaming, and the blackout was like a weight on their minds and spirits. They listened to the news, read the newspapers, with the same look of bewildered but patient courage; and it seemed as if the war was a long, black, noisome tunnel from which they would never emerge.

In the third year Jem fell off a ladder one cold, foggy morning and injured his back. 'It's all right. Rose,' he said. 'I can get back to work all right.'

'You're not working,' she said flatly. 'You're sixty-seven. That's enough now, you've been working since you was fourteen.'

'There won't be enough coming in every week.'

'Won't there?' she said triumphantly. 'You used to go on at me for working. Aren't you glad now? With your bit of pension and what I get, I can still put some away every week if I try. Funny thing,' she said reflectively, not without grim humour: 'It was two pounds a week when there was peace, and I was supposed to be grateful for it. Comes a war and they pay you like you was a queen. I'm getting seven pounds a week now, one way and another. So you take things easy, and if I find you getting back to work, with your back as it is, and your rheumatism, you'll catch it from me, I'm telling you.'

'It's not right for me to sit at home, with the war and all,' he said uneasily.

'Well, did you make the war? No! You have some sense now.'

Now things were not so hard for Rose because when Jem could get out of bed he cleaned the rooms for her and there was a cup of tea waiting when she came in at night. But there was an emptiness in her and she could not pretend to herself there was not. One day she saw George's wife in the street with a little girl of about four, and stopped her. The girl was hostile, but Rose said hurriedly: 'I wanted to know, how's George?' Rather unwillingly came the reply: 'He's all right, so far, he's in North Africa.' She held the child to her as she spoke, as if for comfort, and the tears came into Rose's eyes. The two women stood hesitating on the pavement, then Rose said appealingly: 'It must be hard for you.' 'Well, it'll be over some day – when they've stopped playing soldiers,' was the grim reply; and at this Rose smiled in sympathy and the women suddenly felt friendly towards each other. 'Come over some time if you like,' said George's wife, slowly; and Rose said quickly: 'I'd like to ever so much.'

So Rose got into the habit of going over once a week to the rooms that had originally been got ready for herself. She went because of the little girl, Jill. She was secretly asking herself now: Did I make a mistake then? Should I have married George? But even as she asked the question she knew it was futile: she could have behaved in no other way; it was one of those irrational, emotional things that seem so slight and meaningless, but are so powerful. And yet, time was passing, she was nearly thirty, and when she looked in the mirror she was afraid. She was very thin now, nothing but a white-faced shrimp of a girl, with lank, tired, stringy black hair. Her sombre dark eyes peered anxiously back at her over hollowed and bony cheeks. 'It's because I work so hard,' she comforted herself. 'No sleep, that's what it is, and the bad food, and those chemicals in the factory . . . it'll be better after the war.' It was a question of endurance; somehow she had to get through the war, and then everything would be all right. Soon she looked forward all week to the Sunday night when she went over to George's wife, with a little present for Jill. When she lay awake at nights she thought not of George, nor of the men she met at the factory who might have become interested in her, but of children. 'What with the war and all the men getting killed,' she sometimes worried, 'perhaps it's too late. There won't be any men left by the time they've finished killing them all off.' But if her father could have managed for himself before, he could not now; he was really dependent on her. So she always pushed away her fears and longings with the thought: 'When the war's over we can eat and sleep again, and then I'll look better, and then perhaps . . .'

Not long before the war ended Rose came home late one night, dragging her feet tiredly along the dark pavement, thinking that she had forgotten to buy anything for supper. She turned into her street, was troubled by a feeling that something was wrong, looked down towards the house where she lived, and stopped dead. There were heaps of smoking rubble showing against the reddish glare of fire. At first she thought: 'I must have come to the wrong street in the black-out.' Then she understood and began to run towards her home, clutching her handbag tightly, holding the scarf under her chin. At the edge of the street was a deep crater. She nearly fell into it, but righted herself and walked on stumblingly among bomb refuse and tangling wires. Where her gate had been she stopped. A group of people were standing there. 'Where's my father?' she demanded angrily. 'Where is he?' A young man came forward and said, 'Take it easy, miss.' He laid a hand on her shoulder. 'You live here? I think your Dad was an unlucky one.' The words brought no conviction to her and she stared at him, frowning. 'What have you done with him?' she asked, accusingly. 'They took him away, miss.' She stood passively, then she heavily lifted her head and looked around her. In this part of the street all the houses were gone. She pushed her way through the people and stood looking down at the steps to the basement door. The door was hanging loose from the frame, but the glass of the window was whole. 'It's all right,' she said, half-aloud. She took a key from her handbag and slowly descended the steps over a litter of bricks. 'Miss, miss,' called the young man, 'you can't go down there.' She made no reply, but fitted the key into the door and tried to turn it. It would not turn, so she pushed the door, it swung in on its one remaining hinge, and she went inside. The place looked as it always did, save that the ornaments on the mantelpiece had been knocked to the floor. It was half-lit from the light of burning houses over the street. She was slowly picking up the ornaments and putting them back when a hand was laid on her arm. 'Miss,' said a compassionate voice, 'you can't stay down here.'

'Why shouldn't I?' she retorted, with a flash of stubbornness.

She looked upwards. There was a crack across the ceiling and dust was still settling through the air. But a kettle was boiling on the stove. 'It's all right,' she announced. 'Look, the gas is still working. If the gas is all right then things isn't too bad, that stands to reason, doesn't it now?'

'You've got the whole weight of the house lying on that ceiling,' said the man dubiously.

'The house has always stood over the ceiling hasn't it,' she said, with a tired humour that surprised him. He could not see what was funny, but she was grinning heavily at the joke. 'So nothing's changed,' she said, airily. But there was a look on her face that worried him, and she was trembling in a hard, locked way, as if her muscles were held rigid against the weakness of her flesh. Sudden spasmodic shudders ran through her, and then she shut her jaw hard to stop them. 'It's not safe,' he protested again, and she obediently gazed around her to see. The kettle and the pans stood as they had ever since she could remember; the cloth on the table was one her mother had embroidered, and through the cracked window she would see the black, solid shape of the dustcan, though beyond it there were no silhouettes of grey houses, only grey sky spurting red flame. 'I think it's all right,' she said, stolidly. And she did. She felt safe. This was her home. She lifted the kettle and began making tea. 'Have a cup?' she inquired, politely. He did not know what to do. She took her cup to the table, blew off the thick dust and began stirring in sugar. Her trembling made the spoon tinkle against the cup.

'I'll be back,' he announced suddenly, and went out, meaning to fetch someone who would know how to talk to her. But now there was no one outside. They had all gone over to the burning houses; and after a little indecision he thought: I'll come back later, she's all right for the moment. He helped with the others over at the houses until very late, and he was on his way home when he remembered: That kid, what's she doing? Almost, he went straight home. He had not had his clothes off for nights, he was black and grimy, but he made the effort and returned to the basement under the heap of rubble. There was a faint glow beneath the ruin and, peering low, he saw two candles on the table, while a small figure sat sewing beside them. Well I'll be ... he thought, and went in. She was darning socks. He went beside her and said: 'I've come to see if you're all right.' Rose worked on her sock and replied calmly: 'Yes, of course I'm all right, but thanks for dropping in.' Her eyes were enormous, with a wild look, and her mouth was trembling like that of an old woman. 'What are you doing?' he asked, at a loss. 'What do you think?' she said, tartly. Then she looked wonderingly at the sock which was stretched across her palm and shuddered. 'Your Dad's sock?' he said carefully; and she gave him an angry glance and began to cry. That's better, he thought, and went forward and made her lean against him while he said aloud: 'Take it easy, take it easy, miss.' But she did not cry for long. Almost at once she pushed him away and said: 'Well, there's no need to let the socks go to waste. They'll do for someone.'

'That's right, miss.' He stood hesitantly beside her and, after a moment, she lifted her head and looked at him. For the first time she saw him. He was a slight man, of middle height, who seemed young because of the open, candid face, though his hair was greying. His pleasant grey eyes rested compassionately on her and his smile was warm. 'Perhaps you'd like them,' she suggested. 'And there's his clothes, too – he didn't have anything very special, but he always looked after his things.' She began to cry again, this time more quietly, with small, shuddering sobs. He sat gently beside her, patting her hand as it lay on the table, repeating, 'Take it easy miss, take it easy, it's all right.' The sound of his voice soothed her and soon she came to an end, dried her eyes and said in a matter-of-fact voice: 'There, I'm just silly, what's the use of crying?' She got up, adjusted the candles so that they would not gutter over the cloth, and said: 'Well, we might as well have a cup of tea.' She brought him one, and they sat drinking in silence. He was watching her curiously; there was something about her that tugged at his imagination. She was such an indomitable little figure sitting there staring out of sad, tired eyes, under the ruins of her home, like a kind of waif. She was not pretty, he decided, looking at the small, thin face, at the tired locks of black hair lying tidily beside it. He felt tender towards her; also he was troubled by her. Like everyone who lived through the big cities during the war, he knew a great deal about nervous strain; about shock; he could not have put words around what he knew, but he felt there was still something very wrong with Rose; outwardly, however, she seemed sensible, and so he suggested: 'You'd better get yourself some sleep. It'll be morning soon.'

'I've got to be getting to work. I'm working an early shift.'

He said: 'If you feel like it,' thinking it might be better for her to work. And so he left her, and went back home to get some sleep.

That next evening he came by expecting to find her gone, and saw her sitting at the table, in the yellow glow from the candles, her hands lying idly before her, staring at the wall. Everything was very tidy, and the dust had been removed. But the crack in the ceiling had perceptibly widened. 'Hasn't anyone been to see you?' he asked carefully. She replied evasively: 'Oh, some old nosey-parkers came and said I mustn't stay.' 'What did you tell them?' She hesitated, and then said: 'I said I wasn't staying here, I was with some friends.' He scratched his head, smiling ruefully:

he could imagine the scene. 'Those old nosey-parkers,' she went on resentfully, 'interfering, telling people what to do.'

'You know miss, I think they were right, you ought to move out.'

'I'm staying here,' she announced defiantly, with unmistakable fear. 'Nothing's getting me out. Not all the king's horses.'

'I don't expect they could spare the king's horses,' he said, trying to make her laugh; but she replied seriously, after considering it: 'Well, even if they could.' He smiled tenderly at her literal-mindedness, and suggested on an impulse: 'Come to the pictures with me, doesn't do any good to sit and mope.'

'I'd like to, but it's Sunday, see?'

'What's the matter with a Sunday?'

'Every Sunday I go and see a friend of mine who has a little girl ...' she began to explain; and then she stopped, and went pale. She scrambled to her feet and said: 'Oh oh, I never thought ...'

'What's wrong, what's up?'

'Perhaps that bomb got them too, they were along this street – oh dear, oh dear, I never came to think – I'm wicked, that's what I am. ...' She had taken up her bag and was frantically wrapping her scarf around her head.

'Here, miss, don't go rushing off – I can find out for you, perhaps I know – what was her name?'

She told him. He hesitated for a moment and then said: 'You're having bad luck, and that's a fact. She was killed the same time.'

'She?' asked Rose, quickly.

'The mother was killed, the kid's all right, it was playing in another room.'

Rose slowly sat down, thinking deeply, her hand still holding the scarf together at her chin. Then she said: 'I'll adopt her, that's what I'll do.'

He was surprised that she showed no sort of emotion at the death of the woman, her friend. 'Hasn't the kid got a dad?' he asked. 'He's in North Africa,' she said. 'Well, he'll come back after the war, he might not want you to adopt the kid.' But she was silent, and her face was hard with determination. 'Why this kid in particular?' he asked. 'You'll have kids of your own one day.'

She said evasively: 'She's a nice kid, you should see her.' He left it. He could see that there was something here too deep for him to grasp. Again he suggested: 'Come to the pictures and take your mind off things.' Obediently she rose and placed herself at his disposal, as it were. Walking along the streets she turned this way and that at a touch of his hand, but in spirit she was not with him. He knew that she sat through the film without seeing it. 'She's in a bad way,' he said helplessly to himself. 'It's time she snapped out of it.'

But Rose was thinking only of Jill. Her whole being was now concentrated on the thought of the little girl. To-morrow she would find out where she was. Some nosey-parkers would have got hold of her – that was certain; they were always bossing other people. She would take Jill away from them and look after her – they could stay in the base-ment until the house got rebuilt. ... Rose was awake all night, dreaming of Jill; and next day she did not go to work. She went in search of the child. She found her grandmother had taken her. She had never thought of the grandmother, and the discovery was a such a shock that she came back to the basement not knowing how she walked or what she did. The fact that she could not have the child seemed more terrible than anything else; it was as if she had been de-prived maliciously of something she had a right to; some-thing had been taken away from her – that was how she felt.

Jimmie came that night. He was asking himself why he kept returning, what it would come to; and yet he could not keep away. The image of Rose, the silent, frightened little girl – which was how he saw her – stayed with him all day. When he entered the basement she was sitting as usual by the candles, staring before her. He saw with dismay that she had made no effort to clean the place, and that her hair was untidy. This last fact seemed worse than anything.

He sat beside her, as usual, and tried to think of some way to make her 'snap out of it.' At last he remarked: 'You ought to be making some plans to move, Rose.' At this, she irritably shrugged her shoulders. She wished he would stop pestering her with this sort of reminder. At the same time she was glad to have him there. She would have liked him to stay beside her silently; his warm friendliness wrapped her about like a blanket, but she could never relax into it because there was a part of her mind alert against him for fear of what he might say.

She was afraid, really, that he might talk of her father. Not once had she allowed herself to think of it – her father's death, as it must have been. She said to herself the words: My father's dead, just as she had once said to herself: My mother's dead. Never had she allowed those words to form into images of death. If they had been ordinary deaths, deaths one could understand, it would have been different. People dying of illness or age, in bed; and then the neighbours coming, and then the funeral – that was understandable, that would have been different. But not the senselessness of a black bomb falling out of the sky, dropped by a nice young man in an aeroplane, not the silly business of a lorry running someone over – no, she could not bear to think of it. Underneath the surface of living was a black gulf, full of senseless horror. All day, at the factory (where she helped to make other bombs) or in the basement at night, she made the usual movements, said the expected things, but never allowed herself to think of death. She said: My father's been killed, in a flat, ordinary voice, without letting pictures of death arise into her mind.

And now here was Jimmie, who had come into her life just when she needed his warmth and support most; and even this was two-faced, because it was the same Jimmie who made these remarks, forcing her to think . . . she would not think, she refused to respond. Jimmie noticed that whenever he made a remark connected in any way with the future, or even with the war, a blank, nervous look came on to her face and she turned away her eyes. He did not know what to do. For that evening he left it, and came back next day. This was the sixth day after the bomb, and he saw that the crack in the ceiling was bulging heavily downwards from the weight on top of it, and when a car passed, bits of plaster flaked down in a soft white rain. It was really dangerous. He had to do something. And still she sat there, her hands lying loosely in front of her, staring at the wall. He decided to be cruel. His heart was hammering with fright at what he was going to do; but he announced in a loud and cheerful voice: 'Rose, your father's dead, he's not going to come back.'

She turned her eyes vaguely towards him; it seemed as if she had not heard at all. But he had to go on now. 'Your Dad's had it,' he said brightly. 'He's copped it. He's dead as a doornail, and it's no use staying here.'

'How do you know?' she asked faintly. 'Sometimes there are mistakes. Sometimes people come back, don't they?'

This was much worse than he had thought. 'He won't come back. I saw him myself.'

'No,' she protested, sharply drawing breath.

'Oh, yes I did. He was lying on the pavement, smashed to smithereens.' He was waiting for her face to change. So far, it was obstinate, but her eyes were fixed on him like a scared rabbit's. 'Nothing left,' he announced, jauntily, 'his legs were gone – nothing there at all, and he didn't have a head left either. . . .'

And now Rose got to her feet with a sudden angry movement, and her eyes were small and black. 'You . . .' she began. Her lips shook. Jimmie remained seated. He was trying to look casual, even jaunty He was forcing himself to smile. Underneath he was very frightened. Supposing this was the wrong thing? Supposing she went clean off her rocker . . . supposing . . . He passed his tongue quickly over his lips and glanced at her to see how she was. She was still staring at him. But now she seemed to hate him. He wanted to laugh from fright. But he stood up and, with an appearance of deliberate brutality, said: 'Yes Rosie girl, that's how it is, your Dad's nothing but a bleeding corpse – that's good, bleeding!' And now, he thought, I've done it properly! 'You—' began Rose again, her face contracted with hatred. 'You—' And such a stream of foul language came from her mouth that it took him by surprise. He had expected her to cry, to break down. She shouted and raved at him, lifting her fists to batter at his chest. Gently holding her off he said silently to himself, giving himself courage: 'Ho, ho, Rosie my girl, what language, naughty, naughty!' Out loud he said, with uneasy jocularity: 'Hey, take it easy, it's not my fault now. . . .' He was surprised at her strength. The quiet, composed, neat little Rose was changed into a screaming hag, who scratched and kicked and clawed. 'Get out of here you—' and she picked up a candlestick and threw it at him. Holding his arm across his face, he retreated backwards to the door, gave it a kick with his heel, and went out. There he stood, waiting, with a half-rueful, half-worried smile on his face, listening. He was rubbing the scratches on his face with his handkerchief. At first there was silence, then loud sobbing. He straightened himself slowly. I might have hurt her bad, talking like that, he thought; perhaps she'll never get over it. But he felt reassured; instinctively he knew he had done the right thing. He listened to the persistent crying for a while, and then wondered: Yes, but what do I do now? Should I go back again now, or wait a little? And more persistent than these worries was another: And what then? If I go back now, I'll let myself in for something and no mistake. He slowly retreated from Rose's door, down the damaged street, to a pub at the corner, which had not been hit. Must have a drink and a bit of a think . . . Inside the pub he leaned quietly by the counter, glass in hand, his grey eyes dark with worry. He heard someone say: 'Well handsome, and what's been biting you?' He looked up, smiling, and saw Pearl. He had known her for some time – nothing serious; they exchanged greetings and bits of talk over the counter when he dropped in. He liked Pearl, but now he wanted to be left alone. She lingered and said again: 'How's your wife?' He frowned quickly, and did not reply. She made a grimace as if to say: Well, if you don't want to be sociable I'm not going to force you! But she remained where she was, looking at him closely. He was thinking: I shouldn't have started it, I shouldn't have taken her on. No business of mine what happened to her. . . . And then, unconsciously straightening himself, with a small, desperate smile that was also triumphant: You're in trouble again, my lad, you're in for it now! Pearl remarked in an offhand way: 'You'd better get your face fixed up – been in a fight?' He lifted his hand to his face and it came away covered with blood. 'Yes,' he said, grinning, 'with a spitfire.' She laughed, and he laughed with her. The words presented Rose to him in a new way. Proper little spitfire, he said to himself, caressing his cheek. Who would have thought Rose had all that fire in her? Then he set down the glass, straightened his tie, wiped his cheek with his handkerchief, nodded to Pearl with his debonair smile, and went out. Now he did not hesitate. He went straight back to the basement.

Rose was washing clothes in the sink. Her face was swollen and damp with crying, but she had combed her hair. When she saw him she went red, trying to meet his eyes, but could not. He went straight over to her and put his arms around her. 'Here, Rosie, don't get worked up now.' 'I'm sorry,' she said, with prim nervousness, trying to smile. Her eyes appealed to him. 'I don't know what came over me, I don't really.'

'It's all right, I'm telling you.'

But now she was crying from shame. 'I never use them words. Never. I didn't know I knew them. I'm not like that. And now you'll think . . .' He gathered her to him and felt her shoulders shaking. 'Now don't you waste any more time thinking about it. You were upset – well, I wanted you to be upset. I did it on purpose, don't you see, Rosie? You couldn't go on like that, pretending to yourself.' He kissed the part of her cheek that was not hidden in his shoulder. 'I'm sorry, I'm ever so sorry,' she wept, but she sounded much better.

He held her tight and made soothing noises. At the same time he had the feeling of a man sliding over the edge of a dangerous mountain. But he could not stop himself now. It was much too late. She said, in a small voice: 'You were quite right, I know you were. But it was just that I couldn't bear to think. I didn't have anybody but Dad. It's been him and me together for ever so long. I haven't got anybody at all. . . .' The thought came into her mind and vanished: Only George's little girl. She belongs to me by rights.

Jimmie said indignantly: 'Your Dad – I'm not saying anything against him, but it wasn't right to keep you here looking after him. You should have got out and found yourself a nice husband and had kids.' He did not understand why, though only for a moment, her body hardened and rejected him. Then she relaxed and said submissively: 'You mustn't say anything against my Dad.'

'No,' he agreed, mildly, 'I won't.' She seemed to be waiting. 'I haven't got anything now,' she said, and lifted her face to him. 'You've got me,' he said at last, and he was grinning a little from sheer nervousness. Her face softened, her eyes searched his, and she still waited. There was a silence, while he struggled with common sense. It was far too long a silence, and she was already reproachful when he said: 'You come with me, Rosie, I'll look after you.'

And now she collapsed against him again and wept: 'You do love me, don't you, you do love me?' He held her and said: 'Yes, of course I love you.' Well that was true enough. He did. He didn't know why, there wasn't any sense in it, she wasn't even pretty, but he loved her. Later she said: 'I'll get my things together and come to where you live.'

He temporized, with an anxious glance at the ominous ceiling: 'You stay here for a bit. I'll get things fixed first.'

'Why can't I come now?' She looked in a horrified, caged way around the basement as if she couldn't wait to get out of it – she who had clung so obstinately to its shelter.

'You just trust me now, Rosie. You pack your things, like a good girl. I'll come back and fetch you later.' She clutched his shoulders and looked into his face and pleaded: 'Don't leave me here long – that ceiling – it might fall.' It was as if she had only just noticed it. He comforted her, put her persuasively away from him, and repeated he would be back in half an hour. He left her sorting out her belongings in worried haste, her eyes fixed on the ceiling.

And now what was he going to do? He had no idea. Flats – they weren't hard to find, with so many people evacuated; yes, but here it was after eleven at night, and he couldn't even lay hands on the first week's rent. Besides, he had to give his wife some money tomorrow. He walked slowly through the damaged streets, in the thick dark, his hands in his pockets, thinking: Now you're in a fix, Jimmie boy, you're properly in a fix.

About an hour later his feet took him back. Rose was seated at the table, and on it were two cardboard boxes and a small suitcase – her clothes. Her hands were folded together in front of her.

'It's all right?' she inquired, already on her feet.

'Well, Rosie, it's like this—' he sat down and tried for the right words. 'I should've told you. I haven't got a place really.'

'You've got no place to sleep?' she inquired, incredulously.

He avoided her eyes and muttered: 'Well, there's complications.' He caught a glimpse of her face and saw there – pity! It made him want to swear. Hell, this was a mess, and what was he to do? But the sorrowful warmth of her face touched him and, hardly knowing what he was doing, he let her put her arms around him, while he said: 'I was bombed out last week.'

'And you were looking after me, and you had no place yourself?' she accused him, tenderly. 'We'll be all right. We'll find a place in the morning.'

'That's right, we'll have our own place and – can we get married soon?' she inquired shyly, going pink.

At this, he laid his face against hers, so that she could not look at him, and said: 'Let's get a place first, and we can fix everything afterwards.'

She was thinking. 'Haven't you got no money?' she inquired, diffidently at last. 'Yes, but not the cash. I'll have it later.' He was telling himself again: You're properly in the soup, Jimmie, in – the – soup!

'I've got two hundred pounds in the post-office,' she offered, smiling with shy pride, as she fondled his hair. 'And there's the furniture from here – it's not hurt by the bomb a bit. We can furnish nicely.'

'I'll give you back the money later,' he said desperately.

'When you've got it. Besides, my money is yours now,' she said, smiling tenderly at him. '*Ours*.' She tasted the word delicately, inviting him to share her pleasure in it.


Jimmie was essentially a man who knew people, got around, had irons in the fire and strings to pull; and by next afternoon he had found a flat. Two rooms and a kitchen, a cupboard for the coal, hot and cold water, and a share of the bathroom downstairs. Cheap, too. It was the top of an old house, and he was pleased that one could see trees from Battersea Park over the tops of the buildings opposite. Rose'll like it, he thought. He was happy now. All last night he had lain on the floor beside her in the ruinous basement, under the bulging ceiling, consumed by dubious thoughts; now these had vanished, and he was optimistic. But when Rose came up the stairs with her packages she went straight to the window and seemed to shrink back. 'Don't you like it, Rosie?' 'Yes, I like it, but . . .' Soon she laughed and said, apologetically: 'I've always lived underneath – I mean, I'm not used to being so high up.' He kissed her and teased her and she laughed too. But several times he noticed that she looked unhappily down from the window and quickly came away, with a swift, uncertain glance around at the empty rooms. All her life she had lived underground, with buses and cars rumbling past above eye-level, the weight of the big old house heavy over her, like the promise of protection. Now she was high above streets and houses, and she felt unsafe. Don't be silly, she told herself. You'll get used to it. And she gave herself to the pleasure of arranging furniture, putting things away. She took a hundred pounds of her money out of the post-office and bought – but what she bought was chiefly for him. A chest for his clothes: she teased him because he had so many; a small wireless set; and finally a desk for him to work on, for he had said he was studying for an engineering degree of some kind. He asked her why she bought nothing for herself, and she said, defensively, that she had plenty. She had arranged the new flat to look like her old home. The table stood the same way, the calendar with yellow roses hung on the wall, and she worked happily beside her stove, making the same movements she had used for years; for the cupboard, the drying-line and the draining-board had been fixed exactly as they had been 'at home'. Unconsciously, she still used that phrase. 'Here,' he protested, 'isn't this home now?' She said seriously: 'Yes, but I can't get used to it.' 'Then you'd better get used to it,' he complained, and then kissed her to make amends for his resentment. When this had happened several times he let out: 'Anyway, the basement's fallen in, I passed today, and it's filled with bricks and stuff.' He had intended not to tell her. She shrank away from him and went quite white. 'Well, you knew it wasn't going to stay for long,' he said. She was badly shaken. She could not bear to think of her old home gone; she could imagine it, the great beams slanting into it, filled with dirty water – she imagined it and shut out the vision for ever. She was quiet and listless all that day, until he grew angry with her. He was quite often angry. He would protest when she bought things for him. 'Don't you like it?' she would inquire, looking puzzled. 'Yes, I like it fine, but ...' And later she was hurt because he seemed reluctant to use the chest, or the desk.

There were other points where they did not understand each other. About four weeks after they moved in she said: 'You aren't much of a one for home, are you?' He said, in genuine astonishment: 'What do you mean? I'm stuck here like ...' He stopped, and put a cigarette in his mouth to take the place of speech. From his point of view he had turned over a new leaf; he was a man who hated to be bound, to spend every evening the same way; and now he came to Rose most evenings straight from work, ate supper with her, paid her sincere compliments on her cooking, and then – well, there was every reason why he should come, he would be a fool not to! He was consumed by secret pride in her. Fancy Rose, a girl like her, living with her old man all these years, like a girl shut into a convent, or not much better – you'd think there was something wrong with a girl who got to be thirty before having a man in her bed! But there was nothing wrong with Rose. And at work he'd think of their nights and laugh with deep satisfaction. She was all right, Rose was. And then, slowly, a doubt began to eat into the pride. It wasn't natural that she'd been alone all those years. Besides, she was a good-looker. He laughed when he remembered that he had thought her quite ugly at first. Now that she was happy, and in a place of her own, and warmed through with love, she was really pretty. Her face had softened, she had a delicate colour in her thin cheeks, and her eyes were deep and welcoming. It was like coming home to a little cat, all purring and pliable. And when he took her to the pictures he walked proudly by her, conscious of the other men's glances at her. And yet he was the first man who had had the sense to see what she could be? – hmm, not likely, it didn't make sense.

He talked to Rose, and suddenly the little cat showed its sharp and unpleasant claws. 'What is it you want to know?' she demanded coldly, after several clumsy remarks from him. 'Well, Rosie – it's that bloke George, you said you were going to marry him when you were a kid still?'

'What of it?' she said, giving him a cool glance.

'You were together for a long time?'

'Three years,' she said flatly.

'Three years!' he exclaimed. He had not thought of anything so serious. 'Three years is a long time.'

She looked at him with a pleading reproach that he entirely failed to understand. As far as she was concerned the delight Jimmie had given her completely cancelled out anything she had known before. George was less than a memory. When she told herself that Jimmie was the first man she had loved, it was true, because that was how she felt. The fact that he could now question it, doubting himself, weakened the delight, made her unsure not only of him but of herself. How could he destroy their happiness like this! And into the reproach came contempt. She looked at him with heavy, critical eyes; and Jimmie felt quite wild with bewilderment and dismay – she could look at him like that! – then that proved she had been lying when she said he was the first – if she had said so. ... 'But Rosie,' he blustered, 'it stands to reason. Engaged three years, and you tell me ...'

'I've never told you anything,' she pointed out, and got up from the table and began stacking the dishes ready for washing.

'Well, I've a right to know, haven't I?' he cried out, unhappily.

But this was very much a mistake. 'Right?' she inquired in a prim, disdainful voice. She was no longer Rose, she was something much older. She seemed to be hearing her mother speaking. 'Who's talking about rights?' She dropped the dishes neatly into the hot, soapy water and said: 'Men! I've never asked you what you did before me. And I'm not interested either, if you want to know. And what I did, if I did anything, doesn't interest you neither.' Here she turned on the tap so that the splashing sound made another barrier. Her ears filled with the sound of water, she thought: Men, they always spoil everything. She had forgotten George, he didn't exist. And now Jimmie brought him to life and made her think of him. Now she was forced to wonder: Did I love him as much then? Was it the same as this? And if her happiness with George had been as great as now it was with Jimmie, then that very fact seemed to diminish love itself and make it pathetic and uncertain. It was as if Jimmie were doing it on purpose to upset her. That, at any rate, was how she felt.

But across the din of the running water Jimmie shouted: 'So I'm not interested, is that it?'

'No, you'd better not be interested,' she announced, and looked stonily before her, while her hands worked among the hot, slippery plates. 'So that's how it is?' he shouted again, furiously.

To which she did not reply. He remained leaning at the table, calling Rose names under his breath, but at the same time conscious of bewilderment. He felt that all his possessive masculinity was being outraged and flouted; there was, however, no doubt that she felt as badly treated as he did. As she did not relent he went to her and put his arms around her. It was necessary for him to destroy this aloof and wounded-looking female and restore the loving, cosy woman. He began to tease: 'Spitfire, little cat, that's what you are.' He pulled her hair and held her arms to her sides so that she could not dry the plates. She remained unresponsive. Then he saw that the tears were running down her immobile and stubborn cheeks, and in a flush of triumph picked her up and carried her over to the bed. It was all quite easy, after all.

But maybe not so easy, because late that night, in a studiously indifferent voice, Rose inquired from the darkness at his side: 'When are we going to get married?' He stiffened. He had forgotten – or almost – about this. Hell, wasn't she satisfied? Didn't he spend all his evenings here? He might just as well be married, seeing what she expected of him. 'Don't you trust me, Rosie?' he inquired at last. 'Yes, I trust you,' she said, rather doubtfully, and waited. 'There's reasons why I can't marry you just now.' She remained silent, but her silence was like a question hanging in the dark between them. He did not reply, but turned and kissed her. 'I love you, Rosie, you know that, don't you?' Yes, she knew that; but about a week later he left her one morning saying: 'I can't come tonight, Rosie. I've got to put in some work on this exam.' He saw her glance at the desk she had bought him and which he had never used. 'I'll be along tomorrow as usual,' he said quickly, wanting to escape from the troubled, searching eyes.

She asked suddenly: 'Your wife getting anxious about you?'

He caught his breath and stared at her: 'Who told you?' She laughed derisively. 'Well, who told you?'

'No one told me,' she said, with contempt.

'Then I must have been talking in my sleep,' he muttered, anxiously.

She laughed loudly: ' "Someone told me." "Talking in your sleep" – you must think I'm stupid.' And with a familiar, maddening gesture, she turned away and picked up a dishcloth.

'Leave the dishes alone, they're clean, anyway,' he shouted. 'Don't shout at me like that.'

'Rose,' he appealed after a moment, 'I was going to tell you, I just couldn't tell you – I tried to, often.'

'Yes?' she said, laconically. That *yes* of hers always exasperated him. It was like a statement of rock-bottom disbelief, a basic indifference to himself and the world of men. It was as if she said: There's only one person I can rely on – myself.

'Rosie, she won't divorce me, she won't give me my free-dom.' These dramatic words were supplied straight to his tongue by the memory of a film he had seen the week before. He felt ashamed of himself. But her face had changed. 'You should have told me,' she said; and once again he was dis-concerted because of the pity in her voice. She had instinctively turned to him with a protective movement. Her arms went around him and he let his head sink on her shoulder with that old feeling that he was being swept away, that he had no control over the things he did and said. Hell, he thought, even while he warmed to her tenderness: to hell with it. I never meant to get me and Rosie into this fix. In the meantime she held him comfortingly, bending her face to his hair, but there was a rigidity in her pose that told him she was still waiting. At last she said: 'I want to have kids. I'm not getting any younger.' He tightened his arms around her waist while he thought: I never thought of that. For he had two children of his own. Then he thought: She's right. She should have kids. Remember how she got worked up over that other kid in the blitz? Women need to have kids. He thought of her with his child, and pride stirred in him. He realized he would be pleased if she got pregnant, and felt even more at sea. Rose said: 'Ask her again, Jimmie. Make her divorce you. I know women get spiteful and that about divorces, but if you talk to her nice—' He miserably promised that he would. 'You'll ask her tonight?' she insisted. 'Well . . .' the fact was, that he had not intended to go home tonight. He wanted to have an evening to himself – go to the pub, see some of his pals, even work for an hour or so. 'Weren't you going home tonight?' she asked, incredulously, seeing his face. 'No, I meant it, I want to do some work. I've got to get this exam, Rosie. I know I can take it if I work a little. And then I'm qualified. Just now I'm not one thing and I'm not the other.' She accepted this with a sigh, then pleaded: 'Go home tomorrow then and ask her.'

'But tomorrow I want to come and see you, Rosie, don't you want me.' She sighed again, not knowing that she did, and smiled: 'You're nothing but a baby, Jimmy.' He began coaxing: 'Come on, be nice, Rosie, give me a kiss.' He felt it was urgently necessary for him to have her warm and relaxed and loving again before he could leave her with a quiet mind. And so she was – but not entirely. There was a thoughtful line across her forehead and her mouth was grave and sad. Oh, to hell with it, he thought, as he went off. To hell with them all.

The next evening he went to Rose anxiously. He had drunk himself gay and debonair in the pub, he had flirted a little with Pearl, talked sarcastically about women and marriage, and finally gone home to sleep. He had breakfast with his family, avoided his wife's sardonic eye, and went off to work with a bad hangover. At the factory, as always, he became absorbed in what he was doing. It was a small factory which made precision instruments. He was highly skilled, but in status an ordinary workman. He knew, had known for a long time, that with a little effort he could easily take an examination which would lift him into the middle-classes as far as money was concerned. It was the money he cared about, not the social aspect of it. For years his wife had been nagging at him to better himself, and he had answered impatiently because, for her, what mattered was to outdo their neighbours. This he despised. But she was right for the wrong reasons. It was a question of devoting a year of evenings to study. What was a year of one's life? Nothing. And he had always found examinations easy. That day, at the factory, he had decided to tell Rose that she would not see as much of him in future. He swore angrily to himself that she must understand a man had a duty to himself. He was only forty, after all. . . . And yet, even while he spoke firmly to himself and to the imaginary Rose, he saw a mental picture of the desk she had bought him that stood unused in the living-room of the flat. 'Well, who's stopping you from working?' she would inquire, puzzled. Genuinely puzzled, too. But he could not work in that flat, he knew that; although in the two months before he had met Rose he was working quite steadily in his evenings. That day he was cursing the fate that had linked him with Rose; and by evening he was hurrying to her as if some terrible thing might happen if he were not there by supper-time. He was expecting her to be cold and distant, but she fell into his arms as if he had been away for weeks. 'I missed you,' she said, clinging to him. 'I was so lonely without you.'

'It was only one night,' he said, jauntily, already reassured.

'You were gone two nights last week,' she said, mournfully. At once he felt irritated. 'I didn't know you counted them up,' he said, trying to smile. She seemed ashamed that she had said it. 'I just get lonely,' she said, kissing him guiltily. 'After all . . .'

'After all what?' His voice was aggressive.

'It's different for you,' she defended herself. 'You've got – other things.' Here she evaded his look. 'But I go to work, and then I come home and wait for you. There's nothing but you to look forward to.' She spoke hastily, as if afraid to annoy him, and then she put her arms around his neck and kissed him coaxingly and said: 'I've cooked you something you like – can you smell it?' And she was the warm and affectionate woman he wanted her to be. Later he said: 'Listen, Rosie girl, I've got to tell you something. That exam – I must start working for it.' She said, gaily, at once: 'But I told you already, you can work here at the desk and I'll sew while you work, and it'll be lovely.' The idea seemed to delight her, but his heart chilled at it. It seemed to him quite insulting to their romantic love that she should not mind his working, that she should suggest prosaic sewing – just like a wife. He spent the next few evenings with her, newly in love, absorbed in her. And he felt hurt when she suggested hurriedly – for she was afraid of a rebuff – 'If you want to work tonight, I don't mind, Jimmie.' He said laughing: 'Oh, to hell with work, you're the only work I want.' She was flattered, but the thoughtful line was marked deep across her forehead. About a fortnight after his wife was first mentioned she delicately inquired: 'Have you asked her about the divorce.'

He turned away, saying evasively, 'She wouldn't listen just now.' He was not looking at her, but he could feel her heavy, questioning look on him. His irritation was so strong that he had to make an effort to control it. Also he was guilty, and that guilt he could understand even less than the irritation. He all at once became very gay, so that his mood infected her, and they were giggling and laughing like two children. 'You're just conventional, that's what you are,' he said, pulling her hair. 'Conventional?' she tasted the big word doubtfully. 'Women always want to get married. What do you want to get married for? Aren't we happy? Don't we love each other? Getting married would just spoil it.' But theoretical statements like this always confused Rose. She would consider each of them separately, with a troubled face, rather respectful of the intellectual minds that had formulated them. And while she considered them, the current of her emotions ran steadily and deep, unconnected with words. From the gulf of love in which she was sunk she murmured, fondly: 'Oh, you – you just talk and talk.' 'Men are polygamous,' he said gaily, 'it's a fact, scientists say so.' 'What are women then?' she asked, keeping her end up. 'They aren't polygamous.' She considered this seriously, as was her way, and said doubtfully: 'Yes?' 'Hell,' he expostulated, half seriously, half laughing, 'you're telling me you're polygamous?' But Rose moved uneasily, with a laugh, away from him. To connect a word like polygamous, reeking as it did of the 'nosey-parkers' who were, she felt, her chief enemy in life, with herself, was too much to ask of her. Silence. 'You're thinking of George,' he suddenly shouted, jealously. 'I wasn't doing any such thing,' she said, indignantly. Her genuine indignation upset him. He always hated it when she was serious. As far as he was concerned, he had just been teasing her – he thought.

Once she said: 'Why do you always look cross when I say what I think about something?' Now that surprised him – didn't she always say what she thought? 'I don't get cross, Rosie, but why do you take everything so serious?' To this she remained silent, in the darkness. He could see the small, thoughtful face turned away from him, lit by the bleak light from the window. The thoughtfulness seemed to him like a reproach. He liked her childish and responsive. 'Don't I make you happy, Rose?' He sounded miserable. 'Happy?' she said, testing the word. Then she unexpectedly-laughed and said: 'You talk so funny sometimes you make me laugh.' 'I don't see what's funny, you've no sense of humour, that's what's wrong with you.' But instead of responding to his teasing voice, she thought it over and said seriously: 'Well I laugh at things, don't I? I must be laughing at something then. My Dad used to say I hadn't any sense of humour. I used to say to him: "How do you know what I laugh at isn't as funny as what you laugh at?"' He said, wryly, after a moment, 'When you laugh, It's like you're not laughing at all, it's something nasty.' 'I don't know what you mean.' 'I ask you if you're happy and you laugh – what's funny about being happy?' Now he was really resentful. Again she meditated about it, instead of responding – as he had hoped – with a laugh or some reassurance that he made her perfectly happy. 'Well, it stands to reason,' she concluded, 'people who talk about happy or unhappy, and then the long words – and the things you say, women are like this, and men are like that, and polygamous and all the rest – well . . .' 'Well?' he demanded. 'Well, it just seems funny to me,' she said lamely. For she could have found no words at all for what she felt, that deep knowledge of the dangerousness and the sadness of life. Bombs fell on old men, lorries killed people, and the war went on and on, and the nights when he did not come to her she would sit by herself, crying for hours, not knowing why she was crying, looking down from the high window at the darkened, ravaged streets – a city dark with the shadow of war.

In the early days of their love Jimmie had loved best the

hours of tender, aimless, frivolous talk. But now she was, it seemed, always grave. And she questioned him endlessly about his life, about his childhood. 'Why do you want to know?' he would inquire, unwilling to answer. And then she was hurt. 'If you love someone, you want to know about them, it stands to reason.' So he would give simple replies to her questions, the facts, not the spirit, which she wanted. 'Was your Mum good to you?' she would ask, anxiously. 'Did she cook nice?' She wanted him to talk about the things he had felt; but he would reply, shortly: 'Yes' or 'Not bad.'

'Why don't you want to tell me?' she would ask, puzzled.

He repeated that he didn't mind telling her; but all the same he hated it. It seemed to him that no sooner had one of those long, companionable silences fallen, in which he could drift off into a pleasant dream, than the questions began. 'Why didn't you join up in the war?' she asked once. 'They wouldn't have me, that's why.' 'You're lucky,' she said, fiercely. 'Lucky nothing, I tried over and over. I wanted to join.'

And then, to her obstinate silence, he said: 'You're queer. You've got all sorts of ideas. You talk like a pacifist; it's not right when there's a war on.'

'Pacifist!' she cried, angrily. 'Why do you use all these silly words? I'm not anything.'

'You ought to be careful, Rosie, if you go saying things like that where people can hear you, they'll think you're against the war, you'll get into trouble.'

'Well, I am against the war, I never said I wasn't.'

'But Rosie—'

'Oh, shut up. You make me sick. You all make me sick. Everybody just talks and talks, and those fat old so-and-so's talking away in Parliament, they just talk so they can't hear themselves think. Nobody knows anything and they pretend they do. Leave me alone, I don't want to listen.' He was silent. To this Rose he had nothing to say. She was a stranger to him. Also, he was shocked: he was a talker who liked picking up phrases from books and newspapers and using them in a verbal game. But she, who could not use words, who was so deeply inarticulate, had her own ideas and stuck to them. Because he used words so glibly she tried to become a citizen of his country – out of love for him and because she felt herself lacking. She would sit by the window with the newspapers and read earnestly, line by line, having first overcome her instinctive shrinking from the language of violence and hatred that filled them. But the war news, the slogans, just made her exhausted and anxious. She turned to the more personal. 'War takes toll of marriage,' she would read. 'War disrupts homes.' Then she dropped the paper and sat looking before her, her brow puzzled. That headline was about her, Rose. And again, she would read the divorces; some judge would pronounce: 'This unscrupulous woman broke up a happy marriage and ...' Again the paper dropped while Rose frowned and thought. That meant herself. She was one of those bad women. She was The Other Woman. She might even be that ugly thing, A Co-Respondent. ... But she didn't feel like that. It didn't make sense. So she stopped reading the newspapers, she simply gave up trying to understand.

She felt she was not on an intellectual level with Jimmie, so instinctively she fell back on her feminine weapons – much to his relief. She was all at once very gay, and he fell easily into the mood. Neither of them mentioned his wife for a time. It was their happiest time. After love, lying in the dark, they talked aimlessly, watching the sky change through moods of cloud and rain and tinted light, watching the searchlights. They took no notice of raids or danger. The war was nearly over, and they spoke as if it had already ended. 'If we was killed now, I shouldn't mind,' she said, seriously, one night when the bombs were bad. He said: 'We're not going to get killed, they can't kill us.' It sounded a simple statement of fact: their love and happiness was proof enough against anything. But she said again, earnestly: 'Even if we was killed, it wouldn't matter. I don't see how anything afterwards could be as good as this, now.'

'Ah, Rosie, don't be so serious always.'

It was not long before they quarrelled again – because she was so serious. She was asking questions again about his past. She was trying to find out why the army wouldn't have him. He would never tell her. And then he said, impatiently, one night: 'Well, if you must know, I've got ulcers ... ah, for God's sake, Rosie, don't fuss, I can't stand being fussed.'

For she had given a little cry and was holding him tight. 'Why didn't you tell me? I haven't been cooking the proper things for you.'

'Rose, for crying out aloud, don't go on.'

'But if you've got ulcers you must be fed right, it stands to reason.' And next evening when she served him some milk pudding, saying anxiously: 'This won't hurt your stomach,' he flared up and said, 'I told you, Rosie, I won't have you coddling me.' Her face was loving and stubborn and she said: 'But you've got no sense. . . .'

'For the last time, I'm not going to put up with it.'

She turned away, her mouth trembling, and he went to her and said desperately: 'Now don't take on Rosie, you mean it nicely, but I don't like it, that's why I didn't tell you before. Get it?' She responded to him, listlessly, and he found himself thinking, angrily: 'I've got two wives, not one. . . .' They were both dismayed and unhappy because their happiness was so precarious it could vanish overnight just because of a little thing like ulcers and milk pudding.

A few days later he ate in heavy silence through the supper she had provided, and then sarcasm broke out of him: 'Well, Rosie, you've decided to humour me, that's what it is.' The meal had consisted of steamed fish, baked bread and very weak tea, which he hated. She looked uncomfortable, but said obstinately: 'I went to a friend of mine who's a chemist at the corner, and he told me what it was right for you to eat.' Involuntarily he got up, his face dark with fury. He hesitated, then he went out, slamming the door.

He stood moodily in the pub, drinking. Pearl came across and said: 'What's eating you tonight?' Her tone was light, but her eyes were sympathetic. The sympathy irritated him. He ground out: 'Women!' slammed down his glass and turned to go. 'Doesn't cost you anything to be polite,' she said tartly, and he replied: 'Doesn't cost you anything to leave me alone.' Outside he hesitated a moment, feeling guilty. Pearl had been a friend for so long, and she had a soft spot for him – also, she knew about his wife, and about Rose, and made no comment, seemed not to condemn. She was a nice girl, Pearl was – he went back and said, hastily: 'Sorry,

Pearl, didn't mean it.' Without waiting for a reply he left again, and this time set off for home.

The woman he called his wife looked up from her sewing and asked briefly: 'What do you want now?'

'Nothing.' He sat down, picked up a paper and pretended to read, conscious of her glances. They were not hostile. They had gone a long way beyond that, and the fact that she seemed scarcely interested in him was a relief after Rose's persistent, warm curiosity – like loving white fingers strangling him, he thought involuntarily. 'Want something to eat?' she inquired at last.

'What have you got?' he inquired cautiously, thinking of the tasteless steamed fish and baked bread he had just been offered.

'Help yourself,' she returned, and he went to the cupboard on the landing, filled a plate with bread and mustard pickles and cheese, and came back to the room where she was. She glanced at his plate, but made no comment. After a while he asked sarcastically: 'Aren't you going to tell me I shouldn't eat pickles?'

'Couldn't care less,' she returned equably. 'If you want to kill yourself, it's your funeral.' At this he laughed loudly, and she joined him. Later, she asked: 'Staying here the night?'

'If you don't mind.' At this she gave a snort of derisive laughter, got up and said: 'Well, I'm off to bed. You can't have the sofa because the kids have got a friend and he's got it. You'll have to put a blanket and a cushion on the floor.'

'Thanks,' he said, indifferently. 'How are the kids?' he inquired, as an afterthought.

'Fine – if you're interested.'

'I asked, didn't I? he replied, without heat. All this conversation had been conducted quietly, indifferently, and the undercurrent was almost amiable. An outsider would have said they hardly knew each other. When she had gone he took a blanket from a drawer, wrapped it round his legs, and settled himself in a chair. He had meant to think about himself and Rose, but instead he dropped off at once. He left the house early, before anyone was awake. All day at the factory he thought: About Rose, what must I do about

Rose? After work he went instinctively to the pub. Pearl stood quietly behind the counter, showing him by her manner that she was not holding last night's bad humour against him. He meant to have one drink and go, but he had three. He liked Pearl's cheerful humour. She told him that her young man was playing about with another girl, and added, as if it hardly concerned her: 'There's plenty of fish in the sea after all.'

'That's right,' he said, non-committally.

'Well, we all have our troubles,' she said, with a half-humorous sigh.

'Yes – for what they're worth.' At this he felt a pang of guilt because he had been thinking of Rose. Pearl was giving him a keen look. Then she said: 'I didn't say he hadn't been worth it. But now that other girl's getting all the benefit. . . .' Here she laughed grimly.

He liked this cheerful philosophy, and could not prevent himself saying: 'He's got no sense, turning you up.' He looked with appreciation at her crown of bright yellow curls, at her shapely body. Her eyes brightened, and he said good night quickly, and left. He mustn't get mixed up with Pearl now, he was thinking.

It was after eight. Usually he was with Rose by seven. He lagged down the street, thinking of what he would say to her, and entered the flat with a blank mind. For some reason he was very tired. Rose had eaten by herself, cleared the table, and now sat beside it, frowning over a newspaper. 'What are you reading?' he asked, for something to break the ice. Looking over her shoulder he saw that she had marked a column headed: 'Surplus Women Present Problem to Churches.' He was surprised.

'That's what I am, a surplus woman,' she said, and gave that sudden, unexpected laugh.

'What's funny?' he asked, uncomfortably.

'I've a right to laugh if I want,' she retorted. 'Better than crying, anyhow.'

'Oh, Rose,' he said, helplessly, 'Oh, Rose, stop it now. . . .' She burst into tears and clung to him. But this was not the end, and he knew it. Later that night she said: 'I want to tell you something . . .' and he thought: Now I'm for it – whatever it is.

'You were home last night, weren't you?'

'Yes,' he said, alertly.

A pause, and then she asked: 'What did she say?'

'About what?' It was a fact that he did not immediately understand her. '*Jimmie*,' she said incredulously, under her breath, and he said: 'Rosie, it's no good, I told you that before.'

She did not immediately reply, but when she did her voice was very bitter: 'Well, I see how it is now.'

'You don't see at all,' he said sarcastically.

'Well, then, tell me?' He was silent. Her silence was like a persistent question. Again he felt as if the warm, soft fingers were wrapping around him. He felt suffocated. 'There's nothing to explain, I just can't help it.' A pause, and then she said in the flat, laconic way he hated: 'Yes?' That was all. For the time being, at least. A week later she said, calmly: 'I went to see Jill's Granny to-day.'

His heart faltered and he thought: Now what? 'Well?' he enquired.

'George was killed last month. In Italy.'

He felt triumph, then he said guiltily: 'I'm sorry.' She waved this away and said: 'I told her Granny that I want to adopt Jill.'

'But Rose ...' Then he saw her face and quailed.

'I want kids,' she said fiercely. He dropped his gaze.

'Her Granny won't want to give her up.'

'I'm not so sure. At first she said no, then she thought it over a bit. She's getting old now – eighty next year. She thinks perhaps Jill'd be better with me.'

'You want to have the kid *here*?' he asked, incredulously. 'Why shouldn't I?'

'You're working all day.' She was silent, he looked at her – and slowly coloured.

'Listen a minute,' she began, persuasively – not unpleasantly at all, though every word wounded Jimmie. 'I furnished this place. It was my furniture and my money. And I've got a hundred still in the post-office in case of accidents – I'll need it; now the war's over we won't be earning so much money, if I know anything. So far, I've not been ...' But here her instinctive delicacy overcame her, and she could not go on. She wanted to say that she paid for the food, paid for everything. Lately, even the rent. One week he had said, apologetically, that he hadn't the cash, and that if she could do it this once – but now it was a regular thing.

'You want me to give you the money so you can stay here with the kid?' he inquired, cautiously. She was blushing with embarrassment. 'No, no,' she said, quickly. 'Listen. If you can just pay the rent – that would be enough. I could get a part-time job, just the mornings. Jill goes to school now, and I'd manage somehow.'

He digested this silently. He was thinking, incredulously: She wants to have a kid here, a kid's always in the way – that means she can't love me any more. He said, slowly: 'Well, Rosie, if that's what you want, then go ahead.'

Her face cleared into vivid happiness and she came running to him in the old way and kissed him and said: 'Oh, Jimmie; oh, Jimmie. . . .' He held her and thought, bitterly, that all this joy was not because of him, all she cared about was the kid – women! But at the back of his mind were two other thoughts: First, that he did not know how he would find the money to pay the rent unless he passed that examination soon, and the other was that the authorities would never let Rose have Jill.

Next evening Rose was despondent. 'Did you see the officials?' he asked at last.

'Yes.' She would not look at him. She was staring helpless down from the window.

'Wasn't it any good?'

'They said I must prove myself a fit and proper person. So I said that I was. I told them I'd known Jill since she was born. I said I knew her mother and father.'

'That's true enough,' he could not help interjecting, jealously. She gave him a cold look and said: 'Don't start that now. I told them her Granny was too old, and I could easily look after Jill.'

'Well then?'

She was silent, then, wringing her hands unconsciously, she cried out: 'They wasn't nice, they wasn't nice to me at all. There were two of them, a woman and a man. They said: How could I support Jill? I said I could get money. They said I must show them papers and things. . . .' She was silently crying now, but she did not come to him. She stayed at the window, her back turned, shutting him out of her sorrow. 'They asked me, how could a working girl look after a child, and I said I'd do it easy, and they said, did I have a husband. . . .' Here she leaned her head against the wall and sobbed bitterly. After a time he said: 'Well, Rosie, it looks as if I'm no good for you. Perhaps you'd better give me up and get yourself a proper husband.' At this she jerked her head up, looked incredulously at him and cried: 'Jimmie! How could I give you up. . . .' He went to her, thinking, in relief: 'She loves me better after all.' He meant: better than the child.

It seemed that Rose had accepted her defeat. For some days she talked sorrowfully about 'those nosey-parkers' at the Council. She was even humorous, though in the way that made him uneasy. 'I'll go to them,' she said, smiling grimly, 'I'll go and I'll say: I can't help being a surplus woman. Don't blame me, blame the war, it's not my fault that they keep killing all the men off in their silly wars. . . .'

And then his jealousy grew unbearable and he said: 'You love Jill better than me.' She laughed in amazement, and said 'Don't be a baby, Jimmie.' 'Well, you must. Look how you go on and on about that kid. It's all you think about.'

'There isn't no sense in you being jealous of Jill.'

'Jealous,' he said, roughly. 'Who says I'm jealous?'

'Well, if you're not, what are you then?'

'Oh, go to hell, go to hell,' he muttered to himself, as he put his arms around her. Aloud he said: 'Come on Rosie girl, come on, stop being like this, be like you used to be, can't you?'

'I'm not any different,' she said patiently, submitting to his caresses with a sigh.

'So you're not any different,' he said, exasperatedly. Then, controlling himself with difficulty he coaxed: 'Rosie, Rosie, don't you love me a little . . .'

For the truth was he was becoming obsessed with the difference in Rose. He thought of her continuously as she had been. It was like dreaming of another woman, she was so changed now. At work, busy with some job that needed all his attention, he would start as if stung, and mutter: 'Rose – oh, to hell with her!' He was remembering, with anguish, how she had run across the room to welcome him, how responsive she had been, how affectionate. He thought of her patient kindliness now, and wanted to swear. After work he would go straight to the flat, reaching it even before she did. The lights would be out, the rooms cold, like a reminder of how Rose had changed. She would come in, tired, laden with string-bags, to find him seated at the table staring at her, his eyes black with jealousy. 'This place is as cold as a street-corner,' he would say, angrily. She looked at him, sighed, then said, reasonably: 'But Jimmie, look, here's where I keep the sixpences for the gas – why don't you light the fire?' Then he would go to her, holding down her arms as he kissed her, and she would say: 'Just leave me a minute, Jimmie. I must get the potatoes on or there'll be no supper.'

'Can't the potatoes wait a minute?'

'Let me get my arms free, Jimmie.' He held them, so she would carefully reach them out from under the pressure of his grip, and put the string-bags on the table. Then she would turn to kiss him. He noticed that she would be glancing worriedly at the curtains, which had not been drawn, or at the rubbish-pail, which had not been emptied. 'You can't even kiss me until you've done all the house-work,' he cried, sullenly. 'All right then, you tip me the wink when you've got a moment to spare and you don't mind being kissed.'

To this she replied, listlessly but patiently: 'Jimmie, I come straight from work and there's nothing ready, and before you didn't come so early.'

'So now you're complaining because I come straight here. Before, you complained because I dropped in for a drink somewhere first.'

'I never complained.'

'You sulked, even if you didn't complain.'

'Well, Jimmie,' she said, after a sorrowful pause, as she peeled the potatoes. 'If I went to drink with a boy-friend you wouldn't like it either.'

'That means Pearl, I suppose. Anyway, it's quite different.'

'Why is it different?' she asked, reasonably. 'I don't like to go to pubs by myself, but if I did I don't see why not, I don't see why men should do one thing and women another.'

These sudden lapses into feminism always baffled him.

They seemed so inconsistent with her character. He left that point and said: 'You're jealous of Pearl, that's what it is.'

He wanted her, of course, to laugh, or even quarrel a little, so the thing could be healed by kisses, but she considered it, thoughtfully, and said: 'You can't help being jealous if you love someone.'

'Pearl!' he snorted. 'I've known her for years. Besides, who told you?'

'You always think that nobody ever notices things,' she said, sadly. 'You're always so surprised.'

'Well, how did you know?'

'People always tell you things.'

'And you believe *people*.'

A pause. Then: 'Oh, Jimmie, I don't want to quarrel all the time, there isn't any sense in it.' This sad helplessness satisfied him, and he was able to take her warmly in his arms. 'I don't mean to quarrel either,' he murmured.

But they quarrelled continuously. Every conversation was bound to end, it seemed, either in Pearl or in George. Or their tenderness would lapse into tired silence, and he would see her staring quietly away from him, thinking. 'What are you getting so serious about now, Rosie?' 'I was thinking about Jill. Her Granny's too old. Jill's shut up in that kitchen all day – just think, those old nosey-parkers say I'm not a fit and proper person for Jill, but at least I'd take her for walks on Sundays . . .'

'You want Jill because of George,' he would grind out, gripping her so tight she had to ease her arms free. 'Oh, stop it, Jimmie, stop it.'

'Well, it's true.'

'If you want to think it, I can't stop you.' Then the silence of complete estrangement.

After some weeks of this he went back to the pub one evening. 'Hullo, stranger,' said Pearl. Her eyes shone welcomingly over at him.

'I've been busy, one way or another,' he said.

'I bet,' she said, satirically, challenging him with her look.

He could not resist it. 'Women,' he said, 'women.' And he took a long drain from his glass.

'Don't you talk that way to me,' she said, with a short laugh. 'My boy-friend's just got himself married. Didn't so much as send me an invite to the wedding.'

'He doesn't know what's good for him.'

Her wide, blue eyes swung around and rested obliquely on him before she lowered them to the glasses she was rinsing. 'Perhaps there are others who don't neither.'

He hesitated and said: 'Maybe, maybe not.' Caution held him back. Yet they had been flirting cheerfully for so long, out of sheer good-nature. The new hesitation was dangerous in itself, and gave depth to their casual exchanges. He thought to himself: Careful, Jimmie boy, you're off again if you're not careful. He decided he should go to another pub. Yet he came back, every evening, for he looked forward to the moment when he stood in the doorway, and then she saw him, and her eyes warmed to him as she said lightly: 'Hullo, handsome, what trouble have you been getting yourself into to-day?' He got into the way of staying for an hour or more, instead of the usual half hour. He leaned quietly against the counter, his coat collar turned up round his face, while his grey eyes rested appreciatively on Pearl. Sometimes she grew self-conscious and said: 'Your eyes need a rest,' and he replied, coolly: 'If you don't want people to look at you, better buy yourself another jumper.' He would think, with a sense of disloyalty: Why doesn't Rosie buy herself one like that? But Rose always wore her plain, dark skirts and her neat blouses, pinned at the throat with a brooch.

Afterwards he climbed the stairs to the flat thinking, anxiously: Perhaps today she'll be like she used to be? He would expectantly open the door, thinking: Perhaps she'll smile when she sees me and come running over. . . .

But she would be at the stove, or seated at the table waiting, and she gave him that tired, patient smile before beginning to dish up the supper. His disappointment dragged down his spirits, but he forced himself to say: 'Sorry I'm late, Rosie.' He braced himself for a reproach, but it never came, though her eyes searched him anxiously, then lowered as if afraid he might see a reproach in them.

'That's all right,' she replied, carefully, setting the dishes down and pulling out the chair for him.

Always, he could not help looking to see if she was still 'fussing' about the food. But she was taking trouble to hide the precautions she took to feed him sensibly. Sometimes he would probe sarcastically: 'I suppose your friend the chemist said that peas were good for ulcers – how about a bit of fried onions, Rosie?'

'I'll make you some tomorrow,' she would reply. And she averted her eyes, as if she were wincing, when he pulled the pickle bottle towards him and heaped mustard pickle over his fish. 'You only live once,' he remarked, jocularly.

'That's right.' And then, in a prepared voice: 'It's your stomach, after all.'

'That's what I always said.' To himself he said: Might be my bloody wife. For his wife had come to say at last: 'It's your stomach, if you want to die ten years too soon. . . .'

If he had attacks of terrible pain in the night, after a plateful of fried onions, or chips thick with tomato sauce, he would lie rigid beside her, concealing it, just as he had with his wife. Women fussing! Fussing women!

He asked himself continually why he did not break it off. A dozen times he had said to himself: That's enough now, it's no good, she doesn't love me, anyway. Yet by evening he was back at the pub, flirting tentatively with Pearl, until the time came when he could delay no longer. And back he went, as if dragged, to Rose. He could not understand it. He was behaving badly – and he could not help himself; he should be studying for his exam – and he couldn't bring himself to study; it would be so easy to make Rose happy – and he couldn't take the decisive step; he should decide not to return to Pearl in the evenings, and he could not keep away. What was it all about? Why did people just go on doing things, as if they were dragged along against their will, even against what they enjoyed?

One Saturday evening Rose said: 'Tomorrow I won't be here.'

He clutched at her hand and demanded: 'Why not? Where are you going?'

'I'm going to take Jill out all day and then have supper with her Granny.'

Breathing quickly, his lips set hard, he brought out: 'No time for me anymore, eh?'

'Oh, Jimmie, have some sense.'

Next morning he lay in bed and watched her dress to go

out. She was smiling, her face soft with pleasure. She kissed him consolingly before she left, and said: 'It's only on Sundays, Jimmie.'

So it's going to be every Sunday, he thought, miserably.

In the evening he went to the pub. It was Pearl's evening off. He had thought of asking her along to the pictures, but he didn't know where she lived. He went to his home. The children were in bed and his wife had gone to see a neighbour. He felt as if everyone had let him down. At last he went back to the flat and waited for Rose. When she came he sat quietly, an angry little smile on his face, while she chatted animatedly about Jill. In bed he turned his back on her and lay gazing at the greyish light at the window. It couldn't go on, he thought; what was the point of it? Yet he was back next evening as usual.

Next Sunday she asked him to go with her to see Jill.

'What the hell!' he exclaimed, indignantly.

She was hurt. 'Why not, Jimmie? She's so sweet. She's such a good girl. She's got long golden ringlets.'

'I suppose George had long yellow ringlets, too,' he said, sardonically.

She looked at him blankly shrugged, and said no more. When she had gone he went to Pearl's house – for he had asked for the address – and took her to the pictures. They were careful and polite with each other. She watched him secretly: his face was tight with worry; he was thinking of Rose with that damned brat – she was happy with Jill, when she couldn't even raise a smile for him! When he said good night, Pearl drawled out: 'Do you even know what the film was called?'

He laughed uncomfortably and said: 'Sorry, Pearl, got things on my mind.'

'Thanks for the information.' But she was not antagonistic; she sounded sympathetic. He was grateful for her understanding. He hastily kissed her cheek and said: 'You're a nice kid, Pearl.' She flushed and quickly put her arms around his neck and kissed him again. Afterwards he thought uneasily: If I just lifted my little finger I could have her.

At home Rose was cautious with him and did not mention Jill until he did. She was afraid of him. He saw it, and it made him half-wild with frustration. Anyone'd think that he was cruel to her! 'For crying out aloud, Rose,' he pleaded, 'what's the matter with you, why can't you be nice to me?'

To which she sighed and asked in a dry, tired voice: 'I suppose Pearl is nice to you.'

'Hell, Rosie, I have to do something when you're away.'

'I asked you to come with me, didn't I?'

They were now on the verge of some crisis, and both knew it, and for several days they were treating each other almost like strangers, for fear of an explosion. They hardly dare let their eyes meet.

On the following Saturday evening Rose inquired: 'Made a date with Pearl for tomorrow?'

He was going to deny it, but she went on implacably: 'Things can't go on like this, Jimmie.' He was silent, and then she asked suddenly: 'Jimmie, did you ever really ask your wife to divorce you?'

He exploded: 'Hell, Rosie, are you going back to that now?'

'I suppose you are thinking it's not my affair and I'm interfering,' she said, and laughed with that unexpected, grim humour of hers.

Rose went off to Jill in the morning without another word to him. As for him, he went to Pearl. The girl was gentle with him: 'If you don't feel like the pictures, you don't have to take me,' she said, sympathetically. So they went to a café and he said, abruptly: 'You know, Pearl, it's no good getting to like me, women think I'm poison when they get to know better.' He was was grinning savagely and his hands were clenched. She reached out, took one of them and said: 'It's for me to say what I want, isn't it?'

'Don't say I didn't warn you,' he said at random, putting his arm around her, feeling that he had, by this remark, absolved himself of all responsibility for Pearl. He was thinking of Rose. She'd be back home by now. Well, it'd do her good not to find him there. She just took him for granted, and it was a fact. But after a restless five minutes he said: 'I better be getting along.' When he left her, Pearl said: 'I love you, Jimmie, don't forget that. I'd do anything for you, anything. . . .' She ran into the house, and he saw she was crying. She loves me, at any rate, he thought, thinking angrily of Rose. Slowly he climbed the long, dark stairs. He was very tired again. I must get some sleep, he mused, dimly, this can't go on, it wears a man out, I'll go straight to bed and sleep.

But he opened the door on bright light; she was already in, seated at the table. She was still in her best clothes: a neat, grey suit, white blouse, brooch; and her hair looked as if she had just combed it. Her face was what held him: she looked tight-lipped, determined, even triumphant. What's up? he thought.

'Don't go to bed straight away,' she said – for he was throwing off his shoes and coat. 'There's something we've got to do.'

'It'd better be pretty important,' he said. 'I'm dead on my feet.'

'For once you'd better stay on your feet.' This brutal note was new and astonishing from Rose.

'What's going on?'

'You'll see in a minute.'

He almost ignored her and went to bed; but at last he compromised by pushing the pillows against the wall and leaning on them. 'Wake me up when the mystery's ripe,' he said, and dropped off at once.

Rose remained at the table in a stiff attitude, watching the door and listening. The day before she had made a decision. Or rather, a decision had been made for her. It had come into her head: Why not write and ask? She'll know . . . At first the idea had shocked her. It was a terrible thing to do, contrary to what she felt to be the right way to behave. And yet from the moment it entered her head, the idea gathered strength until she could think of nothing else. At last she sat down and wrote:

Dear Mrs. Pearson, I am writing to you on a matter which is personal to us both, and I hope it gives no offence, because I am not writing in that spirit. I am Rose Johnson, and your husband has been courting me for two years since before the war stopped. He says you live separate and you won't divorce him. I want things to be straight and proper now, and I've been thinking perhaps if we have a little talk, things will be straight. If this meets with your approval, Jimmie will be home tomorrow night, ten or so, and we could all three have a talk. Believing me, I mean no trouble or offence.

This letter she had carried herself to the house and dropped through the letter-slot. Afterwards, she could not go away. She walked guiltily up the street, and then down, her eyes fixed on the windows. That was where *she* lived. Her heart was so heavy with jealous love it was as if her very feet were weighted. That was where Jimmie had lived with *her*. That was where his children lived. She hoped to get a glimpse of them, and looked searchingly at some children playing in the street, trying to find his eyes, his features in their faces. There was a little boy she thought might be his son, and she found herself smiling at the child, her eyes filled with tears. Then, finally, she walked past the house and thought: If only it'd come to an end, I can't bear it no longer, I can't bear it. . . .

There were footsteps, Rose half-rose to open the door, but they went past. Later, when she had given up hope, there were steps again, and they stopped at the door. Now the moment had come Rose was faint with anxiety and could hardly cross the floor. She thought: I mustn't wake Jimmie, he's so tired. She opened the door with an instinctive gesture of warning towards the sleeping man. Mrs. Pearson glanced at him, smiled in a tight-lipped fashion, and came in, making her heels click loudly. Rose had created for herself many pictures of this envied woman, Jimmie's wife. She had imagined her, for some reason, fair, frail, pretty – rather like Pearl, whom she had seen in the street once. But she was not like that at all. She was a big, square woman, heavy on her feet. Her face was square and good-humoured, her brown eyes calm and direct. Her dark, greying hair was tightly waved, too close around her head for the big features. 'Well,' she said in a normal voice, with a good-humoured nod at Rose, 'the prisoner's sleeping before the execution.'

'Oh, no,' breathed Rose, in dismay: 'It's not like that at all.'

Mrs. Pearson looked curiously at her, shrugged, and laid her bag on the table. 'Thanks for the letter,' she said. 'It's about time you found out.'

'Found out what?' asked Rose quickly.

Jimmie stirred, looked blankly over at the women and then scrambled quickly to his feet. 'What the hell?' he asked, involuntarily. And then, very angry: 'What are you poking your nose in for?'

'She asked me to come,' said his wife, quietly. She sat down. 'Come and sit down, Jimmie, and let's talk it over.'

He looked quite baffled. Then he, too, shrugged, lit a cigarette and came to the table. 'O.K., get it over,' he said jauntily. He glanced incredulously at Rose. She could do this to him, he thought, hurt to the very bone – and she says she loves me. . . . He was set hard against Rose, hard against his wife. . . . Well, let them do as they liked.

'Now listen, Jimmie,' said his wife, reasonably, as to a child, 'it seems you've been telling this poor child a lot of lies.' He sat tight and said nothing. She waited, then went on, looking at Rose: 'This is the truth. We've been married ten years. We've got two kids. We were happy at first – well, nothing unusual in that. Then he got fed up. Nothing unusual in that either. In any case, he's not a man who can settle to anything. I used to be unhappy, and then I got used to it. I thought: Well, we can't change our natures. Jimmie doesn't mean any harm, he just drifts into everything. Then the war started, and you know how things were. I was working night-shifts, and he too, and there was a girl at his factory, and they got together.' She paused, looking at Jimmie like a presiding judge, but he said nothing. He smoked, looking down at the table with a small angry smile. 'I got fed up and said we'd better separate. Then he came running back and said it wouldn't happen again, he didn't really want a divorce. Jimmie stirred, opened his mouth to say something, then shut it again. 'You were going to say?' inquired his wife, pleasantly. 'Nothing. Go on, enjoy yourself.'

'Isn't it true?'

He shrugged, she waited and then went on: 'So everything was all right for a month or so. And then he started up with the girl again. . . .'

'Pearl?' Rose suddenly asked.

He snorted derisively: 'Pearl, that's all she can think of.'

'Who's Pearl?' asked Mrs. Pearson, alertly. 'She's a new one on me.'

'Never mind,' said Rose. 'Go on.'

'But this time I'd had enough. I said either me or her.' Addressing Rose, excluding Jimmie, she said: 'If there's one thing he can't do, it's make up his mind to anything.'

'Yes,' agreed Rose, involuntarily. Then she flushed and looked guiltily at Jimmie.

'Go on, enjoy yourselves,' he said, sarcastically.

'*We* haven't been enjoying ourselves, *you* have.'

'That's what you think.'

'Oh, have it your own way. You always do. But now I'm talking to Rose. When I said either her or me, he got into a proper state. The root of the matter was, he wanted both of us. Men are naturally bigamists, he said.'

'Yes,' said Rose again, quickly.

'Oh, for crying out aloud, can't you two ever take a joke. It was a joke. What did you think? I wanted to be married to two women at once? One's enough.'

'You have been married to two women at once,' said his wife, tartly. 'Whether you liked it or not. Or as good as.' The two women were looking at each other, smiling grimly. Jimmie glanced at them, got up and went to the window. 'Let me know when you've finished,' he said.

Rose made an impulsive movement towards him. 'Oh sit down, the trouble with you is you're too soft with him. I was too.'

From the window Jimmie said: 'Soft as concrete.' To Rose he made a gesture indicating his wife: 'Just take a good look at her and see how soft she is.' Rose looked, flushed, and said: 'Jimmie, I didn't mean anything nasty for you.'

'You didn't?' That was contemptuous.

'Well,' said Mrs. Pearson, loudly, interrupting this exchange: 'At last I got the pip and divorced him.'

Rose drew in her breath. Her eyes were frantic. 'You're *divorced*?' She stared at Jimmie, waiting for him to deny it, but he kept his back turned. 'Jimmie, it isn't true, is it?'

Mrs. Pearson, with rough kindliness, 'Now don't get upset Rose. It's time you knew what's what. We got divorced three years ago. I got the kids, and he's supposed to pay me two pounds a week for them. But if the other girl thought he was going to marry her she made a mistake. He was courting me for three years and then I had to put my foot down. He said he couldn't live without me, but at the registry he looked like a man being executed.'

Jimmie said, in cold fury: 'If you want to know the truth, she wouldn't marry me, she married someone else.'

'I daresay. She learned some sense, I expect. You never told her you were married, and she got shocked into her senses when she found out.'

'Go on,' said Rose, 'I want to hear the end of it.'

'There wasn't any end, that's the point. After the divorce Jimmie was popping in and out as if he belonged in the house. "Here," I used to say, "I thought we were divorced." But if he was short of a place to sleep, or he wanted somewhere to read, or his ulcers was bad, he'd drop in for a meal or the use of the sofa. And he still does,' she concluded.

Rose was crying now. 'Why did you lie to me, Jimmie,' she implored, gazing at his impervious back. 'Why? You didn't have to lie to *me*.'

He said miserably: 'What was the use, Rosie? I have to pay two pounds a week to her. I couldn't do that and give you a proper home too.'

Rose gave a helpless sort of gesture and sat silently, while the tears ran steadily down. Mrs. Pearson watched her, not unkindly. 'What's the use of crying?' she inquired. 'He's no good to you. And you say he's got another woman already! Who's this Pearl?'

Rose said: 'He takes her to the pictures and she wants to marry him.'

'How the hell do you know?' he asked, turning around and facing them at last.

Rose glanced pleadingly at him and said softly: 'But Jimmie, everybody knows.'

'I suppose you've been down talking to Pearl,' he said, contemptuously. 'Women!'

'Of course I didn't.' She was shocked. 'I wouldn't do no such thing. But everyone knows about it.'

'Who's everyone this time?'

'Well, there's my friend at the shop at the corner, who keeps my bit extra for me when there's biscuits or something going. He told me Pearl was crazy for you, and he said people said you were going to marry her.'

'Jesus,' he said simply, sitting on the bed. 'Women.'

'Just like him,' commented Mrs. Pearson, dryly. 'He always thinks he's the invisible man. He can just carry on in broad daylight and no one'll notice what he's doing. He's always surprised when they do. He was going out with that other girl for months, and the whole factory knew it, but when I mentioned it he thought I'd have a private detective on to him.'

'Well,' said Rose, helplessly, at last. 'I don't know, I really don't.'

She said again, with that rough warmth: 'Now don't you mind too much, Rosie. You're well out of it, believe me.'

Rose's lips trembled again. Mrs. Pearson got up, sat by her and patted her shoulders. 'There now,' she said, as Rose collapsed. 'Now don't take on. There, there,' she soothed, while over Rose's head she gave her husband a deadly look. Jimmie was sitting on the edge of the bed, smoking, looking badly shaken. What he was thinking was: That Rose could do this to me – how could she do it to me?

'I haven't got nothing,' wailed Rose. 'I haven't got anything or anybody anywhere.'

Mrs. Pearson went on patting. Her face was thoughtful. She made soothing noises, and then she asked suddenly, out of the blue: 'Listen, Rose, how'd you like to come and live with me?'

Rose stopped crying from the shock, lifted her face and said: 'What did you say?'

'I expect you're surprised.' Mrs. Pearson looked surprised at herself. 'I just thought of it – I'm starting a cake shop next month. I saved a bit during the war. I was looking for someone to help me with it. You could live in my place if you like. It's only got three rooms and a kitchen, but we'd manage.'

'The house isn't yours?'

Mrs. Pearson laughed: 'I suppose my lord told you he owned the whole house? Not on your life. I've got the basement.'

'The basement,' said Rose, intently.

'Well, it's warm and dry and in one piece, more than can be said for most basements.'

'It's safer, too,' said Rose, slowly.

'Safer?'

'If there's bombing or something.'

'I suppose so,' said Mrs. Pearson, rather puzzled at this. Rose was gazing eagerly into her face. 'You've got the kids,' said Rose, slowly.

'They're no trouble, really. They're at school.'

'I didn't mean that – could I have a kid – no, listen, I'd be wanting to adopt a kid if I came to you. If I lived with you I'd be a fit and proper person and those nosey-parkers would let me have her.'

'You want to adopt a kid?' said Mrs. Pearson, rather put out. She glanced at Jimmie, who said: 'You say things about me – but look at her. She was engaged to a man, and he was killed and all she thinks about is his kid.'

'Jimmie . . .' began Rose, in protest. But Mrs. Pearson asked: 'Hasn't the kid got a mother?'

'The blitz,' said Rose, simply.

After a pause Mrs. Pearson said thoughtfully: 'I suppose there's no reason why not.'

Rose's face was illuminated. 'Mrs. Pearson,' she prayed, 'Mrs Pearson – if I could have Jill, if only I could have Jill . . .'

Mrs. Pearson said dryly: 'I can't see me cluttering myself up with kids if I didn't have to. You wouldn't catch me marrying and getting kids if I had my chance over again, but it takes all sorts to make a world.'

'Then it'd be all right?'

Mrs. Pearson hesitated: 'Yes, why not?'

Jimmie gave a short laugh. 'Women,' he said. 'Women.'

'You can talk,' said his wife.

Rose looked shyly at him. 'What are you going to do now?' she asked.

'A fat lot you care,' he said, bitterly.

'He s going to marry Pearl, I don't think,' commented his wife.

Rose said slowly: 'You ought to marry Pearl, you know, Jimmie. You did really ought to marry her. It's not right. You shouldn't make her unhappy, like me.'

Jimmie stood before them, hands in pockets, trying to look nonchalant. He was slowly nodding his head as if his worst suspicions were being confirmed. 'So now you've decided to marry me off,' he said, savagely.

'Well, Jimmie,' said Rose, 'she loves you, everyone knows that, and you've been taking her out and giving her ideas – and – and – you could have this flat now, I don't want it. You better have it, anyway, you can't get flats now the war's finished. And you and Pearl could live here.' She sounded as if she were pleading for herself.

'For crying out aloud,' said Jimmie, astonished, gazing at her.

Mrs. Pearson was looking shrewdly at him. 'You know, Jimmie, it's not a bad idea, Rose is quite right.'

'Wha-a-at? You too?'

'It's about time you stopped messing around. You messed around with Rose here, and I told you time and time again, you should either marry her or not, I said.'

'You *knew* about me?' said Rose, dazedly.

'Well, no harm in that,' said Mrs. Pearson, impatiently. 'Be your age, Rose. Of course, I knew. When he came home I used to say to him: You do right by that poor girl. You can't expect her to go hanging about, missing her chances, just to give you an easy life and somewhere to play nicely at nights.'

'I told Rose,' he said, abruptly. 'I told her often enough I wasn't good enough for her, I said.'

'I bet you did,' said his wife, shortly.

'Didn't I, Rose?' he asked her.

Rose was silent. Then she shrugged. 'I just don't understand,' she said at last. And then, after a pause: 'I suppose you're just made that way.' And then, after a longer pause: 'But you ought to marry Pearl now.'

'Just to please you, I suppose!' He turned challengingly to his wife: 'And you, too, I suppose. You want to see me safely tied up to someone, don't you?'

'No one's going to marry me, stuck with two kids,' said his wife. 'I don't see why you shouldn't be tied too, if we're going to look at it that way.'

'And you can't see why I shouldn't marry Pearl when I've got to pay you two pounds a week?'

Mrs. Pearson said on an impulse: 'If you marry Pearl, I'll let you off the two pounds. I'm going to make a good thing out of my cake shop, I expect, and I won't need your bit.'

'And if I don't marry her, then I must go on paying you the two pounds?'

'Fair enough,' she said, calmly.

'Blackmail,' he said, bitterly. 'Blackmail, that's what it is.'

'Call it what you like.' She got up and lifted her handbag from the table. 'Well, Rose,' she said. 'All this has been sudden, spur of the moment sort of thing. Perhaps you'd like to think about it. I'm not one for rushing into things myself, in the usual way. I wouldn't like you to come and then be sorry after.'

Rose had unconsciously risen and was standing by her. 'I'll come with you now, if it's all right. I'll get my things tomorrow. I wouldn't want to stay here tonight.' She glanced at Jimmie, then averted her face.

'She's afraid of staying here with me,' said Jimmie with bitter triumph.

'Quite right. I know you.' She mimicked his voice: *'Don't go back on me, Rose, don't you trust me?'*

Rose winced and muttered: 'Don't do that.'

'Oh, I know him, I know him. And you'd have to put chains on him and drag him to the registry. It's not that he doesn't want to marry you. I expect he does, when all's said. But it just kills him to make up his mind.'

'Staying with me, Rosie?' asked Jimmie, suddenly – the gambler playing his last card. He watched her with bright eyes, waiting, almost sure of his power to make her stay.

Rose looked unhappily from him to Mrs. Pearson.

Mrs. Pearson watched her with a half-smile; that smile seemed to say: I'm not implicated, settle it for yourself, it makes no difference to me. But aloud she said: 'You're a fool if you stay, Rosie.'

'Let her decide,' said Jimmie, quietly. He was thinking: If she cares anything she'll stay with me, she'll stand by me. Rose gazed pitifully at him and wavered. It flashed across her mind: He's just trying to prove something to his wife, he doesn't really want me at all. But she could not take her eyes away. There he sat, upright but easy, his hair ruffled lightly on his forehead, his handsome grey eyes watching her. She thought, wildly: Why does he just sit there waiting? If he loved me he'd come across and put his arms around me and ask nicely to stay with him, and I would – if he'd only do that. . . .

But he remained quiet, challenging her to move; and slowly the tension shifted and Rose drooped away from him with a sigh. She turned to Mrs. Pearson. He couldn't really love her or he wouldn't have just sat there – that's what she felt.

'I'll come with you,' she said, heavily.

'That's a sensible girl, Rose.'

Rose followed the older woman with dragging feet.

'You won't regret it,' said Mrs. Pearson. 'Men – they're more trouble than they're worth, when all is said. Women have to look after themselves these days, because if they don't, no one will.'

'I suppose so,' said Rose, reluctantly. She stood hesitating at the door, looking hopefully at Jimmie. Even now – she thought – even now, if he said one word she'd run back to him and stay with him.

But he remained motionless, with that bitter little smile about his mouth.

'Come on, Rose,' said Mrs. Pearson. 'Come, if you're coming. We'll miss the Underground.'

And Rose followed her. She was thinking, dully: 'I'll have Jill, that's something. And by the time she grows up perhaps there won't be wars and bombs and things, and people won't act silly any more.'

# Eldorado

# Eldorado

HUNDREDS of miles South were the gold-bearing reefs of Johannesburg; hundreds of miles North, the rich copper mines. These the two lodestars of the great central plateau, these the magnets which drew men, white and black; drew money from the world's counting-houses; concentrated streets, shops, gardens; attracted riches and misery – particularly misery.

But this, here, was farming country, true farming land, a pocket of good, dark, rich soil in the wastes of the light sandveld. A 'pocket' some hundreds of miles in depth, and only to be considered in such midget terms by comparison with those eternal sandy wastes which fed cattle, though poorly, and satisfied that shallow weed tobacco. For that is how a certain kind of farmer sees it; a man of the old-fashioned sort will think of farming as the making of food, and of tobacco as a nervous, unsatisfactory crop, geared to centres in London and New York; he will watch the fields fill and crowd with new, bright leaf, and imagine it crushed through factory and warehouse to end in a wisp of pale smoke; he will not like to imagine the substance of his soil dissipating in smoke. And if sensible people argue: Yes, but people must smoke, you smoke yourself, you're not being reasonable; he is likely to reply (rather irritably perhaps): 'Yes, of course, you're right – but I want to grow food, the others can grow tobacco.'

When Alec Barnes came searching for a farm, he chose the rich maize soil, though cleverer, experienced men told him the big money was to be found only in tobacco. Tobacco and gold, gold and tobacco – these were the moneymakers. For this country had gold too, a great deal of it; but perhaps there is only room in one's mind for one symbol, one type; and when people say 'gold' they think of the Transvaal, and so it was with Alec. There were many ways of seeing this new country, and Alec Barnes chose to see it with the eye of the food producer. He had not left England, he said, to worry about money and chase success. He wanted a slow, satisfying life, taking things easy.

He bought a small farm, about two thousand acres, from a man who had gone bankrupt. There was a house already built. It was a pleasant house, in the style of the country, of light red brick with a corrugated iron roof, big, bare rooms and a wide verandah. Shrubs and creepers, now rather neglected, showed scarlet against the dull green scrub, or hung in showers of gold and purple from the trees. The rainy season had sprung new grass high and thick over paths, over flower-beds. When the Barnes family came in they had to send a native ahead with a scythe to cut an opening through thickets of growth; and in the front room the bricks of the floor were being tumbled aside by the shoots from old tree-roots. There was a great deal to do before the place could be comfortable, and Maggie Barnes set herself to work. She was the daughter of a small Glasgow shopkeeper, and it might be thought that everything would be strange to her; but her grandparents had farmed, and she remembered visiting the old people as a child, playing with a shaggy old cart-horse, feeding the chickens. That way of farming could hardly be compared to this, but in a sense it was like returning to her roots. At least, that was how she thought of it. She would pause in her work, duster in hand, at a window or on the verandah, and look over the scrub to the mealie-fields, and it did not seem so odd that she should be here, in this big house, with black servants to wait on her, not *so* outlandish that she might walk an hour across country and call the soil underfoot her soil. There was no domesticated cart-horse to take sugar from her hand, only teams of sharp-horned and wild-eyed oxen; but there were chickens and turkeys and geese – she had no intention of paying good money for what she could grow herself, not she who knew the value of money! Besides, a busy woman has no time for fainthearted comparisons, and there was so much to do; and she intended that all this activity should earn its proper reward. She had gone beyond her grandparents, with their tight, frugal farm, which earned a living but no more; had gone beyond her parents, counting their modest profits in the back rooms of the grocery shop. In a sense she included both generations, could see the merits and failings of both, but – she and her husband would 'get on,' they would be prosperous as the farmers around them were prosperous.

It was true that when the neighbours made doubtful faces at their growing small-scale maize, and said there could be no 'taking it easy' on that farm, she felt a little troubled. But she approved her husband's choice; the growing of food satisfied her ideas of what was right, and connected her with her religious and respectable grandparents. Besides, many of the things Alec said she simply did not take seriously. When he said, fiercely, how glad he was to be out of England, out of the fight for success and the struggle to be better than one's neighbours, she merely smiled: what was the matter with getting on, and bettering oneself? They were just words to her. She would say, in her bluff, affectionate way, of Alec: 'He's a queer man, being English, I canna get used to the way of him.' For she put down his high-flown notions to his being English. Also, he was strange to her because of his gentleness: the men of her people were outspoken and determined and did not defer to their women. Alec deferred to her. Sometimes she could not understand him; but she was happy with him, and with her son, who was still a small child.

She sent Paul out with a native servant to play in the veld, while she worked, whitewashing the house, even climbing the roof herself to see to the guttering. Paul learned a new way of playing. He spread himself, ranging over the farm, so that the native youth who had the care of him found himself kept running. His toys, the substitutes for the real thing, mechanical lorries and bricks and dolls, were left in cupboards; and he made dams in the mud of the fields, plunged fearfully on the plough behind the oxen, rode high on the sacks of the waggons. He lost the pretty, sheltered look of the child from 'home,' who must be nervous of streets and traffic, always conscious of the pressure of the neighbours. He grew fast and tall, big-boned and muscular, and lean and burnt. Sometimes Maggie would say, with that good-natured laugh: 'Well, and I don't know myself with this change-child!' Perhaps the laugh was a little uneasy, too. For she was not as thick-fibred as she looked. She was that Scots type, rather short, but finely made, even fragile, with the great blue eyes and easily-freckling fair skin and a mass of light black curls. Even after the hard work and the sunlight, which thickened her into a sturdy, energetic body of a woman, she kept, under the appearance of strength, that fine-boned delicacy and a certain shy charm. And here was her son shooting up into a lanky, bony youngster, the whites of his eyes always a little reddened by glare, his dark hair tumbling rough over his head with rusty bleached locks where the sun had struck. She looked at him in the bath, showing smooth dark-brown all over, save for the tender, milky skin like a loincloth where the strong khaki shorts kept the sun off. She felt a little perturbed, as if in some way he was most flagrantly betraying her by growing so, away from the fair, clear, open looks of her good Scots ancestors. There was something stubborn and secretive about him – perhaps even something a little coarse. But then – she reminded herself – he was half-English, too, and Alec was tall, long-headed, with a closed English face, and slow English speech which concealed more than it said. For a time she tried to change the child, to make him more dependent, until Alec noticed it and was angry. She had never seen him so angry before. He was a mild, easy man, who noticed very little, content to work at the farm and leave the rest to her. But now they fought. 'What are you coddling him for?' Alec shouted. 'What's the good of bringing him here to a country where he can grow up a man if you're going to fuss and worry all the time?' She gave him back as good; for to her women friends she would expound her philosophy of men: 'You've got to stand against them once in a way, it doesnae do to be too sweet to them.' But these remarks, she soon understood, sounded rather foolish; for when did she need to 'stand against' Alec? She had her own way over everything. Except in this, for the very country was against her. Soon she left the boy to do as he liked on the veld. He was at an age when children at 'home' would be around their mothers, but at seven and eight he was quite independent, had thrown off the attendant servant, and would spend all day on the fields, coming in for meals as if – so Maggie complained in that soft, pretty, Scots voice: 'As if I'm no better than a restaurant!' But she accepted it, she was not the complaining sort; it was only a comfortable grumble to her women friends. Besides, living here had hardened her a little. Perhaps hardened was not the right word? It was a kind of fatalism, the easy atmosphere of the country, which might bring in Paul and her husband an hour late for a meal, looking at her oddly if she complained of the time. What's an hour? they seemed to be asking; even: 'What's time at all?' She could understand it, she was beginning to feel a little that way herself. But in her heart she was determined that Paul would not grow up lax and happy-go-lucky, like a Colonial. Soon he would be going to school and he would 'have it knocked out of him.' She had that good sturdy Scottish attitude towards education. She expected children to work and win scholarships. And indeed, it would be necessary for the farm could hardly support a son through the sort of schooling she visualized for him. She was beginning to understand that it never would. At the end of the first five years she understood that their neighbours had been right: This farm would never do more than make a scanty living.

When she spoke to Alec he seemed to turn against her, not noisily, in a healthy and understandable quarrel, but in a stubborn, silent way. Surely he wanted Paul to make something of himself? she demanded. Put like that, of course, Alec had to agree, but he agreed vaguely. It was this vagueness that upset Maggie, for there was no way of answering it. It seemed to be saying: All these things are quite irrelevant; I don't understand you.

Alec had been a clerk in a bank until the first world war. After the upheaval he could not go back into an office. He married Maggie and came to this new country. There were farmers in his family, too, a long way back, though he had only come to remember this when he felt a need to explain, even excuse, that dissident streak which had made a conventional English life impossible. He would talk of a certain great-uncle, who had ridden a wild black horse around the shires, fathering illegitimate children and drinking and behaving so that he ended in prison for smuggling. Yes, this was all very well, thought Maggie, but what has that old rascal got to do with Alec, and what with *my* son? For Alec would talk of this unsatisfactory ancestor with pride and his eyes would rest speculatively on Paul – it gave Maggie goose-flesh to see him.

Alec grew even vaguer as time went by. He used to stand at the edge of a field, gazing dimly across it at a ridge of bush which rose sharp to the great blue sky; or at the end of the big vlei, which cut across the farm in a shallow, golden swathe of rustling grasses, with a sluggish watercourse showing green down its centre. He would stand on a moonlight night staring across the fields which now appeared like a diffusing green sea, the white crests of the maize shifting like foam; or at midday, looking over the stretching acres of brown and heaving clods, warm and rich with sunlight; or at sunset, when the miles of bush flared gold and red. Distance – that was what he needed. It was what he had left England to find.

He cleared new ground every year. When he first came it was mostly bush, with a few cleared patches. The house was bedded in trees. Now one walked from the house through Maggie's pretty garden, and the mealies stood like a green wall on three sides of the homestead. From a little hillock behind the house, the swaying green showed solid and unbroken, hundreds of acres of it, beautiful to look at until one remembered that the experts were warning against this kind of planting. Better small fields with trees to guard them from wind; better girdles of grass, so that the precious soil might be held by the roots and not wash away with the flooding storm-waters. But Alec's instinct was for space. and soon half the surface of the farm was exposed, and the ploughs drove a straight line from boundary to boundary, and the labourers worked in a straight line, like an advancing army, their hoes rising and falling and flashing like spears in the sun. The vivid green of the leaves rippled and glittered, or shone soft with moonlight; or at reaping time the land lay bare and hard, and over it the tarnished litter of the fallen husks; or at planting a wide sweep of dark-brown clods which turned to harsh red under the rain. Beautiful it was, and Maggie could understand Alec's satisfaction in it; but it was disturbing when the rains drove the soil along the gulleys; when the experts came from town and told Alec he was ruining his farm; when at the season's end the yield rose hardly at all, in spite of the constantly increased acreage. But Alec set that obstinate face of his against the experts and the evidence of the books, and cut more trees, exposing the new soil which fed fine, strong plants, showing the richness of their growth in the heavy cobs. One could mark the newly-cleared area in the great field every year;

the maize stood a couple of feet shorter on the old soil. Alec sent gangs of workers into the trees, and through the dry season the dull thud-thud of axes sounded across the wide, clean air, and the trees crashed one after another into the wreckage of their branches. Always a new field, or rather the old one extended; always fine new soil ready for the planting. But there came a time when it was not possible to cut more trees, for where would the cattle graze? There must be sufficient veld left to feed them, for without them the ploughs and waggons could not move, and there wasn't sufficient capital for a tractor. So Alec rested on his laurels for a couple of years, working the great field, and Maggie sent her son off to school in town a hundred miles away. He would return only for the holidays – would return, she hoped, brisker, with purpose, the languor of the farm driven out of him. She missed him badly, but it was a relief that he was with other children, and this relief made up for the loss. As for Alec, Paul's going made him uneasy. Now he was actually at school, he must face his responsibility for the child's future. He wandered over his farm rather less vaguely and wondered how Paul thought of the town. For that was how he saw it; not that he was at school, but in town; and it was the reason why he had been so reluctant for him to go. He did not want him to grow into an office-worker, a pen-user, a city-cypher, the sort of person he had been himself and now disowned. But what if Paul did not feel as he did? Alec would stand looking at a tree, or a stretch of water, thinking: What does this mean to Paul, what does he think when he swims here? – in the secretive, nostalgic way of parents trying to guess at their children's souls. What sort of a creature *was* Paul? When he came to it, he had no idea at all, although the child was so like him, a long, lean dark, silent boy, with contemplative dark eyes and a slow way of speaking. And here was Maggie, with such plans for him, determined that he must be an engineer, a scientist, a doctor, and nothing less than famous. The fame could be discounted tolerantly, with her maternal pride and possessiveness, but scientists of any kind are not produced on the sort of profits he was making.

He thought worriedly about the farm. Perhaps he could lease adjoining land and graze his beasts there, and leave his own good land free for cutting? But all the land was taken up. He knew quite well, too, that the problem was deeper. He should change his way of farming. There were all sorts of things he could do *should* do, at once; but at the idea of them a lassitude crept over him and he thought, obstinately: Why should I, why fuss and worry, when I'm free of all that, free of the competition in the Old Country? I didn't come here to fight myself into a shadow over getting rich. . . . But the truth was, though he did not admit it to himself, not for a second, he was very bored. He had come to the limits of his old way, and now, to succeed, it would be going over the same ground, but in a different way – nothing *new*; that was the point. Rather guiltily he found himself daydreaming about pulling up his roots here and going off somewhere else – South America, China – why not? Then he pulled himself together. To postpone the problem he cut another small area of trees, and the cutting of them exposed all the ground to where the ridge lifted itself; they could see clear from the house across the vlei and up the other side; all mealies, all a shimmering mass of green; and on the ridge was the boundary of the next farm, a low, barbed-wire fence, and against the fence was a small mine. It was nothing very grand, just a two-stamp affair, run by a single man who got what gold he could from a poor but steady seam. The mine had been there for years. The mine-stamps thudded day and night, coming loud or soft, according to the direction of the wind. But to Alec there was something new and even terrible about seeing the black dump of the mine buildings, seeing the black smoke drifting up into the blue, fresh sky. His deep and thoughtful eyes would often turn that way. How strange that from that cluster of black ugliness, under the hanging smoke, gold should come from the earth. It was unpleasant, too. This was farming land. It was outrageous that the good soil should be covered, even for a mere five acres or so, by buildings and iron gear and the sordid mine compound.

Alec felt as he did when people urged him to grow tobacco. It would be a betrayal, though what he would be betraying he could not say. And this mine was a betrayal of everything decent. They fetched up the ore, they washed the gold out, melted it to conveniently-handled shapes, thousands of workers spent their lives on it when they might be doing something useful on the land; and ultimately the gold was shipped off to America. He often made the old joke, these days, about digging up gold from one hole in the ground and sending it to America to be buried in another. Maggie listened and wondered at him. What a queer man he was! He noticed nothing until he was faced with it. For years she had been talking about Paul's future; and only when she packed him off to school did Alec begin to talk, just as if he had only that moment come to consider it, of how he should be educated. For years he had been living a couple of miles from a mine, with the sound of it always in his ears, but it was not until he could see it clear on the next ridge that he seemed to notice it. And yet for years the old miner had been dropping in of an evening. Alec would make a polite inquiry or two and then start farm-talk, which could not possibly interest him. 'Poor body,' Maggie had been used to say, half-scornfully, 'what's the use of talking seasons and prices to *him*?' For she shared Alec's feeling that mining was not a serious way of living – not this sort of mining, scratching in the dirt for a little gold. That was how she thought of it. But at least she had thought of it; and here was Alec like a man with a discovery.

When Paul came home for his holiday and saw the mine lifted black before him on the long, green ridge, he was excited, and made his longest journey afield. He spent a day at the mine and came home chattering about pennyweights and ounces of gold; about reefs and seams and veins; about ore and slimes and cyanide – a whole new language. Maggie poured brisk scorn on the glamour of gold; but she was secretly pleased at this practical new interest. He was at least talking about *things,* he wasn't mooning about the farm like a waif returned from exile. She dreamed of him becoming a mining engineer or a geologist. She sent to town for books about famous men of science and left them lying about. Paul hardly glanced at them. His practical experience of handling things, watching growth, seeing iron for implements shaped in a fire, made it so that his knowledge must come first-hand, and afterwards he confirmed by reading. And he was roused to quite different thoughts. He would kick at an exposed rock, so that the sparks fell dull red under his boot-soles, and say: 'Daddy, perhaps this is gold rock?' Or he would come running with bits of decomposed stone that showed dull gleams of metal and say: 'Look, this is gold, isn't it?'

'Maybe,' said Alec, reluctantly. 'This is all gold country. The prospectors used to come through here. There is a big reef running across that ridge which is exactly the same formation as one of the big reefs on the Rand; once they thought they'd find a mine as big as that one, here. But it didn't come to anything.'

'Perhaps we'll find it,' said Paul, obstinately.

'Perhaps,' said Alec, indulgently. But he was stirred, whether he liked it or not. He thought of the old prospectors wandering over the country with their meagre equipment, panning gold from the sand of river-beds, crushing bits of rock, washing the grit for those tiny grains that might proclaim a new Rand. Sometimes, when he came on a projecting ledge of rock, instead of cursing it for being on farmland at all, he would surreptitiously examine it, thinking: That bit there looks as if it had been broken off – perhaps one of the old hands used his hammer here twenty years ago. Or he might find an old digging, half-filled in by the rains, where someone had tried his luck; and he stood looking down at the way the rock lay in folds under the earth, sometimes flat, packed tidily one above the other, sometimes slanting in a crazy plunge where the subterranean forces had pushed and squeezed. And then he would shake himself and turn back to the business of farming, to the visible surfaces, the tame and orderly top-soil that was a shallow and understandable layer responsive to light and air and wetness, where the worms and air-bringing roots worked their miracles of decomposition and growth. He puts his thoughts back to this malleable surface of the globe, the soil – or imagined that he did; and suppressed his furtive speculation about the fascinating underground structures – but not altogether. There was slowly growing in him another vision, another need; and he listened to the regular thud-thud of the mine-stamps from the opposite ridge as if they were drums beating from a country whose frontier he was forbidden to cross.

One evening an old weather-stained man appeared at the

door and unslung from his back a great bundle of equipment and came in for the night, assuming the traveller's privilege of hospitality. He was, in fact, one of the vanishing race of wandering prospectors; and for most of the night he talked about his life on the veld. It was like a story from a child's adventure book in its simplicities of luck and bad fortune and persistent courage rewarded only by the knowledge of right-doing. For this old man spoke of the search for gold as a scientist might of discovery, or an artist of his art. Twice he had found gold and sold his riches trustingly, so that he was tricked by unscrupulous men who were now rich, while he was as poor as he had been forty years before. He spoke of this angrily, it is true, but it was that kind of anger we maintain from choice, like a relation whose unpleasantness has become, through the years, almost a necessity. There had been one brief period of months when he was very rich indeed, and squandered he did not know how much money in the luxury hotels of the golden city. He spoke of this indifferently, as of a thing which had chosen to visit him, and then as arbitrarily chosen to withdraw. Maggie, listening, was thankful that Paul was not there. And yet this was a tale any child might remember all his life, grateful for a glimpse of one of the old kind of adventurer, bred when there were still parts of the world unknown to map-makers and instrument-users. This was a character bound to fire any boy; but Maggie thought, stubbornly: There is enough nonsense as it is. And by this she meant, making no bones about it: Alec is enough of a bad influence. For she had come to understand that if Paul was to have that purpose she wanted in him, she must plant it and nurture it herself. She did not like the way Alec listened to this old man, who might be a grand body in his way, but not in *her* way. He was listening to a siren song, she could see that in his face. And later he began talking again about that nuisance of a great-uncle of his who, in some queer way, he appeared to link with the prospector. What more did the man want? Most sensible people would think that gallivanting off to farm in Africa was adventure enough, twice as adventurous as being a mere waster and ruffian, deceiving honest girls and taking honest people's goods, and ending as a common criminal!

Maggie, that eminently sensible woman, wept a little that night when Alec was asleep, and perhaps her courage went a little numb. Or rather, it changed its character, becoming more like a shield than a spear, a defensive, not an attacking thing. For when she thought of Alec she felt helpless; and the old man asleep in the next room made her angry. Why did he have to come to *this* farm, why not take his dangerous gleam elsewhere? Long afterwards, she remembered that night and said, tartly, to Alec: 'Yes, that was when the trouble started, when that old nuisance came lolloping along here with his long tongue wagging. . . .' But 'the trouble' started long before; who could say when? With the war, that so unsettled men and sent them flying off to new countries, new women? With whatever forces they were that bred men's silly wars? Something in Alec himself: his long-dead ancestor stirring in him and whispering along his veins of wildness and adventure? Well, she would leave all that to Alec and see that *her* son became a respectable lawyer, or a bridge-builder. That was enough adventure for her.

When the old man left next day, trudging off through the mealie fields with his pack over his shoulder, Alec watched him from the verandah. And that evening he climbed the hillock behind the house and saw the small red glow of a fire down in the vlei. There he was, after his day of rock-searching, rock-chipping. He would be cooking his supper, or perhaps already lying wrapped in his blanket beside the embers, a fold of it across his face so that the moon would not trouble his eyelids with its shifting, cold gleams. The old man was alone; he did not even take a native with him to interpret the veld; he no longer needed this intermediary; he understood the country as well as the black men who lived on it. Alec went slowly to bed, thinking of the old prospector who was free, bound to no one, owning nothing but a blanket and a frying-pan and his clothes.

Not long afterwards a package arrived from the station and Maggie watched Alec open it. It was a gold pan. Alec held it clumsily between his palms, as he had seen the prospector do. He had not yet got the feel of the thing. It was like a deep frying-pan, without a handle, of heavy black metal, with a fine groove round the inside of the rim. This groove was to catch the runnels of silt that should hold grains of gold, if there was any gold. Alec brought back fragments of rock from the lands and crushed them in a mortar and stood beside the water tanks swirling the muddy mixture around and around endlessly, swearing with frustration, because he was still so clumsy and could not get the movements right. Each sample took a long time, and he could not be sure, when he had finished, if it had been properly done. First the handful of crushed rock, as fine as face-powder, must be placed in the pan and then the water run in. Afterwards it must be shaken so that the heavy metals should sink, and then with a strong sideways movement the lighter grit and dust must be flung out, with the water. Then more water added and the shaking repeated. Finally, there should be nothing but a wash of clean water, and the loose grit and bits of metal sliding along the groove: the dull, soft black of iron, a harder shine for chrome, the false glitter of pyrites, that might be taken for gold by a greenhorn, and finally, and in almost every sample, dragging slow and heavy behind the rest, would be the few dully-shining grains of true gold. But the movements had to be learned. The secret was a subtle little sideways jerk at the end, which separated the metals from the remnants of lighter rock. So stood Alec, methodically practising, with the heavy pan between his palms, the packets of crushed rock on the ground beside him, and on the other side the dripping water-taps. He was squandering the precious water that had to be brought from the well three times a week in the water-cart. The household was always expected to be niggardly with water, and now here was Alec swilling away gallons of it every day. An aggrieved Maggie watched him through the kitchen window.

But it was still a hobby. Alec worked as usual on the farm, picking up interesting bits of rock if he came across them, and panned them at evening, or early in the morning before breakfast. The house was littered with lumps of rocks, and Maggie handled them wonderingly when she was alone, for she did not intend to encourage Alec in 'this nonsense'. She was fascinated by the rocks, and she did not want to be fascinated. There were round stones, worn smooth by the wash of water; red stones, marbled with black; green stones, dull like rough jade; blue stones, with a fire of metal when they were shifted against a light. They were beautiful enough to be cut and worn as jewels. Then there were lumps of rough substance, half-way between soil and rock, the colour of ox-blood; and some so rich with metal that they weighed the hand low. Most promising were the decomposing rocks, where the soft parts had been rotted out by wind and water, leaving a crumbling, veiny substance, like a skeleton of the soil, and in some of these the gold could be seen lying thick and close, like dirt along the seams of a garment.

Alec did not yet know the names of the rocks and minerals, and he was troubled by his ignorance. He sent for books; and in the meantime he moved like an explorer over the farm he imagined he knew as well as it could be known, learning to see it in a new way. That rugged jut of reef, for instance, which intersected the big vlei like the wall of a natural dam – what was the nature of that hard and determined rock, and what happened to it beneath the ground? Why was the soil dark and red at one end of the big field and a sullen orange at the other? He looked at this field when it was bared ready for the planters, and saw how the soil shaded and modulated from acre to acre, according to the varieties of rock from which it had been formed, and he no longer saw the field, he saw the reefs and shales and silts and rivers of the underworld. He lifted his eyes from this vision and saw the kopjes six miles away; hard granite, they were; and the foothills, tumbled outposts of granite boulders almost to his own boundary – rock from another era, mountains erupted from an older time. On another horizon could be seen the long mountain where chrome was mined and exported to the countries which used it for war. Along the flanks of the mountain showed the scars and levels of the workings – it was another knowledge, another language of labour. He felt as if he had been blind half his life and only just discovered it. And on the slopes of his own farm were the sharp quartz reefs that the prospector told him were promise of gold. Quartz, that most lovely of rocks, coloured and weathered to a thousand shapes and tints, sometimes standing cold and glittering, like miniature snow mountains; sometimes milky, like slabs of opal, or delicate pink and amber with a smoky flush in its depths, as if a fire burnt there invisibly; marbled black, or mottled blue – there was no end to the strangeness and variety of those quartz reefs which for years he had been cursing because they made whole acres of his land unfit for the plough. Now he wandered there with a prospector's hammer, watching the fragments of rock fly off like chips of ice, or like shattering jewels. When he panned these pieces they showed traces of gold. But not enough: he had already learned how to measure the richness of a sample.

He sent for a geological map and tacked it to the wall of his farm office. Maggie found it and stood in front of it, studying it when he couldn't see her. Here was Africa, but in a new aspect. Instead of the shaded greens and browns and blues of the map she was accustomed to see, the colours of earth and growth, the colours of leaf and soil and grass and moving water, now they were harsh colours, like the metallic hues of rock. An arsenic green showed the copper deposits of Northern Rhodesia, a cold yellow the gold of the Transvaal – but not only the Transvaal. She had had no idea how much gold there was, worked everywhere; the patches of yellow mottled the sub-continent. But Maggie had no feeling for gold; her sound instincts were against the useless stuff. She looked with interest at the black of the coalfields – one of the richest in the world, Alec said, and hardly touched; at the dull grey of the chrome deposits, whole mountains of it, lying unused; at the glittering light green of the asbestos, at the iron and the manganese and – but most of these names she had never heard, could not even pronounce.

When Alec's books came, she would turn over the pages curiously, gaining not so much a knowledge as an intimation of the wonderful future of this continent. Perhaps Alec should have been a scientist, she thought, and not a farmer at all? Perhaps, with this capacity of his for completely losing himself (as he had become lost) he might have been a great man? For this was how the vision narrowed down in her: all the rich potentialities of Africa she saw through her son, who might one day work with coal, or with copper; or through Alec, the man, who 'might have done well for himself' if he had had a different education.

Education, that was the point. And she turned her thoughts steadily towards her son. All her interests had narrowed to him. She set her will hard, like a prayer, towards him, as if her dammed forces could work on him a hundred miles away at school in the city.

When he came home from school he found his father using a new vocabulary. Alec was still attending to the farm with half his attention, but his passion was directed into this business of gold-finding. He had taken half a dozen labourers from the fields and they were digging trenches along the quartz reef on the ridge. Maggie made no direct comment, but Paul could feel her disapproval. The child was torn between loyalty to his mother and fascination for his new interest, and the trenches won. For some days Maggie hardly saw him, he was with his father, or over at the mine on the ridge.

'Perhaps we'll have a mine on our farm, too,' said Paul to Maggie; and then, scornfully: 'But we won't have a silly mine like that one, we'll have a big one, like Johannesburg.' And Maggie's heart sank, listening to him. Now was the time, she thought, to mould him, and she showed him the coloured map on the office wall and tried to make it come alive for him, as it had for her. She spoke of the need for engineers and experts, but he looked and listened without kindling. 'But my bairn,' said Maggie reproachfully, using the old endearment which was falling out of use now, with her other Scots ways of speech, 'my bairn, it's time you were making your mind to what you want. You must know what you want to be.' He looked sulky and said if they found 'a big mine, like Johannesburg', he would be a gold-miner. 'Oh, no,' said Maggie, indignantly. 'That's just luck. Anyone can have a stroke of luck. It takes a clever man to be educated and know about things.' So Paul evaded this and said all right then, he'd be a tobacco farmer. 'Oh, no,' said Maggie again; and wondered herself at the passion she put into it. Why should he not be a tobacco farmer? But it wasn't what she dreamed of for him. He would become a rich tobacco farmer? He would make his thousands and study the international money-juggling and buy more farms and more farms and have assistants until he sat in an office and directed others, just as if he were a business man? For with tobacco there seemed to be no half-way place, the tobacco farmers drove themselves through night-work and long hours on the fields, as if an invisible whip threatened them, and then they failed, or they succeeded suddenly, and paid others to do the slaving ... it was no sort of a life, or at least, not for *her* son. 'What's matter with having money?' asked Paul at last, in hostility. 'Don't you see,' said Maggie, desperately, trying to convey something of her solid and honest values; 'anyone can be lucky, anyone can do it. Young men come out from England, with a bit of money behind them, and they needn't be anything, just fools maybe, and then the weather's with them, and the prices are good, and they're rich men – but there's nothing in that, you want to try something more worthwhile than that, don't you?' Paul swung the dark and stubborn eyes on her and asked, dourly: 'What do you think of my father, then?' She caught her breath, looked at him in amazement – surely he couldn't be criticizing his father! But he was; already his eyes were half-ashamed, however, and he said quickly, 'I'll think about it,' and made his escape. He went straight off to the diggings, and seemed to avoid his mother for a time. As for Alec, Maggie thought he'd lost his senses. He came rushing in and out of the house with bits of rock and announcements of imminent riches so that Paul became as bad, and spent half his day crushing stones and watching his father panning. Soon he learned to use the pan himself. Maggie watched the intent child at work beside the water-tanks, while the expensive water went sloshing over to the dry ground, so that there were always puddles, in spite of the strong heat. The tanks ran dry and Alec had to give orders for the water-carts to make an extra journey. Yes, thought Maggie, bitterly, all these years I've been saving water and now, over this foolishness, the water-carts can make two or three extra trips a week. Because of this, Alec began talking of sinking a new well; and Maggie grew more bitter still, for she had often asked for a well to be sunk close at the back of the house, and there had never been time or money to see to it. But now, it seemed, Alec found it justified.

People who lived on the veld for a long time acquire an instinct for the places where one must sink for water. An old-timer will go snuffing and feeling over the land like a dog, marking the fall of the earth, the lie of a reef, the position of an anthill, and say at last: Here is the place. Likely enough he will be right, and often enough, of course, quite wrong.

Alec went through just such a morning of scenting and testing, through the bush at the back of the house, where the hillock erupted its boulders. If the underground forces had broken here, then there might be fissures where water could push its way; water was often to be found near a place of reefs and rocks. And there were antheaps; and ant galleries mostly ended, perhaps a hundred feet down, in an underground river. And there was a certain promising type of tree – yes, said Alec, this would be a good place for a well. And he had already marked the place and taken two labourers from the farm to do the digging when there appeared yet another of those dangerous visitors; another vagrant old man, just as stained and weatherworn as the last; with just such a craziness about him, only this time even worse, for he claimed he was a water-diviner and would find Alec Barnes a well for the sum of one pound sterling.

That night Paul was exposed until dawn to the snares of magical possibilities. He could not be made to go to bed. The old man had many tales of travel and danger; for he had spent his youth as a big-game hunter, and later, when he was too old for that, became a prospector; and later still, by chance, found that the forked twig of a tree had strength in his hands. Chance! – it was always chance, thought Maggie, listening dubiously. These men lived from one stroke of luck to the next. It was bad luck that the elephant charged and left the old man lame for life, with the tusk-scars showing white from ankle to groin. It was good luck that he 'fell in' with old Thompson, who had happened to 'make a break' with diamonds in the Free State. It was bad luck that malaria and then blackwater got him, so that he could no longer sleep in the bush at nights. It was good luck that made him try his chances with the twig, so that now he might move from farm to farm, with an assured welcome for a night behind mosquito netting. ... What an influence for Paul!

Paul sat quietly beside her and missed not a word. He blinked slow attention through those dark and watchful eyes: and he was critical, too. He rejected the old man's boasting, his insistence on the scientific certainties of the magic wand, all the talk of wells and watercourses, of which he spoke as if they were a species of underground animal that could be stalked and trapped. Paul was fixed by something else, by what kept his father still and alert all night, his eyes fixed on his guest. That *something else* – how well Maggie knew it! and how she distrusted it, and how she grieved for Paul, whose heart was beating (she could positively hear it) to the pulse of that dangerous *something else*. It was not the elephants and the lions and the narrow escapes; not the gold; not underground rivers; none of these things in themselves, and perhaps not even the pursuit of them. It was that oblique, unnameable quality in life which Maggie, trying to pin it down safely in homely words, finally dismissed in the sour and nagging phrase: Getting something for nothing. That's all they wanted, she said to herself, sadly; and when she kissed Paul and put him to bed she said, in her sensible voice: 'There isn't anything to be proud of in getting something for nothing.' She saw that he did not know what she meant; and so she left him.

Next morning, when they all went off to the projected well, Maggie remained a little way off, her apron lifted over her head against the sun, arms folded on her breast, in that ancient attitude of a patient and ironic woman; and she shook her head when the diviner offered her the twig and suggested she should try. But Paul tried, standing on his two planted feet, elbows tight into his sides, as he was shown, with the angles of the fork between palm and thumb. The twig turned over for him and he cried, delightedly: 'I'm a diviner, I'm a diviner,' and the old man agreed that he had the gift.

Alec indicated the place, and the old man walked across and around it with the twig, and at last he gave his sanction to dig – the twig turned down, infallibly, at just that spot. Alec paid him twenty shillings, and the old man wandered off to the next farm. Maggie said: 'In a country the like of this, where everyone is parched for water, a man who could tell for sure where the water is would be nothing but a millionaire. And look at this one, his coat all patches and his boots going.' She knew she might as well save her breath, for she found two pairs of dark and critical eyes fixed on her, and it was as good as if they said: Well, woman, and what has the condition of his boots got to do with it?

Late that evening she saw her husband go secretly along the path to the hillock with a twig, and later still he came back with an excited face, and she knew that he, too, 'had the gift'.

It was that term that Maggie got a letter from Paul's headmaster saying that Paul was not fitted for a practical education, nor yet did he have any especial facility for examinations. If he applied himself, he might win a scholarship, however, and become academically educated ... and so on. It was a tactful letter, and its real sense Maggie preferred not to examine, for it was too wounding to her maternal pride. Its surface sense was clear: it meant that Paul was going to cost them a good deal of money. She wrote to say that he must be given special coaching, and went off to confront Alec. He was rather irritable with her, for his mind was on the slow descent of the well. He spent most of his time watching the work. And what for? Wells were a routine. One set a couple of men to dig, and if there was no water by a certain depth, one pulled them out and tried again elsewhere. No need to stand over the thing like a harassed mother hen. So thought Maggie as she watched her husband walking in his contemplative way around the well with his twig in his hands. At thirty feet they came on water. It was not a very good stream, and might even fail in the dry season, but Alec was delighted. 'And if that silly old man hadnae come at all, the well would have been sunk just that place, and no fiddle-faddle with the divining rod,' Maggie pointed out. Alec gave her a short answer and went off to the mine on the ridge, taking his twig with him. The miner said, tolerantly, that he could divine a well if he liked. Alec chose a place, and came home to tell Maggie he would earn a guinea if there turned out to be water. 'But man,' said Maggie in amazement, 'you aren't going to keep the family in shoe-leather on guineas earned that way!' She asked again about the money for Paul's coaching, and Alec said: 'What's the matter with the boy, he's doing all right.' She persisted, and he gave in; but he seemed to resent it, this fierce determination of hers that her son must be some-thing special in the world. But when it came to the point, Alec could not find the money, it was just not in the bank. Maggie roused herself and sold eggs and poultry to the store at the station, to earn the extra few pounds that were needed. And she went on scraping shillings together and hoarding them in a drawer, though money from chickens and vegetables would not send Paul through university.

She said to Alec: 'The wages of the trench-boys would save up for Paul's education.' She did not say, since she could not think of herself as a nagging woman: And if you put your mind to it there'd be more money at the end of a season. But although she did not say it, Alec heard it, and replied with an aggrieved look and dogged silence. Later he said: 'If I find another Rand here the boy can go to Oxford, if you want that.' There was not a grain of humour in it, he was quite in earnest.

He spent all his time at the mine while the well was being sunk. They found water and he earned his guinea, which he put carefully with the silver for paying the labourers. What Maggie did not know was that during that time he had been walking around the mine-shaft with his divining rod. It was known how the reefs lay underground, and how much gold they carried.

He remarked, thoughtfully: 'Lucky the mine is just over the way for testing. The trouble with this business is it's difficult to check theories.'

Maggie did not at first understand; for she was thinking of water. She began: 'But the well on the mine is just the same as this one. . . .' She stopped, and her face changed as the outrageous suspicion filled her. 'But Alec,' she began, indignantly; and saw him turning away, shutting out her carping and doubt. 'But Alec,' she insisted, furiously, 'surely you aren't thinking of . . .'

'People have been divining for water for centuries,' he said simply, 'so why not gold?' She saw that it was all quite clear to him, like a religious faith, and that nothing she could say would reach him at all. She remained silent; and it was at that moment the last shreds of her faith in him dissolved; and she was filled with the bitterness of a woman who has no life of her own outside husband and children, and must see everything that she could be destroyed. For herself she did not mind; it was Paul – he would have to pay for this lunacy. And she must accept that too; she had married him, and that was the end of it; for the thought of leaving him did not enter her mind: Maggie was too old-fashioned for divorce. There was nothing she could do; one could not argue with a possessed person, and Alec was possessed. And in this acceptance, which was like a slow shrug of the shoulders, was something deeper, as if she felt that the visionary moon-chasing quality in Alec – even though it was ridiculous – was something necessary, and that there must always be a moment when the practical-minded must pay tribute to it. From that day, Alec found Maggie willing to listen, though ironically; she might even inquire spontaneously after his 'experiments'. Well, why not? she would catch herself thinking; perhaps he may discover something new after all. Then she pulled herself up, rather angrily; she was becoming infected by the lunacy. In her mind she was lowering the standards she had for Paul.

When Paul next returned from school he found the atmosphere again altered. The exhilaration had gone out of Alec; the honeymoon phase of discovery was past; he was absorbed and grim. His divining rod had become an additional organ; for he was never seen without it. Now it was made of iron wire, because of some theory to do with the attraction of gold for iron; and this theory and all the others were difficult to follow. Maggie made no comment at all; and this Paul would have liked to accept at its surface value, for it would have left him free to move cheerfully from one parent to the other without feeling guilt. But he was deeply disturbed. He saw his mother, with the new eyes of adolescence, for the first time, as distinct from feeling her, as the maternal image. He saw her, critically, as a fading, tired woman, with grey hair. He watched her at evening, sitting by the lamp, with the mending on her lap, in the shabby living-room; he saw how she knitted her brows and peered to thread a needle; and how the sock or shirt might lie forgotten while she went off into some dream of her own which kept her motionless, her face sad and pinched, for half an hour at a time, while her hands rubbed unconsciously in a hard and nervous movement over the arms of the chair. It is always a bad time when a son grows up and sees his mother as an elderly lady; but this did not last longer than a few days with Paul; because at once the pathos and tiredness of her gripped him, and with it, a sullen anger against his own father. Paul had become a young man when he was hardly into his teens; he took a clear look at his father and hated him for murdering the gay and humorous Maggie. He looked at the shabby house, at the neat but faded clothes of the family, and at the neglected farm. That holiday he spent down on the lands with the labourers, trying to find out what he should do. To Maggie, the new protective gentleness of her son was sweet, and also very frightening, because she did not know how to help him. He would come to her and say: 'Mother, there's a gulley down the middle of that land, what should I tell the boss-boy to do?' or 'We should plant some trees, there's hardly any timber on the place, *he's* gone and cut it all down.' He referred to his father, with hostility, as *he*; all those weeks, and Maggie said over and over again that he should not worry, he was too young. She was mortally afraid he would become absorbed by the farm and never be able to escape. When he went back to school he wrote desperate letters full of appeals like this one: 'Do, please, *make* him see to that fence before the rains, please mother, don't be soft and good-natured with him.' But Alec was likely to be irritable about details such as fences; and Maggie would send back the counter-appeal: 'Be patient, Paul. Finish your studies first, there'll be plenty of time for farming.'

He scraped through his scholarship examination with three marks to spare, and Maggie spoke to him very seriously. He appeared to be listening and perhaps he tried to; but in the end he broke in impatiently: 'Oh, mother, what's the use of me wasting time on French and Latin and English Literature. It just doesn't make sense in this country, you must see that.' Maggie could not break through this defence of impatient common sense, and planned to write him a long, authoritative letter when he got back to school. She still kept a touching belief in what schools could put in and knock out of children. At school, she thought, he might be induced into a serious consideration of his future, for the scholarship was a very small one, and would only last two years.

In the meantime he went to his father, since Maggie could not or would not help him, for advice about the farm. But Alec hardly listened to warnings about drains that needed digging and trees that should be planted; and in a fit of bitter disappointment, Paul wandered off to the mine: the boy needed a father, and had to find one somewhere. The miner liked the boy, and spoiled him with sweets and gave him the run of the workings, and let him take rides in the iron lift down the mine-shaft that descended through the soiled and sour-smelling earth. He went for a tour through the underground passages where the mine-boys worked in sodden grey loincloths, the water from the roof dripping and mingling with their running sweat. The muffled thudding of their picks sounded like marching men, a thudding that answered the beat of the mine-stamps overhead; and the lamps on their foreheads, as they moved cautiously through the half-dark tunnels, made them seem like a race of groping Cyclops. At evening he would watch the cage coming up to the sunlight full of labourers, soaked with dirt and sweat, their forehead lamps blank now, their eyes blinking painfully at the glare. Then everyone stood around expectantly for the blasting. At the very last moment the cage came racing up, groaning with the strain, and discharged the two men who had lit the fuse; and almost at once there was a soft, vibrating roar from far under their feet, and the faces and bodies of the watchers relaxed. They yawned and stretched, and drifted off in groups for their meal. Paul would lean over the shaft to catch the acrid whiff from the blasting; and then went off to eat with James, the miner. He lived in a little house with a native woman to cook for him. It was unusual to have a woman working in the house, and this plump creature, who smiled and smiled and gave him biscuits and called him darling, fascinated Paul. It was terrible cheek for a kaffir, and a kaffir woman at that, to call him darling; and Paul would never have dreamed of telling his mother, who had become so critical and impatient, and might forbid him to come again.

Several times his father appeared from the trenches down the ridge, walking straight and fast through the bush with his divining rod in his hand. 'So there you are, old son,' he would say to Paul, and forgot him at once. He nodded to James, asked: 'Do you mind?' and at once began walking back and forth around the mine-shaft with his rod. Sometimes he was pleased, and muttered: 'Looks as if I'm on the right track.' Or he might stand motionless in the sun, his old hat stuck on the back of his head, eyes glazed in thought. 'Contradictory,' he would mutter. 'Can't make it out at all.' Then he said, briefly, 'Thanks!' nod again at James and Paul as if at strangers, and walk back just as fast and determined to the 'experimental' trenches. James watched him expressionlessly, while Paul avoided his eyes. He knew James found his father ridiculous, and he did not intend to show that he knew it. He would stare off into the bush, chewing at a grass-stem, or down at the ground, making patterns in the dust with his toes, and his face was flushed and unhappy. James, seeing it, would say, kindly: 'Your father'll make it yet, Paul.'

'Do you think there could be gold?' Paul asked, eagerly, for confirmation, not of the gold, but of his father's good sense.

'Why not? There's a mine right here, isn't there? There's half a dozen small-workers round about.'

'How did you find this reef?'

'Just luck. I was after a wild pig, as it happened. It disappeared somewhere here and I put my rifle down against a rock to have a smoke, and when I picked it up the rock caught my eye, and it seemed a likely bit, so I panned it and it showed up well; I dug a trench or two and the reef went down well, and – so here I am.'

But Paul was still thinking of his father. He was looking away through the trees, over the wire fence to where the trenches were. '*My* father says if he proves right he'll divine mines for everyone, all over the world, and not only gold but diamonds and coal – and everything!' maintained Paul, proudly, with a defiant look at the miner.

'That's right, son,' said James nicely, meeting the look seriously. 'Your Dad's all right,' he added, to comfort the boy. And Paul was grateful. He used to go over to James every day just after breakfast and return late in the evening when the sun had gone. Maggie did not know what to say to him. He could not be blamed for taking his troubles to someone who was prepared to spend time with him. It was not his fault for having Alec as a father – thus Maggie, secretly feeling disloyal.

One evening she paid a visit to Alec's trenches. The reef lay diagonally down the slope of the ridge for about a mile, jutting up slantingly, like a rough ledge. At intervals, trenches had been dug across it and in places it had been blown away by a charge of gelignite.

Maggie was astonished at the extent of the work. There were about twelve labourers, and the sound of picks on flinty earth sounded all around her. From shallow trenches protruded the shoulders and heads of some of the men, but others were out of sight, twelve or more feet down. She stood looking on, feeling sad and tired, computing what the labour must cost each month, let alone the money for gelignite and fuses and picks. Alec was moving through the scrub with his wire. He had a new way of handling it. As a novice he had gripped it carefully, elbows tight at his sides, and walked cautiously as if he were afraid of upsetting the magnetism. Now he strode fast over the ground, his loose bush-shirt flying around him, the wire held lightly between his fingers. He was zigzagging back and forth in a series of twenty-foot stretches, and Maggie saw he was tracking the course of a reef, for at the centre of each of these stretches the wire turned smartly downwards. Maggie could not help thinking there was something rather perfunctory in it. 'Let me try,' she asked, and for the first time she held the magic wand. 'Walk along here,' her husband ordered, frowning with the concentration he put into it; and she walked as bidden. It was true that the wire seemed to tug and strain in her hands; but she tried again and it appeared to her that if she pulled the two ends apart, pressure tugged the point over and down, whereas if she held it without tension it remained unresponsive. Surely it could not be as simple as that? Surely Alec was not willing the wire to move as he wanted? He saw the doubt in her face and said quickly: 'Perhaps you haven't the electricity in you.' 'I daresay not,' she agreed, drily; and then asked quickly, trying to sound interested, because at once he reacted like a child to the dry note in her voice: 'Is this water or a reef?'

'A reef.' His face had brightened pathetically at this sign of interest, and he explained: 'I've worked out that either an iron rod or a twig works equally well for water, but if you neutralize the current with an iron nut on the end there must be mineral beneath, but I don't know whether gold or just any mineral.'

Maggie digested this, with difficulty, and then said: 'You say an iron rod, but this is just called galvanized iron, its just a name, it might be made of anything really, steel or tin – or anything,' she concluded lamely, her list of metals running out.

His face was perturbed. She saw that this, after all, very simple idea had never occurred to him. 'It doesn't matter,' he said, quickly, 'The point is that it works. I've proved it on the reefs at the mine.' She saw that he was looking thoughtful, nevertheless, and could not prevent herself thinking sarcastically that she had given birth to a new theory, probably based on the word *galvanized*. 'How do you know it isn't reacting to water? That mine is always having trouble with water, they say there's an underground river running parallel to the main reef.' But this was obvious enough to be insulting, and Alec said, indignantly: 'Give me credit for some sense. I checked that a long time ago.' He took the wire, slipped an iron nut on each bent end and gripped the ends tight. 'Like that,' he said. 'The iron neutralizes, do you see?' She nodded, and he took off the iron nuts and then she saw him reach into his pocket and take out his signet ring and put that on the wire.

'What are you doing?' asked Maggie, with the most curious feeling of dismay. That signet ring she had given him when they were married. She had bought it with money saved from working as a girl in her parents' shop, and it represented a great deal of sacrifice to her then. Even now, for that matter. And here he was using it as an implement, not even stopping to think how she might feel about it. When he had finished he slipped the gold ring, together with  the two iron nuts, back into the pocket of his bush-shirt. 'You'll lose it,' she said, anxiously, but he did not hear her. 'If the iron neutralizes the water, which I've proved,' he said, worriedly, 'then the gold ring should neutralize the gold.' She did not follow the logic of this, though she could not doubt it all had been worked out most logically. He took her slowly along the great reef, talking in that slow, thoughtful way of his. She felt a thwarted misery – for what was the use of being miserable? She did not believe in emotions that were not useful in some way.

Later he began flying back and forth again over a certain vital patch of earth, and he dropped the signet ring and it rolled off among the long grasses, and she helped him to find it again. 'As a matter of fact,' he mused aloud, 'I'll give up the trenches here, I think, and sink a proper shaft. Not here. It's had a fair chance. I'll try somewhere new.'

Before they left at sundown she walked over to one of the deep trenches and stood looking down. It was like a grave, she thought. The mouth was narrow, a slit among the long, straggling grass, with the mounds of rubble banked at the ends, and the rosy evening sun glinted red on the grass-stems and flashed on the pebbles. The trees glowed, and the sky was a wash of colour. The side of the trench showed the strata of soil and stone. First a couple of feet of close, hard, reddish soil, hairy with root-structure; then a slab of pinkish stuff mixed with round white pebbles; then a narrow layer of smooth white that resembled the filling in a cake; and then a deep plunge of greyish shale that broke into flakes at the touch of the pick. There was no sign of any reef at the bottom of the trench; and as Alec looked down he was frowning; and she could see that there should have been a reef, and this trench proved something unsettling to the theory.

Some days later he remarked that he was taking the workers off the reef to a new site. She did not care to ask where; but soon she saw a bustle of activity in the middle of the great mealie-field. Yes, he had decided to sink a shaft just there, he, who had once lost his temper if he found even a small stone in a furrow which might nick the plough-shares.

It was becoming a very expensive business. The cases of explosive came out from the station twice a month on the waggon; and she had to order boxes of mining candles, instead of packets, from the store. And when Alec panned the samples there were twenty or more, instead of the half-dozen, and he would be working at the water-tanks half the morning. He was very pleased with the shaft; he thought he was on the verge of success. There were always a few grains of gold in the pan, and one day a long trail of it, which he estimated at almost as much as would be worth working. He sent a sample into the Mines Department for a proper test, and it came back confirmed. But this was literally a flash in the pan, for nothing fresh happened; and soon that shaft was abandoned. Workers dragged an untidy straggle of barbed wire around the shaft so that cattle should not stray into it; and the ploughs detoured there; and in the centre of the once unbroken field stood a tall thicket of grass and scrub, which made Paul furious when he came home for the holidays. He remonstrated with his father, who replied that it had been justified, because from that shaft he had learned a great deal, and one must be prepared to pay for knowledge. He used just those words, very seriously, like a scientist. Maggie remarked that the shaft had cost at least a hundred pounds to sink, and she hoped the knowledge was worth that much. It was the sort of remark she never made these days; and she understood she had made it now because Paul was there, who supported her. As soon as Paul came home she always had the most uncomfortable feeling that his very presence tugged her away from her proper loyalty to Alec. She found herself becoming critical and nagging; while the moment Paul had gone she drifted back into a quiet acceptance, like fatalism. It was not long after that bitter remark that Alec finally lost his signet ring; and because it was necessary to work with a gold ring, asked her for her wedding ring. She had never taken it off her finger since they married, but she slipped it off now and handed it to him without a word. As far as she was concerned it was a moment of spiritual divorce; but a divorce takes two, and if the partner doesn't even notice it, what then?

He lost that ring too, of course, but it did not matter by then, for he had amended his theory, and gold rings had become a thing of the past. He was now using a rod of fine copper wire with shreds of asbestos wound about it. Neither Maggie nor Paul asked for explanations, for there were pages of detailed notes on his farm desk, and books about magnetic fields and currents and the sympathy of metals, and they could not have understood the terms he used, for his philosophy had become the most extraordinary mixture of alchemy and magic and the latest scientific theories. His office, which for years had held nothing but a safe for money and a bookshelf of farming magazines, was now crammed with lumps of stone, crucibles, mortars, and the walls were covered with maps and diagrams, while divining rods in every kind of metal hung from nails. Next to the newest geological map from the Government office was an old map imagined by a seventeenth-century explorer, with mammoth-like beasts scrolling the border; and the names of the territories were fabulous, like El Dorado, and Golconda, and Queen Sheba's Country. There were shelves of retorts and test-tubes and chemicals, and in a corner stood the skull of an ox, for there was a period of months when Alec roamed the farm with that skull dangling from his divining rod, to test a belief that the substances of bone had affinities with probable underground deposits of lime. The books ranged from the latest Government publications to queer pamphlets with titles such as *Metallurgy and the Zodiac*, or *Gold Deposits on Venus*.

It was in this room that Maggie confronted him with a letter from Paul's headmaster. The scholarship money was finished. Was it intended that the boy should try for a fresh one to take him through university. In this case, he must change his attitude, for while he could not be described as stupid, he 'showed no real inclination for serious application'. If not, there was 'no immediate necessity for reviewing the state of affairs', but a list of employers was enclosed with whom Mrs. Barnes might care to communicate. In short, the headmaster thought Paul was thick-witted. Maggie was furious. *Her* son become a mere clerk! She informed Alec, peremptorily, that they must find the money to send Paul through university. Alec was engaged in making a fine diagram of his new shaft in cross-section, and he lifted a blank face to say: 'Why spoon-feed the boy? If he was any good he'd work.' The words struck Maggie painfully, for they summed up her own belief; but she found herself thinking that it was all Alec's fault for being English and infecting her son with laziness. She controlled this thought and said they must find the money, even if Alec curtailed his experimenting. He looked at her in amazement and anger. She saw that the anger was against her false scale of values. He was thinking: What is one child's future (even if he happens to be my own, which is a mere biological accident, after all) against a discovery which might change the future of the world? He maintained the silence necessary when dealing with little-minded people. But she would not give in. She argued and even wept, and gave him no peace, until his silence crumbled into violence and he shouted: 'Oh, all right then, have it your own way.'

At first Maggie thought that she should have done this before 'for his own good'. It was not long before she was sorry she had done it. For Alec went striding anxiously about the farm, his eyes worriedly resting on the things he had not really seen for so long – eroded soil, dragging fences, blocked drains – he had been driven out of that inward refuge where everything was clear and meaningful, and there was a cloud of fear on his face like a child with night-terrors. It hurt Maggie to look at him; but for a while she held out, and wrote a proud letter to the headmaster saying there was no need to trouble about a scholarship, they could pay the money. She wrote to Paul himself, a nagging letter, saying that his laziness was making his father ill, and the very least he could do 'after all his father had done for him' was to pass his matriculation well.

This letter shocked Paul, but not in the way she had intended. He knew quite well that his father would never notice whether he passed an examination or not. His mother's dishonesty made him hate her; and he came home from school in a set and defiant mood, saying he did not want to go to university. This betrayal made Maggie frantic. Physically she was passing through a difficult time, and the boy hardly recognized this hectoring and irritable mother. For the sake of peace he agreed to go to university, but in a way which told Maggie that he had no intention at all of doing any work. But his going depended, after all, on Alec, and when Maggie confronted him with the fact that money for fees was needed, he replied, vaguely, that he would have it in good time. It was not quite the old vagueness, for there was a fever and urgency in him that seemed hopeful to Maggie, and she looked every day at the fields for signs of reorganization. There were no changes yet. Weeks passed, and again she went to him, asking what his new plans were. Alec replied, irritably, that he was doing what he could, and what did she expect, a miracle to order? There was something familiar in this tone and she looked closely at him and demanded: 'Alec, what exactly are you doing?'

He answered in the old, vague way: 'I'm on to it now, Maggie, I'm certain I'll have the answer inside a month.'

She understood that she had spurred him, not into working on the farm, but into putting fresh energies behind the gold-seeking. It was such a shock to her that she felt really ill, and for some days she kept to her bed. It was not real illness, but a temporary withdrawal from living. She pulled the curtains and lay in the hot half-dark. The servants took in her meals, for she could not bear the sight of either her son or her husband. When Paul entered tentatively, after knocking and getting no reply, he found her lying in her old dressing-gown, her eyes averted, her face flushed and exhausted, and she replied to his questions with nervous dislike. But it was Paul who coaxed her back into the family, with that gentle, protective sympathy which was so strange in a boy of his age. She came back because she had to; she took her place again and behaved sensibly, but in a tight and controlled way which upset Paul, and which Alec ignored, for he was quite obsessed. He would come in for meals, his eyes hot and glittering, and eat unconsciously, throwing out remarks like: Next week I'll know. I'll soon know for sure.

In spite of themselves, Paul and Maggie were affected by his certainty. Each was thinking secretly: Suppose he's right? After all, the great inventors are always laughed at to begin with.

There was a day when he came triumphantly in, loaded with pieces of rock. 'Look at this,' he said, confidently. Maggie handled them, to please him. They were of rough, heavy, crumbling substance, like rusty honeycomb. She could see the minerals glistening. She asked: 'Is this what you wanted?'

'You'll see,' said Alec, proudly, and ordered Paul to come with him to the shaft, to help bring more samples. Paul went, in his rather sullen way. He did not want to show that he half-believed his father. They returned loaded. Each piece of rock was numbered according to the part of the reef it had been taken from. Half of each piece was crushed in the mortar, and father and son stood panning all the afternoon.

Paul came to her and said, reluctantly: 'It seems quite promising, mother.' He was appealing to her to come and look. Silently she rose, and went with him to the water-tanks. Alec gave her a defiant stare and thrust the pan over to her. There was the usual trail of mineral, and behind was a smear of dull gold, and behind that big grits of the stuff. She looked with listless irony over at Paul, but he nodded seriously. She accepted it from him, for he knew quite a lot by now. Alec saw that she trusted his son when she dis-believed him, and gave her a baffled and angry look. She hastened to smooth things over. 'Is it a lot?' she asked.

'Quite enough to make it workable.'

'I see,' she said, seriously. Hope flicked in her and again she looked over at Paul. He gave an odd, humorous grimace, which meant: Don't get excited about it yet; but she could see that he was really excited. They did not want to admit to each other that they were aroused to a half-belief, so they felt awkward. If this madness turned out to be no madness at all, how foolish they would feel!

'What are you going to do now?' she asked Alec.

'I'm sending in all these samples to the Department for proper assaying.'

'*All* of them . . .' she checked the protest, but she was thinking: That will cost an awful lot of money. 'And when will you hear?'

'In about a week.'

Again Paul and she exchanged glances, and they went in-doors, leaving Alec to finish the panning. Paul said, with that grudging enthusiasm: 'You know, mother, if it's true . . .'

'If . . .' she scoffed.

'But he says if this works it means he can divine anything. He says Governments will be sending for him to divine their coalfields, water, gold – everything!'

'But Paul,' she said, wearily, 'they can find coalfields and minerals with scientific instruments, they don't need black magic.' She even felt a little mean to damp the boy in this way. 'Can they?' he asked, doubtfully. He didn't want to believe it, because it sounded so dull to him. 'But mother, even if he can't divine, and it's all nonsense, we'll have a rich mine on this farm.'

'That won't satisfy your father,' she said. 'He'll rest at nothing less than a universal theory.'

The rocks were sent off that same day to the station; and now they were restless and eager, even Maggie, who tried not to show it. They all went to examine this vital shaft one afternoon. It was in a thick patch of bush and they had to walk along a native path to reach the rough clearing, where a simple windlass and swinging iron bucket marked the shaft. Maggie leaned over. There being no gleam of water, as in a well, to mark the bottom, she could see nothing at first. For a short distance the circular hole plunged rockily, with an occasional flash of light from a faceted pebble; then a complete darkness. But as she looked there was a glow of light far below and she could see the tiny form of a man against the lit rock face. 'How deep?' she asked, shuddering a little.

'Over a hundred now,' said Alec, casually. 'I'll just go down and have a look.' The natives swung the bucket out into the centre of the shaft and Alec pulled the rope to him, so that the bucket inclined at the edge, slid in one leg and thrust himself out, so that he hung in space, clinging to the rope with one hand and using an arm and a leg to fend off the walls as the rope unwound him down into the blackness. Maggie found it frightening to watch so she pulled her head back from the shaft so as not to look; but Paul lay on his stomach and peered over.

At last Alec came up again. He scrambled lightly from the rocking bucket to safety, and Maggie suppressed a sigh of relief. 'You should see that reef,' he said, proudly. 'It's three feet wide. I've cross-cut in three places and it doesn't break at all.'

Maggie was thinking: Only three days of waiting gone! They were all waiting now, in a condition of hallucinatory calm, for the result to come back from the Assay Department. When only five days had passed Alec said: 'Let's send the boy in for the post.' She had been expecting this, and although she said 'Silly to send so soon', she was eager to do so; after all, they *might* have replied, one never knew – and so the houseboy made the trip in to the station. Usually they only sent twice a week for letters. Next day he went again – nothing. And now a week had passed and the three of them hanging helplessly about the house, watching the road for the post-boy. Eight days: Alec could not work, could not eat; and Paul lounged about the verandah, saying: 'Won't it be funny to have a big mine just down there, on our own farm. There'll be a town around it, and think what this land will be worth then!'

'Don't count your chickens,' said Maggie. But all kinds of half-suppressed longings were flooding up in her. It would be nice to have good clothes again; to buy nice linen, instead of the thin, washed-out stuff they had been using for years. Perhaps she could go to the doctor for her headaches, and he would prescribe a holiday, and they could go to Scotland for a holiday and see the old people. . . .

Nine days. The tension was no longer pleasant. Paul and Alec quarrelled. Alec said he would refuse to allow a town to be built around the mine; it would be a pity to waste good farming land. Paul said he was mad – look at Johannesburg, the building lots there were worth thousands the square inch. Maggie again told them not to be foolish; and they laughed at her and said she had no imagination.

The tenth day was a regular mail-day. If there was no letter then Alec said he would telephone the Department; but this was a mere threat, because the Department dealt with hundreds of samples from hopeful gold-searchers all over the country, and could not be expected to make special arrangements for one person. But Alec said: 'I'm surprised they haven't telephoned before. Just like a Government department not to see the importance of something like this.' The post was late. They sat on the darkening verandah, gazing down the road through the mealie-fields, and when the man came at last there was still no letter. They had all three expected it.

And now there was a feeling of anti-climax, and Maggie found a private belief confirmed: that nothing could happen to this family in neat, tidy events; everything must always drag itself out, everything declined and decayed and muddled itself along. Even if there is gold, she thought, secretly, there'll be all kinds of trouble with selling it, and it'll drag out for months and months! That eleventh day was a long torture. Alec sat in his office, anxiously checking his calculations, drinking cup after cup of strong, sweet tea. Paul pretended to read, and yawned and watched the clock until Maggie lost her temper with him. The houseboy, now rather resentful because of these repeated trips of seven miles each way on foot, set off late after lunch to the station. They tried to sleep the afternoon away, but could not keep their eyes closed. When the sun was hanging just over the mountains, they again arranged themselves on the verandah to wait. The sun sank, and Maggie telephoned the station: Yes, the train had been two hours late. They ate supper in tense silence and went back to the verandah. The moon was up and everything flooded with that weird light which made the mealie-fields lose solidity, so that there was a swaying and murmuring like a sea all around them. At last Paul shouted: 'Here he comes!' And now, when they could see the swinging hurricane lamp, that sent a dim, red flicker along the earth across the bright moonlight, they could hardly bring themselves to move. They were thinking: Well, it needn't be today, after all – perhaps we'll have this waiting tomorrow, too.

The man handed in the sack. Maggie took it, removed the bundle of letters and handed them to Alec; she could see a Government envelope. She was feeling sick, and Paul was white, the bones of his face showed too sharply. Alec dropped the letters and then clumsily picked them up. He made several attempts to open the envelope and at last ripped it across, tearing the letter itself. He straightened the taper, held it steady and – but Maggie had averted her eyes and glanced at Paul. He was looking at her with a sickly and shamed smile.

Alec held the piece of paper loose by one corner, and he was sitting rigid, his eyes dark and blank. 'No good,' he said at last, in a difficult, jerking voice. He seemed to have shrunk, and the flesh of his face was tight. His lips were blue. He dropped the paper and sat staring. Then he muttered: 'I can't understand it, I simply can't understand it.'

Maggie whispered to Paul. He jumped up, relieved to

get away, and went to the kitchen and soon returned with a tray of tea. Maggie poured out a big cup, sugared it heavily and handed it to Alec. Those blue lips worried her. He put it at his side, but she took it again and held it in front of him and he drank it off, rather impatiently. It was that impatient movement which reassured her. He was now sitting more easily and his face was flushed. 'I can't understand it,' he said again, in an aggrieved voice, and Maggie understood that the worst was over. She was aching with pity for him and for Paul, who was pretending to read. She could see how badly the disappointment had gripped him. But he was only a child, she thought; he would get over it.

'Perhaps we should go to bed,' she suggested, in a small voice; but Alec said: 'That means . . .' he paused, then thought for a moment and said: 'I must have been wrong over – all this time I've been over-estimating the amount in a sample. I thought that was going ounces to the ton. And it means that my theory about the copper was . . .' He sat leaning forward, arms hanging loosely before him; then he jumped up, strode through to his office and returned with a divining wire. She saw it was one of the old ones, a plain iron rod. 'Have you anything gold about you?' he asked, impatiently.

She handed him a brooch her mother had given her. He took it and went towards the verandah. 'Alec,' she protested, 'not tonight.' But he was already outside. Paul put down his book and smiled ruefully at her. She smiled back. She did not have to tell him to forget all the wild-goose daydreams. Life would seem flat and grey for a while, but not for long – that was what she wanted to say to him; she would have liked, too, to add a little lecture about working for what one wanted in life, and not to trust to luck; but the words stuck. 'Get yourself to bed,' she suggested; but he shook his head and handed his cup for more tea. He was looking out at the moonlight, where a black, restless shape could be seen passing backwards and forwards.

She went quietly to a window and looked out, shielding herself with a curtain, though she felt ashamed of this anxious supervision which Alec would most certainly resent if he knew. But he did not notice. The moon shone monotonously down; it looked like a polished silver sixpence; and

Alec's shadow jerked and lengthened over the rough ground as he walked up and down with his divining rod. Sometimes he stopped and stood thinking. She went back to sit by Paul. She slipped an arm around him, and so they remained for a time, thinking of the man outside. Later she went to the window again, and this time beckoned to Paul and he stood with her, silently watching Alec.

'He's a very brave man,' she found herself saying, in a choked voice; for she found that determined figure in the moonlight unbearably pathetic. Paul felt awkward because of her emotion, and looked down when she insisted: 'Your father's a very brave man and don't you ever forget it.' His embarrassment sent him off to bed. He could not stand her emotion as well as his own.

Afterwards she understood that her pity for Alec was a false feeling – he did not need pity. It flashed through her mind, too – though she suppressed the thought – that words like brave were as false.

Until the moon slid down behind the house and the veld went dark, Alec remained pacing that patch of ground before the house. At last he came morosely to bed, but without that look of exposed and pitiful fear she had learned to dread; he was safe in that orderly inner world he had built for himself. She heard him remark from the bed on the other side of the room where he was sitting smoking in the dark: 'If that reef outside the front door is what I think it is, then I've found where I was wrong. Quite a silly little mistake, really.'

Cautiously she inquired: 'Are you going on with that shaft?'

'I'll see in the morning. I'll just check up on my new idea first.' They exchanged a few remarks of this kind; and then he crushed out his cigarette and lay down. He slept immediately; but she lay awake, thinking drearily of Paul's future.

In the morning Alec went straight off down to his shaft, while Paul forced himself to go and interview the boss-boys about the farmwork. Maggie was planning a straight talk with the boy about his school, but his present mood frightened her. Several times he said, scornfully, just as if he had not himself been intoxicated: 'Father's crazy. He's got no sense left.' He laughed in an arrogant, half-ashamed way;

and she controlled her anger at this youthful unfairness. She was tired, and afraid of her own irritability, which these days seemed to explode in the middle of the most trifling arguments. She did not want to be irritable with Paul because, when this happened, he treated her tolerantly, as a grown man would, and did not take her seriously. She waited days before the opportunity came, and then the discussion went badly after all.

'Why do you want me to be different, mother?' he asked, sullenly, when she insisted he should study for a scholarship. 'You and father were just like everybody else, but I've got to be something high and mighty.' Maggie already found herself growing angry. She said, as her mother might have done: 'Everybody has the duty to better themselves and get on. If you try you can be anything you like.' The boy's face was set against her. There was something in the air of this country which had formed him that made that other, older voice seem like an anachronism. Maggie persisted: 'Your great-grandparents were small farmers. They rented their land from a lord. But they saved enough to give your grandfather fifty pounds to take to the city. He got his own shop by working for it. Your father was just an ordinary clerk, but he took his opportunities and made his way here. But you see no shame in accepting a nobody's job, wherever someone's kind enough to offer it to you.' He seemed embarrassed, and finally remarked: 'All that class business doesn't mean anything out here. Besides, my father's a small farmer, just like his grandparents. I don't see what's so new about that.' At this, as if his words had released a spring marked *anger*, she snapped out: 'So, if that's what you are, the way you look at things, it's a waste of time even . . .' She checked herself, but it was too late. Her loss of control had ended the contact between them. Afterwards she wondered if perhaps he was right. In a way, the wheel had come the circle: the difference between that old Scotsman and Alec was that one worked his land with his own hands; he was limited only by his own capacities; while the other worked through a large labour-force: he was as much a slave to his ill-fed, backward and sullen labourers as they were to him. Well then, and if this were true, and Paul could see it as clearly as she did, why could he not decide to break the circle and join the men who had power because they had knowledge: the free men, that was how she saw them. Knowledge freed a man; and to that belief she clung, because it was her nature; and she was to grieve all her life because such a simple and obvious truth was not simple for Paul.

Some days later she said, tartly, to Paul: 'If you're not going back to school, then you might as well put your mind to the farmwork.' He replied that he was trying to; to her impatience he answered with an appeal: 'It's difficult, mother. Everything's in such a mess. I don't know where to start. I haven't the experience.' Maggie tried hard to control that demon of disappointment and anger in her that made her hard, unsympathetic; but her voice was dry: 'You'll get experience by working.'

And so Paul went to his father. He suggested, practically, that Alec should spend a month ('only a month, Dad, it's not so long') showing him the important things. Alec agreed, but Paul could see that as they went from plough to waggon, field to grazing land, that Alec's thoughts were not with him. He would ask a question, and Alec did not hear. And at the end of three days he gave it up. The boy was seething with frustration and misery. 'What do they expect me to do?' he kept muttering to himself, 'what do they want?' His mother was like a cold wall; she would not love him unless he became a college boy; his father was amiably uninterested. He took himself off to neighbouring farmers. They were kind, for everyone was sorry for him. But after a week or so of listening to advice, he was more dismayed than before. 'You'd better do something about your soil, lad,' they said. 'Your Dad's worked it out.' Or: 'The first thing is to plant trees, the wind'll blow what soil there is away unless you do something quickly.' Or: 'That big, vlei of yours: do you know it was dry a month before the rains last year? Your father has ploughed up the catchment area; you'd better sink some wells quickly.' It meant a complete reorganization. He could do it, of course, but ... the truth was he had not the heart to do it, when no one was interested in him. They just don't care, he said to himself; and after a few weeks of desultory work he took himself off to James, his adopted father. Part of the day he would spend on the lands, just to keep things going, and then he drifted over to the mine.

James was a big, gaunt man, with a broad and bony face. Small grey eyes looked steadily from deep sockets, his mouth was hard. He stood loosely, bending from the shoulders, and his hands swung loose beside him so that there was something of a gorilla-look about him. Strength – that was the impression he gave, and that was what Paul found in him. And yet there was also a hesitancy, a moment of indecision before he moved or spoke, and a sardonic note in his drawl – it was strength on the defensive, a watchful and precarious strength. He smoked heavily, rough cigarettes he rolled for himself between yellow-stained fingers; and regularly drank just a little too much. He would get really drunk several times a year, but between these indulgences kept to his three whiskies at sundown. He would toss these back, standing, one after another, when he came in from work; and then give the bottle a long look, a malevolent look, and put it away where he could not see it. Then he took his dinner, without pleasure, to feed the drink; and immediately went to bed. Once Paul found him at a week-end lying sodden and asleep sprawled over the table, and he was sickened; but afterwards James was simple and kindly as always; nor did he apologize, but took it as a matter of course that a man needed to drink himself blind from time to time. This, oddly enough, reassured the boy. His own father never drank, and Maggie had a puritan horror of it; though she would offer visitors a drink from politeness. It was a problem that had never touched him; and now it was presented crudely to him and seemed no problem at all.

He asked questions about James' life. James would give him that shrewd, slow look, hesitate a little, and then in a rather tired voice, as if talking were disagreeable, answer the boy's clumsy questions. He was always very patient with Paul; but behind the good-natured patience was another emotion, like a restrained cruelty; it was not a personal cruelty, directed against Paul, but the self-punishment of fatalism, in which Paul was included.

James' mother was Afrikaans and his father English. He had the practicality, the humour, the good sense of his mother's people, and the inverted and tongue-tied poetry of the English, which expressed itself in just that angry fatalism and perhaps also in the drink. He had been raised in a suburb of Johannesburg, and went early to the mines. He spoke of that city with a mixture of loathing and fascination, so that to Paul it became an epitome of all the great and glamorous cities of the world. But even while Paul was dreaming of its delights he would hear James drawl: 'I got out of it in time, I had that much sense.' And though he did not want to have his dream darkened, he had to listen: 'When you first go down, you get paid like a prince and the world's your oyster. Then you get married and tie yourself up with a houseful of furniture on the hire-purchase and a house under a mortgage. Your car's your own, and you exchange it for a new one every year. It's a hell of a life, money pouring in and money pouring out, and your wife loves you, and everything's fine; parties and a good time for one and all. And then your best friend finds his chest is giving him trouble and he goes to the doctor, and then suddenly you find he's dropped out of the crowd; he's on half the money and all the bills to pay. His wife finds it no fun and off she goes with someone else. Then you discover it's not just one of your friends, but half the men you know are in just that position, crocks at thirty and owning nothing but the car, and they soon sell that to pay alimony. You find you drink too much – there's something on your mind, as you might say. Then, if you've got sense, you walk out while the going's good. If not, you think: It can't happen to me, and you stay on.' He allowed a minute to pass while he looked at the boy to see how much had sunk in. Then he repeated, firmly: 'That's not just my story, son, take it from me. It's happened to hundreds.'

Paul thought it over and said: 'But you didn't have a wife?'

'Oh, yes, I had a wife all right,' said James, grim and humourous. 'I had a fine wife, but only while I was underground raking in the shekels. When I decided it wasn't good enough and I wanted to save my lungs, and I went on surface work at less money, she transferred to one of the can't-happen-to-me boys. She left him when the doctor told him he was fit for the scrap-heap, and then she used her brains and married a man on the stock exchange.'

Paul was silent, because this bitter note against women was not confirmed by what he felt about his mother. 'Do you ever want to go back?' he asked.

'Sometimes,' conceded James, grudgingly. 'Johannesburg's a mad house, but it's got something – but when I get the hankering I remember I'm still alive and kicking when my crowd's mostly dead or put out to grass.' He was speaking of the city as men do of the sea, or travel, or of drugs; and it gripped Paul's imagination. But James looked sharply at him and said: 'Hey, sonnie, if you've got any ideas about going South to the golden city, then think again. You don't want to get any ideas about getting rich quick. If you want to mix yourself up in that racket, then you buy yourself an education and stay on the surface bossing the others, and not underground being bossed. You take it from me, son.'

And Paul took it from him, though he did not want to. The golden city was shimmering in his head like a mirage. But what was the alternative? To stay on this shabby little farm? In comparison, James' life seemed daring and wonderful and dangerous. It seemed to him that James was telling him everything but what was essential; he was leaving something out – and soon he came back again for another dose of the astringent common-sense that left him unfed, acknowledging it with his mind but not his imagination.

He found James sitting on a heap of shale at the shaft-head, rolling cigarettes, his back to the evening sun. Paul stepped over the long, black shadow and seated himself on the shale. It was loose and shifted under him to form a warm and comfortable hollow. He asked for a cigarette and James good-humouredly gave him one. 'Are you glad you became a small-worker?' he asked at once.

There was a shrewd look and the slow reply: 'No complaints, there's a living as long as the seam lasts – looks as if it won't last much longer at that.' Paul ignored that last remark and persisted: 'If you had your life again, how would you change it?'

James grimaced and asked: 'Who's offering me my life again?'

The boy's face was strained with disappointment. 'I want to know,' he said, stubbornly, like a child.

'Listen, sonnie,' said James, quietly, 'I'm no person to ask for advice. I've nothing much to show. All I've got to pat myself on the back for is I had the sense to pull out of the big money in time to save my lungs.' Paul let these words go past him and he looked up at the big man, who seemed so kindly and solid and sensible, and asked: 'Are you happy?' At last the question was out. James positively started; then he gave that small, humorous grimace and put back his head and laughed. It was painful. Then he slapped Paul's knee and said, tolerantly, still laughing: 'Sonnie, you're a nice kid, don't you let any of them get you down.'

Paul sat there, shamefaced, trying to smile, feeling badly let down. He felt as if James, too, had rejected him. But he clung to the man, since there was no one else; he came over in the evenings to talk, while he decided to put his mind to the farm. There was nothing else to do.

Yet while he worked he was daydreaming. He imagined himself travelling South, to the Rand, and working as James had done, saving unheard of sums of money and then leaving, a rich man, in time to save his health. Or did not leave, but was carried out on a stretcher, with his mother and James as sorrowing witnesses of this victim of the gold industry. Or he saw himself as the greatest mine expert of the continent, strolling casually among the mine-dumps and headgear of the Reef, calmly shedding his pearls of wisdom before awed financiers. Or he bought a large tobacco farm, made fifty thousand the first season and settled vast sums on James and his parents.

Then he took himself in hand, refusing himself even the relief of daydreams, and forced himself to concentrate on the work. He would come back full of hopeful enthusiasm to Maggie, telling her that he was dividing the big field for a proper rotation of crops and that soon it would show strips of colour, from the rich, dark green of maize to the blazing yellow of the sunflower. She listened kindly, but without responding as he wanted. So he ceased to tell her what he was doing – particularly as half the time he felt uneasily that it was wrong, he simply did not know. He set his teeth over his anger and went to Alec and said: 'Now listen, you've got to answer a question.' Alec, divining rod in hand, turned and said: 'What now?' 'I want to know, should I harrow the field now or wait until the rains?' Alec, hesitated and said: 'What do you think?' Paul shouted: 'I want to know what *you* think – you've had the experience, haven't you?' And then Alec lost his temper and said: 'Can't you see I'm working this thing out? Go and ask – well go and ask one of the neighbours.'

Paul would not give in. He waited until Alec had finished, and then said: 'Now come on, father, you're coming with me to the field. I want to know.' Reluctantly, Alec went. Day after day, Paul fought with his father; he learned not to ask for general advice, he presented Alec with a definite problem and insisted until he got an answer. He was beginning to find his way among the complexities of the place, when Maggie appealed to him: 'Paul, I know you'll think I'm hard, but I want you to leave your father alone.'

The boy said, in amazement: 'What do you mean? I don't ask him things oftener than once or twice a day? He's got all the rest of the time to play with his toys.'

Maggie said: 'He should be left. I know you won't understand, but I'm right Paul.' For several days she had been watching Alec; she could see that cloud of fear in his eyes that she had seen before. When he was forced to look outside him and his private world, when he was made to look at the havoc he had created by his negligence, then he could not bear it. He lay tossing at night, complaining endlessly: 'What does he want? What more can I do? He goes on and on, and he knows I'm on to the big thing. I'll have it soon, Maggie, I know I will. This new reef'll be full of gold, I am sure. . . .' It made her heart ache with pity for him. She had decided, firmly, to support her husband against her son. After all, Paul was young, he'd his life in front of him. She said, quietly: 'Leave him, Paul. You don't understand. When a person's a failure, it's cruel to make them see it.'

'I'm not making him see anything,' said Paul, bitterly. 'I'm only asking for advice, that's all, that's all!' And the big boy of sixteen burst into tears of rage; and after a helpless, wild look at his mother, ran off into the bush, stumbling as he ran. He was saying to himself: I've had enough, I'm going to run away. I'm going South. . . . But after a while he quietened and went back to work. He left Alec alone. But it was not so easy. Again he said to Maggie: 'He's dug a trench right across my new contour ridges; he didn't even ask me. . . .' And later: 'He's put a shaft clean in the middle of the sunflowers, he's ruined half an acre – can't you talk to him, mother.' Maggie promised to talk to her husband, and when it came to the point, lost her courage. Alec was like a child, what was the use of talking?

Later still, Paul came and said: 'Do you realize what he's spent this last year on his nonsense?'

'Yes, I know,' sighed Maggie.

'Well, he can't spend so much, and that's all there is to it.'

'What are you going to do?' said Maggie. And then quickly: 'Be gentle with him, Paul. Please. . . .'

Paul insisted one evening that Alec 'should listen to him for a moment'. He made his father sit at one end of the table while he placed books of account before him and stood over him while he looked through them. 'You can't do it, father,' said Paul, reasonably, patiently; 'you've got to cut it down a bit.'

It hurt Maggie to see them. It hurt Paul, too – it was like pensioning off his own father. For he was simply making conditions, and Alec had to accept them. He was like a petitioner, saying: 'You're not going to take it all away from me, are you? You can't do that?' His face was sagging with disappointment, and in the end it brightened pathetically at the concession that he might keep four labourers for his own use and spend fifty pounds a year. 'Not a penny more,' said Paul. 'And you've got to fill in all the abandoned diggings and shafts. You can't walk a step over the farm now without risking your neck.'

Maggie was tender with Alec afterwards, when he came to her and said: 'That young know-all, turning everything upside down, all theories and no experience!' Then he went off to fill in the trenches and shafts, and afterwards to a distant part of the farm where he had found a new reef.

But now he tended to make sarcastic remarks to Paul; and Maggie had to be careful to keep the peace between them, feeling a traitor to both, for she would agree first with one man, then with the other – Paul was a man now, and it hurt her to see it. Sixteen, thin as a plank, sunburn dark on a strained face, much too patient with her. For Paul would look at the tired old woman who was his mother and think that by rights she should still be a young one, and he shut his teeth over the reproaches he wanted to make: Why do you support him in this craziness; why do you agree to everything he says? And so he worried through that first season; and there came the time to balance the farm books; and there happened something that no one expected.

When all the figuring and accounting was over, Alec, who had apparently not even noticed the work, went into the office and spent an evening with the books. He came out with a triumphant smile and said to Paul: 'Well, you haven't done much better than I did, in spite of all your talk.'

Paul glanced at his mother, who was making urgent signs at him to keep his temper. He kept it. He was white, but he was making an effort to smile. But Alec continued: 'You go on at me, both of you, but when it comes to the point you haven't made any profit either.' It was so unfair that Paul could no longer remain silent. 'You let the farm go to pieces,' he said, bitterly, 'You won't even give me advice when I ask for it, and then you accuse me . . .'

'Paul,' said Maggie, urgently.

'And when I find a goldmine,' said Alec, magnificently, 'and it won't be long now, you'll come running to me, you'll be sorry then! You can't run a farm, and you haven't got the sense to learn elementary geology from me. You've been with *me* all these years and you don't even know one sort of reef from another. You're too damned lazy to live.' And with this he walked out of the room.

Paul was sitting still, head dropped a little, looking at the floor. Maggie waited for him to smile with her at this child who was Alec. She was arranging the small, humorous smile on her lips that would take the sting out of the scene, when Paul slowly rose, and said quietly: 'Well, that's the end.'

'No, Paul,' cried Maggie, 'you shouldn't take any notice; you can't take it seriously. . . .'

'Can't I?' said Paul, bitterly. 'I've had enough.'

'Where are you going? What are you going to do?'

'I don't know.'

'You can't leave,' Maggie found herself saying. 'You haven't got the education to . . .' She stopped herself, but not in time. Paul's face was so hurt and abandoned that she cried out to herself: What's the matter with me? Why did I say it? Paul said: 'Well, that's that.' And he went out of the room after his father.

Paul went over to the mine, found James sitting on his verandah, and said at once: 'James, can I come as a partner with you?'

James' face did not change. He looked patiently at the boy and said 'Sit down.' Then, when Paul had set, and was leaning forward waiting, he said: 'There isn't enough profit for a partner here, you know that. Otherwise I'd like to have you. Besides, it looks as if the reef is finished.' He waited and asked: 'What's gone wrong?'

Paul made an impatient movement, dismissing his parents, the farm, and his past, and said: 'Why is your reef finished.'

'I told you that a long time ago.'

He had, but Paul had not taken it in. 'What are you going to do?' he inquired.

'Oh, I don't know,' said James, comfortably, lighting a cigarette. 'I'll get along.'

'Yes, but . . .' Paul was very irritated. This laxness was like his father. 'You've got to do something,' he insisted.

'Well, what do you suggest?' asked James, humorously, with the intention of loosening the lad up. But Paul gripped his hands together and shouted: 'Why should I suggest anything? Why does everyone expect me to suggest things?'

'Hey, take it easy,' soothed James. 'Sorry,' said Paul. He relaxed and said: 'Give me a cigarette.' He lit it clumsily and asked: 'Yes, but if there's no reef, there's no profit, so how are you going to live?'

'Oh, I'll get a job, or find another reef or something,' said James, quite untroubled.

Paul could not help laughing. 'Do you mean to say you've known the reef was finished and you've been sitting here without a care in the world.'

'I didn't say it was finished. It's just dwindling away. I'm not losing money and I'm not making any. But I'll pull out in a week or so, I've been thinking,' said James, puffing clouds of lazy smoke.

'Going prospecting?' asked the boy, persistently.

'Why not?'

'Can I come with you?'

'What do you mean by prospecting?' temporized James. 'If you think I'm going to wander around with a pan and a hammer, romantic-like, you're wrong. I like my comfort. I'll take my time and see what I can find.'

Paul laughed again at James' idea of comfort. He glanced into the two little rooms behind the verandah, hardly furnished at all, with the kitchen behind where the slovenly and good-natured native woman cooked meat and potatoes, potatoes and boiled fowl, with an occasional plate of raw tomatoes as relish.

James said: 'I met an old pal of mine at the station last week. He found a reef half a mile from here last month. He's starting up when he can get the machinery from town. The country's lousy with gold, don't worry.'

And with this slapdash promise of a future Paul was content. But before they started prospecting James deliberately arranged a drinking session. 'About time I had a holiday,' he said, quite seriously. James went through four bottles of whisky in two days. He drank, slowly and persistently, until he became maudlin and sentimental, a phase which embarrassed the boy. Then he became hectoring and noisy, and complained about his wife, the mine owners of the Rand, and his parents, who had taken him from school at fifteen to make his way as he could. Then, having worked that out of his system, nicely judging his own condition, he took a final half-glass of neat whisky, lay comfortably down on the bed and passed out. Paul sat beside his friend and waited for him to wake, which he did, in five or six hours, quite sober and very depressed. Then the process was repeated.

Maggie was angry when Paul came home after three days' absence, saying that James had had malaria and needed a nurse. At the same time she was pleased that her son could sit up three nights with a sick man and then come walking quietly home across the veld, without any fuss or claim for attention, to demand a meal and eat it and then take himself off to bed; all very calm and sensible, like a grown person.

She wanted to ask him if he intended to run the farm, but

did not dare. She could not blame him for feeling as he did, but she could not approve his running away either. In the end it was Alec who said to Maggie, in his son's presence: 'Your precious Paul. He runs off the farm and leaves it standing while he drinks himself under the table.' He had heard that James was in a drinking bout from one of the natives.

'Paul doesn't drink,' said Maggie finally, telling Alec with her eyes that she was not going to sit there and hear him run down his son. Alec looked away. But he said derisively to Paul: 'Been beaten by the farm already? You can't stick it more than one season?'

Paul replied, calmly: 'As you like.'

'What are you going to do now?' asked Maggie, and Paul said: 'You'll know in good time.' To his father he could not resist saying: 'You'll know soon enough for your peace of mind!'

When he had gone, Maggie sat thinking for a long time: if he was with James it meant he was going mining; he was as bad as his father, in fact. Worse, he was challenging his father. With the tired thought that she hoped at least Alec would not understand his son was challenging him, she walked down to the fields to tell her husband that he should spend a little of his time keeping the farm going. She found him at work beside his new shaft, and sat quietly on a big stone while he explained some new idea to her. She said nothing about the farm.

As for Paul, he said to James: 'Let's start prospecting.' James said: 'There's no hurry.' 'Yes, there is, there is,' insisted the boy, and with a shrug James went to find his hammer.

Together they spent some days working over the nearer parts of the bush. At this stage they did not go near the Barnes' farm, but kept on the neighbouring farm. This neighbour was friendly because he hoped that a really big reef would be found and then he could sell his land for what he chose to ask for it. Sometimes he sent a native to tell them that there was a likely reef in such and such a place, and the man and the boy went over to test it. Nothing came of these suggestions. Mostly Paul slept in James' house. Once or twice, for the sake of peace, he went home, looking defiant. But Maggie greeted him pleasantly. She had gone beyond caring. She was listless and ironic. All she feared was that Alec would find out that Paul was prospecting. Once she said, trying to joke: 'What'd you do if Paul found gold?' Alec responded, magnificently: 'Any fool can find gold. It takes intelligence to use the divining rod properly.' Maggie smiled and shrugged. Then she found another worry: that if Paul knew that his father did not think enough of him to care, he might give up the search; and she felt it better for him to be absorbed in prospecting than in running away down South, or simply drinking his time away. She thought sadly that Paul had made for himself an image of a cruel and heartless father, whereas he was more like a shadow. To fight Alec was shadow-boxing, and she remembered what she had felt over the wedding rings. He had lost her ring, she felt as if the bottom had dropped out of their marriage, and all he said was: 'Send to town for another one, what's in a ring, after all?' And what *was* in a ring? He was right. With Alec, any emotion always ended in a shrug of the shoulders.

And then, for a time, there was excitement. Alec found a reef that carried gold; not much, but almost as much as the mine on the ridge. And of course he wanted to work it. Maggie would not agree. She said it was too risky; and anyway, where would they find the capital? Alec said, calmly, that money could be borrowed. Maggie said it would be hanging a millstone around their necks ... and so on. At last experts came from town and gave a verdict: it was under the workable minimum. The experts went back again, but oddly enough, Alec seemed encouraged rather than depressed. 'There you are,' he said, 'I always said there was gold, didn't I?' Maggie soothed him, and he went off to try another reef.

Paul, who had not been home for a couple of weeks, got wind of this discovery and came striding over with a fevered look to demand: 'Is it true that father's found gold?'

'No,' said Maggie. And then, with sad irony: 'Wouldn't you be pleased for his sake if he did?' At that look he coloured, but he could not bring himself to say he would be pleased. Suddenly Maggie asked: 'Are you drinking, Paul?' He did not look well, but that was due to the intensity of his search for gold, not to drink. James would not let him drink: 'You can do what you like when you're twenty-one,' he said, just like a father. 'But you're not drinking when you're with me till then.'

Paul did not want to tell his mother that he allowed James to order him about, and he said: 'You've got such a prejudice against drink.'

'Plenty of people'd be pleased if they'd been brought up with *that* prejudice,' she said, dryly. 'Look how many ruin themselves in this country with drink.'

He said, obstinately: 'James is all right, isn't he? There's nothing wrong with him – and he drinks off and on.'

'Can't you be "all right" without drinking off and on?' inquired Maggie, with that listless irony that upset Paul because it was not like her. He kissed her and said: 'Don't worry about me, I'm doing fine.' And back he went to James.

For now he and James spent every spare moment prospecting. It was quite different from Alec's attitude. James seemed to assume that since this was gold country, gold could be found; it was merely a question of persistence. Quite calmly, he closed down his mine, and dismissed his labour force, and set himself to find another. It had a convincing ring to Paul; it was not nearly as thrilling as with Alec, who was always on the verge of a discovery that must shake the world, no less; but it was more sensible. Perhaps, too, Paul was convinced because it was necessary; and what is necessary has its own logic.

When they had covered the neighbour's farm they hesitated before crossing the boundary on to Alec's. But one evening they straddled over the barbed fence, while Paul lagged behind, feeling unaccountably guilty. James wanted to go to the quartz reef. He glanced inquiringly back at the boy, who slowly followed him, persuading himself there was no need to feel guilty. Prospecting was legal, and he had a right to it. They slowly made their way to the reef. The trenches had been roughly filled in, and the places where the stone had been hammered and blasted were already weathering over. They worked on the reef for several days, and sometimes James said, humorously: 'When your father does a thing he does it thoroughly. . . .' For there was hardly a piece of that mile-long reef which had not been examined. Soon they left it, and worked their way along the ridge. The ground was broken by jutting reefs, outcrops, boulders, but here, it seemed, Alec had not been.

'Well, sonnie,' said James, 'this looks likely, hey?'

There was no reason why it should be any more likely than any other place, but Paul was trusting to the old miner's instinct. He liked to watch him move slowly over the ground, pondering over a slant of rock, a sudden scattering of sparkling white pebbles. It seemed like a kind of magic, as ways of thinking do that have not yet been given names and classified. Yet it was based on years of experience of rock and minerals and soil; although James did not consciously know why he paused beside this outcrop and not the next; and to Paul it appeared an arbitrary process.

One morning they met Alec. At first Paul hung back; then he defiantly strode forward. Alec's face was hostile and he demanded: 'What are you two doing here?'

'It's legal to prospect, Mr. Barnes,' said James.

Alex frowned and said: 'You didn't have the common decency to ask.' He was looking at Paul and not at James. Then, when Paul could not find words, he seemed to lose interest and began moving away. They were astounded to hear him remark: 'You're quite right to try here, though. It always did seem a likely spot. Might have another shot here myself one day.' Then he walked slowly off.

Paul felt bad; he had been imagining his father as an antagonist. So strong was his reaction that he almost lost interest in the thing; he might even have gone back to the farm if James had not been there to keep him to it. For James was not the sort of man to give up a job once he had started.

Now he glanced at Paul and said: 'Don't you worry, son. Your Dad's a decent chap, when all's said. He was right, we should have asked, just out of politeness.'

'It's all very well,' said Paul, hugging his old resentment. 'He sounds all right now, but you should have heard the things he said.'

'Well, well, we all lose our tempers,' said James, tolerantly.

Several days later James remarked: 'This bit of rock

looks quite good, let's pan it.' They panned it, and it showed good gold. 'Doesn't prove anything,' said James. 'We'd better dig a trench or two.' A trench or two were dug, and James said, casually: 'Looks as if this might be it.' It did not immediately come home to Paul that this was James' way of announcing success. It was too unheroic. He even found himself thinking: If this is all it is, what's the point of it? *To find gold* – what a phrase it is! Impossible to hear it without a quickening of the pulse. And so through the rest: I might find gold, you could find gold; they, most certainly, always seem to find gold. But not only was it possible to drop the words, as if they were the most ordinary in the world, it did not occur to James that Paul might be disappointed. 'Yes, this is it,' he confirmed himself, some days later, and added immediately: 'Let's get some food, no point in being uncomfortable for nothing.'

So flat was the scene, just a few untidy diggings in the low greenish scrub, with the low, smoky September sky pressing down, that Paul was making the thing verbally dramatic in his mind, thus: 'We have found gold. James and I have found gold. And won't my father be cross!' But it was no use at all; and he obediently followed James back to the little shack for cold meat and potatoes. It all went on for weeks, while James surveyed the whole area, digging cross-trenches, sinking a small shaft. Then he sent some rocks in to the Assay people and their assessment was confirmed. Surely this should be a moment for rejoicing, but all James said was: 'We won't get rich on this lot, but it could be worse.' It seemed as if he might even shrug the whole thing off and start again somewhere else.

Once again the experts came out, standing over the diggings making their cautious pronouncements; city men, dressed in the crisp khaki they donned for excursions into the veld. 'Yes, it was workable. Yes, it might even turn out quite prosperous, with luck.' Paul felt cheated of glory, and there was no one who would understand this feeling. Not even Maggie; he tried to catch her eye and smile ruefully, but her eye would not be caught. For she was there on her son's invitation. She walked over to see Paul's triumph without telling Alec. And all the time she watched the experts, watched Paul and James, she was thinking of Alec, who would have to be told. After all these years of work with his divining rods and his theories; after all that patient study of the marsh light, gold, it seemed too cruel that his son should casually walk over the ridge he had himself prospected so thoroughly and find a reef within a matter of weeks. It was so cruel that she could not bring herself to tell him. Why did it have to be there, on that same ridge? Why not anywhere else in the thousands of acres of veld? And she felt even more sad for Alec because she knew quite well that the reef's being there, on that ridge, was part of Paul's triumph. She was afraid that Alec would see that gleam of victory in his son's eyes.

In the meantime the important piece of ground lay waiting, guarded by the prescribed pegging notices that were like sign-boards on which were tacked the printed linen notices listing fines and penalties against any person – even Alec himself – who came near to the still invisible gold without permission. Then out came the businessmen and the lawyers, and there was a long period of signing documents and drinking toasts to everyone concerned.

Paul came over to supper one evening, and Maggie sat in suspense, waiting for him to tell his father, waiting for the cruel blow to fall. The boy was restless, and several times opened his mouth to speak, fell silent, and in the end said nothing. When Alec had gone to his office to work out some calculations for a new reef, Maggie said: 'Well, I suppose you're very pleased with yourself.'

Paul grinned and said: 'Shouldn't I be?'

'Your poor father – can't you see how he's going to feel about it?'

All she could get out of him was: 'All right, you tell him then. I won't say anything.'

'I'm glad you've got some feeling for him.'

So Paul left and she was faced with the task of telling Alec. She marvelled that he did not know it already. All he had to do was lift his eyes and look close at the ridge. There, among the bare, thinned trees of the September veld, were the trenches, like new scars, and a small black activity of workers.

Then one day Paul came again and said – and now he sounded apologetic: 'You'll have to tell him, you know.

We're moving the heavy machinery tomorrow. He'll see for himself.'

'I really will tell him,' she promised.

'I don't want him to feel bad, really I don't, mother.' He sounded as insistent as a child who needs to be forgiven.

'You didn't think of it before,' she said, dryly.

He protested: 'But surely, mother – you've never said you were glad, not once. Don't you understand? This might turn out to be a really big thing; the experts said it might, I might be a partner of a really big mine quite soon.'

'And you're not eighteen yet,' she said, smiling to soften the words. She was thinking that it was a sad falling-off from what she had hoped. What was he? A small-worker. Half-educated, without ambition, dependent on that terrible thing, luck. He might be a small-worker all his life, with James for companion, drinking at weekends, the native woman in the kitchen – oh, yes, she knew what went on, although he seemed to think she was a fool. And if they were lucky, he would become a rich man, one of the big financiers of the sub-continent. It was possible, anything was possible – she smiled tolerantly and said nothing.

That night she lay awake, trying to arouse in herself the courage to tell Alec. She could not. At breakfast she watched his absorbed, remote face, and tried to find the words. They would not come. After the meal he went into his office, and she went quickly outside. Shading her eyes she looked across the mealie-fields to the ridge. Yes, there went the heavy waggons, laden with the black bulk of the headgear, great pipes, pulleys: Alec had only to look out of his window to see. She slowly went inside and said: 'Alec, I want to tell you something.' He did not lift his eyes. 'What is it?' he asked, impatiently.

'Come with me for a minute.' He looked at her, frowned, then shrugged and went after her. She pointed at the red dust track that showed in the scrub and said: 'Look.' Her voice sounded like a little girl's.

He glanced at the laden waggons, then slowly moved his eyes along the ridge to where the diggings showed.

'What is it?' he asked. She tried to speak and found that her lips were trembling. Inside she was crying: Poor thing;

poor, poor thing! 'What is it?' he demanded again. Then, after a pause: 'Have they found something?'

'Yes,' she brought out at last.

'Any good?'

'They say it might be very good.' She dared to give him a sideways glance. His face was thoughtful, no more, and she was encouraged to say: 'James and Paul are partners.'

'And on that ridge,' he exclaimed at last. There was no resentment in his voice. She glanced at him again. 'It seems hard, doesn't it?' he said, slowly; and at once she clutched his arm and said: 'Yes, my dear, it is, it is, I'm so very sorry. . . .' And here she began to cry. She wanted to take him in her arms and comfort him. But he was still gazing over at the ridge. 'I never tried just that place,' he said, thoughtfully. She stopped crying. 'Funny, I was going to sink a trench just there, and then – I forget why I didn't.'

'Yes?' she said, in a little voice. She was understanding that it was all right. Then he remarked: 'I always said there was gold on that ridge, and there is. I always said it, didn't I?'

'Yes, my dear, you did – where are you going?' she added, for he was walking away, the divining rod swinging from his hand.

'I'll just drop over and do a bit of work around their trenches, she heard as he went. 'If they know how the reefs lie, then I can test. . . .'

He vanished into the bush, walking fast, the tails of his bush shirt flying.

When Paul saw him coming he went forward to meet him, smiling a rather sickly smile, his heart beating with guilt, and all Alec said was: 'Your mother told me you'd struck it lucky. Mind if I use my rod around here for a bit?' And then, as Paul remained motionless from surprise, he said, impatiently: 'Come on, there's a good kid, I'm in a hurry.'

And as the labourers unloaded the heavy machinery and James and Paul directed the work, Alec walked in circles and in zigzags, the rod rising and falling in his hands like a variety of trapped insect, his face rapt with thought. He was oblivious to everything. They had to pull him aside to avoid being crushed by the machinery. When, at midday, they asked him to share their cold meat, and broke it to him that they had found a second reef, even richer than the first, with every prospect of 'going as deep as China,' all he said was, and in a proud, pleased voice: 'Well, that proves it. I told you, didn't I? I always told you so.'

# The Antheap

# The Antheap

BEYOND the plain rose the mountains, blue and hazy in a strong blue sky. Coming closer they were brown and grey and green, ranged heavily one beside the other. But the sky was still blue. Climbing up through the pass the plain flattened and diminished behind, and the peaks rose sharp and dark grey from lower heights of heaped granite boulder, and the sky overhead was deeply blue and clear and the heat came shimmering off in waves from every surface. 'Through the range, down the pass, and into the plain the other side – let's go quickly, there it will be cooler, the walking easier.' So thinks the traveller. So the traveller has been thinking for many centuries, walking quickly to leave the stifling mountains, to gain the cool plain where the wind moves freely. But there is no plain. Instead, the pass opens into a hollow which is closely surrounded by kopjes: the mountains clench themselves into a fist here, and the palm is a mile-wide reach of thick bush, where the heat gathers and clings, radiating from boulders, rocking off the trees, pouring down from a sky which is not blue, but thick and yellow, because of the smoke that rises, and has been rising so long from this mountain-imprisoned hollow. For though it is hot and close and arid half the year, and then warm and steamy and wet in the rains, there is gold here, so there are always people, and everywhere in the bush are pits and slits where the prospectors have been, or shallow holes, or even deep shafts. They say that the Bushmen were here, seeking gold, hundreds of years ago. Perhaps it is possible. They say that trains of Arabs came from the coast, with slaves and warriors, looking for gold to enrich the courts of the Queen of Sheba. No one has proved they did not.

But it is at least certain that at the turn of the century there was a big mining company which sunk half a dozen fabulously deep shafts, and found gold going ounces to the ton sometimes, but it is a capricious and chancy piece of ground, with the reefs all broken and unpredictable, and so this company loaded its heavy equipment into lorries and off they went to look for gold somewhere else, and in a place where the reefs lay more evenly.

For a few years the hollow in the mountains was left silent, no smoke rose to dim the sky, except perhaps for an occasional prospector, whose fire was a single column of wavering blue smoke, as from the cigarette of a giant, rising into the blue, hot sky.

Then all at once the hollow was filled with violence and noise and activity and hundreds of people. Mr. Macintosh had bought the rights to mine this gold. They told him he was foolish, that no single man, no matter how rich, could afford to take chances in this place.

But they did not reckon with the character of Mr. Macintosh, who had already made a fortune and lost it, in Australia, and then made another in New Zealand, which he still had. He proposed to increase it here. Of course, he had no intention of sinking those expensive shafts which might or might not reach gold and hold the dipping, chancy reefs and seams. The right course was quite clear to Mr. Macintosh, and this course he followed, though it was against every known rule of proper mining.

He simply hired hundreds of African labourers and set them to shovel up the soil in the centre of that high, enclosed hollow in the mountains, so that there was soon a deeper hollow, then a vast pit, then a gulf like an inverted mountain. Mr. Macintosh was taking great swallows of the earth, like a gold-eating monster, with no fancy ideas about digging shafts or spending money on roofing tunnels. The earth was hauled, at first, up the shelving sides of the gulf in buckets, and these were suspended by ropes made of twisted bark fibre, for why spend money on steel ropes when this fibre was offered free to mankind on every tree? And if it got brittle and broke and the buckets went plunging into the pit, then they were not harmed by the fall, and there was plenty of fibre left on the trees. Later, when the gulf grew too deep, there were trucks on rails, and it was not unknown for these, too, to go sliding and plunging to the bottom, because in all Mr. Macintosh's dealings there was a fine, easy good-humour, which meant he was more likely to laugh at such an accident than grow angry. And if someone's head got in the way of falling buckets or trucks, then there were plenty of black heads and hands for the hiring. And if the loose, sloping bluffs of soil fell in landslides, or if a tunnel, narrow as an ant-bear's hole, that was run off sideways from the main pit like a tentacle exploring for new reefs, caved in suddenly, swallowing half a dozen men – well, one can't make an omelette without breaking eggs. This was Mr. Macintosh's favourite motto.

The natives who worked this mine called it 'The pit of death', and they called Mr. Macintosh 'The Gold Stomach'. Nevertheless, they came in their hundreds to work for him, thus providing free arguments for those who said: 'The native doesn't understand good treatment, he only appreciates the whip, look at Macintosh, he's never short of labour.'

Mr. Macintosh's mine, raised high in the mountains, was far from the nearest police station, and he took care that there was always plenty of kaffir beer brewed in the compound, and if the police patrols came searching for criminals, these could count on Mr. Macintosh facing the police for them and assuring them that such and such a native, Registration Number Y2345678 had never worked for him. Yes, of course they could see his books.

Mr. Macintosh's books and records might appear to the simple-minded as casual and ineffective, but these were not the words used of his methods by those who worked for him, and so Mr. Macintosh kept his books himself. He employed no book-keeper, no clerk. In fact, he employed only one white man, an engineer. For the rest, he had six overseers or boss-boys whom he paid good salaries and treated like important people.

The engineer was Mr. Clarke, and his house and Mr. Macintosh's house were on one side of the big pit, and the compound for the natives was on the other side. Mr. Clarke earned fifty pounds a month, which was more than he would earn anywhere else. He was a silent, hardworking man, except when he got drunk, which was not often. Three or four times in the year he would be off work for a week, and then Mr. Macintosh did his work for him till he recovered, when he greeted him with the good-humoured words: 'Well, laddie, got that off your chest?'

Mr. Macintosh did not drink at all. His not drinking was a passionate business, for like many Scots people he ran to extremes. Never a drop of liquor could be found in his house. Also, he was religious, in a reminiscent sort of way, because of his parents, who had been very religious. He lived in a two-roomed shack, with a bare wooden table in it, three wooden chairs, a bed and a wardrobe. The cook boiled beef and carrots and potatoes three days a week, roasted beef three days, and cooked a chicken on Sundays.

Mr. Macintosh was one of the richest men in the country, he was more than a millionaire. People used to say of him: But for heaven's sake, he could do anything, go anywhere, what's the point of having so much money if you live in the back of beyond with a parcel of blacks on top of a big hole in the ground?

But to Mr. Macintosh it seemed quite natural to live so, and when he went for a holiday to Cape Town, where he lived in the most expensive hotel, he always came back again long before he was expected. He did not like holidays. He liked working.

He wore old, oily khaki trousers, tied at the waist with an old red tie, and he wore a red handkerchief loose around his neck over a white cotton singlet. He was short and broad and strong, with a big square head tilted back on a thick neck. His heavy brown arms and neck sprouted thick black hair around the edges of the singlet. His eyes were small and grey and shrewd. His mouth was thin, pressed tight in the middle. He wore an old felt hat on the back of his head, and carried a stick cut from the bush, and he went strolling around the edge of the pit, slashing the stick at bushes and grass or sometimes at lazy natives, and he shouted orders to his boss-boys far below him in the bottom of the pit, and then he would go to his little office and make up his books, and so he spent his day. In the evenings he sometimes asked Mr. Clarke to come over and play cards.

Then Mr. Clarke would say to his wife: 'Annie, he wants me,' and she nodded and told her cook to make supper early.

Mrs. Clarke was the only white woman on the mine. She did not mind this, being a naturally solitary person. Also, she had been profoundly grateful to reach this haven of fifty pounds a month with a man who did not mind her husband's bouts of drinking. She was a woman of early middle age, with a thin, flat body, a thin, colourless face, and quiet blue eyes. Living here, in this destroying heat, year after year, did not make her ill, it sapped her slowly, leaving her rather numbed and silent. She spoke very little, but then she roused herself and said what was necessary.

For instance, when they first arrived at the mine it was to a two-roomed house. She walked over to Mr. Macintosh and said: 'You are alone, but you have four rooms. There are two of us and the baby, and we have two rooms. There's no sense in it.' Mr. Macintosh gave her a quick, hard look, his mouth tightened, and then he began to laugh. 'Well, yes, that is so,' he said laughing, and he made the change at once, chuckling every time he remembered how the quiet Annie Clarke had put him in his place.

Similarly, about once a month Annie Clarke went to his house and said: 'Now get out of my way, I'll get things straight for you.' And when she'd finished tidying up she said: 'You're nothing but a pig, and that's the truth.' She was referring to his habit of throwing his clothes everywhere, or wearing them for weeks unwashed, and also to other matters which no one else dared to refer to, even as indirectly as this. To this he might reply, chuckling with the pleasure of teasing her: 'You're a married woman, Mrs. Clarke,' and she said: 'Nothing stops you getting married that I can see.' And she walked away very straight, her cheeks burning with indignation.

She was very fond of him, and he of her. And Mr. Clarke liked and admired him, and he liked Mr. Clarke. And since Mr. Clarke and Mrs. Clarke lived amiably together in their four-roomed house, sharing bed and board without ever quarrelling, it was to be presumed they liked each other too. But they seldom spoke. What was there to say?

It was to this silence, to these understood truths, that little Tommy had to grow up and adjust himself.

Tommy Clarke was three months when he came to the mine, and day and night his ears were filled with noise, every day and every night for years, so that he did not think of it as noise, rather, it was a different sort of silence. The mine-stamps thudded *gold*, gold, *gold*, gold, *gold*, gold, on and on, never changing, never stopping. So he did not hear them. But there came a day when the machinery broke, and it was when Tommy was three years old, and the silence was so terrible and so empty that he went screeching to his mother: 'It's stopped, it's stopped,' and he wept, shivering, in a corner until the thudding began again. It was as if the heart of the world had gone silent. But when it started to beat, Tommy heard it, and he knew the difference between silence and sound, and his ears acquired a new sensitivity, like a conscience. He heard the shouting and the singing from the swarms of working natives, reckless, noisy people because of the danger they always must live with. He heard the picks ringing on stone, the softer, deeper thud of picks on thick earth. He heard the clang of the trucks, and the roar of falling earth, and the rumbling of trolleys on rails. And at night the owls hooted and the night-jars screamed, and the crickets chirped. And when it stormed it seemed the sky itself was flinging down bolts of noise against the mountains, for the thunder rolled and crashed, and the lightning darted from peak to peak around him. It was never silent, never, save for that awful moment when the big heart stopped beating. Yet later he longed for it to stop again, just for an hour, so that he might hear a true silence. That was when he was a little older, and the quietness of his parents was beginning to trouble him. There they were, always so gentle, saying so little, only: That's how things are; or: You ask so many questions; or: You'll understand when you grow up.

It was a false silence, much worse than that real silence had been.

He would play beside his mother in the kitchen, who never said anything but Yes, and No, and – with a patient, sighing voice, as if even his voice tired her: You talk so much, Tommy!

And he was carried on his father's shoulders around the big, black working machines, and they couldn't speak because of the din the machines made. And Mr. Macintosh would say: Well, laddie? and give him sweets from his pocket, which he always kept there, especially for Tommy. And once he saw Mr. Macintosh and his father playing cards in the evening, and they didn't talk at all, except for the words that the game needed.

So Tommy escaped to the friendly din of the compound

across the great gulf, and played all day with the black children, dancing in their dances, running through the bush after rabbits, or working wet clay into shapes of bird or beast. No silence there, everything noisy and cheerful, and at evening he returned to his equable, silent parents, and after the meal he lay in bed listening to the *thud,* thud, *thud*, thud, *thud*, thud, of the stamps. In the compound across the gulf they were drinking and dancing, the drums made a quick beating against the slow thud of the stamps, and the dancers around the fires yelled, a high, ululating sound like a big wind coming fast and crooked through a gap in the mountains. That was a different world, to which he belonged as much as to this one, where people said: Finish your pudding; or: It's time for bed; and very little else.

When he was five years old he got malaria and was very sick. He recovered, but in the rainy season of the next year he got it again. Both times Mr. Macintosh got into his big American car and went streaking across the thirty miles of bush to the nearest hospital for a doctor. The doctor said quinine, and be careful to screen for mosquitoes. It was easy to give quinine, but Mrs. Clarke, that tired, easy-going woman, found it hard to say: Don't, and Be in by six; and Don't go near water; and so, when Tommy was seven, he got malaria again. And now Mrs. Clarke was worried, because the doctor spoke severely, mentioning blackwater.

Mr. Macintosh drove the doctor back to his hospital and then came home, and at once went to see Tommy, for he loved Tommy very deeply.

Mrs. Clarke said: 'What do you expect, with all these holes everywhere, they're full of water all the wet season.'

'Well, lassie, I can't fill in all the holes and shafts, people have been digging up here since the Queen of Sheba.'

'Never mind about the Queen of Sheba. At least you could screen our house properly.'

'I pay your husband fifty pounds a month,' said Mr. Macintosh, conscious of being in the right.

'Fifty pounds and a proper house,' said Annie Clarke.

Mr. Macintosh gave her that quick, narrow look, and then laughed loudly. A week later the house was encased in fine wire mesh all round from roof-edge to verandah-edge, so that it looked like a new meat safe, and Mrs. Clarke went over to Mr. Macintosh's house and gave it a grand cleaning, and when she left she said: 'You're nothing but a pig, you're as rich as the Oppenheimers, why don't you buy yourself some new vests at least. And you'll be getting malaria, too, the way you go traipsing about at nights.'

She returned to Tommy, who was seated on the verandah behind the grey-glistening wire-netting, in a big deck-chair. He was very thin and white after the fever. He was a long child, bony, and his eyes were big and black, and his mouth full and pouting from the petulances of the illness. He had a mass of richly-brown hair, like caramels, on his head. His mother looked at this pale child of hers, who was yet so brightly coloured and full of vitality, and her tired will-power revived enough to determine a new regime for him. He was never to be out after six at night, when the mosquitoes were abroad. He was never to be out before the sun rose.

'You can get up,' she said, and he got up, thankfully throwing aside his covers.

'I'll go over to the compound,' he said at once.

She hesitated, and then said: 'You mustn't play there any more.'

'Why not?' he asked, already fidgeting on the steps outside the wire-netting cage.

Ah, how she hated these Whys, and Why nots! They tired her utterly. 'Because I say so,' she snapped.

But he persisted: 'I always play there.'

'You're getting too big now, and you'll be going to school soon.'

Tommy sank on to the steps and remained there, looking away over the great pit to the busy, sunlit compound. He had known this moment was coming, of course. It was a knowledge that was part of the silence. And yet he had not known it. He said: 'Why, why, why, why?' singing it out in a persistent wail.

'Because I say so.' Then, in tired desperation: 'You get sick from the natives, too.'

At this, he switched his large black eyes from the scenery to his mother, and she flushed a little. For they were derisively scornful. Yet she half-believed it herself, or rather, must believe it, for all through the wet season the bush would lie waterlogged and festering with mosquitoes, and nothing could be done about it, and one has to put the blame on something.

She said: 'Don't argue. You're not to play with them. You're too big now to play with a lot of dirty kaffirs. When you were little it was different, but now you're a big boy.'

Tommy sat on the steps in the sweltering afternoon sun that came thick and yellow through the haze of dust and smoke over the mountains, and he said nothing. He made no attempt to go near the compound, now that his growing manhood depended on his not playing with the black people. So he had been made to feel. Yet he did not believe a word of it, not really.

Some days later, he was kicking a football by himself around the back of the house when a group of black children called to him from the bush, and he turned away as if he had not seen them. They called again and then ran away. And Tommy wept bitterly, for now he was alone.

He went to the edge of the big pit and lay on his stomach looking down. The sun blazed through him so that his bones ached, and he shook his mass of hair forward over his eyes to shield them. Below, the great pit was so deep that the men working on the bottom of it were like ants. The trucks that climbed up the almost vertical sides were like matchboxes. The system of ladders and steps cut in the earth, which the workers used to climb up and down, seemed so flimsy across the gulf that a stone might dislodge it. Indeed, falling stones often did. Tommy sprawled, gripping the earth tight with tense belly and flung limbs, and stared down. They were all like ants and flies. Mr. Macintosh, too, when he went down, which he did often, for no one could say he was a coward. And his father, and Tommy himself, they were all no bigger than little insects.

It was like an enormous ant-working, as brightly tinted as a fresh antheap. The levels of earth around the mouth of the pit were reddish, then lower down grey and gravelly, and lower still, clear yellow. Heaps of the inert, heavy yellow soil, brought up from the bottom, lay all around him. He stretched out his hand and took some of it. It was unresponsive, lying lifeless and dense on his fingers, a little damp from the rain. He clenched his fist, and loosened it, and now the mass of yellow earth lay shaped on his palm, showing the marks of his fingers. A shape like – what? A bit of root? A fragment of rock rotted by water? He rolled his palms vigorously around it, and it became smooth like a water-ground stone. Then he sat up and took more earth, and formed a pit, and up the sides flying ladders with bits of stick, and little kips of wetted earth for the trucks. Soon the sun dried it, and it all cracked and fell apart. Tommy gave the model a kick and went moodily back to the house. The sun was going down. It seemed that he had left a golden age of freedom behind, and now there was a new country of restrictions and time-tables.

His mother saw how he suffered, but thought: Soon he'll go to school and find companions.

But he was only just seven, and very young to go all the way to the city to boarding-school. She sent for school-books, and taught him to read. Yet this was for only two or three hours in the day, and for the rest he mooned about, as she complained, gazing away over the gulf to the compound, from where he could hear the noise of the playing children. He was stoical about it, or so it seemed, but underneath he was suffering badly from this new knowledge, which was much more vital than anything he had learned from the school-books. He knew the word loneliness, and lying at the edge of the pit he formed the yellow clay into little figures which he called Betty and Freddy and Dirk. Playmates. Dirk was the name of the boy he liked the best among the children in the compound over the gulf.

One day his mother called him to the back door. There stood Dirk, and he was holding between his hands a tiny duiker, the size of a thin cat. Tommy ran forward, and was about to exclaim with Dirk over the little animal, when he remembered his new status. He stopped, stiffened himself, and said: 'How much?'

Dirk, keeping his eyes evasive, said: 'One shilling, Baas.'

Tommy glanced at his mother and then said, proudly, his voice high: 'Damned cheek, too much.'

Annie Clarke flushed. She was ashamed and flustered. She came forward and said quickly: 'It's all right, Tommy,

I'll give you the shilling.' She took the coin from the pocket of her apron and gave it to Tommy, who handed it at once to Dirk. Tommy took the little animal gently in his hands, and his tenderness for this frightened and lonely creature rushed up to his eyes and he turned away so that Dirk couldn't see – he would have been bitterly ashamed to show softness in front of Dirk, who was so tough and fearless.

Dirk stood back, watching, unwilling to see the last of the buck. Then he said: 'It's just born, it can die.'

Mrs. Clarke said, dismissingly: 'Yes, Tommy will look after it.' Dirk walked away slowly, fingering the shilling in his pocket, but looking back at where Tommy and his mother were making a nest for the little buck in a packing-case. Mrs. Clarke made a feeding-bottle with some linen stuffed into the neck of a tomato sauce bottle and filled it with milk and water and sugar. Tommy knelt by the buck and tried to drip the milk into its mouth.

It lay tremblingly lifting its delicate head from the crumbled, huddled limbs, too weak to move, the big eyes dark and forlorn. Then the trembling became a spasm of weakness and the head collapsed with a soft thud against the side of the box, and then slowly, and with a trembling effort, the neck lifted the head again. Tommy tried to push the wad of linen into the soft mouth, and the milk wetted the fur and ran down over the buck's chest, and he wanted to cry.

'But it'll die, mother, it'll die,' he shouted, angrily.

'You mustn't force it,' said Annie Clarke, and she went away to her household duties. Tommy knelt there with the bottle, stroking the trembling little buck and suffering every time the thin neck collapsed with weakness, and tried again and again to interest it in the milk. But the buck wouldn't drink at all.

'Why?' shouted Tommy, in the anger of his misery. 'Why won't it drink? Why? why?'

'But it's only just born,' said Mrs. Clarke. The cord was still on the creature's navel, like a shrivelling, dark stick.

That night Tommy took the little buck into his room, and secretly in the dark lifted it, folded in a blanket, into his bed. He could feel it trembling fitfully against his chest, and he cried into the dark because he knew it was going to die.

In the morning when he woke, the buck could not lift its head at all, and it was a weak, collapsed weight on Tommy's chest, a chilly weight. The blanket in which it lay was messed with yellow stuff like a scrambled egg. Tommy washed the buck gently, and wrapped it again in new coverings, and laid it on the verandah where the sun could warm it.

Mrs. Clarke gently forced the jaws open and poured down milk until the buck choked. Tommy knelt beside it all morning, suffering as he had never suffered before. The tears ran steadily down his face and he wished he could die too, and Mrs. Clarke wished very much she could catch Dirk and give him a good beating, which would be unjust, but might do something to relieve her feelings. 'Besides,' she said to her husband, 'it's nothing but cruelty, taking a tiny thing like that from its mother.'

Later that afternoon the buck died, and Mr. Clarke who had not seen his son's misery over it, casually threw the tiny, stiff corpse to the cookboy and told him to go and bury it. Tommy stood on the verandah, his face tight and angry, and watched the cookboy shovel his little buck hastily under some bushes, and return whistling.

Then he went into the room where his mother and father were sitting and said: 'Why is Dirk yellow and not dark brown like the other kaffirs?'

Silence. Mr. Clarke and Annie Clarke looked at each other. Then Mr. Clarke said 'They come different colours.'

Tommy looked gracefully at his mother, who said: 'He's a half-caste.'

'What's a half-caste?'

'You'll understand when you grow up.'

Tommy looked from his father, who was filling a pipe, his eyes lowered to the work, then at his mother, whose cheekbones held that proud, bright flush.

'I understand now,' he said, defiantly.

'Then why do you ask?' said Mrs. Clarke, with anger. Why she was saying, do you infringe the rule of silence?

Tommy went out, and to the brink of the great pit. There he lay, wondering why he had said he understood when he did not. Though in a sense he did. He was remembering, though he had not noticed it before, that among the gang of children in the compound were two yellow children. Dirk was one, and Dirk's sister another. She was a tiny child, who came toddling on the fringe of the older children's games. But Dirk's mother was black, or rather, dark-brown like the others. And Dirk was not really yellow, but light copper-colour. The colour of this earth, were it a little darker. Tommy's fingers were fiddling with the damp clay. He looked at the little figures he had made, Betty and Freddy. Idly, he smashed them. Then he picked up Dirk and flung him down. But he must have flung him down too carefully, for he did not break, and so he set the figure against the stalk of a weed. He took up a lump of clay, and as his fingers experimentally pushed and kneaded it, the shape grew into the shape of a little duiker. But not a sick duiker, which had died because it had been taken from its mother. Not at all, it was a fine strong duiker, standing with one hoof raised and its head listening, ears pricked forward.

Tommy knelt on the verge of the great pit, absorbed, while the duiker grew into its proper form. He became dissatisfied – it was too small. He impatiently smashed what he had done, and taking a big heap of the yellowish, dense soil shook water on it from an old rusty railway sleeper that had collected rainwater and made the mass soft and workable. Then he began again. The duiker would be half life-size.

And so his hands worked and his mind worried along its path of questions: Why? Why? Why? And finally: If Dirk is half black, or rather half white and half dark-brown, then who is his father?

For a long time his mind hovered on the edge of the answer, but did not finally reach it. But from time to time he looked across the gulf to where Mr. Macintosh was strolling, swinging his big cudgel, and he thought: There are only two white men on this mine.

The buck was now finished, and he wetted his fingers in rusty rainwater, and smoothed down the soft clay to make it glisten like the surfaces of fur, but at once it dried and dulled, and as he knelt there he thought how the sun would crack it and it would fall to pieces, and an angry dissatisfaction filled him and he hung his head and wanted very much to cry. And just as the first tears were coming he heard a soft whistle from behind him, and turned, and there was Dirk, kneeling behind a bush and looking out through the parted leaves.

'Is the buck all right?' asked Dirk.

Tommy said: 'It's dead,' and he kicked his foot at his model duiker so that the thick clay fell apart in lumps.

Dirk said: 'Don't do that, it's nice,' and he sprang forward and tried to fit the pieces together.

'It's no good, the sun'll crack it,' said Tommy, and he began to cry, although he was so ashamed to cry in front of Dirk. 'The buck's dead,' he wept, 'it's dead.'

'I can get you another,' said Dirk, looking at Tommy rather surprised. 'I killed it's mother with a stone. It's easy.'

Dirk was seven, like Tommy. He was tall and strong, like Tommy. His eyes were dark and full, but his mouth was not full and soft, but long and narrow, clenched in the middle. His hair was very black and soft and long, falling uncut around his face, and his skin was a smooth, yellowish copper. Tommy stopped crying and looked at Dirk. He said: 'It's cruel to kill a buck's mother with a stone.' Dirk's mouth parted in surprised laughter over his big white teeth. Tommy watched him laugh, and he thought: Well, now I know who his father is.

He looked away to his home, which was two hundreds yards off, exposed to the sun's glare among low bushes of hibiscus and poinsettia. He looked at Mr. Macintosh's house, which was a few hundred yards further off. Then he looked at Dirk. He was full of anger, which he did not understand, but he did understand that he was also defiant, and this was a moment of decision. After a long time he said: 'They can see us from here,' and the decision was made.

They got up, but as Dirk rose he saw the little clay figure laid against a stem, and he picked it up. 'This is me,' he said at once. For crude as the thing was, it was unmistakably Dirk, who smiled with pleasure. 'Can I have it? he asked, and Tommy nodded, equally proud and pleased.

They went off into the bush between the two houses, and then on for perhaps half a mile. This was the deserted part of the hollow in the mountains, no one came here, all the bustle and noise was on the other side. In front of them rose a sharp peak, and low at its foot was a high anthill, draped with Christmas fern and thick with shrub.

The two boys went inside the curtains of fern and sat down. No one could see them here. Dirk carefully put the little clay figure of himself inside a hole in the roots of a tree. Then he said: 'Make the buck again.' Tommy took his knife and knelt beside a fallen tree, and tried to carve the buck from it. The wood was soft and rotten, and was easily carved, and by night there was the clumsy shape of the buck coming out of the trunk. Dirk said: 'Now we've got something.'

The next day the two boys made their way separately to the antheap and played there together, and so it was every day.

Then one evening Mrs. Clarke said to Tommy just as he was going to bed: 'I thought I told you not to play with the kaffirs?'

Tommy stood very still. Then he lifted his head and said to her, with a strong look across at his father: 'Why shouldn't I play with Mr. Macintosh's son?'

Mrs. Clarke stopped breathing for a moment, and closed her eyes. She opened them in appeal at her husband. But Mr. Clarke was filling his pipe. Tommy waited and then said good night and went to his room.

There he undressed slowly and climbed into the narrow iron bed and lay quietly listening to the thud, thud, gold, gold, thud, thud, of the mine-stamps. Over in the compound they were dancing, and the tom-toms were beating fast, like the quick beat of the buck's heart that night as it lay on his chest. They were yelling like the wind coming through gaps in a mountain and through the window he could see the high, flaring light of the fires, and the black figures of the dancing people were wild and active against it.

Mrs. Clarke came quickly in. She was crying. 'Tommy,' she said, sitting on the edge of his bed in the dark.

'Yes?' he said, cautiously.

'You mustn't say that again. Not ever.'

He said nothing. His mother's hand was urgently pressing his arm. 'Your father might lose his job,' said Mrs. Clarke, wildly. 'We'd never get this money anywhere else. Never. You must understand, Tommy.'

'I do understand,' said Tommy, stiffly, very sorry for his

mother, but hating her at the same time. 'Just don't say it, Tommy, don't ever say it.' Then she kissed him in a way that was both fond and appealing, and went out, shutting the door. To her husband she said it was time Tommy went to school, the next day she wrote to make the arrangements.

And so now Tommy made the long journey by car and train into the city four times a year, and four times a year he came back for the holidays. Mr. Macintosh always drove him to the station and gave him ten shillings pocket money, and he came to fetch him in the car with his parents, and he always said: 'Well, laddie, and how's school?' And Tommy said: 'Fine, Mr. Macintosh.' And Mr. Macintosh said: 'We'll make a college man of you yet.'

When he said this, the flush came bright and proud on Annie Clarke's cheeks, and she looked quickly at Mr. Clarke, who was smiling embarrassed. But Mr. Macintosh laid his hands on Tommy's shoulders and said: 'There's my laddie, there's my laddie,' and Tommy kept his shoulders stiff and still. Afterwards, Mrs. Clarke would say, nervously: 'He's fond of you, Tommy, he'll do right by you.' And once she said: 'It's natural, he's got no children of his own.' But Tommy scowled at her and she flushed and said: 'There's things you don't understand yet, Tommy, and you'll regret it if you throw away your chances.' Tommy turned away with an impatient movement. Yet it was not so clear at all, for it was almost as if he were a rich man's son, with all that pocket money, and the parcels of biscuits and sweets that Mr. Macintosh sent into school during the term, and being fetched in the great rich car. And underneath it all he felt as if he were dragged along by the nose. He felt as if he were part of a conspiracy of some kind that no one ever spoke about. Silence. His real feelings were growing up slow and complicated and obstinate underneath that silence.

At school it was not at all complicated, it was the other world. There Tommy did his lessons and played with his friends and did not think of Dirk. Or rather, his thoughts of him were proper for that world. A half-cast, ignorant, living in the kaffir location – he felt ashamed that he played with Dirk in the holidays, and he told no one. Even on the train coming home he would think like that of Dirk, but the nearer he reached home the more his thoughts wavered and darkened. On the first evening at home he would speak of the school, and how he was first in the class, and he played with this boy or that, or went to such fine houses in the city as a guest. The very first morning he would be standing on the verandah looking at the big pit and at the compound away beyond it, and his mother watched him, smiling in nervous supplication. And then he walked down the steps, away from the pit, and into the bush to the antheap. There Dirk was waiting for him. So it was every holiday. Neither of the boys spoke, at first, of what divided them. But, on the eve of Tommy's return to school after he had been there a year, Dirk said: 'You're getting educated, but I've nothing to learn.' Tommy said: 'I'll bring back books and teach you.' He said this in a quick voice, as if ashamed, and Dirk's eyes were accusing and angry. He gave his sarcastic laugh and said: 'That's what you say, white boy.'

It was not pleasant, but what Tommy said was not pleasant either, like a favour wrung out of a condescending person.

The two boys were sitting on the antheap under the fine lacy curtains of Christmas fern, looking at the rocky peak soaring into the smoky yellowish sky. There was the most unpleasant sort of annoyance in Tommy, and he felt ashamed of it. And on Dirk's face there was an aggressive but ashamed look. They continued to sit there, a little apart, full of dislike for each other, and knowing that the dislike came from the pressue of the outside world. 'I said I'd teach you, didn't I?' said Tommy, grandly, shying a stone at a bush so that leaves flew off in all directions. 'You white bastard,' said Dirk, in a low voice, and he let out that sudden ugly laugh, showing his white teeth. 'What did you say?' said Tommy, going pale and jumping to his feet. 'You heard,' said Dirk, still laughing. He too got up. Then Tommy flung himself on Dirk and they overbalanced and rolled off into the bushes, kicking and scratching. They rolled apart and began fighting properly, with fists. Tommy was better-fed and more healthy. Dirk was tougher. They were a match, and they stopped when they were too tired and battered to go on. They staggered over to the antheap and sat there side by side, panting, wiping the blood off their faces. At last they lay on their backs on the rough slant of the anthill and looked up at the sky. Every trace of dislike had vanished, and they felt easy and quiet. When the sun went down they walked together through the bush to a point where they could not be seen from the houses, and there they said, as always: 'See you tomorrow.'

When Mr. Macintosh gave him the usual ten shillings, he put them into his pocket thinking he would buy a football, but he did not. The ten shillings stayed unspent until it was nearly the end of the term, and then he went to the shops and bought a reader and some exercise books and pencils, and an arithmetic. He hid these at the bottom of his trunk and whipped them out before his mother could see them.

He took them to the antheap next morning, but before he could reach it he saw there was a little shed built on it, and the Christmas fern had been draped like a veil across the roof of the shed. The bushes had been cut on the top of the anthill, but left on the sides, so that the shed looked as if it rose from the tops of the bushes. The shed was of unbarked poles pushed into the earth, the roof was of thatch, and the upper half of the front was left open. Inside there was a bench of poles and a table of planks on poles. There sat Dirk, waiting hungrily, and Tommy went and sat beside him, putting the books and pencils on the table.

'This shed is fine,' said Tommy, but Dirk was already looking at the books. So he began to teach Dirk how to read. And for all that holiday they were together in the shed while Dirk pored over the books. He found them more difficult than Tommy did, because they were full of words for things Dirk did not know, like curtains or carpet, and teaching Dirk to read the word carpet meant telling him all about carpets and the furnishings of a house. Often Tommy felt bored and restless and said: 'Let's play,' but Dirk said fiercely: 'No, I want to read.' Tommy grew fretful, for after all he had been working in the term and now he felt entitled to play. So there was another fight. Dirk said Tommy was a lazy white bastard, and Tommy said Dirk was a dirty half-caste. They fought as before, evenly matched and to no conclusion, and afterwards felt fine and friendly, and even made jokes about the fighting. It was arranged that they should work in the mornings only and leave the afternoons for play. When Tommy went back home that evening his mother saw the scratches on his face and the swollen nose, and said hopefully: 'Have you and Dirk been fighting?' But Tommy said no, he had hit his face on a tree.

His parents, of course, knew about the shed in the bush, but did not speak of it to Mr. Macintosh. No one did. For Dirk's very existence was something to be ignored by everyone, and none of the workers, not even the overseers, would dare to mention Dirk's name. When Mr. Macintosh asked Tommy what he had done to his face, he said he had slipped and fallen.

And so their eighth year and their ninth went past. Dirk could read and write and do all the sums that Tommy could do. He was always handicapped by not knowing the different way of living, and soon he said, angrily, it wasn't fair, and there was another fight about it, and then Tommy began another way of teaching. He would tell how it was to go to a cinema in the city, every detail of it, how the seats were arranged in such a way, and one paid so much, and the lights were like this, and the picture on the screen worked like that. Or he would describe how at school they ate such things for breakfast and other things for lunch. Or tell how the man had come with picture slides talking about China. The two boys got out an atlas and found China, and Tommy told Dirk every word of what the lecturer had said. Or it might be Italy or some other country. And they would argue that the lecturer should have said this or that, for Dirk was always hotly scornful of the white man's way of looking at things, so arrogant, he said. Soon Tommy saw things through Dirk; he saw the other life in town clear and brightly-coloured and a little distorted, as Dirk did.

Soon, at school, Tommy would involuntarily think: I must remember this to tell Dirk. It was impossible for him to do anything, say anything, without being very conscious of just how it happened, as if Dirk's black, sarcastic eye had got inside him, Tommy, and never closed. And a feeling of unwillingness grew in Tommy, because of the strain of fitting these two worlds together. He found himself swearing at niggers or kaffirs like the other boys, and more violently than they did, but immediately afterwards he would find himself thinking: I must remember this so as to tell Dirk. Because of all this thinking, and seeing everything clear all the time, he was very bright at school, and found the work easy. He was two classes ahead of his age.

That was the tenth year, and one day Tommy went to the shed in the bush and Dirk was not waiting for him. It was the first day of the holidays. All the term he had been remembering things to tell Dirk, and now Dirk was not there. A dove was sitting on the Christmas fern, cooing lazily in the hot morning, a sleepy, lonely sound. When Tommy came pushing through the bushes it flew away. The mine-stamps thudded heavily, gold, gold, and Tommy saw that the shed was empty even of books, for the case where they were usually kept was hanging open.

He went running to his mother: 'Where's Dirk?' he asked.

'How should I know?' said Annie Clarke, cautiously. She really did not know.

'You do know, you do!' he cried, angrily. And then he went racing off to the big pit. Mr. Macintosh was sitting on an upturned truck at the edge, watching the hundreds of workers below him, moving like ants on the yellow bottom. 'Well, laddie?' he asked, amiably, and moved over for Tommy to sit by him.

'Where's Dirk?' asked Tommy, accusingly, standing in front of him.

Mr. Macintosh topped his old felt hat even further back and scratched at his front hair and looked at Tommy.

'Dirk's working,' he said, at last.

'Where?'

Mr. Macintosh pointed at the bottom of the pit. Then he said again: 'Sit down, laddie, I want to talk to you.'

'I don't want to,' said Tommy, and he turned away and went blundering over the veld to the shed. He sat on the bench and cried, and when dinner-time came he did not go home. All that day he sat in the shed, and when he had finished crying he remained on the bench, leaning his back against the poles of the shed, and stared into the bush. The doves cooed and cooed, kru-kruuuu, kru-kruuuuu, and a woodpecker tapped, and the mine-stamps thudded. Yet it was very quiet, a hand of silence gripped the bush, and he could hear the borers and the ants at work in the poles of the bench he sat on. He could see that although the anthill seemed dead, a mound of hard, peaked, baked earth, it was very much alive, for there was a fresh outbreak of wet, damp earth in the floor of the shed. There was a fine crust of reddish, lacey earth over the poles of the walls. The shed would have to be built again soon, because the ants and borers would have eaten it through. But what was the use of a shed without Dirk?

All that day he stayed there, and did not return until dark, and when his mother said: 'What's the matter with you, why are you crying?' he said angrily, 'I don't know,' matching her dishonesty with his own. The next day, even before breakfast, he was off to the shed, and did not return until dark, and refused his supper although he had not eaten all day.

And the next day it was the same, but now he was bored and lonely. He took his knife from his pocket and whittled at a stick, and it became a boy, bent and straining under the weight of a heavy load, his arms clenched up to support it. He took the figure home at supper-time and ate with it on the table in front of him.

'What's that?' asked Annie Clarke, and Tommy answered: 'Dirk.'

He took it to his bedroom, and sat in the soft lamplight, working away with his knife, and he had it in his hand the following morning when he met Mr. Macintosh at the brink of the pit. 'What's that, laddie?' asked Mr. Macintosh, and Tommy said: 'Dirk.'

Mr. Macintosh's mouth went thin, and then he smiled and said: 'Let me have it.'

'No, it's for Dirk.'

Mr. Macintosh took out his wallet and said: 'I'll pay you for it.'

'I don't want any money,' said Tommy, angrily, and Mr. Macintosh, greatly disturbed, put back his wallet. Then Tommy, hesitating, said: 'Yes, I do.' Mr. Macintosh, his values confirmed, was relieved, and he took out his wallet again and produced a pound note, which seemed to him very generous. 'Five pounds,' said Tommy, promptly. Mr. Macintosh first scowled, then laughed. He tipped back his head and roared with laughter. 'Well, laddie, you'll make a business man yet. Five pounds for a little bit of wood!'

'Make it for yourself then, if it's just a bit of wood.'

Mr. Macintosh counted out five pounds and handed them over. 'What are you going to do with that money?' he asked, as he watched Tommy buttoning them carefully into his shirt pocket. 'Give them to Dirk,' said Tommy, triumphantly, and Mr. Macintosh's heavy old face went purple. He watched while Tommy walked away from him, sitting on the truck, letting the heavy cudgel swing lightly against his shoes. He solved his immediate problem by thinking: He's a good laddie, he's got a good heart.

That night Mrs. Clarke came over while he was sitting over his roast beef and cabbage, and said: 'Mr. Macintosh, I want a word with you.' He nodded at a chair, but she did not sit. 'Tommy's upset,' she said, delicately, 'he's been used to Dirk, and now he's got no one to play with.'

For a moment Mr. Macintosh kept his eyes lowered, then he said: 'It's easily fixed Annie, don't worry yourself.' He spoke heartily, as it was easy for him to do, speaking of a worker, who might be released at his whim for other duties.

That bright protesting flush came on to her cheeks, in spite of herself, and she looked quickly at him, with real indignation. But he ignored it and said: 'I'll fix it in the morning, Annie.'

She thanked him and went back home, suffering because she had not said those words which had always soothed her conscience in the past: You're nothing but a pig, Mr. Macintosh. . . .

As for Tommy, he was sitting in the shed, crying his eyes out. And then, when there were no more tears, there came such a storm of anger and pain that he would never forget it as long as he lived. What for? He did not know, and that was the worst of it. It was not simply Mr. Macintosh, who loved him, and who thus so blackly betrayed his own flesh and blood, nor the silences of his parents. Something deeper, felt working in the substance of life as he could hear those ants working away with those busy jaws at the roots of the poles he sat on, to make new material for their different forms of life. He was testing those words which were used, or not used – merely suggested – all the time, and for a ten-year-old boy it was almost too hard to bear. A child may say of a companion one day that he hates so and so, and the next: He is my friend. That is how a relationship is, shifting and changing, and children are kept safe in their hates and loves by the fabric of social life their parents make over their heads. And middle-aged people say: This is my friend, this is my enemy, including all the shifts and changes of feeling in one word, for the sake of an easy mind. In between these ages, at about twenty perhaps, there is a time when the young people test everything, and accept many hard and cruel truths about living, and that is because they do not know how hard it is to accept them finally, and for the rest of their lives. It is easy to be truthful at twenty.

But it is not easy at ten, a little boy entirely alone, looking at words like friendship. What, then, was friendship? Dirk was his friend, that he knew, but did he like Dirk? Did he love him? Sometimes not at all. He remembered how Dirk had said: 'I'll get you another baby buck. I'll kill its mother with a stone. He remembered his feeling of revulsion at the cruelty. Dirk was cruel. But – and here Tommy unexpectedly laughed, and for the first time he understood Dirk's way of laughing. It was really funny to say that Dirk was cruel, when his very existence was a cruelty. Yet Mr. Macintosh laughed in exactly the same way, and his skin was white, or rather, white browned over by the sun. Why was Mr. Macintosh also entitled to laugh, with that same abrupt ugliness? Perhaps somewhere in the beginnings of the rich Mr. Macintosh there had been the same cruelty, and that had worked its way through the life of Mr. Macintosh until it turned into the cruelty of Dirk, the coloured boy, the half-caste? If so, it was all much deeper than differently coloured skins, and much harder to understand.

And then Tommy thought how Dirk seemed to wait always, as if he, Tommy, were bound to stand by him, as if this were a justice that was perfectly clear to Dirk; and he, Tommy, did in fact fight with Mr. Macintosh for Dirk, and he could behave in no other way. Why? Because Dirk was his friend? Yet there were times when he hated Dirk, and certainly Dirk hated him, and when they fought they could have killed each other easily, and with joy.

Well, then? Well, then? What was friendship, and why were they bound so closely, and by what? Slowly the little boy sitting alone on his antheap came to an understanding which is proper to middle-aged people, that resignation in knowledge which is called irony. Such a person may know, for instance, that he is bound most deeply to another person, although he does not like that person, in the way the word is ordinarily used, or the way he talks, or his politics, or anything else. And yet they are friends and will always be friends, and what happens to this bound couple affects each most deeply, even though they may be in different continents, or may never see each other again. Or after twenty years they may meet, and there is no need to say a word, everything is understood. This is one of the ways of friendship, and just as real as amiability or being alike.

Well, then? For it is a hard and difficult knowledge for any little boy to accept. But he accepted it, and knew that he and Dirk were closer than brothers and always would be so. He grew many years older in that day of painful struggle, while he listened to the mine-stamps saying gold, gold, and to the ants working away with their jaws to destroy the bench he sat on, to make food for themselves.

Next morning Dirk came to the shed, and Tommy, looking at him, knew that he, too, had grown years older in the months of working in the great pit. Ten years old – but he had been working with men and he was not a child.

Tommy took out the five pound notes and gave them to Dirk.

Dirk pushed them back. 'What for?' he asked.

'I got them from *him*,' said Tommy, and at once Dirk took them as if they were his right.

And at once, inside Tommy, came indignation, for he felt he was being taken for granted, and he said: 'Why aren't you working?'

'He said I needn't. He means, while you are having your holidays.'

'I got you free,' said Tommy, boasting.

Dirk's eyes narrowed in anger. 'He's my father,' he said, for the first time.

'But he made you work,' said Tommy, taunting him. And then: 'Why do you work? I wouldn't. I should say no.'

'So you would say no?' said Dirk in angry sarcasm.

'There's no law to make you.'

'So there's no law, white boy, no law ...' But Tommy had sprung at him, and they were fighting again, rolling over and over, and this time they fell apart from exhaustion and lay on the ground panting for a long time.

Later Dirk said: 'Why do we fight, it's silly?'

'I don't know,' said Tommy, and he began to laugh, and Dirk laughed too. They were to fight often in the future, but never with such bitterness, because of the way they were laughing now.

It was the following holidays before they fought again. Dirk was waiting for him in the shed.

'Did he let you go?' asked Tommy at once, putting down new books on the table for Dirk.

'I just came,' said Dirk. 'I didn't ask.'

They sat together on the bench, and at once a leg gave way and they rolled off on to the floor laughing. 'We must mend it,' said Tommy. 'Let's build the shed again.'

'No,' said Dirk at once, 'don't let's waste time on the shed. You can teach me while you're here, and I can make the shed when you've gone back to school.'

Tommy slowly got up from the floor, frowning. Again he felt he was being taken for granted. 'Aren't you going to work on the mine during the term?'

'No, I'm not going to work on the mine again. I told him I wouldn't.'

'You've got to work,' said Tommy, grandly.

'So I've got to work,' said Dirk, threateningly. 'You can go to school, white boy, but I've got to work, and in the holidays I can't just take time off to please you.'

They fought until they were tired, and five minutes afterwards they were seated on the anthill talking. 'What did you do with the five pounds?' asked Tommy.

'I gave them to my mother.'

'What did she do with them?'

'She bought herself a dress, and then food for us all, and bought me these trousers, and she put the rest away to keep.'

A pause. Then, deeply ashamed, Tommy asked: 'Doesn't *he* give her any money?'

'He doesn't come any more. Not for more than a year.'

'Oh, I thought he did still,' said Tommy casually, whistling.

'No.' Then, fiercely, in a low voice: 'There'll be some more half-castes in the compound soon.'

Dirk sat crouching his fierce black eyes on Tommy, ready to spring at him. But Tommy was sitting with his head bowed, looking at the ground. 'It's not fair,' he said. 'It's not fair.'

'So you've discovered that, white boy?' said Dirk. It was said good-naturedly, and there was no need to fight. They went to their books and Tommy taught Dirk some new sums.

But they never spoke of what Dirk would do in the future, how he would use all this schooling. They did not dare.

That was the eleventh year.

When they were twelve, Tommy returned from school to be greeted by the words: 'Have you heard the news?'

'What news?'

They were sitting as usual on the bench. The shed was newly built, with strong thatch, and good walls, plastered this time with mud, so as to make it harder for the ants.

'They are saying you are going to be sent away.'

'Who says so?'

'Oh, everyone,' said Dirk, stirring his feet about vaguely under the table. This was because it was the first few minutes after the return from school, and he was always cautious, until he was sure Tommy had not changed towards him. And that 'everyone' was explosive. Tommy nodded, however, and asked apprehensively: 'Where to?'

'To the sea.'

'How do they know?' Tommy scarcely breathed the word *they*.

'Your cook heard your mother say so ...' And then Dirk added with a grin, forcing the issue: 'Cheek, dirty kaffirs talking about white men.'

Tommy smiled obligingly, and asked: 'How, to the sea, what does it mean?'

'How should we know, dirty kaffirs.'

'Oh, shut up,' said Tommy, angrily. They glared at each other, their muscles tensed. But they sighed and looked away. At twelve it was not easy to fight, it was all too serious.

That night Tommy said to his parents: 'They say I'm going to sea. Is it true?'

His mother asked quickly: 'Who said so?'

'But is it true?' Then, derisively: 'Cheeky, dirty kaffirs talking about *us*.'

'Please don't talk like that, Tommy, it's not right.'

'Oh, mother, please, how am I going to sea?'

'But be sensible Tommy, it's not settled, but Mr. Macintosh . . .'

'So it's Mr. Macintosh!'

Mrs. Clarke looked at her husband, who came forward and sat down and settled his elbows on the table. A family conference. Tommy also sat down.

'Now listen, son. Mr. Macintosh has a soft spot for you. You should be grateful to him. He can do a lot for you.'

'But why should I go to sea?'

'You don't have to. He suggested it – he was in the Merchant Navy himself once.'

'So I've got to go just because he did.'

'He's offered to pay for you to go to college in England, and give you money until you're in the Navy.'

'But I don't want to be a sailor. I've never ever seen the sea.'

'But you're good at your figures, and you have to be, so why not?'

'I won't,' said Tommy, angrily. I won't, I won't.' He glared at them through tears. 'You just want to get rid of me, that's all it is. You want me to go away from here, from . . .'

The parents looked at each other and sighed.

'Well, if you don't want to, you don't have to. But it's not every boy who has a chance like this.'

'Why doesn't he send Dirk?' asked Tommy, aggressively.

'Tommy,' cried Annie Clarke, in great distress.

'Well, why doesn't he? He's much better than me at figures.'

'Go to bed,' said Mr. Clarke suddenly, in a fit of temper. 'Go to bed.'

Tommy went out of the room, slamming the door hard. He must be grown-up. His father had never spoken to him like that. He sat on the edge of the bed in stubborn rebellion, listening to the thudding of the stamps. And down in the compound they were dancing, the lights of the fires flickered red on his window-pane.

He wondered if Dirk were there, leaping around the fires with the others.

Next day he asked him: 'Do you dance with the others?' At once he knew he had blundered. When Dirk was angry, his eyes darkened and narrowed. When he was hurt, his mouth set in a way which made the flesh pinch thinly under his nose. So he looked now.

'Listen, white boy. White people don't like us half-castes. Neither do the blacks like us. No one does. And so I don't dance with them.'

'Let's do some lessons,' said Tommy, quickly. And they went to their books, dropping the subject.

Later Mr. Macintosh came to the Clarke's house and asked for Tommy. The parents watched Mr. Macintosh and their son walk together along the edge of the great pit. They stood at the window and watched, but they did not speak.

Mr. Macintosh was saying easily: 'Well, laddie, and so you don't want to be a sailor.'

'No, Mr. Macintosh.'

'I went to sea when I was fifteen. It's hard, but you aren't afraid of that. Besides, you'd be an officer.'

Tommy said nothing.

'You don't like the idea?'

'No.'

Mr. Macintosh stopped and looked down into the pit. The earth at the bottom was as yellow as it had been when Tommy was seven, but now it was much deeper. Mr. Macintosh did not know how deep, because he had not measured it. Far below, in this man-made valley, the workers were moving and shifting like black seeds tilted on a piece of paper.

'Your father worked on the mines and he became an engineer working at nights, did you know that?'

'Yes.'

'It was very hard for him. He was thirty before he was qualified, and then he earned twenty-five pounds a month until he came to this mine.'

'Yes.'

'You don't want to do that, do you.'

'I will if I have to,' muttered Tommy, defiantly.

Mr. Macintosh's face was swelling and purpling. The veins along nose and forehead were black. Mr. Macintosh was asking himself why this lad treated them like dirt, when he was offering to do him an immense favour. And yet, in spite of the look of sullen indifference which was so ugly on that young face, he could not help loving him. He was a fine boy, tall, strong, and his hair was the soft, bright brown, and his eyes clear and black. A much better man than his own father, who was rough and marked by the long struggle of his youth. He said: 'Well, you don't have to be a sailor, perhaps you'd like to go to university and be a scholar.'

'I don't know,' said Tommy, unwilling, although his heart had moved suddenly. Pleasure – he was weakening. Then he said suddenly: 'Mr. Macintosh, why do you want to send me to college?'

And Mr. Macintosh fell right into the trap. 'I have no children,' he said, sentimentally. 'I feel for you like my own son.' He stopped. Tommy was looking away towards the compound, and his intention was clear.

'Very well then,' said Mr. Macintosh, harshly. 'If you want to be a fool.'

Tommy stood with his eyes lowered and he knew quite well he was a fool. Yet he could not have behaved in any other way.

'Don't be hasty,' said Mr. Macintosh, after a pause. 'Don't throw away your chances, laddie. You're nothing but a lad, yet. Take your time.' And with this tone, he changed all the emphasis of the conflict, and made it simply a question of waiting. Tommy did not move, so Mr. Macintosh went on quickly: 'Yes, that's right, you just think it over.' He hastily slipped a pound note from his pocket and put it into the boy's hand.

'You know what I'm going to do with it?' said Tommy, laughing suddenly, and not at all pleasantly.

'Do what you like, do just as you like, it's your money,' said Mr. Macintosh, turning away so as not to have to understand.

Tommy took the money to Dirk, who received it as if it

were his right, a feeling in which Tommy was not an accomplice, and they sat together in the shed. 'I've got to be something,' said Tommy angrily. 'They're going to make me be something.'

'They wouldn't have to *make* me be anything,' said Dirk, sardonically. 'I know what I'd be.'

'What?' asked Tommy, enviously.

'An engineer.'

'How do you know what you've got to do?'

'That's what I want,' said Dirk, stubbornly.

After a while Tommy said: 'If you went to the city, there's a school for coloured children.'

'I wouldn't see my mother again.'

'Why not?

'There's laws, white boy, laws. Anyone who lives with and after the fashion of the natives is a native. Therefore I'm a native, and I'm not entitled to go to school with the half-castes.'

'If you went to the town, you'd not be living with the natives so you'd be classed as a Coloured.'

'But then I couldn't see my mother, because if she came to town she'd still be a native.'

There was a triumphant conclusiveness in this that made Tommy think: He intends to get what he wants another way ... And then: Through me. ... But he had accepted that justice a long time ago, and now he looked at his own arm that lay on the rough plank of the table. The outer side was burnt dark and dry with the sun, and the hair glinted on it like fine copper. It was no darker than Dirk's brown arm, and no lighter. He turned it over. Inside, the skin was a smooth, dusky white, the veins running blue and strong across the wrist. He looked at Dirk, grinning, who promptly turned his own arm over, in a challenging way. Tommy said, unhappily: 'You can't go to school properly because the inside of your arm is brown. And that's that!' Dirk's tight and bitter mouth expanded into a grin that was also his father's, and he said: 'That is so, white boy, that is so.'

'Well, it's not my fault,' said Tommy, aggressively, closing his fingers and banging the fist down again and again.

'I didn't say it was your fault,' said Dirk at once.

Tommy said, in that uneasy, aggressive tone: 'I've never even seen your mother.'

To this, Dirk merely laughed, as if to say: You have never wanted to.

Tommy said, after a pause: 'Let me come and see her now.'

Then Dirk said, in a tone which was uncomfortable, almost like compassion: 'You don't have to.'

'Yes,' insisted Tommy. 'Yes, now.' He got up, and Dirk rose too. 'She won't know what to say,' warned Dirk. 'She doesn't speak English.' He did not really want Tommy to go to the compound; Tommy did not really want to go. Yet they went.

In silence they moved along the path between the trees, in silence skirted the edge of the pit, in silence entered the trees on the other side, and moved along the paths to the compound. It was big, spread over many acres, and the huts were in all stages of growth and decay, some new, with shining thatch, some tumbledown, with dulled and sagging thatch, some in the process of being built, the peeled wands of the roof-frames gleaming like milk in the sun.

Dirk led the way to a big square hut. Tommy could see people watching him walking with the Coloured boy, and turning to laugh and whisper. Dirk's face was proud and tight, and he could feel the same look on his own face. Outside the square hut sat a little girl of about ten. She was bronze, Dirk's colour. Another little girl, quite black, perhaps six years old, was squatted on a log, finger in mouth, watching them. A baby, still unsteady on its feet, came staggering out of the doorway and collapsed, chuckling, against Dirk's knees. Its skin was almost white. Then Dirk's mother came out of the hut after the baby, smiled when she saw Dirk, but went anxious and bashful when she saw Tommy. She made a little bobbing curtsey, and took the baby from Dirk, for the sake of something to hold in her awkward and shy hands.

'This is Baas Tommy,' said Dirk. He sounded very embarrassed.

She made another little curtsey and stood smiling.

She was a large woman, round and smooth all over, but her legs were slender, and her arms, wound around the child, thin and knotted. Her round face had a bashful curiosity, and her eyes moved quickly from Dirk to Tommy and back while she smiled and smiled, biting her lips with strong teeth, and smiled again.

Tommy said: 'Good morning,' and she laughed and said 'Good morning.'

Then Dirk said: 'Enough now, let's go.' He sounded very angry. Tommy said: 'Good-bye.' Dirk's mother said: 'Good-bye,' and made her little bobbing curtsey, and she moved her child from one arm to another and bit her lip anxiously over her gleaming smile.

Tommy and Dirk went away from the square mud hut where the variously-coloured children stood staring after them.

'There now,' said Dirk, angrily. 'You've seen my mother.'

'I'm sorry,' said Tommy uncomfortably, feeling as if the responsibility for the whole thing rested on him. But Dirk laughed suddenly and said: 'Oh, all right, all right, white boy, it's not your fault.'

All the same, he seemed pleased that Tommy was upset.

Later, with an affectation of indifference, Tommy asked, thinking of those new children: 'Does Mr. Macintosh come to your mother again now?'

And Dirk answered 'Yes,' just the one word.

In the shed Dirk studied from a geography book, while Tommy sat idle and thought bitterly that they wanted him to be a sailor. Then his idle hands protested, and he took a knife and began slashing at the edge of the table. When the gashes showed a whiteness from the core of the wood, he took a stick lying on the floor and whittled at it, and when it snapped from thinness he went out to the trees, picked up a lump of old wood from the ground, and brought it back to the shed. He worked on it with his knife, not knowing what it was he made, until a curve under his knife reminded him of Dirk's sister squatting at the hut door, and then he directed his knife with a purpose. For several days he fought with the lump of wood, while Dirk studied. Then he brought a tin of boot polish from the house, and worked the bright brown wax into the creamy white wood, and soon there was a bronze-coloured figure of the little girl, staring with big, curious eyes while she squatted on spindly legs.

Tommy put it in front of Dirk, who turned it around, grinning a little. 'It's like her,' he said at last. 'You can have it if you like,' said Tommy. Dirk's teeth flashed, he hesitated, and then reached into his pocket and took out a bundle of dirty cloth. He undid it, and Tommy saw the little clay figure he had made of Dirk years ago. It was crumbling, almost worn to a lump of mud, but in it was still the vigorous challenge of Dirk's body. Tommy's mind signalled recognition – for he had forgotten he had ever made it – and he picked it up. 'You kept it?' he asked shyly, and Dirk smiled. They looked at each other, smiling. It was a moment of warm, close feeling, and yet in it was the pain that neither of them understood, and also the cruelty and challenge that made them fight. They lowered their eyes unhappily. 'I'll do your mother,' said Tommy, getting up and running away into the trees, in order to escape from the challenging closeness. He searched until he found a thorn tree, which is so hard it turns the edge of an axe, and then he took an axe and worked at the felling of the tree until the sun went down. A big stone near him was kept wet to sharpen the axe, and next day he worked on until the tree fell. He sharpened the worn axe again, and cut a length of tree about two feet, and split off the tough bark, and brought it back to the shed. Dirk had fitted a shelf against the logs of the wall at the back. On it he had set the tiny, crumbling figure of himself, and the new bronze shape of his little sister. There was a space left for the new statue. Tommy said, shyly: 'I'll do it as quickly as I can so that it will be done before the term starts.' Then, lowering his eyes, which suffered under this new contract of shared feeling, he examined the piece of wood. It was not pale and gleaming like almonds, as was the softer wood. It was a gingery brown, a close-fibred, knotted wood, and down its centre, as he knew, was a hard black spine. He turned it between his hands and thought that this was more difficult than anything he had ever done. For the first time he studied a piece of wood before starting on it, with a desired shape in his mind, trying to see how what he wanted would grow out of the dense mass of material he held.

Then he tried his knife on it and it broke. He asked Dirk for his knife. It was a long piece of metal, taken from a pile of scrap mining machinery, sharpened on stone until it was razor-fine. The handle was cloth wrapped tight around.

With this new and unwieldy tool Tommy fought with the wood for many days. When the holidays were ending, the shape was there, but the face was blank. Dirk's mother was full-bodied, with soft, heavy flesh and full, naked shoulders above a tight, sideways draped cloth. The slender legs were planted firm on naked feet, and the thin arms, knotted with work, were lifted to the weight of a child who, a small, helpless creature swaddled in cloth, looked out with large, curious eyes. But the mother's face was not yet there.

'I'll finish it next holidays,' said Tommy, and Dirk set it carefully beside the other figures on the shelf. With his back turned he asked cautiously: 'Perhaps you won't be here next holidays?'

'Yes I will, ' said Tommy, after a pause. 'Yes I will.'

It was a promise, and they gave each other that small, warm, unwilling smile, and turned away, Dirk back to the compound and Tommy to the house, where his trunk was packed for school.

That night Mr. Macintosh came over to the Clarke's house and spoke with the parents in the front room. Tommy, who was asleep, woke to find Mr. Macintosh beside him. He sat on the foot of the bed and said: 'I want to talk to you, laddie.' Tommy turned the wick of the oil-lamp, and now he could see in the shadowy light that Mr. Macintosh had a look of uneasiness about him. He was sitting with his strong old body balanced behind the big stomach, hands laid on his knees, and his grey Scots eyes were watchful.

'I want you to think about what I said,' said Mr. Macintosh, in a quick, bluff good-humour. 'Your mother says in two years' time you will have matriculated, you're doing fine at school. And after that you can go to college.'

Tommy lay on his elbow, and in the silence the drums came tapping from the compound, and he said: 'But Mr. Macintosh, I'm not the only one who's good at his books.'

Mr. Macintosh stirred, but said bluffly: 'Well, but I'm talking about you.'

Tommy was silent, because as usual these opponents were so much stronger than was reasonable, simply because of their ability to make words mean something else. And then, his heart painfully beating, he said: 'Why don't you send Dirk to college. You're so rich, and Dirk knows everything I know. He's better than me at figures. He's a whole book ahead of me, and he can do sums I can't.'

Mr. Macintosh crossed his legs impatiently, uncrossed them, and said: 'Now why should I send Dirk to college?' For now Tommy would have to put into precise words what he meant, and this Mr. Macintosh was quite sure he would not do. But to make certain, he lowered his voice and said: 'Think of your mother laddie, she's worrying about you, and you don't want to make her worried, do you?'

Tommy looked towards the door, under it came a thick yellow streak of light: in that room his mother and his father were waiting in silence for Mr. Macintosh to emerge with news of Tommy's sure and wonderful future.

'You know why Dirk should go to college,' said Tommy in despair, shifting his body unhappily under the sheets, and Mr. Macintosh chose not to hear it. He got up, and said quickly: 'You just think it over, laddie. There's no hurry but by next holidays I want to know.' And he went out of the room. As he opened the door, a brightly-lit, painful scene was presented to Tommy: his father and mother sat, smiling in embarrassed entreaty at Mr. Macintosh. The door shut, and Tommy turned down the light, and there was darkness.

He went to school next day. Mrs. Clarke, turning out Mr. Macintosh's house as usual, said unhappily: 'I think you'll find everything in its proper place,' and slipped away, as if she were ashamed.

As for Mr. Macintosh, he was in a mood which made others, besides Annie Clarke, speak to him carefully. His cook-boy, who had worked for him twelve years, gave notice that month. He had been knocked down twice by that powerful, hairy fist, and he was not a slave, after all, to remain bound to a bad-tempered master. And when a load of rock slipped and crushed the skulls of two workers, and the police came out for an investigation, Mr. Macintosh met them irritably, and told them to mind their own business. For the first time in that mine's history of scandalous recklessness, after many such accidents, Mr. Macintosh heard the indignant words from a police officer: 'You speak as if you were above the law, Mr. Macintosh. If this happens again, you'll see . . .'

Worst of all, he ordered Dirk to go back to work in the pit, and Dirk refused.

'You can't make me,' said Dirk.

'Who's the boss on this mine?' shouted Mr. Macintosh.

'There's no law to make children work,' said the thirteen-year-old, who stood as tall as his father, a straight, lithe youth against the bulky strength of the old man.

The word *law* whipped the anger in Mr. Macintosh to the point where he could feel his eyes go dark, and the blood pounding in that hot darkness in his head. In fact, it was the power of this anger that sobered him, for he had been very young when he had learned to fear his own temper. And above all, he was a shrewd man. He waited until his sight was clear again, and then asked, reasonably: 'Why do you want to loaf around the compound, why not work and earn money?'

Dirk said: 'I can read and write, and I know my figures better than Tommy – Baas Tommy,' he added, in a way which made the anger rise again in Mr. Macintosh, so that he had to make a fresh effort to subdue it.

But Tommy was a point of weakness in Mr. Macintosh, and it was then that he spoke the words which afterwards made him wonder if he'd gone suddenly crazy. For he said: 'Very well, when you're sixteen you can come and do my books and write the letters for the mine.'

Dirk said: 'All right,' as if this were no more than his due, and walked off, leaving Mr. Macintosh impotently furious with himself. For how could anyone but himself see the books? Such a person would be his master. It was impossible, he had no intention of ever letting Dirk, or anyone else, see them. Yet he had made the promise. And so he would have to find another way of using Dirk, or – and the words came involuntarily – getting rid of him.

From a mood of settled bad temper, Mr. Macintosh dropped into one of sullen thoughtfulness, which was entirely foreign to his character. Being shrewd is quite different from the processes of thinking. Shrewdness, particularly the money-making shrewdness, is a kind of instinct.

While Mr. Macintosh had always known what he wanted to do, and how to do it, that did not mean he had known why he wanted so much money, or why he had chosen these ways of making it. Mr. Macintosh felt like a cat whose nose has been rubbed into its own dirt, and for many nights he sat in the hot little house, that vibrated continually from the noise of the mine-stamps, most uncomfortably considering himself and his life. He reminded himself, for instance, that he was sixty, and presumably had no more than ten or fifteen years to live. It was not a thought that an unreflective man enjoys, particularly when he had never considered his age at all. He was so healthy, strong, tough. But he was sixty nevertheless, and what would be his monument? An enormous pit in the earth, and a million pounds worth of property. Then how should he spend those ten or fifteen years? Exactly as he had the preceding sixty, for he hated being away from this place, and this gave him a caged and useless sensation, for it had never entered his head before that he was not as free as he felt himself to be.

Well, then – and this thought gnawed most closely to Mr. Macintosh's pain – why had he not married? For he considered himself a marrying sort of man, and had always intended to find himself the right sort of woman and marry her. Yet he was already sixty. The truth was that Mr. Macintosh had no idea at all why he had not married and got himself sons; and in these slow, uncomfortable ponderings the thought of Dirk's mother intruded itself only to be hastily thrust away. Mr. Macintosh, the sensualist, had a taste for dark-skinned women; and now it was certainly too late to admit as a permanent feature of his character something he had always considered as a sort of temporary whim, or makeshift, like someone who learns to enjoy an inferior brand of tobacco when better brands are not available.

He thought of Tommy, of whom he had been used to say: 'I've taken a fancy to the laddie.' Now it was not so much fancy as a deep, grieving love. And Tommy was the son of his employee, and looked at him with contempt, and he, Mr. Macintosh, reacted with angry shame as if he were guilty of something. Of what? It was ridiculous.

The whole situation was ridiculous, and so Mr. Macintosh allowed himself to slide back into his usual frame of mind. Tommy's only a boy, he thought, and he'll see reason in a year or so. And as for Dirk, I'll find him some kind of a job when the time comes. . . .

At the end of the term, when Tommy came home. Mr. Macintosh asked, as usual, to see the school report, which usually filled him with pride. Instead of heading the class with approbation from the teachers and high marks in all subjects, Tommy was near the bottom, with such remarks as Slovenly, and Lazy, and Bad-mannered. The only subject in which he got any marks at all was that called Art, which Mr. Macintosh did not take into account.

When Tommy was asked by his parents why he was not working, he replied, impatiently: 'I don't know,' which was quite true; and at once escaped to the anthill. Dirk was there, waiting for the books Tommy always brought for him. Tommy reached at once up to the shelf where stood the figure of Dirk's mother, lifted it down and examined the unworked space which would be the face. 'I know how to do it,' he said to Dirk, and took out some knives and chisels he had brought from the city.

That was how he spent the three weeks of that holiday, and when he met Mr. Macintosh he was sullen and uncomfortable. 'You'll have to be working a bit better,' he said, before Tommy went back, to which he received no answer but an unwilling smile.

During that term Tommy distinguished himself in two ways besides being steadily at the bottom of the class he had so recently led. He made a fiery speech in the debating society on the iniquity of the Colour Bar, which rather pleased his teachers, since it is a well-known fact that the young must pass through these phases of rebellion before settling down to conformity. In fact, the greater the verbal rebellion, the more settled was the conformity likely to be. In secret Tommy got books from the city library such as are not usually read by boys of his age, on the history of Africa, and on comparative anthropology, and passed from there to the history of the moment – he ordered papers from the Government Stationery Office, the laws of the country. Most particularly those affecting the relations between black and white and coloured. These he bought in order to take back to Dirk. But in addition to all this ferment, there was that subject Art, which in this school meant a drawing lesson twice a week, copying busts of Julius Caesar, or it might be Nelson, or shading in fronds of fern or leaves, or copying a large vase or a table standing diagonally to the class, thus learning what he was told were the laws of Perspective. There was no modelling, nothing approaching sculpture in this school, but this was the nearest thing to it, and that mysterious prohibition which forbade him to distinguish himself in Geometry or English, was silent when it came to using the pencil.

At the end of the term his Report was very bad, but it admitted that he had An Interest in Current Events, and a Talent for Art.

And now this word Art, coming at the end of two successive terms, disturbed his parents and forced itself on Mr. Macintosh. He said to Annie Clarke: 'It's a nice thing to make pictures, but the lad won't earn a living by it.' And Mrs. Clarke said reproachfully to Tommy: 'It's all very well, Tommy, but you aren't going to earn a living drawing pictures.'

'I didn't say I wanted to earn a living with it,' shouted Tommy, miserably. 'Why have I got to *be* something, you're always wanting me to *be* something.'

That holidays Dirk spent studying the Acts of Parliament and the Reports of Commissions and Sub-Committees which Tommy had brought him, while Tommy attempted something new. There was a square piece of soft white wood which Dirk had pilfered from the mine, thinking Tommy might use it. And Tommy set it against the walls of the shed, and knelt before it and attempted a frieze or engraving – he did not know the words for what he was doing. He cut out a great pit, surrounded by mounds of earth and rock, with the peaks of great mountains beyond, and at the edge of the pit stood a big man carrying a stick, and over the edge of the pit wound a file of black figures, tumbling into the gulf. From the pit came flames and smoke. Tommy took green ooze from leaves and mixed clay to colour the mountains and edges of the pit, and he made the little figures black with charcoal, and he made the flames writhing up out of the pit red with the paint used for parts of the mining machinery.

'If you leave it here, the ant'sll eat it,' said Dirk, looking with grim pleasure at the crude but effective picture.

To which Tommy shrugged. For while he was always solemnly intent on a piece of work in hand, afraid of anything that might mar it, or even distract his attention from it, once it was finished he cared for it not at all.

It was Dirk who had painted the shelf which held the other figures with a mixture that discouraged ants, and it was now Dirk who set the piece of square wood on a sheet of tin smeared with the same mixture, and balanced it in a way so it should not touch any part of the walls of the shed, where the ants might climb up.

And so Tommy went back to school, still in that mood of obstinate disaffection, to make more copies of Julius Caesar and vases of flowers, and Dirk remained with his books and his Acts of Parliament. They would be fourteen before they met again, and both knew that crises and decisions faced them. Yet they said no more than the usual: Well, so long, before they parted. Nor did they ever write to each other, although this term Tommy had a commission to send certain books and other Acts of Parliament for a purpose which he entirely approved.

Dirk had built himself a new hut in the compound, where he lived alone, in the compound but not of it, affectionate to his mother, but apart from her. And to this hut at night came certain of the workers who forgot their dislike of the half-caste, that cuckoo in their nest, in their common interest in what he told them of the Acts and Reports. What he told them was what he had learnt himself in the proud loneliness of his isolation. 'Education,' he said, 'Education, that's the key' – and Tommy agreed with him, although he had, or so one might suppose from the way he was behaving, abandoned all idea of getting an education for himself. All that term parcels came to 'Dirk, c/o Mr. Macintosh,' and Mr. Macintosh delivered them to Dirk without any questions.

In the dim and smoky hut every night, half a dozen of the workers laboured with stubs of pencil and the exercise books sent by Tommy, to learn to write and do sums and understand the Laws.

One night Mr. Macintosh came rather late out of that other hut, and saw the red light from a fire moving softly on the rough ground outside the door of Dirk's hut. All the others were dark. He moved cautiously among them until he stood in the shadows outside the door, and looked in. Dirk was squatting on the floor, surrounded by half a dozen men, looking at a newspaper.

Mr. Macintosh walked thoughtfully home in the starlight. Dirk had he known what Mr. Macintosh was thinking, would have been very angry, for all his flaming rebellion, his words of resentment, were directed against Mr. Macintosh and his tyranny. Yet for the first time Mr. Macintosh was thinking of Dirk with a certain, rough, amused pride. Perhaps it was because he was a Scot, after all, and in every one of his nation is an instinctive respect for learning and people with the determination to 'get on'. A chip off the old block, thought Mr. Macintosh, remembering how he, as a boy, had laboured to get a bit of education. And if the chip was the wrong colour – well, he would do something for Dirk. Something, he would decide when the time came. As for the others who were with Dirk, there was nothing easier than to sack a worker and engage another. Mr. Macintosh went to his bed, dressed as usual in vest and pyjama trousers, unwashed and thrifty in candlelight.

In the morning he gave orders to one of the overseers that Dirk should be summoned. His heart was already soft with thinking about the generous scene which would shortly take place. He was going to suggest that Dirk should teach all the overseers to read and write – on a salary from himself, of course – in order that these same overseers should be more useful in the work. They might learn to mark pay-sheets, for instance.

The overseer said that Baas Dirk spent his days studying in Baas Tommy's hut – with the suggestion in his manner that Baas Dirk could not be disturbed while so occupied, and that this was on Tommy's account.

The man, closely studying the effect of his words, saw how Mr. Macintosh's big, veiny face swelled, and he stepped back a pace. He was not one of Dirk's admirers.

Mr. Macintosh, after some moments of heavy breathing, allowed his shrewdness to direct his anger. He dismissed the man, and turned away.

During that morning he left his great pit and walked off into the bush in the direction of the towering blue peak. He had heard vaguely that Tommy had some kind of a hut, but imagined it as a child's thing. He was still very angry because of that calculated 'Baas Dirk'. He walked for a while along a smooth path through the trees, and came to a clearing. On the other side was an anthill, and on the anthill a well-built hut, draped with Christmas fern around the open front, like curtains. In the opening sat Dirk. He wore a clean white shirt, and long smooth trousers. His head, oiled and brushed close, was bent over books. The hand that turned the pages of the books had a brass ring on the little finger. He was the very image of an aspiring clerk: that form of humanity which Mr. Macintosh despised most.

Mr. Macintosh remained on the edge of the clearing for some time, vaguely waiting for something to happen, so that he might fling himself, armoured and directed by his contemptuous anger, into a crisis which would destroy Dirk for ever. But nothing did happen. Dirk continued to turn the pages of the book, so Mr. Macintosh went back to his house, where he ate boiled beef and carrots for his dinner.

Afterwards he went to a certain drawer in his bedroom, and from it took an object carelessly wrapped in cloth which, exposed, showed itself as that figure of Dirk the boy Tommy had made and sold for five pounds. And Mr. Macintosh turned and handled and pored over that crude wooden image of Dirk in a passion of curiosity, just as if the boy did not live on the same square mile of soil with him, fully available to his scrutiny at most hours of the day.

If one imagines a Judgement Day with the graves giving up their dead impartially, black, white, bronze and yellow, to a happy reunion, one of the pleasures of that reunion might well be that people who have lived on the same acre or street all their lives will look at each other with incredulous recognition. 'So that is what you were like,' might be the gathering murmur around God's heaven. For the glass wall between colour and colour is not only a barrier against touch, but has become thick and distorted, so that black men, white men, see each other through it, but see – what? Mr. Macintosh examined the image of Dirk as if searching for some final revelation, but the thought that came persistently to his mind was that the statue might be of himself as a lad of twelve. So after a few moments he rolled it again in the cloth and tossed it back into the corner of a drawer, out of sight, and with it that unwelcome and tormenting knowledge.

Late that afternoon he left his house again and made his way towards the hut on the antheap. It was empty, and he walked through the knee-high grass and bushes till he could climb up the hard, slippery walls of the antheap and so into the hut.

First he looked at the books in the case. The longer he looked, the faster faded that picture of Dirk as an oiled and mincing clerk, which he had been clinging to ever since he threw the other image into the back of a drawer. Respect for Dirk was reborn. Complicated mathematics, much more advanced than he had ever done. Geography. History. 'The Development of the Slave Trade in the Eighteenth Century.' 'The Growth of Parliamentary Institutions in Great Britain.' This title made Mr. Macintosh smile – the free-booting buccaneer examining a coastguard's notice perhaps. Mr. Macintosh lifted down one book after another and smiled. Then, beside these books, he saw a pile of slight, blue pamphlets, and he examined them. 'The Natives Employment Act'. 'The Natives Juvenile Employment Act'. 'The Native Passes Act'. And Mr. Macintosh flipped over the leaves and laughed, and had Dirk heard that laugh it would have been worse to him than any whip.

For as he patiently explained these laws and others like them to his bitter allies in the hut at night, it seemed to him that every word he spoke was like a stone thrown at Mr. Macintosh, his father. Yet Mr. Macintosh laughed, since he despised these laws, although in a different way, as much as Dirk did. When Mr. Macintosh, on his rare trips to the city, happened to drive past the House of Parliament, he turned on it a tolerant and appreciative gaze. 'Well, why not?' he seemed to be saying. 'It's an occupation, like any other.'

So to Dirk's desperate act of retaliation he responded with a smile, and tossed back the books and pamphlets on the shelf. And then he turned to look at the other things in the shed, and for the first time he saw the high shelf where the statuettes were arranged. He looked, and felt his face swelling with that fatal rage. There was Dirk's mother, peering at him in bashful sensuality from over the baby's head, there the little girl, his daughter, squatting on spindly legs and staring. And there, on the edge of the shelf, a small, worn shape of clay which still held the vigorous strength of Dirk. Mr. Macintosh, breathing heavily, holding down his anger, stepped back to gain a clearer view of those figures, and his heel slipped on a slanting piece of wood. He turned to look, and there was the picture Tommy had carved and coloured of his mine. Mr. Macintosh saw the great pit, the black little figures tumbling and sprawling over into the flames, and he saw himself, stick in hand, astride on his two legs at the edge of the pit, his hat on the back of his head.

And now Mr. Macintosh was so disturbed and angry that he was driven out of the hut and into the clearing, where he walked back and forth through the grass, looking at the hut while his anger growled and moved inside him. After some time he came close to the hut again and peered in. Yes, there was Dirk's mother, peering bashfully from her shelf, as if to say: 'Yes, it's me, remember? And there on the floor was the square, tinted piece of wood which said what Tommy thought of him and his life. Mr. Macintosh took a box of matches from his pocket. He lit a match. He understood he was standing in the hut with a lit match in his hand to no purpose. He dropped the match and ground it out with his foot. Then he put a pipe in his mouth, filled it and lit it, gazing all the time at the shelf and at the square carving. The second match fell to the floor and lay spurting a small white flame. He ground his heel hard on to it. Anger heaved up in him beyond all sanity, and he lit another match, pushed it into the thatch of the hut, and walked out of it and so into the clearing and away into the bush. Without looking behind him he walked back to his house where his supper of boiled beef and carrots was waiting for him. He was amazed, angry, resentful. Finally he felt aggrieved, and wanted to explain to someone what a monstrous injustice was Tommy's view of him. But there was no one to explain it to; and he slowly quietened to a steady, dulled sadness, and for some days remained so, until time restored him to normal. From this condition he looked back at his behaviour and did not like it. Not that he regretted burning the hut, it seemed to him unimportant. He was angry at himself for allowing his anger to dictate his actions. Also he knew that such an act brings its own results.

So he waited, and thought mainly of the cruelty of fate in denying him a son who might carry on his work – for he certainly thought of his work as something to be continued. He thought sadly of Tommy, who denied him. And so, his affection for Tommy was sprung again by thinking of him, and he waited, thinking of reproachful things to say to him.

When Tommy returned from school he went straight to the clearing and found a mound of ash on the antheap that was already sifted and swept by the wind. He found Dirk, sitting on a tree trunk in the bush waiting for him.

'What happened?' asked Tommy. And then, at once: 'Did you save your books?'

Dirk said: '*He* burnt it.'

'How do you know?'

'I know.'

Tommy nodded. 'All your books have gone,' he said, very grieved, and as guilty as if he had burnt them himself.

'Your carving and your statues are burnt too.'

But at this Tommy shrugged, since he could not care about his things once they were finished. 'Shall we build the hut again now?' he suggested.

'My books are burnt,' said Dirk, in a low voice, and Tommy, looking at him, saw how his hands were clenched. He instinctively moved a little aside to give his friend's anger space.

'When I grow up I'll clear you all out, all of you, there won't be one white man left in Africa, not one.'

Tommy's face had a small, half-scared smile on it. The hatred Dirk was directing against him was so strong he nearly went away. He sat beside Dirk on the tree trunk and said: 'I'll try and get you more books.'

'And then he'll burn them again.'

'But you've already got what was in them inside your

head,' said Tommy, consolingly. Dirk said nothing, but sat like a clenched fist, and so they remained on that tree trunk in the quiet bush while the doves cooed and the mine-stamps thudded, all that hot morning. When they had to separate at midday to return to their different worlds, it was with a deep sadness, knowing that their childhood was finished, and their playing, and something new was ahead.

And at that meal Tommy's mother and father had his school report on the table, and they were reproachful. Tommy was at the foot of his class, and he would not matriculate that year. Or any year if he went on like this.

'You used to be such a clever boy,' mourned his mother, 'and now what's happened to you?'

Tommy, sitting silent at the table, moved his shoulders in a hunched, irritable way, as if to say: Leave me alone. Nor did he feel himself to be stupid and lazy, as the Report said he was.

In his room were drawing blocks and pencils and hammers and chisels. He had never said to himself he had exchanged one purpose for another, for he had no purpose. How could he, when he had never been offered a future he could accept? Now, at this time, in his fifteenth year, with his reproachful parents deepening their reproach, and the knowledge that Mr. Macintosh would soon see that Report, all he felt was a locked stubbornness, and a deep strength.

In the afternoon he went back to the clearing, and he took his chisels with him. On the old, soft, rotted tree trunk that he had sat on that morning, he sat again, waiting for Dirk. But Dirk did not come. Putting himself in his friend's place he understood that Dirk could not endure to be with a white-skinned person – a white face, even that of his oldest friend, was too much the enemy. But he waited, sitting on the tree trunk all through the afternoon, with his chisels and hammers in a little box at his feet in the grass, and he fingered the soft, warm wood he sat on, letting the shape and texture of it come into the knowledge of his fingers.

Next day, there was still no Dirk.

Tommy began walking around the fallen tree, studying it. It was very thick, and its roots twisted and slanted into the air to the height of his shoulder. He began to carve the root. It would be Dirk again.

That night Mr. Macintosh came to the Clarke's house and read the Report. He went back to his own, and sat wondering why Tommy was set so bitterly against him. The next day he went to the Clarke's house again to find Tommy, but the boy was not there.

He therefore walked through the thick bush to the ant-heap, and found Tommy kneeling in the grass working on the tree root.

Tommy said: 'Good morning,' and went on working, and Mr. Macintosh sat on the trunk and watched.

'What are you making?' asked Mr. Macintosh.

'Dirk,' said Tommy, and Mr. Macintosh went purple and almost sprang up and away from the tree trunk. But Tommy was not looking at him. So Mr. Macintosh remained, in silence. And then the useless vigour of Tommy's concentration on that rotting bit of root goaded him, and his mind moved naturally to a new decision.

'Would you like to be an artist?' he suggested.

Tommy allowed his chisel to rest, and looked at Mr. Macintosh as if this were a fresh trap. He shrugged, and with the appearance of anger, went on with his work.

'If you've a real gift, you can earn money by that sort of thing. I had a cousin back in Scotland who did it. He made souvenirs, you know, for travellers.' He spoke in a soothing and jolly way.

Tommy let the souvenirs slide by him, as another of these impositions on his independence. He said: 'Why did you burn Dirk's books?'

But Mr. Macintosh laughed in relief. 'Why should I burn his books?' It really seemed ridiculous to him, his rage had been against Tommy's work, not Dirk's.

'I know you did,' said Tommy. 'I know it. And Dirk does too.'

Mr. Macintosh lit his pipe in good humour. For now things seemed much easier. Tommy did not know why he had set fire to the hut, and that was the main thing. He puffed smoke for a few moments and said: 'Why should you think I don't want Dirk to study? It's a good thing, a bit of education.'

Tommy stared disbelievingly at him.

'I asked Dirk to use his education, I asked him to teach

some of the others. But he wouldn't have any of it. Is that my fault?'

Now Tommy's face was completely incredulous. Then he went scarlet, which Mr. Macintosh did not understand. Why should the boy be looking so foolish? But Tommy was thinking: We were on the wrong track.... And then he imagined what this offer must have done to Dirk's angry, rebellious pride, and he suddenly understood. His face still crimson, he laughed. It was a bitter, ironical laugh, and Mr. Macintosh was upset – it was not a boy's laugh at all.

Tommy's face slowly faded from crimson, and he went back to work with his chisel. He said, after a pause: 'Why don't you send Dirk to college instead of me? He's much more clever than me. I'm not clever, look at my Report.'

'Well, laddie ...' began Mr. Macintosh reproachfully – he had been going to say: 'Are you being lazy at school simply to force my hand over Dirk?' He wondered at his own impulse to say it; and slid off into the familiar obliqueness which Tommy ignored: 'But you know how things are, or you ought to by now. You talk as if you didn't understand.'

But Tommy was kneeling with his back to Mr. Macintosh working at the root, so Mr. Macintosh continued to smoke. Next day he returned and sat on the tree trunk and watched. Tommy looked at him as if he considered his presence an unwelcome gift, but he did not say anything.

Slowly, the big fanged root which rose from the trunk was taking Dirk's shape. Mr. Macintosh watched with uneasy loathing. He did not like it, but he could not stop watching. Once he said: 'But if there's a veld fire, it'll get burnt. And the ants'll eat it in any case.' Tommy shrugged. It was the making of it that mattered, not what happened to it afterwards, and this attitude was so foreign to Mr. Macintosh's accumulating nature that it seemed to him that Tommy was touched in the head. He said: 'Why don't you work on something that'll last? Or even if you studied like Dirk it would be better.'

Tommy said: 'I like doing it.'

'But look, the ants are already at the trunk – by the time you get back from your school next time there'll be nothing left of it.'

'Or someone might set fire to it,' suggested Tommy. He looked steadily at Mr. Macintosh's reddening face with triumph. Mr. Macintosh found the words too near the truth. For certainly, as the days passed, he was looking at the new work with hatred and fear and dislike. It was nearly finished. Even if nothing were done to it, it could stand as it was, complete.

Dirk's long, powerful body came writhing out of the wood like something struggling free. The head was clenched back, in the agony of the birth, eyes narrowed and desperate, the mouth – Mr. Macintosh's mouth – tightened in obstinate purpose. The shoulders were free, but the hands were held; they could not pull themselves out of the dense wood, they were imprisoned. His body was free to the knees, but below them the human limbs were uncreated, the natural shapes of the wood swelled to the perfect muscled knees.

Mr. Macintosh did not like it. He did not know what art was, but he knew he did not like this at all, it disturbed him deeply, so that when he looked at it he wanted to take an axe and cut it to pieces. Or burn it, perhaps. . . .

As for Tommy, the uneasiness of this elderly man who watched him all day was a deep triumph. Slowly, and for the first time, he saw that perhaps this was not a sort of game that he played, it might be something else. A weapon – he watched Mr. Macintosh's reluctant face, and a new respect for himself and what he was doing grew in him.

At night, Mr. Macintosh sat in his candle-lit room and he thought, or rather *felt*, his way to a decision.

There was no denying the power of Tommy's gift. Therefore, it was a question of finding the way to turn it into money. He knew nothing about these matters, however, and it was Tommy himself who directed him, for towards the end of the holidays he said: 'When you're so rich you can do anything. You could send Dirk to college and not even notice it.'

Mr. Macintosh, in the reasonable and persuasive voice he now always used, said: 'But you know these Coloured people have nowhere to go.'

Tommy said: 'You could send him to the Cape. There are Coloured people in the university there. Or to Johannesburg.' And he insisted against Mr. Macintosh's silence:

'You're so rich you can do anything you like.'

But Mr. Macintosh, like most rich people, thought not of money as things to buy, things to do, but rather how it was tied up in buildings and land.

'It would cost thousands,' he said. 'Thousands for a Coloured boy.'

But Tommy's scornful look silenced him, and he said hastily: 'I'll think about it.' But he was thinking not of Dirk, but of Tommy. Sitting alone in his room he told himself it was simply a question of paying for knowledge.

So next morning he made his preparations for a trip to town. He shaved, and over his cotton singlet he put a striped jacket, which half-concealed his long, stained khaki trousers. This was as far as he ever went in concessions to the city life he despised. He got into his big American car and set off.

In the city he took the simplest route to knowledge.

He went to the Education Department, and said he wanted to see the Minister of Education. 'I'm Macintosh,' he said, with perfect confidence; and the pretty secretary who had been patronizing his clothes, went at once to the Minister and said: 'There is a Mr. Macintosh to see you.' She described him as an old, fat, dirty man with a large stomach, and soon the doors opened, and Mr. Macintosh was with the spring of knowledge.

He emerged five minutes later with what he wanted, the name of a certain expert. He drove through the deep green avenues of the city to the house he had been told to go to, which was a large and well-kept one, and comforted Mr. Macintosh in his faith that art properly used could make money. He parked his car in the road and walked in.

On the verandah, behind a table heaped with books, sat a middle-aged man with spectacles. Mr. Tomlinson was essentially a scholar with working hours he respected, and he lifted his eyes to see a big, dirty man with black hair showing above the dirty whiteness of his vest, and he said sharply: 'What do you want?'

'Wait a minute, laddie,' said Mr. Macintosh easily, and he held out a note from the Minister of Education, and Mr. Tomlinson took it and read it, feeling reassured. It was worded in such a way that his seeing Mr. Macintosh could be felt as a favour he was personally doing the Minister.

'I'll make it worth your while,' said Mr. Macintosh, and at once distaste flooded Mr. Tomlinson, and he went pink, and said: 'I'm afraid I haven't the time.'

'Damn it, man, it's your job, isn't it? Or so Wentworth said.'

'No,' said Mr. Tomlinson, making each word clear, 'I advise on ancient Monuments.'

Mr. Macintosh stared, then laughed, and said: 'Wentworth said you'd do, but it doesn't matter, I'll get someone else.' And he left.

Mr. Tomlinson watched this hobo go off the verandah and into a magnificent car, and his thought was: 'He must have stolen it.' Then, puzzled and upset, he went to the telephone. But in a few moments he was smiling. Finally he laughed. Mr. Macintosh was the Mr. Macintosh, a genuine specimen of the old-timer. It was the phrase 'old-timer' that made it possible for Mr. Tomlinson to relent. He therefore rang the hotel at which Mr. Macintosh, as a rich man, would be bound to be staying, and said he had made an error, he would be free the following day to accompany Mr. Macintosh.

And so next morning Mr. Macintosh, not at all surprised that the expert was at his service after all, with Mr. Tomlinson, who preserved a tolerant smile, drove out to the mine.

They drove very fast in the powerful car, and Mr. Tomlinson held himself steady while they jolted and bounced, and listened to Mr. Macintosh's tales of Australia and New Zealand, and thought of him rather as he would of an ancient Monument.

At last the long plain ended, and foothills of greenish scrub heaped themselves around the car, and then high mountains piled with granite boulders, and the heat came in thick, slow waves into the car, and Mr. Tomlinson thought: I'll be glad when we're through the mountains into the plain. But instead they turned into a high, enclosed place with mountains all around, and suddenly there was an enormous gulf in the ground, and on one side of it were two tiny tin-roofed houses, and on the other acres of kaffir huts. The mine-stamps thudded regularly, like a pulse of the heat, and Mr. Tomlinson wondered how anybody, white or black, could bear to live in such a place.

He ate boiled beef and carrots and greasy potatoes with one of the richest men in the sub-continent, and thought how well and intelligently he would use such money if he had it – which is the only consolation left to the cultivated man of moderate income. After lunch, Mr. Macintosh said: 'And now, let's get it over.'

Mr. Tomlinson expressed his willingness, and smiling to himself, followed Mr. Macintosh off into the bush on a kaffir path. He did not know what he was going to see. Mr. Macintosh had said: 'Can you tell if a youngster has got any talent just by looking at a piece of wood he has carved?'

Mr. Tomlinson had said he would do his best.

Then they were beside a fallen tree trunk, and in the grass knelt a big lad with untidy brown hair falling over his face, labouring at the wood with a large chisel.

'This is a friend of mine,' said Mr. Macintosh to Tommy, who got to his feet and stood uncomfortably, wondering what was happening. 'Do you mind if Mr. Tomlinson sees what you are doing?'

Tommy made that shrugging movement, and felt that things were going beyond his control. He looked in awed amazement at Mr. Tomlinson, who seemed to him rather like a teacher or professor, and certainly not at all what he had imagined an artist to be.

'Well?' said Mr. Macintosh to Mr. Tomlinson, after a space of half a minute.

Mr. Tomlinson laughed, in a way which said: 'Now don't be in such a hurry.' He walked around the carved tree root, looking at the figure of Dirk from this angle and that.

Then he asked Tommy: 'Why do you make these carvings?'

Tommy very uncomfortably shrugged, as if to say: What a silly question; and Mr. Macintosh hastily said: 'He gets high marks for Art at school.'

Mr. Tomlinson smiled again, and walked around to the other side of the trunk. From here he could see Dirk's face flattened back on the neck, eyes half-closed and strained, the muscles of the neck shaped from the natural veins of the wood.

'Is this someone you know?' he asked Tommy in an easy intimate way, one artist to another.

'Yes,' said Tommy, briefly; he resented the question.

Mr. Tomlinson looked at the face and then at Mr. Macintosh. 'It has a look of you,' he observed dispassionately, and coloured himself as he saw Mr. Macintosh grow angry. He walked well away from the group, to give Mr. Macintosh space to hide his embarrassment. When he returned, he asked Tommy: 'And so you want to be a sculptor?'

'I don't know,' said Tommy, defiantly.

Mr. Tomlinson shrugged, rather impatiently, and with a nod at Mr. Macintosh suggested it was enough. He said goodbye to Tommy, and went back to the house with Mr. Macintosh.

There he was offered tea and biscuits, and Mr. Macintosh asked: 'Well, what do you think?'

But by now Mr. Tomlinson was certainly offended at this casual cash-on-delivery approach to art, and he said: 'Well, that rather depends, doesn't it?'

'On what? 'demanded Mr. Macintosh.

'He seems to have talent,' conceded Mr. Tomlinson.

'That's all I want to know,' said Mr. Macintosh, and suggested that now he could run Mr. Tomlinson back to town.

But Mr. Tomlinson did not feel it was enough, and he said: 'It's quite interesting, that statue. I suppose he's seen pictures in magazines. It has quite a modern feeling.'

'Modern?' said Mr. Macintosh, 'what do you mean?'

Mr. Tomlinson shrugged again, giving it up. 'Well,' he said, practically, 'what do you mean to do?'

'If you say he has talent, I'll send him to the University and he can study art.'

After a long pause, Mr. Tomlinson murmured: 'What a fortunate boy he is.' He meant to convey depths of disillusionment and irony, but Mr. Macintosh said: 'I always did have a fancy for him.'

He took Mr. Tomlinson back to the city, and as he dropped him on his verandah, presented him with a cheque for fifty pounds, which Mr. Tomlinson most indignantly returned. 'Oh, give it to charity,' said Mr. Macintosh impatiently, and went to his car, leaving Mr. Tomlinson to heal his susceptibilities in any way he chose.

When Mr. Macintosh reached his mine again it was midnight, and there were no lights in the Clarke's house, and so his need to be generous must be stifled until the morning.

Then he went to Annie Clarke and told her he would send Tommy to university, where he could be an artist, and Mrs. Clarke wept gratitude, and said that Mr. Macintosh was much kinder than Tommy deserved, and perhaps he would learn sense yet and go back to his books.

As far as Mr. Macintosh was concerned it was all settled. He set off through the trees to find Tommy and announce his future to him.

But when he arrived at seeing distance there were two figures, Dirk and Tommy, seated on the trunk talking, and Mr. Macintosh stopped among the trees, filled with such bitter anger at this fresh check to his plans that he could not trust himself to go on. So he returned to his house, and brooded angrily – he knew exactly what was going to happen when he spoke to Tommy, and now he must make up his mind, there was no escape from decision.

And while Mr. Macintosh mused bitterly in his house, Tommy and Dirk waited for him; it was now all as clear to them as it was to him.

Dirk had come out of the trees to Tommy the moment the two men left the day before. Tommy was standing by the fanged root, looking at the shape of Dirk in it, trying to understand what was going to be demanded of him. The word 'artist' was on his tongue, and he tasted it, trying to make the strangeness of it fit that powerful shape struggling out of the wood. He did not like it. He did not want – but what did he not want? He felt pressure on himself, the faint beginnings of something that would one day be like a tunnel of birth from which he must fight to emerge; he felt the obligations working within himself like a goad which would one day be a whip perpetually falling just behind him so that he must perpetually move onwards.

His sense of fetters and debts was confirmed when Dirk came to stand by him. First he asked: 'What did they want?'

'They want me to be an artist, they always want me to be something,' said Tommy, sullenly. He began throwing stones at the trees, and shying them off along the tops of the grass.

Then one hit the figure of Dirk, and he stopped.

Dirk was looking at himself. 'Why do you make me like that?' he asked. The narrow, strong face expressed nothing but that familiar, sardonic antagonism, as if he said: 'You, too – just like the rest!'

'Why? What's the matter with it?' challenged Tommy at once.

Dirk walked around it, then back. 'You're just like all the rest,' he said.

'Why? Why don't you like it?' Tommy was really distressed. Also, his feeling was: What's it got to do with him? Slowly he understood that his emotion was that belief in his right to freedom which Dirk always felt immediately, and he said in a different voice: 'Tell me what's wrong with it?'

'Why do I have to come out of the wood? Why haven't I any hands or feet?'

'You have, but don't you see ...' But Tommy looked at Dirk standing in front of him and suddenly gave an impatient movement: 'Well, it doesn't matter, it's only a statue.'

He sat on the trunk and Dirk beside him. After a while he said: 'How should you be, then?'

'If you made yourself, would you be half wood?'

Tommy made an effort to feel this, but failed. 'But it's not me, it's you.' He spoke with difficulty, and thought: But it's important, I shall have to think about it later. He almost groaned with the knowledge that here it was, the first debt, presented for payment.

Dirk said suddenly: 'Surely it needn't be wood. You could do the same thing if you put handcuffs on my wrists.' Tommy lifted his head and gave a short, astonished laugh. 'Well, what's funny?' said Dirk, aggressively. 'You can't do it the easy way, you have to make me half wood, as if I was more a tree than a human being.'

Tommy laughed again, but unhappily. 'Oh, I'll do it again,' he acknowledged at last. 'Don't fuss about that one, it's finished. I'll do another.'

There was a silence.

Dirk said: 'What did that man say about you?'

'How do I know?'

'Does he know about art?'

'I suppose so.'

'Perhaps you'll be famous,' said Dirk at last. 'In that book you gave me, it said about painters. Perhaps you'll be like that.'

'Oh, shut up,' said Tommy, roughly. 'You're just as bad as *he* is.'

'Well, what's the matter with it?'

'Why have I got to *be* something. First it was a sailor, and then it was a scholar, and now it's an artist.'

'They wouldn't *have* to make me be anything,' said Dirk sarcastically.

'I know,' admitted Tommy, grudgingly. And then, passionately: 'I shan't go to university unless he sends you too.'

'I know,' said Dirk at once, 'I know you won't.'

They smiled at each other, that small, shy revealed smile, which was so hard for them, because it pledged them to such a struggle in the future.

Then Tommy asked: 'Why didn't you come near me all this time?'

'I get sick of you,' said Dirk. 'I sometimes feel I don't want to see a white face again, not ever. I feel that I hate you all, every one.'

'I know,' said Tommy, grinning. Then they laughed, and the last strain of dislike between them vanished.

They began to talk, for the first time, of what their lives would be.

Tommy said: 'But when you've finished training to be an engineer, what will you do? They don't let Coloured people be engineers.'

'Things aren't always going to be like that,' said Dirk.

'It's going to be very hard,' said Tommy, looking at him questioningly, and was at once reassured when Dirk said, sarcastically: 'Hard, it's *going* to be hard? Isn't it hard now, white boy?'

Later that day Mr. Macintosh came towards them from his house.

He stood in front of them, that big, shrewd, rich man, with his small, clever grey eyes, and his narrow, loveless mouth; and he said aggressively to Tommy: 'Do you want to go to the University and be an artist.'

'If Dirk comes too,' said Tommy immediately.

'What do you want to study?' Mr. Macintosh asked Dirk, direct.

'I want to be an engineer,' said Dirk at once.

'If I pay your way through the University then at the end of it I'm finished with you. I never want to hear from you and you are never to come back to this mine once you leave it.'

Dirk and Tommy both nodded, and the instinctive agreement between them fed Mr. Macintosh's bitter unwillingness in the choice, so that he ground out viciously: 'Do you think you two can be together in the University? You don't understand. You'll be living separate, and you can't go around together just as you like.'

The boys looked at each other, and then, as if some sort of pact had been made between them, simply nodded.

'You can't go to University, anyway, Tommy, until you've done a bit better at school. If you go back for another year and work you can pass your matric. and go to University, but you can't go now, right at the bottom of the class.'

Tommy said: 'I'll work.' He added at once: 'Dirk'll need more books to study here till we can go.'

The anger was beginning to swell Mr. Macintosh's face, but Tommy said: 'It's only fair. You burnt them, and now he hasn't any at all.'

'Well,' said Mr. Macintosh heavily. 'Well, so that's how it is!'

He looked at the two boys, seated together on the tree trunk. Tommy was leaning forward, eyes lowered, a troubled but determined look on his face. Dirk was sitting erect, looking straight at his father with eyes filled with hate.

'Well,' said Mr. Macintosh, with an effort at raillery which sounded harsh to them all: 'Well, I send you both to University and you don't give me so much as a thank you!'

At this, both faced towards him, with such bitter astonishment that he flushed.

'Well, well,' he said. 'Well, well . . .' And then he turned to leave the clearing, and cried out as he went, so as to give the appearance of dominance: 'Remember, laddie, I'm not sending you unless you do well at school this year. . . .'

And so he left them and went back to his house, an angry old man, defeated by something he did not begin to understand.

As for the boys, they were silent when he had gone.

The victory was entirely theirs, but now they had to begin again, in the long and difficult struggle to understand what they had won and how they would use it.

*Fifth Novel*

# Hunger

NOTE
**Skellum**—*a wicked person*
**Kraal**—*a native village*
**Matsotsis**—*a spiv*

IT IS dark inside the hut, and very cold. Yet around the oblong shape that is the doorway where a sack hangs, for the sake of comely decency, is a diffusing yellow glare, and through holes in the sack come fingers of yellow warmth, nudging and prodding at Jabavu's legs. 'Ugh,' he mutters, drawing up his feet and kicking at the blanket to make it stretch over him. Under Jabavu is a reed mat, and where its coolness touches him he draws back, grumbling in his sleep. Again his legs sprawl out, again the warm fingers prod him, and he filled with a rage of resentment. He grabs at sleep, as if a thief were trying to take it from him; he wraps himself in sleep like a blanket that persists in slipping off; there is nothing he has ever wanted, nothing he will ever want again as he wants sleep at this moment. He leans as greedily towards it as towards a warm drink on a cold night. He drinks it, guzzles it, and is sinking contentedly into oblivion when words come dropping through it like stones through thick water. 'Ugh!' mutters Jabavu again. He lies as still as a dead rabbit. But the words continue to fall into his ears, and although he has sworn to himself not to move, not to sit up, to hold to this sleep which they are trying to take from him, he nevertheless sits up, and his face is surly and unwilling.

His brother, Pavu, on the other side of the dead ashes of the fire, which is in the middle of the mud floor, also sits up. He too, is sulking. His face is averted and he blinks slowly as he rises to his feet, lifting the blanket with him. Yet he remains respectfully silent while his mother scolds.

'Children, your father has already been waiting for you as long as it takes to hoe a field.' This intended to remind them of their duty, to put back into their minds what their minds have let slip – that already, earlier, they have been awakened, their father laying his hand silently first on one shoulder and then on another.

Pavu guiltily folds his blanket and lays it on the low earth mound on one side of the hut, and then stands waiting for Jabavu.

But Jabavu is leaning on his elbow by the ashen smudge of last night's fire, and he says to his scolding mother: 'Mother, you make as many words as the wind brings grains of dust.' Pavu is shocked. He would never speak any way but respectfully to his parents. But also, he is not shocked, for this is Jabavu the Big Mouth. And if the parents say with sorrow that in their day no child would speak to his parents as Big Mouth speaks, then it is true, too, that now there are many children who speak thus – and how can one be shocked by something that happens every day?

Jabavu says, breaking into a shrill whirl of words from the mother: 'Ah, mother, *shut up!*' The words 'shut up' are in English. And now Pavu is really shocked, with the whole of himself, not merely with that part of him that pays tribute to the old forms of behaviour. He says quickly, to Jabavu: 'And now that is enough. Our father is waiting.' He is so ashamed that he lifts the sacking from the door and steps outside, blinking into the sunlight. The sun is pale bright gold, and quickly gathering heat. Pavu moves his stiff limbs in it as if it were hot water, and then stands beside his father. 'Good morning, my father,' he says; and the old man greets him: 'Good morning, my son.'

The old man wears a brown blanket striped with red, folded over his shoulder and held with a large steel safety-pin. He carries a hoe for the fields, and the spear of his fore-fathers with which to kill a rabbit, or buck if one should show itself. The boy has no blanket. He wears a vest that is rubbed into holes tucked into a loincloth. He also carries a hoe.

From inside the hut come voices. The mother is still scolding. They can hear scraping sounds and the small knock of wood – she is kneeling to remove the dead ash and to build the new fire. It is as if they can see her crouching there, coaxing the new day's fire to life. And it is as if they can see Jabavu huddled on his mat, his face sullenly turned away from her while she scolds.

They look at each other, ashamed; then they look away past the little huts of the native village; they see disappearing among the trees a crowd of their friends and relatives from these huts. The other men are already on their way to the fields. It is nearly six in the morning. The father and Pavu, avoiding each other's eyes because of their shame, move off after them. Jabavu must come by himself – if he comes at all. Once the men from this hut were first at the fields, once their fields were first hoed, first planted, first reaped. Now they are the last, and it is because of Jabavu who works or does not work as he feels inclined.

Inside the hut the mother kneels at the fire, watching a small glow of flame rise inside the hollow of her sheltering hand. The warmth contents her, melts her bitterness.

'Ah, my Big Mouth, get up now,' she says with tender reproach. 'Are you going to lie there all day while your father and brother work?' She lifts her face, ready to smile forgiveness at the bad son. But Jabavu leaps from the blanket as if he had found a snake there, and roars: 'My name is Jabavu, not Big Mouth. Even my own, my given name, you take from me!' He stands there stiff, accusing, his eyes quivering with unhappy anger. And his mother slowly drops her eyes, as if guilty.

Now this is strange, for Jabavu is a hundred times in the wrong; while she has always been a proper mother, a good wife. Yet for that moment it is between these two, mother and son, as if she has done wrong and he is justly accusing her. Soon his body loses the stiffness of anger and he leans idly against the wall, watching her; and she turns towards the crescent-shaped earth shelf behind her for a pot. Jabavu watches intently. Now there is a new thought, a new need – which kind of utensil will she bring out? When he sees what it is, he quivers out a sigh of relief, and his mother hears that sigh and wonders and marvels. She has brought out not the cooking pot for the morning porridge, but the petrol tin in which she heats water for washing.

The father and Pavu, all the men of the village, will wash when they return from the fields for the first meal, or in the river by the place where they work. But Jabavu's whole being, every atom of his brain and body is concentrated on the need that she should serve him thus – should warm water especially so that he may wash in it now. And yet at other times Jabavu is careless of his cleanness.

The mother sets the half-tin on the stones in the clump of red and roaring flames, and almost at once a wisp of blueish steam curls off the rocking water. She hears Jabavu sigh again. She keeps her head lowered, wondering. She is thinking that it is as if inside Jabavu, her son, some kind of hungry animal is living, looking out of his eyes, speaking from his mouth. She loves Jabavu. She thinks of him as brave, affectionate, clever, strong and respectful. She believes that he is all these things, that the fierce animal which has made its lair inside Jabavu is not her son. And yet her husband, her other children, and indeed the whole village call him Jabavu the Big Mouth, Jabavu the greedy, the boastful, the bad son, who will certainly one day run off to the white man's town and become one of the matsotsis, the criminal youth. Yes, that is what they say, and she knows it. There are even times when she says so herself. And yet – fifteen years ago there was a year of famine. It was not a famine as is known in other countries that this woman has never heard of, China perhaps, or India. But it was a season of drought, and some people died, and many were hungry.

The year before the drought they had sold their grain as was usual to the native store, keeping sufficient for themselves. They were given the prices that were fair for that year. The white man at that store, a Greek, stored the grain, as was his custom, for resale to these same natives when they ran short, as they often did – a shiftless lot, always ready to sell more than they should for the sake of the glittering shillings with which they could buy head-cloths or bangles or cloth. And that year, in the big markets in America and Europe there was a change of prices. The Greek sold all the maize he had to the big stores in town, and sent his men around the native villages, coaxing them to sell everything they had. He offered a little more money than they had been used to get. He was buying at half of what he could get in the city. And all would have been well if there had not been that season of drought. For the mealies wilted in the fields, the cobs struggled towards fullness, but remained as small as a fist. There was panic in the villages and the people came streaming towards the Greek store and to all the other native stores all over the country. The Greek said, Yes, yes, he had the maize, he always had the maize, but of course at the new price laid down by the Government. And of course the people did not have the money to buy this newly expensive maize.

So in the villages there was a year of hunger. That year, Jabavu's elder sister, three years old, came running playfully to her mother's teats, and found herself smacked off, like a troublesome puppy. The mother was still feeding Jabavu, who had always been a demanding, hungry child, and there was a new baby a month old. The winter was cold and dusty. The men went hunting for hares and buck, the women searched through the bush all day for greens and roots, and there was hardly any grain for the porridge. The dust filled the villages, the dust hung in sullen clouds in the air, blew into the huts and into the nostrils of the people. The little girl died – it was sad because she had breathed too much dust. And the mother's breasts hung limp, and when Jabavu came tugging at her dress she smacked him off. She was sick with grief because of the death of the child, and also with fear for the baby. For now the buck and hares were scarce, they had been hunted so relentlessly, and one cannot keep life on leaves and roots. But Jabavu did not relinquish his mother's breasts so easily. At night, as she lay on her mat, the new baby beside her, Jabavu came pushing and struggling to her milk, and she woke, startled, saying: 'Ehhh, but this child of mine is strong.' He was only a year old, yet she had to use all her strength to fend him off. In the dark of the hut her husband woke and lifted Jabavu, screaming and kicking, away from her, and away from the tender new baby. That baby died, but by then Jabavu had turned sullen and was fighting like a little leopard for what scraps of food there were. A little skeleton he was, with loose brown skin and enormous, frantic eyes, nosing around in the dust for fallen mealies or a scrap of sour vegetable.

This is what the mother thinks of, as she crouches watching the wisps of steam curl off the water. For her Jabavu is three children, she loves him still with all the bereaved passion of that terrible year. She thinks: It was then, when he was so tiny, that Jabavu the Big Mouth was made – yes, the people called him the Big Mouth even then. Yes, it is the fault of the Long Hunger that Jabavu is as he is.

But even while she is excusing him thus, she cannot help

remembering how he was as a new baby. The women used to laugh as they watched him suck. 'That one was born hungry,' they said, 'that one will make a big man!' For he was such a big child, so fierce in his sucking, always crying for food ... and again she excuses him, fondly: If he had not been so, if he had not fed his strength from the time he was born, he too would have died, like the others. And at this thought she lifts her eyes, filled with love and pride – but she lowers them again quickly. For she knows that a big lad, like Jabavu, who is nearly seventeen years old, resents it when a mother looks at him, remembering the baby he was. Jabavu only knows what he is, and that very confusedly. He is still leaning against the mud wall. He does not look at his mother, but at the water which is heating for his use. And inside there is such a storm of anger, love, pain, and resentment: he feels so much, and all at once, that it is as if a wind-devil had got into him. He knows quite well that he does not behave as he ought, yet there is no other way he can behave; he knows that among his own people he is like a black bull in a herd of goats – yet he was bred from them; he wants only the white man's town, yet he knows nothing of it save what he has heard from travellers. And suddenly into his head comes the thought: If I go to the white man's town my mother will die of grief.

Now he looks at his mother. He does not think of her as young, old, pretty, ugly. She is his mother, who came properly endowed to her husband, after a proper amount of cattle had been paid for her. She has borne five children three of whom live. She is a good cook and respectful to her husband. She is a mother, as a mother should be, according to the old ideas. Jabavu does not despise these ideas: simply, they are not for him. There is no need to despise something from which one is already freed. Jabavu's wife will not be like his mother; he does not know why, but he knows it.

His mother is, in fact, according to the new ideas, not yet thirty-five years old, a young woman who would still look pretty in a dress such as the townswomen wear. But she wears some cotton stuff, blue, bound around her breasts leaving her shoulders bare, and a blue cotton skirt bunched in such a way that the heat will not scorch her legs.

She has never thought of herself as old, young, modern or old-fashioned. Yet she, too, knows that Jabavu's wife will not be as she is, and towards this unknown woman her mind lifts in respectful but fearful wonder. She thinks: Perhaps if this son of mine finds a woman who is like him, then he will no longer be like a wild bull among oxen ... this thought comforts her; she allows her skirt to fall as it will, steps back from the scorching heat, and lifts the tin off the flames. 'Now you may wash, my son,' she says. Jabavu grabs the tin, as if it might run away from him, and carries it outside. And then he stops and slowly sets it down. Sullenly, as if ashamed of this new impulse, he goes back into the hut, lifts his blanket which lies where he let it drop, folds it and lays it on the earthen shelf. Then he rolls his reed mat, sets it against the wall, and also rolls and places his brother's mat. He glances at his mother, who is watching him in silence, sees her soft and compassionate eyes ... but this he cannot bear. Rage fills him; he goes out.

She is thinking: See, this is my son! How quickly and neatly he folds the blanket, sets the mats against the wall! How easily he lifts the tin of heavy water! How strong he is, and how kind! Yes, he thinks of me, and returns to tidy the hut, he is ashamed of his thoughtlessness. So she muses, telling herself again and again how kind her Jabavu is, although she knows he is not kind, and particularly not to himself; and that when a kind impulse takes him, such as it has now, Jabavu behaves as if he has performed a bad deed and not a good one. She knows that if she thanks him he will shout at her. She glances through the door of the hut and sees her son, strong and powerful, his bronze skin shining with health in the new morning's sun. But his face is knotted with anger and resentment. She turns away so as not to see it.

Jabavu carries the tin of water to the shade of a big tree, strips off his loincloth and begins to wash. The comforting hot water flows over him, he likes the tingle of the strong soap: Jabavu was the first in all the village to use the white man's soap. He thinks: I, Jabavu, wash in good, warmed water, and with proper soap. Not even my father washes when he wakes.... He sees some women walking past, and pretends he does not see them. He knows what they are thinking, but says to himself: Stupid Kraal women, they don't know anything. But I know that Jabavu is like a white man, who washes when he leaves his sleep.

The women slowly go past and their faces are sorrowful. They look at the hut where his mother is kneeling to cook, and they shake their heads and speak their compassion for this poor woman, their friend and sister, who has bred such a son. But in their voices is another note of emotion, and Jabavu knows it is there, though he cannot hear them speak. Envy? Admiration? Neither of these. But it is not the first time a child like Jabavu has been bred by the villages. And these women know well that the behaviour of Jabavu can be understood only by thinking of the world of the white man. The white man has brought evil and good, things to admire and things to fear, and it is hard to know one from the other. But when an aeroplane flies far overhead like a shining beetle through the air; and when the big motor cars drive past on the road North, they think also of Jabavu and of the young people like him.

Jabavu has finished washing. He stands idle under the big tree, his back turned to the huts of the village, quite naked, covering what should not be seen of his body with his cupped hand. The yellow patches of sunlight tremble and sway on his skin. He feels the shifting warmth and begins to sing with pleasure. Then an unpleasant thought stops the singing: he has nothing to wear but the loincloth which is the garb of a kraal-boy. He owns an old pair of shorts which were too small for him years ago. They once belonged to the son of the Greek at the store when that son was ten years old.

Jabavu takes the shorts from the crotch of the tree and tries to tug them over his hips. They will not go. Suddenly they split behind. Cautiously he twists himself to see how big the tear is. His buttock is sticking out of the material. He frowns, takes a big needle such as is used for sewing grain sacks, threads it with fine strands of fibre stripped from under the bark of a tree, and begins to make a lacework of the fibre across his behind. He does this without taking the shorts off: he stands twisted, using the needle with one hand and holding the edges of frayed material with the other. At last it is done. The shorts decently cover him. They are old, they grip him as tight as the bark of a tree grips the white wood underneath, but they are trousers and not a loincloth.

Now he carefully slides the needle back under the bark of the tree, rolls his loincloth into the crotch of the trunk, then lifts down a comb from where it is laced through a frond of leaves. He kneels before a tiny fragment of mirror that he found in a rubbish-heap behind the Greek store, and combs his thick hair. He combs until his arm is tired, but at last the parting shows clear down his scalp. He sticks the steel comb jauntily at the back of his head, like the comb of a fine cock, and looks at himself happily in the mirror. Now his hair is done like a white man's.

He lifts the tin and throws the water in a fine, gleaming curve over the bushes, watching the drops fall in a glittering shower; and an old hen, which was seeking shelter from the heat, runs away squawking. He roars with laughter, seeing that flapping old hen. Then he tosses the tin away into the bushes. It is new and glints among the green leaves. He looks at the tin, while an impulse stirs in him – that same impulse that always hurts him so, leaving him limp and confused. He is thinking that his mother, who paid a shilling for the tin in the Greek store will now know where it is. Secretly, as if he were doing something wicked, he lifts the tin carries it to the door of the hut and, stretching his hand carefully around the opening, sets it inside. His mother, who is stirring meal into boiling water for the porridge, does not turn around. Yet he knows that she knows what he is doing. He waits for her to turn – if she does and thanks him, then he will shout at her; already he feels the anger crowding his throat. And when she does not turn he feels even more anger, and a hot blackness rocks across his eyes. He cannot endure that anyone, not even his mother, should understand why he creeps like a thief to do a kind thing. He walks swaggering back to the shade of the tree, muttering: I am Jabavu, I am Jabavu – as if this were the answer to any sad look or reproachful words or understanding silence.

He squats under the tree, but carefully, so that his trousers may not fall completely to pieces. He looks at the village. It is a native kraal such as one may see anywhere in Africa, a casual arrangement of round mud huts with conical grass roofs. A few are square, influenced by the angled dwellings of the white man. Beyond the kraal is a belt of trees, and beyond them, the fields. Jabavu thinks: This is my village – and immediately his thoughts leave it and go to the white man's town. Jabavu knows everything about this town, although he has never been there. When someone returns, or passes through this village, Jabavu runs to listen to the tales of the wonderful living, the adventure, the excitement. He has a very clear picture in his mind of the place. He knows the white man's house is always of brick, not of mud. He has seen such a house. The Greek at the store has a brick house, two fine rooms, with chairs in them, and tables, and beds lifted off the floor on legs. Jabavu knows the white man's town will be of such houses, many many houses, perhaps as many as will reach from where he is sitting to the big road going North that is half a mile away. His mind is bright with wonder and excitement as he imagines it, and he looks at his village with impatient dissatisfaction. The village is for the old people, it is right for them. And Jabavu can remember no time when he has not felt as he does now; it is as if he were born with the knowledge that the village was his past, not his future. Also, that he was born longing for the moment when he could go to the town. A hunger rages in him for that town. What is this hunger? Jabavu does not know. It is so strong that a voice speaks in his ear, I want, I want, as if his fingers curl graspingly in a movement, We want, as if every fibre of his body sings and shouts, I want, I want, I want . . .

He wants everything and nothing. He does not say to himself: I want a motor car, an aeroplane, a house. Jabavu is intelligent, and knows that the black man does not own such things. But he wants to be near them, to see them, touch them, perhaps serve them. When he thinks of the white man's town he sees something beautiful, richly coloured, strange. A rainbow to him means the white man's town, or a fine warm morning, or a clear night when there is a dancing. And this exciting life waits for him, Jabavu, he was born for it. He imagines a place of light and warmth and laughter, and people saying: Hau! Here is our friend Jabavu! Come, Jabavu, and sit with us.

This is what he wants to hear. He does not want to hear

any longer the sorrowful voices of the old people: The Big Mouth, look at the Big Mouth, listen to the Big Mouth hatching out words again.

He wants so terribly that his body aches with wanting. He begins to day-dream. This is his dream, slipping, half-ashamed, through his mind. He sees himself walking to town, he enters the town, a black policeman greets him: 'Why, Jabavu, so there you are, I come from your village, do you remember me?' 'My friend,' answered Jabavu, 'I have heard of you from our brothers, I have been told that you are now a son of the Government.' 'Yes, Jabavu, now I serve the Government. See, I have a fine uniform, and a place to sleep, and friends. I am respected both by the white people and the black. I can help you.' This son of the Government takes Jabavu to his room and gives him food – bread perhaps, white bread, such as the white man eats, and tea with milk. Jabavu has heard of such food from people returning to the village. Then the son of the Government takes Jabavu to the white man whom he serves. 'This is Jabavu,' he says, 'my friend from my village.' 'So this is Jabavu,' says the white man. 'I have heard of you, my son. But no one told me how strong you were, how clever. You must put on this uniform and become a son of the Government.' Jabavu has seen such policemen, because once a year they come gathering taxes from the villages. Big men, important men, black men in uniform. . . . Jabavu sees himself in this uniform, and his eyes dazzle with wanting. He sees himself walking around the white man's town. Yes, Baas, no Baas; and to his own people he is very kind. They say, Yes, that is our Jabavu, from our village, do you remember? He is our good brother, he helps us . . . .

Jabavu's dream has flown so high that it crashes and he blinks his eyes in waking. For he has heard things about the town which tell him this dream is nonsense. One does not become a policeman and a son of the Government so easily. One must be clever indeed – and Jabavu gets up and goes to a big, flat stone, first looking around in case anyone is watching. He flips the stone over, brings from under it a roll of paper, quickly replaces the stone and sits on it. He has taken the paper off parcels of things he has bought from the Greek store. Some are all print, some have little coloured pictures, many together, making a story. The bright sheets of pictures are what he likes best.

They have taught Jabavu to read. He spreads them out on the ground and bends over them, his lips forming the words. The very first picture shows a big white man on a big black horse, with a great gun that spits red fire. 'Bang!' say the letters above. 'Bang,' says Jabavu slowly. 'B-a-n-g.' That was the first word he learned. The second picture shows a beautiful white girl, with her dress slipping off her shoulder, her mouth open. 'Help!' say the letters. 'Help' says Jabavu, 'help, help.' He goes on to the next. Now the big white man has caught the girl around the waist and is lifting her on to the horse. Some wicked white men with big black hats are pointing guns at the girl and the good white man. 'Hold me, honey,' say the letters. Jabavu repeats the words. He slowly works his way to the foot of the page. He knows this story by heart and loves it. But the story on the next page is not so easy. It is about some yellow men with small, screwed-up faces. They are wicked. There is another big white man who is good and carries a whip. It is that whip that troubles Jabavu, for he knows it; he was slashed himself by the Greek at the store for being cheeky. The words say: 'Grrrrrr, you Gooks, this'll teach you!' The white man beats the little yellow men with the whip, and Jabavu feels nothing but confusion and dismay. For in the first story he is the white man on the horse who rescues the beautiful girl from the bad men. But in this story he cannot be the white man because of the whip.... Many many hours has Jabavu spent puzzling over that story, and particularly over the words which say: 'You little yellow snakes....' There goes the whip-lash curling over the picture, and for a long time Jabavu thought the word snake meant that whip. Then he saw the yellow men were the snakes.... And in the end, just as he has done often before, he turns the page, giving up that difficult story, and goes to another.

Jabavu cannot merely read the stories in pictures, but also simple print. On the rubbish heap behind the Greek store he once found a child's alphabet, or rather, half of one. It was a long time before he understood it was half only. He used to sit, hour after hour, fitting the letters in the alphabet to words like Bang! and later, to English words he already knew, from the sorrowful, admiring stories that were told about the white men. Black, white, colour, native, kaffir, mealiemeal, smell, bad, dirty, stupid, work. These were some of the words he knew how to speak before he could read them. After a long time he completed the alphabet for himself. A very long time – it took him over a year of sitting under that tree thinking and thinking while the people of the village laughed and called him lazy. Later still he tried the print without pictures. And it was so hard it was as if he had learned nothing. Months passed. Slowly, very slowly, the sheet of black letters put on meaning. Jabavu will never forget, as long as he lives, that day when he first puzzled out a whole sentence. This was the sentence. 'The African must eat beans and vegetables as well as meat and nuts to keep him healthy.' When he understood that long and difficult sentence, he rolled on the ground with pride, laughing and saying: 'The white men write that we must eat these things all the time! That's what I shall eat when I go to white man's town.'

Some of the words he cannot understand, no matter how hard he tries. 'Any person who contravenes any provision of any of the regulations (which contains fifty clauses) is liable to a fine of £25 or three months imprisonment.' Jabavu has spent many hours over that sentence, and it still means nothing to him. Once he walked five miles to the next village to ask a clever man who knew English what it meant. He did not know either. But he taught Jabavu a great deal of English to speak. Jabavu speaks it now quite well. And he has marked all the difficult words on the newspaper with a piece of charcoal, and will ask someone what they mean, when he finds such a person. Perhaps when a traveller returns for a visit from the town? But there is no one expected. One of the young men, the son of Jabavu's father's brother was to have come, but he went to Johannesburg instead. Nothing has been heard of him for a year. In all, there are seven young men from this village working in the town, and two in Johannesburg at the mines. Any one of them may come next week or perhaps next year.... The hunger in Jabavu swells and mutters: When will I go, when, when, when. I am sixteen, I am a man. I can speak English,

I can read the newspaper. I can understand the pictures – but at this thought he reminds himself he does not understand all the pictures. Patiently he turns back the sheet and goes to the story about the little yellow men. What have they done to be beaten with the whip? Why are some men yellow, some white, some black, some bronze, like himself? Why is there a war in the country of the little yellow men? Why are they called snakes and Gooks? Why, why, why? But Jabavu cannot frame the questions to which he needs the answers, and the frustration feeds that hunger in him. I must go to the white man's town, there I will know, there I will learn.

He thinks, half-heartedly: Perhaps I should go by myself? But it is a frightening thought, he does not have the courage. He sits loose and listless under the tree, letting his hand stir patterns in the dust, and thinks: Perhaps someone will return soon from the town and I may go back with him? Or perhaps I can persuade Pavu to come with me? But his heart stirs painfully at the thought: surely his mother and father will die of grief if both sons go at once! For their daughter left home three years before to work as a nanny at the farm twenty miles away, so that they only see her two or three times a year, and that only for a day.

But the hunger swells up until his regret for his parents is consumed by it, and he thinks: I shall speak to Pavu. I shall make him come with me.

Jabavu is still sitting under the tree thinking when the men come back from the fields, his father and brother with them. At the sight of them he at once gets up and goes to the hut. Now his hunger is for food, or rather that he should be there first and served first.

His mother is laying the white porridge on each plate. The plates are of earthenware, made by herself, and decorated with black patterns on the red. They are beautiful, but Jabavu longs for tin plates such as he has seen in the Greek store. The spoons are of tin, and it gives him much pleasure to touch them.

After she has slapped the porridge on to the plates, she carefully smooths the surfaces with the back of the spoon to make them nice and shiny. She has cooked a stew of roots and leaves from the bush, and she pours a little of this over each white mound. She sets the plates on a mat on the floor. Jabavu at once begins to eat. She looks at him; she wants to ask: Why do you not wait, as is proper, until your father is eating? She does not say it. When the father and brother come in, setting their hoes and the spear against the wall, the father looks at Jabavu, who is eating in disagreeable silence, eyes lowered, and says: 'One who is too tired to work is not too tired to eat.'

Jabavu does not reply. He has almost finished the porridge. He is thinking that there is enough for another big plateful. He is consumed with a craving to eat and eat until his belly is heavy. He hastily gulps down the last mouthfuls and pushes his plate towards his mother. She does not at once take it up to refill it, and rage surges in Jabavu, but before the words can come bubbling out of his mouth, the father, who has noticed, begins to talk. Jabavu lets his hands fall and sits listening.

The old man is tired and speaks slowly. He has said all this very often before. His family listen and yet do not listen. What he says already exists, like words on a piece of paper, to be read or not, to be listened to or not.

'What is happening to our people?' he asks, sorrowfully. 'What is happening to our children? Once, in our kraals, there was peace, there was order. Every person knew what it was they should do and how that thing should be done. The sun rose and sank, the moon changed, the dry season came, then the rains, a man was born and lived and died. We knew, then, what was good and what was evil.'

His wife, the mother, thinks: He longs so much for the old times, which he understood, that he has forgotten how one tribe harried another, he has forgotten that in this part of the country we lived in terror because of the tribes from the South. Half our lives were spent like rabbits in the kopjes, and we women used to be driven off like cattle to make wives for men of other tribes. She says nothing of what she thinks, only: 'Yes, yes, my husband, that is very true.' She lifts more porridge from the pot and lays it on his plate, although he has hardly touched his food. Jabavu sees this; his muscles tighten and his eyes, fixed on his mother, are hungry and resentful.

The old man goes on: 'And now it is as if a great storm

is among our people. The young men go to the towns and to the mines and farms, they learn bad ways, and when they return to us they are strangers, with no respect for their elders. The young women become prostitutes in the towns, they dress like white women, they will take any man for husband, regardless of the laws of relationship. And the white man uses us for servants, and there is no limit set to this time of bondage.'

Pavu has finished his porridge. He looks at his mother. She lays some porridge on his plate and pours vegetable relish over it. Now, having served the men who work, she serves the one who has not. She gives Jabavu what is left, which is not much, and scrapes out what is left of the relish. She does not look at him. She knows of the pain, a child's pain, that sears him because she served him last. And Jabavu does not eat it, simply because he was served last. His stomach does not want it. He sits, sullenly, and listens to his father. What the old man says is true, but there is a great deal he does not say, and can never say, because he is old and belongs to the past. Jabavu looks at his brother, sees the thoughtful, frowning face, and knows that Pavu's thoughts are his own.

'What will become of us? When I look into the future it is as if I see a night that has no end. When I hear the tales that are brought from the white man's towns my heart is as dark as a valley under a raincloud. When I hear how the white man corrupts our children it is as if my head were filled with a puddle of muddy water, I cannot think of these things, they are too difficult.'

Jabavu looks at his brother and makes a small movement of his head. Pavu excuses himself politely to his father and his mother, and this politeness must be enough for both, for Jabavu says nothing at all.

The old man stretches himself on his mat in the sun for half an hour's rest before returning to the fields. The mother takes the plates and pot to wash them. The young men go out to the big tree.

'It was heavy work without you, my brother,' are the re-proachful words that Jabavu hears. He has been expecting them, but he frowns, and says: 'I have been thinking.' He wants his brother to ask eagerly after these important and wonderful thoughts, but Pavu goes on: 'There is half a field to finish, and it is right that you should work with us this afternoon.'

Jabavu feels that extraordinary resentment rising in him, but he manages to shut it down. He understands that it is not reasonable to expect his brother to see the importance of the pictures on the paper and the words that are printed. He says: 'I have been thinking about the white man's town.' He looks importantly at his brother, but all Pavu says is: 'Yes, we know that it will soon be time for you to leave us.'

Jabavu is indignant that his secret thoughts should be spoken of so casually. 'No one has said I must leave. Our father and mother speak all the time, until their jaws must ache with saying it, that good sons stay in the village.'

Pavu says, gently, with a laugh: 'Yes, they talk like all the old people, but they know that the time will come for both of us to go.'

First Jabavu frowns and stares; then he exults: 'You will come with me!'

But Pavu lets his head droop. 'How can I come with you,' he temporizes. 'You are older, it is right that you should go. But our father cannot work the fields by himself. I may come later, perhaps.'

'There are other fathers who have no sons. Our father talks of the custom, but if a custom is something that happens all the time, then it is now a custom with us that young men leave the villages and go to the city.'

Pavu hesitates. His face puckered with distress. He wants to got to the city. Yet he is afraid. He knows Jabavu will go soon, and travelling with his big, strong, clever brother will take the fear from it.

Jabavu can see it all on his face, and suddenly he feels nervous, as if a thief were abroad. He wonders if this brother dreams and plans for the white man's city as he does; and at the thought he stretches out his arms in a movement which suggests he is keeping something for himself. He feels that his own wanting is so strong that nothing less than the whole of the white man's city will be enough for him, not even a little left over for his brother! But then his arms fall and he says, cunningly: 'We will go together. We will help each other. We will not be alone in that place where travellers say a stranger may be robbed and even killed.'

He glances at Pavu, who looks as if he were listening to lovers' talk.

'It is right for brothers to be together. A man who goes alone is like a man who goes hunting alone into dangerous country. And when we are gone, our father will not need to grow so much food, for he will not have our stomachs to fill. And when our sister marries, he will have her cattle and her lobola money. . . .' He talks on and on, trying to keep his voice soft and persuasive, although it keeps rising on waves of passionate desire for those good things in the city. He tries to talk as a reasonable man talks of serious things, but his hands twitch and his legs will not keep still.

He is still making words while Pavu listens when the father comes out of the hut and looks across at them. Both rise and follow him to the fields. Jabavu goes because he wants to win Pavu over, for no other reason, and he talks softly to him as they wind through the trees.

There are two rough patches in the bush. Mealies grow there and between the mealies are pumpkins. The plants are straggly, the pumpkins few. Not long ago a white man came from the city in a car, and was angry when he saw these fields. He said they were farming, like ignorant people, and that in other parts of the country the black people were following the advice of the white, and in consequence their crops were thick and fruitful. He said that the soil was poor because they kept too many cattle on it – but at this their ears were closed to his talk. It was well-known in the villages that when the white men said they should reduce their cattle to benefit the soil, it was only because they wanted these cattle themselves. Cattle were wealth, cattle were power; it was the thought of an alien mind that one good cow is worth ten poor ones. Because of this misunderstanding over the cattle the people of this village are suspicious of everything they hear from the sons of the Government, black or white. This suspicion is a terrible burden, like a cloud on their lives. And it is being fed by every traveller from the towns. There are whispers and rumours of new leaders, new thoughts, a new anger. The young people, like

Jabavu, and even Pavu, in his own fashion, listen as if this is nothing terrible, but the old people are frightened.

When the three reach the field they are to hoe, the old man makes a joke about the advice given them by the man from the city; Pavu laughs politely, Jabavu says nothing. It is part of his impatience with his life here that his father insists on the old ways of farming. He has seen the new ways in the village five miles distant. He knows that the white man is right in what he says.

He works beside Pavu and mutters: 'Our father is stupid. This field would grow twice as much if we did what the sons of the Government tell us.'

Pavu says, gently: 'Quiet, he will hear. Leave him to his own knowledge. An old ox follows the path to water that he learned as a calf.'

'Ah, *shut up*,' mutters Jabavu, and he quickens his work so as to be by himself. What is the use of taking a child like his brother to the city? he is asking himself, crossly. Yet he must, for he is afraid. And he tries to make it up, to attract Pavu's attention so they may work together. And Pavu pretends not to notice, but works quietly beside his father.

Jabavu hoes as if there is a devil in him. He has finished as much as a third more than the others when the sun goes down. The father says approvingly: 'When you do work, my son, you work as if you were fed only on meat.'

Pavu is silent. He is angry with Jabavu, but also he is waiting, half with longing, half with fear, for the moment when the sweet and dangerous talks begins again. And after the evening meal the brothers go out into the dark and stroll among the cooking fires, and Jabavu talks and talks. And so it is for a long time, a week passes and then a month. Sometimes Jabavu loses his temper and Pavu sulks. Then Jabavu comes back, making his words quiet and gentle. Sometimes Pavu says 'Yes,' then again he says 'No, and how can we both leave our father?' And still Jabavu the Big Mouth talks his eyes restless and glittering, his body tense with eagerness. During this time the brothers are together more than they have been in years. They are seen under the tree at night, walking among the huts, sitting at the hut door. There are many people who say: Jabavu is talking so that his brother may go with him.

Yet Jabavu does not know that what he is doing is clear to others, since he never thinks of the others – he sees only himself and Pavu.

There comes a day when Pavu agrees, but only if they first tell their parents; he wishes this unpleasantness to be softened by at least the forms of obedience. Jabavu will not hear of it. Why? He does not know himself, but it seems to him that this flight into the new life will be joyless unless it is stolen. Besides, he is afraid that his father's sorrow will weaken Pavu's intention. He argues. Pavu argues. Then they quarrel. For a whole week there is an ugly silence between them, broken only by intervals of violent words. And the whole village is saying: 'Look – Pavu the good son is resisting the talk of Jabavu the Big Mouth.' The only person who does not know is the father, and this is perhaps because he does not wish to know anything so terrible.

On the seventh day Jabavu comes in the evening to Pavu and shows him a bundle which he has ready. In it is his comb, his scraps of paper with words and pictures, a piece of soap. 'I shall go tonight,' he says to Pavu, and Pavu replies: 'I do not believe it.' Yet he half believes it. Jabavu is fearless, and if he takes the road by himself there may never be another chance for Pavu. Pavu seats himself in the door of the hut, and his face shows the agony of his indecision. Jabavu sits near him saying, 'And now my brother you must surely make up your mind, for I can wait no longer.'

It is then that the mother comes and says: 'And so my sons, you are going to the city?' She speaks sadly, and at the tone of her voice the younger brother wishes only to assure her that the thought of leaving the village has never entered his mind. But Jabavu shouts, angrily: 'Yes, yes, we are leaving. We cannot live any longer in this village where there are only children and women and old men.'

The mother glances to where the father is seated with some friends at a fire by another hut. They make dark shapes against the red fire, and the flames scatter sparks up into the blackness. It is a dark night, good for running away. She says: 'Your father will surely die.' She thinks: He will not die, any more than the other fathers whose sons go to the towns.

Jabavu shouts: 'And so we must be shut here in this village until we die, because of the foolishness of an old man who can see nothing in the life of the white men but what is bad.'

She says, quietly: 'I cannot prevent you from leaving, my sons. But if you go, go now, for I can no longer bear to see you quarrelling and angry day after day.' And then, because her sorrow is filling her throat she quickly lifts a pot and walks off with it, pretending she needs to fetch water for the cooking. But she does not go further than the first patch of deep shadow under the big tree. She stands there, looking into the dim and flickering lights that come from the many fires, and at the huts which show sharp and black, and at the far glow of the stars. She is thinking of her daughter. When the girl left she, the mother, wept until she thought she would die. Yet now she is glad she left. She works for a kind white woman, who gives her dresses, and she hopes to marry the cook, who earns good money. The life of this daughter is something far beyond the life of the mother, who knows that if she were younger she, too, would go to the town. And yet she wishes to weep from misery and loneliness. She does not weep. Her throat aches because of the tears locked in it.

She looks at her two sons, who are talking fast and quiet, their heads close together.

Jabavu is saying: 'Now let us go. If we do not, our mother will tell our father and he will prevent us.' Pavu rises slowly to his feet. He says: 'Ah, Jabavu, my heart is weak for this thing.'

Jabavu knows that this is the moment of final decision. He says:

'Now consider, our mother knows of our leaving and she is not angry, and we can send back money from the city to soften the old age of our parents.'

Pavu enters the hut, and from the thatch takes his mouth organ, and from the earthen shelf his hatchet. He is ready. They stand in the hut looking fearfully at each other, Jabavu in his torn shorts, naked from the waist, Pavu in his loincloth and his vest with holes in it. They are thinking that they will be figures of fun when they reach the town. All the tales they have heard of the matsotsis who thieve and murder, the tales of the recruiting men for the mines, the stories of the women of the towns who are like no women they have ever met – these crowd into their seething heads and they cannot move. Then Jabavu says jauntily: 'Come now, my brother. This will not carry our feet along the road.' And they leave the hut.

They do not look at the tree where their mother is standing. They walk past like big men, swinging their arms. And when they heard quick steps, their mother runs to them and says: 'Wait, my sons.' They feel how she fumbles for their hands, and in them they feel something hard and cold. She has given them each a shilling. 'This is for your journey. And wait – Now, in each hand is a little bundle, and they know she has cooked them food for the journey and kept it for the moment.

The brother turns his face away in shame and sorrow. Then he embraces his mother and hurries on. Jabavu is filled first with gratitude, then with resentment – again his mother has understood him too well, and he dislikes her for it. He is stuck to the piece of ground where he stands. He knows if he says one word he will weep like a little child. His mother says, softly, out of the darkness: 'Do not let your brother come to harm. You are headstrong and fearless and may go into danger where he may not.' Jabavu shouts: 'My brother is my brother, but he is also a man –' Her eyes glint softly at him from the dark, and then he hears the apologetic words: 'And your father, he will surely die if he does not hear word of you. You must not do as so many of the children do – send us word through the Native Commissioner what has happened to you.' And Jabavu shouts: 'The Native Commissioner is for the baboons and the ignorant. I can write letters and you will have letters from me two -- no three times a week!' At this boast the mother sighs, and Jabavu, although he had no intention of doing any such thing, grabs her hand, clings to it, then gives it a little push away from him as if it were her desire to clasp his hand – and so he walks away, whistling, through the shadows of the trees.

The mother watches him until she can see her sons walking together, then she waits a little while, then turns towards the light of the fires, wailing first softly, then, as her sorrows grows strength with use, very loudly. She is wailing that her sons have left the kraal for the wickedness of the city. This is for her husband, and with him she will mourn bitterly, and for many days. She saw their backs as they stole away with their bundles – so she will say, and her voice will be filled with a bitter reproach and anguish. For she is a wife as well as a mother, and a woman feels one thing as a mother, another as wife, and both may be true and heartfelt.

As for Jabavu and Pavu, they walk in silence and fear because of the darkness of the bush till on the very outskirts of the village they see a hut that has been abandoned. They do not like to walk at night; their plan had been to leave at dawn; and so now they creep into this hut and lie there, sleepless, until the light comes first grey and then yellow.

The road runs before them fifty miles to the city; they intend to reach it by night, but the cold shortens their steps. They walk, crouching their loins and shoulders against it, and their teeth are clenched so as not to confess their shivering. Around them the grass is tall and yellow, and hung with throngs of glittering diamonds that slowly grow few and then are gone, and now the sun is very hot on their bodies. They straighten, the skin of their shoulders loosens and breathes. Now they swing easily along, but in silence. Pavu turns his narrow, cautious face this way and that for new sights, new sounds. He is arming his courage to meet them, for he is afraid. Already his thoughts have returned to the village for comfort: Now my father will be walking alone to the fields, slowly, because of the weight of grief in his legs; now my mother will be setting water to heat on the fire for the porridge . . .

Jabavu walks confidently. His mind is entirely on the big city. Jabavu! he hears, Look, here is Jabavu come to the town!

A roar grows in their ears, and they have to leap aside to avoid a great lorry. They land in the thick grass on hands and knees, so violently did they have to jump. They look up, open-mouthed, and see the white driver leaning out and grinning at them. They do not understand that he has swerved his lorry so that they have to jump for his amusement. They do not know he is laughing now because he thinks they look very funny, crouching in the grass, staring like yokels. They stand up and watch the lorry disappearing in clouds of pale dust. The back of it is filled with black men, some of them shout, some wave and laugh. Jabavu says: 'Hau! But that was a big lorry.' His throat and chest are filled with wanting. He wants to touch the lorry, to look at the wonder of its construction, perhaps even to drive it . . . There he stands, his face tense and hungry, when there is a roar, a shrill sound like the crowing of a cock – and again the brothers jump aside, this time landing on their feet, while the dust eddies and swirls about them.

They look at each other, then drop their eyes so as not to confess they do not know what to think. But they are wondering: Are those lorries trying to frighten us on purpose? But why? They do not understand. They have heard tales of how an unpleasant white man may make a fool of a black one, so that he may laugh, but that is quite different from what has just happened. They think: We were walking along, we mean no harm, and we are rather frightened, so why does he frighten us even more? But now they are walking slowly, glancing back over their shoulders so as not to be taken by surprise. And when a car or lorry comes up behind they move away on to the grass and stand waiting until it has gone. There are few cars, but many lorries, and these are filled with black men. Jabavu thinks: Soon, maybe tomorrow when I have a job, I will be carried in such a lorry . . . He is so impatient for this wonderful thing to happen that he walks quickly, and once again has to make a sudden jump aside when a lorry screeches at him.

They have been walking for perhaps an hour when they overtake a man who is travelling with his wife and children. The man walks in front with a spear and an axe, the woman behind, carrying the cooking pots and a baby on her back, and another little child holds her skirt. Jabavu knows that these people are not from the town, but travelling from one village to another, and so he is not afraid of them. He greets them, the greetings are returned, and they go together, talking.

When Jabavu says he is making the long journey to the city, the man says: 'Have you never been before?' Jabavu, who cannot bear to confess his ignorance says: 'Yes, many times,' and the reply is: 'Then there is no need to warn you against the wickedness of the place.' Jabavu is silent, regretting he has not told the truth. But it is too late, for a path leads off the road, and the family turn on to it. As they are making their good-byes, another lorry sweeps by, and the dust swirls up around them. The man looks after the lorry and shakes his head. 'Those are the lorries that carry our brothers to the mines,' he says, brushing the dust from his face and shaking it from his blanket. 'It is well you know the dangers of the road, for otherwise by now you would be in one of them filling the mouths of honest people with dust, and laughing when they shake with fright because of the loud noise of the horn.' He has settled his blanket again over his shoulders now he turns away, followed by his wife and children.

Jabavu and Pavu slowly walk on, and they are thinking. How often have they heard of the recruiters for the mines! Yet these stories, coming through many mouths, grow into something like the ugly pictures that flit through sleep when it is difficult and uneasy. It is hard to think of them now, with the sun shining down. And yet this companion of the road spoke with horror of these lorries? Jabavu is tempted; he thinks: This man is a village man and, like my father, he sees only the bad things. Perhaps I and my brother may travel on one of these lorries to the city? And then the fear swells up in him and so his feet are slow with indecision, and when another lorry comes sweeping past he is standing on the very edge of the road, looking after it with big eyes, as if he wishes it to stop. And when it slows, his heart beats so fast he does not know whether it is with fear, excitement or desire. Pavu tugs at his arm and says: 'Let us run quickly,' and he replies: 'You are afraid of everything, like a child who still smells the milk of its mother.'

The white man who drives the lorry puts his head out and looks back. He looks long at Jabavu and at his brother, and then his head goes inside. Then a black man gets out of the front and walks back. He wears clothes like the white men and walks jauntily. Jabavu, seeing this smart fellow, thinks of his own torn trousers and he hugs his elbows around his hips to hide them. But the smart fellow advances, grinning, and says: 'Yes, yes – you boys there! Want a lift?'

Jabavu takes a step forward, and feels Pavu clutching his elbow from behind. He takes no notice of that clutching grip, but it is like a warning, and he stands still and plants his two feet hard in the dust like the feet of an ox who resists the yoke.

'How much?' he asks, and the smart fellow laughs and says: 'You clever boy, you! No money. Lift to town. And you can put your name on a piece of paper like a white man and travel in the big lorry and there will be a fine job for you.' He laughs and swaggers and his white teeth glisten. He is a very fine fellow indeed, and Jabavu's hunger is like a hand clutching at his heart as he thinks that he, too, will be like this man. 'Yes,' he says, eagerly, 'I can make my name, I can write and I can read, too, and with the pictures.'

'So,' says the fine fellow, laughing more than ever. 'Then you are a clever, clever boy. And your job will be a clever one, with writing in an office, with nice white man, plenty money – ten pounds, perhaps fifteen pounds a month!'

Jabavu's brain goes dark, it is as if his thoughts run into water. His eyes have a yellow dazzling in them. He finds he has taken another step forward and the fine fellow is holding out a sheet of paper covered all over with letters Jabavu takes the paper and tries to make out the words. Some he knows, other he has never seen. He stands for a long time looking at the paper.

The fine fellow says: 'Now, you clever boy, do you want to understand that all at once? And the lorry is waiting? Now just put your cross at the foot there and come quickly to the lorry.'

Jabavu says, resentfully: 'I can make my own name like a white man and I do not need to make a cross. My brother will make a cross and will make my own name, Jabavu.' And he kneels on the ground, and puts the paper on a stone, and takes the stub of pencil that the fine fellow is holding out to him, and then thinks where to put the first letter of his name. And then he hears that the fine fellow is saying: Your brother is not strong enough for this work.' Jabavu, turning around, sees that Pavu's face is yellow with fear, but also very angry. He is looking with horror at Jabavu. Jabavu rests his pencil and thinks: Why is my brother not big enough? Many of us go to town when we are still children, and work. A memory comes into his head of how someone has told him that when they recruit for the mines they take only strong men with fine shoulders. He, Jabavu, has the bulky strength of a young bull – he is filled with pride: Yes, he will go to the mines, why not? But then, how can he leave his brother? He looks up at the fine fellow, who is now impatient, and showing it; he looks at the black men in the back of the lorry. He sees one of these men shake his head at him as if in warning. But others are laughing. It seems to Jabavu that it is a cruel laughter, and suddenly he gets to his feet, hands the paper back to the fine fellow and says: 'My brother and I travel together. Also you try to cheat me. Why did you not tell me this lorry was for the mines?'

And now the fine fellow is very angry. His white teeth are hidden behind a closed mouth. His eyes flash. 'You ignorant nigger,' he says, 'You waste my time, you waste my bosses' time, I'll get the policeman to you!' He takes a big step forward and his fists are raised. Jabavu and his brother turn as if their four legs were on a single body, and they rush off into the trees. As they go they hear a roar of laughter from the men on the lorry, and they see the fine fellow going back to the lorry. He is very angry – the two brothers see that the men are laughing at him, and not at them, and they crouch in the bushes, well hidden, thinking about the meaning of these things. When the lorry has sped off into its dust, Jabavu says: 'He called us nigger, and yet his skin is like ours. That is not easy to understand.'

Pavu speaks for the first time: 'He said I was not strong enough for the work!' Jabavu looks at him in surprise. He sees that his brother is offended. 'I am fifteen years old, so the Native Commissioner has said, and for five years already I have been working for my father. And yet this man says I am not strong enough.' Jabavu sees that the fear and the anger in his brother are having a fight, and it is by no means certain which will win. He says: 'Did you understand, my brother, that this was a recruiter for the mines in Johannesburg?'

Pavu is silent. Yes, he understood it, but his pride is speaking too loudly to allow any other voice to be heard. Jabavu decides to say nothing. For his own thoughts are moving too fast. First he thinks: That was a fine fellow with his smart white clothes! Then he thinks: Am I mad to be thinking of the mines? For this city we are going to is hard and dangerous, yet it is small in comparison with Johannesburg, or so the travellers tell us – and now my brother who has the heart of a chicken is so wounded in his pride that he is ready not only for the small city, but for Johannesburg!

The brothers linger under the bushes, though the road is empty. The sun comes from overhead and their stomachs begin to speak of food. They open the bundles their mother has made for them and find small, flat cakes of mealie-meal, baked in the ashes. They eat the cakes, and their stomachs are only half-silenced. They are a long way from proper food and the city, and yet they stay in the safety of the bushes. The sun has shifted so that it strikes on their right shoulders when they come out of the bushes. They walk slowly, and every time a lorry passes they turn their faces away as they walk through the grass at the edge of the road. Their faces are so firmly turned that it is a surprise to them when they understand that another lorry has stopped, and they peer cautiously around to see yet another fine fellow grinning at them.

'Want a nice job?' he says, smiling politely.

'We do not wish to go to the mines,' says Jabavu.

'Who said the mines?' laughs the man. 'Job in office, with pay seven pounds a month, perhaps ten, who knows?' His laughter is not the kind one may trust, and Jabavu's eyes lift from the beautiful black boots this dandy is wearing, and he is about to say 'no,' when Pavu asked, suddenly: 'And there is a job for me also?'

The fellow hesitates, and it is for as long as it would take him to say 'Yes' several times. Jabavu can see the pride strong on Pavu's face.

Then the fellow says: 'Yes, yes, there is a job for you also. In time you will grow to be as strong as your brother.' He is looking at Jabavu's shoulders and thick legs. He brings out a piece of paper and hands it to the brother, not to Jabavu. And Pavu is ashamed because he has never held a pencil and the paper feels light and difficult to him, and he clutches it between his fingers as if it might blow away. Jabavu is glowing with anger. It is he who should have been asked; he is the older, and the leader, and he can write. 'What is written on this paper?' he asks.

'The job is written on this paper,' says the fellow, as if it were of no importance.

'Before we put our names on the paper we shall see what this job is,' says Jabavu, and the fellow's eyes shift, and then he says: 'Your brother has already made his cross, so now you make your name also, otherwise you will be separated.' Jabavu looks at Pavu, who is smiling a half-proud, half-sickly smile, and he says softly: 'That was a foolish thing, my brother, the white man makes an important thing of such crosses.'

Pavu looks in fear at the paper where he has put his cross, and the fine fellow rocks on his feet with laughter and says: 'That is true. You have signed this paper, and so have agreed to work for two years at the mines, and if you do not it means a broken contract, and that is prison. 'And now' – this he says to Jabavu – 'you sign also, for we shall take your brother in the lorry, since he has signed the paper.'

Jabavu sees that the hand of the fine fellow is reaching out to grasp Pavu's shoulder. In one movement he butts his head into the fellow's stomach and pushes Pavu away, and then both turn and run. They run leaping through the bushes till they have run a long way. Fearful glances over their shoulders show that the fine fellow does not attempt to chase them, but stands looking after them, for the breath being shaken from his stomach has darkened his eyes. After a while they hear the lorry growl, then rumble, then purr into silence along the road.

Jabavu says, after a long long time of thinking: 'It is true that when our people go to the city they change so that their own family would not know them. That man, he who told us the lies, would he have been such a skellum in his own village?' Pavu does not reply, and Jabavu follows his thoughts until he begins to laugh. 'Yet we were cleverer than he was!' he says, and as he remembers how he butted his head into the fine fellow's stomach he rolls on the ground with laughing. Then he sits up again – for Pavu is not laughing, and on his face is a look that Jabavu knows well. Pavu is still so frightened that he is trembling all over, and his face is turned away so that Jabavu may not see it. Jabavu speaks to him as gently as a young man to a girl. But Pavu has had enough. It is in his mind to go back home, and Jabavu knows it. He pleads until the darkness comes filtering through the trees and they must find a place to sleep. They do not know this part of the country, it is more than six hours walking from home. They do not like to sleep in the open where the light of their fire might be seen, but they find some big rocks with a cleft between, and here they build a fire and light it as their fathers did before them, and they lie down to sleep, cold because of the naked shoulders and legs, very hungry, and no prospect of waking to a meal of good, warm porridge. Jabavu falls asleep thinking that when they wake in the morning with the sun falling kindly through the trees, Pavu will have regained his courage and forgotten the recruiter. But when he wakes, Jabavu is alone. Pavu has run away very early, as soon as the light showed, as much afraid of Jabavu the Big Mouth's clever tongue as he is of the recruiters. By now he will have run half-way back along the road home. Jabavu is so angry that he flings stones at the trees, calling the trees Pavu. He is so angry that he exhausts himself with dancing and shouting, and finally he quietens and wonders whether he should run after his brother and make him turn around. Then he says to himself it is too late, and that anyway Pavu is nothing but a frightened child and no help to a brave man like himself. For a moment he thinks that he too will return home, because of his very great fear of going on to the city alone. And then he decides to go alone, and immediately: he, Jabavu, is afraid of nothing.

And yet it is not so easy to leave the sheltering trees and take the road. He lingers there, encouraging himself, saying that yesterday he outwitted the recruiters when so many fail. I am Jabavu, he says, I am Jabavu, who is too clever for the tricks of bad white men and bad black men. He thumps himself on the chest. He dances a little, kicking up the leaves and grass until they make a little whirlpool around him. 'I am Jabavu, the Big Mouth. . . .' It turns into a song.

> Here is Jabavu,
> Here is the Big Mouth of the clever true words.
> I am coming to the city,

To the big city of the white man.
I walk alone, hau! hau!
I fear no recruiter,
I trust no one, not even my brother.
I am Jabavu, who goes alone.

And with this he leaves the bush and takes the road, and when he hears a lorry he runs into the bush and waits until it has gone past.

Because he has so often to hide in the bush his progress is very slow, and when the sun turns red that evening he has still not reached the city. Perhaps he has taken the wrong road? He does not dare ask anyone. If someone walks along the road and greets him he remains silent, for fear of a trap. He is so hungry that it can no longer be called hunger. His stomach has got tired of speaking to him of its emptiness and has become silent and sulky, while his legs tremble as if the bones inside have gone soft, and his head is big and light as if a wind has got into it. He creeps off into the bush to look for roots and leaves, and he gnaws at them while his stomach mutters: Eh, Jabavu! So you offer me leaves after so long a fasting? Then he crouches under a tree, his head lowered, hands dangling limp, and for the first time his fear of what he might find in the big city goes through him again and again like a spear and he wishes he has not left home. Pavu will be sitting by the fire now, eating the evening meal. ... The dusk settles, the trees first loom huge and black, then settle into general darkness, and from quite close Jabavu sees a glow of fire. Caution stiffens his limbs. Then he drags himself to his feet and walks towards the fire as carefully as if he were stalking a hare. From a safe distance he kneels to peer through the leaves at the fire. Three people, two men and a woman sit by it, and they are eating. Jabavu's mouth fills with water like a tin standing in heavy rain. He spits. His heart is hammering at him: Trust no one, trust no one! Then his hunger yawns inside him and he thinks: With us it has always been that a traveller may ask for hospitality at a fire – it cannot be that everyone has become cold and unfriendly. He steps forward, his hunger pushing him, his fear dragging him back. When the three people see him they stiffen and stare and speak together, and Jabavu understands that they are afraid he comes for harm. Then they look at his torn trousers – no longer so tight on him now, and they greet him kindly, as one from the villages. Jabavu returns the greetings and pleads: 'My brothers, I am very hungry.'

The woman at once lays out for him some white, flat cakes, and some pieces of yellowish substance, which Jabavu eats like a hungry dog, and they tell him this is food from the city, he has eaten fish and buns. Jabavu now looks at them and sees that they are dressed well, they wear shoes – even the woman – they have proper shirts and trousers and the woman has a red dress with a yellow crocheted cap on her head. For a moment the fear returns: These are people from the city, perhaps skellums? His muscles tense, his eyes glare, but they speak to him, laughing, telling him they are respectable people. Jabavu is silent, for he is wondering why they travel on foot like village people, instead of by train or lorry service, as is usual for city people. Also, he is annoyed that they have so quickly understood what he is thinking. But his pride is soothed when they say: 'When people from the villages first come to the city they see a skellum in every person. But that is much wiser than trusting everyone. You do well to be cautious.'

They pack away what food is left in a square, brown case that has a shiny metal clasp. Jabavu is fascinated to see how it works, and asks if he may also move the clasp, and they smile and say he may. Then they pile more wood on the fire and they talk quietly while Jabavu listens. What they say is only half-understood by him. They are speaking of the city and of the white man, not as do the people of the villages, with voices that are sad, admiring, fearful. Nor do they speak as Jabavu feels, as of a road to an exciting new country where everything is possible. No, they measure their words, and there is a quiet bitterness that hurts Jabavu, for it says to him: What a fool you are with your big hopes and dreams.

He understands that the woman is wife to one of the men, Mr. Samu, and sister to the other. This woman is like no woman he has met or heard about. When he tried to measure her difference he cannot, because of his inexperience. She wears smart clothes, but she is not a coquette, as he has heard are all the women of the towns. She is young and newly married, but she is serious and speaks as if what she says is as important as what the men say, and she does not use words like Jabavu's mother: Yes, my husband, that is true, my husband, no, my husband. She is a nurse at the hospital for women in the location at the city, and Jabavu's eyes grow big when he hears it. She is educated! She can read and write! She understands the medicine of the white man! And Mr. Samu and the other are also educated. They can read, not only words like yes, no, good, bad, black and white, but also long words like regulation and document. As they talk, words such as these fill their mouths, and Jabavu decides he will ask them what mean the words on the paper in his bundle which he has marked with charcoal. But he is ashamed to ask, and continues to listen. It is Mr. Samu who speaks most, but it is all so difficult that Jabavu's brain grows heavy and he pokes the edges of the fire with a green twig, listening to the sizzle of the sap, watching the sparks snap up and fade into the dark. The stars are still and brilliant overhead. Jabavu thinks, sleepily, that the stars perhaps are the sparks from all the fires people make – they drift up and up until they come against the sky and there they must remain like flies crowding together looking for a way out. . . .

He shakes himself awake and gabbles: 'Sir, will you explain to me . . .' He has taken the folded, stained piece of paper from his pocket and, kneeling, spreads it before Mr. Samu, who has stopped talking and is perhaps a little cross at being interrupted so irreverently.

He reads the difficult words. He looks at Jabavu. Then, before explaining, he asks questions. How did Jabavu learn to read? Was he all by himself? He was? Why did he want to read and write? What does he think of what he reads? – Jabavu answers clumsily, afraid of the laughter of these clever people. They do not laugh. They lean on their elbows looking at him, and their eyes are soft. He tells of the torn alphabet, how he finished the alphabet himself, how he learned the words that explained the pictures, and finally the words that are by themselves without pictures. As he speaks, his tongue slips into English, out of sympathy with what he is saying, and he tells of the hours and weeks and months of years he has spent, beneath the big tree, teaching himself, wondering, asking questions.

The three clever people look at each other, and their eyes say something Jabavu does not at once understand. And then Mrs. Samu leans forward and explains what the difficult sentence means, very patiently, in simple words, and also how the newspapers are, some for white people, some for black. She explains about the story of the little yellow people, and how wicked a story it is – and it seems to Jabavu that he learns more in a few minutes from this woman about the world he lives in, than he has in all his life. He wants to say to her: Stop, let me think about what you have said, or I shall forget it. But now Mr. Samu interrupts, leaning forward, speaking to Jabavu. After some moments of talking, it seems to Jabavu that Mr. Samu sees not only him, but many other people – his voice has lifted and grown strong, and his sentences swing up and down, as if they have been made often before, and in exactly the same way. So strong is this feeling that Jabavu looks over his shoulder to see if perhaps there are people behind him, but no, there is nothing but darkness and the trees showing a glint of starlight on their leaves.

'This is a sad and terrible time for the people of Africa,' Mr. Samu is saying. 'The white man has settled like a locust over Africa and, like the locusts in early morning, cannot take flight for the heaviness of the dew on their wings. But the dew that weights the white man is the money that he makes from our labour. The white man is stupid and clever, brave or cowardly, kind or cruel, but all, all say one thing, if they say it in different ways. They may say that the black man has been chosen by God to serve as a drawer of water and a hewer of wood until the end of time; they may say that the white man protects the black from his own ignorance until that ignorance is lightened; two hundred years, five hundred, or a thousand – he will only be allowed free when he has learned to stand on his two feet like a child who lets go his mother's skirts. But whatever they say, their actions are the same. They take us, men and women, into their houses to cook, clean, and tend their children; into their factories and mines; their lives are built on our work, and yet every day and every hour of every day they insult us, call us pigs and kaffirs or children, lazy, stupid and ignorant. Their ugly names for us are as many as leaves on that tree, and every day the white people grow more rich and the black more poor. Truly it is an evil time, and many of our people become evil, they learn to steal and to murder, they learn the ways of easy hatred, they become the pigs the white man says they are. And yet, though it is a terrible time, we should be proud that we live now, for our children and the children of our children will look back and say: 'If it were not for them, those people who lived in the terrible time, and lived with courage and wisdom, our lives would be the lives of slaves. We are free because of them.'

The first part of his speech Jabavu has understood very well, for he has often heard it before. So does his father speak, so all the travellers who come from the city. He was born with such words in his ears. But now they are becoming difficult. In a different tone does the voice of Mr. Samu continue, his hand is lifting and falling, he says trade union, organization, politics, committee, reaction, progress, society, patience, education. And as each new and heavy word enters Jabavu's mind he grabs at it, clutches it, examines it, tries to understand – and by that time a dozen such words have flown past his ears, and he is lost in bewilderment. He looks dazedly at Mr. Samu, who is leaning forward, that hand rising and falling, his steady, intent eyes fixed on his own, and it seems to him that those eyes sink into him, searching for his secret thoughts. He turns his own away, for he wishes them to remain secret. In the kraal I was always hungry, always waiting for when I would reach the plenty of the white man's town. All my life my body has been speaking with the voices of hunger: I want, I want, I want. I want excitement and clothes and food, such as the fish and buns I have eaten tonight; I want a bicycle and the women of the town; I want, I want ... And if I listen to these clever people, straight away my life will be bound to theirs, and it will not be dancing and music and clothes and food, but work, work, work, and trouble, danger and fear. For Jabavu has only just understood that these people travel so, at night, through the bush on foot, because they are going to another town with books, which speak of such matters as committees and organizations, and these books are not liked by the police.

These clever people, rich people, good people, with clothes on their bodies and nice food in their bellies, travel like village natives on foot – the hunger in Jabavu rises and says in a loud voice: No, not for Jabavu.

Mr. Samu sees his face and stops. Mrs. Samu says, pleasantly: 'My husband is so used to making speeches that he cannot stop himself.' The three laugh, and Jabavu laughs with them. Then Mr. Samu says it is very late and they should sleep. But first he writes on a piece of paper and gives it to Jabavu, saying: 'I have written here the name of a friend of mine, Mr. Mizi, who will help you when you reach the city. He will be very impressed when you tell him you learned to read and write all by yourself in the kraal.' Jabavu thanks him and puts the paper in his bundle, and then they all four lie around the fire to sleep. The others have blankets. Jabavu is cold, and the flesh of his chest and back is tight with shivering. Even his bones seem to shiver. The lids of his eyes, weighted with sleep, fly open in protest at the cold. He puts more wood on the fire and then looks at the shape of the woman huddled under her blanket. He suddenly desires her. That's a silly woman, he thinks. She needs a man like me, not a man who talks only. But he does not believe in this thought, and when the woman moves he hastily turns his eyes away in case she sees what is in them and is angry. He looks at the brown suitcase on the other side of the fire, lying on the grass. The metal clasp glints and glimmers in the flickering red glow. It dazzles Jabavu. His lids sink. He is asleep. He dreams.

Jabavu is a policeman in a fine uniform with bright brass buttons. He walks down the road swinging a whip. He sees the three ahead of him, the woman carrying the suitcase. He runs after them, catches the woman by the shoulder and says: 'So, you have stolen that suitcase. Open it, let me see what is inside.' She is very frightened. The other two men have run away. She opens the suitcase. Inside are buns and fish, and a big black book with the name *Jabavu* written on it, Jabavu says: 'You have stolen my book. You are a thief.' He takes her to the Native Commissioner who punishes her.

Jabavu wakes. The fire has sunk low, a heap of grey with red glimmering beneath. The clasp of the suitcase no longer shines. Jabavu crawls on his belly through the grass until he reaches the suitcase. He lays his hand on it, looks around. No one has moved. He lifts it, rises soundlessly to his feet and steals away down the path into the dark. Then he runs. But he does not run far. He stops, for it is very dark and he is afraid of the dark. He asks himself suddenly: Jabavu, why have you stolen this case? They are good people who wish only to help you and they gave you food when you were sick with hunger. But his hand tightens on the case as if it spoke a different language. He stands motionless in the dark, his whole being clamorous with desire for the suitcase, while small, frightened thoughts go through his mind. It will be four or five hours before the sun comes, and all that time he will be alone in the bush. He shivers with terror. Soon his body is clenched in cold and fear. He wishes he still lies beside the fire, he wishes he never touched the case. Kneeling in the dark, his knees painful on rough grass, he opens the case and feels inside it. There are the soft, damp shapes of food, and the hard shapes of books. It is too dark to see, he can only feel. For a long time he kneels there. Then he fastens the case and creeps back until he can see the faint glow of the fire and three bodies, quite still. He moves like a wild cat across the ground, lays the case down where it was, and then lies down himself. 'Jabavu is not a thief,' he says, proudly. 'Jabavu is a good boy.' He sleeps and dreams, but he does not know what he dreams, and wakes suddenly, alert, as if there were an enemy close by. A grey light is struggling through the trees, showing a heap of grey ashes and the three sleepers. Jabavu's body is aching with cold, and his skin is rough like soil. He slowly rises, remains poised for a moment in the attitude of a runner about to take the first great leap. The hunger in him is now saying: 'Get away Jabavu, quickly, before you too become like these, and live in terror of the police.' He springs away through the bushs with big, flying leaps, and the dew soaks him in clinging cold. He runs until he has reached the road, which is deserted because it is so early. Then, when the first cars and lorries come, much later, he moves a little way into the bush beside the road, and so travels out of sight. Today he will reach the city. Each time he climbs a rise he looks for it: surely it must appear, a bright dream of richness over the hill! And towards the middle of the morning he sees a house. Then another house. The houses continue, scattered, at small distances, for half an hour's walking. Then he climbs a rise, and down the other side of it he sees – but Jabavu stands still and his mouth falls open.

Ah, but it is beautiful, how beautiful is the city of the white man! Look how the houses run in patterns, the smooth grey streets making patterns between them like the marks of a clever finger. See how the houses rise, white and coloured, the sun shining on them so that they dazzle. And see how big they are, why, the house of the Greek is the house of a dog compared with them. Here the houses rise as if three or four were on top of each other, and gardens lie around each with flowers of red and purple and gold, and in the gardens are stretches of water, gleaming dark, and on the water flowers are floating. And see how this city stretches down the valley and even up the other side! Jabavu walks on, his feet putting themselves down one after the other with no help from his eyes, so that he goes straying this way and that until there is a shriek of warning from a car, and once again he leaps aside and stands staring, but now there is no dust, only smooth, warm asphalt. He walks on slowly, down the slope, up the other side, and then he reaches the top of the next rise, and now he stands for a long time. For the houses continue as far as he can see in front of him, and also to either side. There is no end to the houses. A new feeling has come into him. He does not say he is afraid, but his stomach is heavy and cold. He thinks of the village, and Jabavu, who has longed for so many years for just this moment, believing he has no part in the village, now hears it saying softly to him: Jabavu, Jabavu, I made you, you belong to me, what will you do in this great and bewildering city that must surely be greater than every other city. For by now he has forgotten that this is nothing compared with Johannesburg and other cities in the South, or rather, he does not dare to remember it, it is too frightening.

The houses are now of different kinds, some big, some

as flimsy as the house of the Greek. There are different kinds of white men, says Jabavu's brain slowly, but it is a hard idea to absorb all at once. He has thought of them, until now, as all equally rich, powerful, clever.

Jabavu says to his feet: Now walk on, walk. But his feet do not obey him. He stands there while his eyes move over the streets of houses, and they are the eyes of a small child. And then there is a slurring sound, wheels of rubber slowing, and beside him is an African policeman on a bicycle. He rests one foot on the road and looks at Jabavu. He looks at the old, torn trousers and at the unhappy face. He says, kindly: 'Have you lost your way?' He speaks in English.

At first Jabavu says no, because even at this moment it goes against the grain not to know everything. Then he says sullenly: 'Yes, I do not know where to go.'

'And you are looking for work?'

'Yes, son of the Government, I seek work.' He speaks in his own language, the policeman, who is from another district, does not understand, and Jabavu speaks again in English.

'Then you must go to the office for passes and get a pass to seek work.'

'And where is this office?'

The policeman gets off his bicycle and, taking Jabavu's arm, speaks to him a long time, thus: 'Now you must go straight on for half a mile, and then where the five roads meet turn left, and then turn again and go straight on and ...' Jabavu listens and nods and says Yes and Thank you, and the policeman bicycles away and Jabavu stands helplessly, for he has not understood. And then he walks on, and he does not know whether his legs tremble from fear or from hunger. When he met the policeman, the sun came from behind on his back, and when his legs stop of their own accord from weakness, the sun is overhead. The houses are all around him, and white women sit on the verandahs with their children, and black men work in the gardens, and he sees more in the sanitary lanes talking and laughing. Sometimes he understands what they say, and sometimes not. For in this city are people from Nyasaland and from Northern Rhodesia and from the country of the Portuguese, and not one word of their speech does he know, and he fears them. But when he hears his own tongue he knows that these people point at his torn trousers and his bundle, and laugh, saying: 'Look at that raw boy from the kraal.'

He stands where two streets cross, looking this way and that way. He has no idea where the policeman told him to go. He walks on a little, then sees a bicycle leaning against a tree. There is a basket at the back, and in it are loaves of bread and buns, such as he has eaten the night before. He looks at them, while his mouth fills with water. Suddenly his hand reaches out and takes a bun. He looks around. No one has seen. He puts the bun in his pocket and moves away. When he has left that street behind, he takes it out and walks along eating the bun. But when it is finished his stomach seems to say: What, one small bun after being empty all morning! Better that you give me nothing!

Jabavu walks on, looking for another basket on a bicycle. Several times he turns up a street after one that looks the same but is not. It is a long time before he finds what he wants. And now it is not easy as before. Then his hand went out by itself and took the bun, while now his mind is warning him: Be careful, Jabavu, careful! He is standing near the basket, looking around, when a white woman in her garden shouts at him over the hedge, and he runs until he has turned a corner and is in another street. There he leans against a tree, trembling. It is a narrow street, full of trees, quiet and shady. He can see no one. Then a nanny comes out of a house with her arms full of clothes, and she hangs them on a line, looking over the hedge at Jabavu. 'Hi, kraal boy, what do you want?' she shouts at him, laughing; 'look at that stupid kraal boy.' 'I am not a kraal boy,' he says, sullenly, and she says: 'Look at your trousers – ohhhhh, what can I see there!' and she goes inside, looking scornful. Jabavu remains leaning against a tree, looking at his trousers. It is true that they are nearly falling off him. But they are still decent.

There is nothing to be seen. The street seems empty. Jabavu looks at the clothes hanging on the line. There are many: dresses, shirts, trousers, vests. He thinks: That girl was cheeky ... he is shocked at what she said. Again he clasps his elbows, crouching, around his hips to cover his trousers. His eyes are on the clothes – then Jabavu has leaped over the hedge and is tugging at a pair of trousers. They will not come off the line, there is a little wooden stick holding them. He pulls, the stick falls off, he holds the trousers. They are hot and smooth, they have just been ironed. He pulls at a yellow shirt, the cloth tears under the wooden peg, but it comes free, and in a moment he has leaped back over the hedge and is running. At the turn of the street he glances back; the garden is quiet and empty, it appears no one has seen him. Jabavu walks soberly along the street, feeling the fine warm cloth of the shirt and trousers. His heart is beating, first like a small chicken tottering as it comes out of the shell, then, as it strengthens, like a strong wind banging against a wall. The violence of his heart exhausts Jabavu and he leans against a tree to rest. A policeman comes slowly past on a bicycle. He looks at Jabavu. Then he looks again, makes a wide circle and comes to rest beside him. Jabavu says nothing, he only stares.

'Where did you get those clothes?' asks the policeman.

Jabavu's brain whirls and from his mouth come words: 'I carry them for my master.'

The policeman looks at Jabavu's torn shorts and his bundle. 'Where does your master live?' he asks cunningly. Jabavu points ahead. The policeman looks where Jabavu is pointing and then at Jabavu's face. 'What is the number of your master's house?'

Again Jabavu's brain faints and comes to life. 'Number three,' he says.

'And what is the name of the street?'

And now nothing comes from Jabavu's tongue. The policeman is getting off his bicycle in order to look at Jabavu's papers, when suddenly there is a commotion in the street which Jabavu has come from. The theft has been discovered. There are voices scolding, high and shrill, it is the white mistress telling the nanny to fetch the missing clothes, the nanny is crying, and there is the word police repeated many times. The policeman hesitates, looks at Jabavu, looks back at the other street, and then Jabavu remembers the recruiter. He butts his head into the policeman's stomach, the bicycle falls over on top of him, and, Jabavu leaps away and into a sanitary lane, vaults over a rubbish bin, then another, darts across a garden which is empty, then over another which is not, so that people start up and stare at him, then over into another sanitary lane and comes to rest between a rubbish bin and the wall of a lavatory. There he quickly pulls off his shorts, pulls on the trousers. They are long, grey, of fine stuff such as he has never seen. He pulls on the yellow shirt, but it is difficult, since he has never worn one, and it gets caught around the arms before he discovers the right hole in which to put his head. He stuffs the shirt, which is too small for him, inside the trousers, which are a little too long, thinking sadly of the hole in the shirt, which is due entirely to his ignorance about those little wooden pegs. He quickly pushes the torn shorts under the lid of a rubbish bin and walks up the sanitary lane, careful not to run, although his feet are itching to run. He walks until that part of the city is well left behind, and then he thinks: Now I am safe; with so many people no one will notice grey trousers and a yellow shirt. He remembers how the policeman looked at the bundle, and he puts the soap and the comb into his pockets, together with the papers, and stuffs the rag of the bundle under the low branches of a hedge. And now he is thinking: I came to this city only this morning and already I have grey trousers like a white man, and a yellow shirt, and I have eaten a bun. I have not spent the shilling my mother gave me. Truly it is possible to live well in the white man's town! And he lovingly handles the hard shape of the shilling. At this moment, for no reason that he understands, comes into his head a memory of the three he met last night, and suddenly Jabavu is muttering Skellums! Bad people! Damn, hell, bloody. For these are words he knows of the white people's swearing, and he thinks them very wicked. He says them again and again, till he feels like a big man, and not like the little boy at whom his mother used to look, saying sorrowfully: Ah, Jabavu, my Big Mouth, what white man's devil has got into you!

Jabavu swaggers himself into such a condition of pride that when a policeman stops him and asks for his pass, Jabavu cannot at once stop swaggering, but says haughtily: 'I am Jabavu.'

'So you are Jabavu,' says the policeman, at once getting

in front of him. 'So, my fine clever boy. And who is Jabavu and where is his pass?'

The madness of pride sinks in Jabavu, and he says humbly: 'I have no pass yet. I have come to seek work.'

But the policeman looks more suspicious than ever. Jabavu wears very fine clothes, although there is one small rent in the shirt, and he speaks good English. How then can he have just arrived from the kraals? So he looks at Jabavu's situpa, which is the paper that every African native must carry all the time, and he reads: Native Jabavu. District so and so. Kraal so and so. Registration Certificate No. X078910312. He copies this down in a little book, and gives the situpa to Jabavu saying: 'Now I shall tell you the way to the Pass Office, and if by this time tomorrow you have no pass to seek work, then there will be big trouble for you.' He goes away.

Jabavu follows the streets which have been shown to him and soon he comes to a poor part of the town, full of houses like that of the Greek, and in them are people of half-colour, such as he has heard about but never seen, who are called in this country the Coloured People. And soon he comes to a big building, which is the Pass Office, with many black people waiting in long files that lead to windows and doors in the building. Jabavu joins one of these files, thinking that they are like cattle waiting to enter the dip, and then he waits. The file moves very slowly. The man in front of him and the woman behind him do not understand his questions, until he speaks in English, and then he finds he is in the wrong file and must go to another. And now he goes politely to a policeman who is standing by to see there is no trouble or fighting, and he asks for help and is put in the right queue. And now he waits again, and because he must stand, without moving, he has time to hear the voices of his hunger, and particularly the hunger of his stomach, and soon it seems as if darkness and bright light are moving like shifting water across his brain, and his stomach says again that since he left home, three days ago, he has eaten very little, and Jabavu tries to quieten the pain in his stomach by saying I shall eat soon, I shall eat soon, but the light swirls violently across his eyes, is swallowed by heavy, nauseating blackness, and then he finds he is lying on a cold, hard floor, and there are faces bending over him, some white, some dark.

He has fainted and has been carried inside the Pass Office. The faces are kind, but Jabavu is terrified and scrambles to his feet. Arms support him, and he is helped into an inner room, which is where he must wait to be examined by a doctor before he may receive a pass to seek work. There are many other Africans there, and they have no clothes on at all. He is told to take off his clothes, and everyone turns to look at him, amazed, because he clutches his arms across his chest, protecting the clothes, imagining they will be taken from him. His eyes roll in despair, and it is some time before he understands and takes them off and waits, naked, in a line with the others. He is cold because of his hunger, although outside the sun is at its hottest. One after another the Africans go up to be examined and the doctor puts a long, black thing to their chests and handles their bodies. Jabavu's whole being is crying out in protest, and there are many voices. One says: Am I an ox to be handled as that white doctor handles us? Another says, anxiously: If I had not been told that the white men have many strange and wonderful things in their medicine I would think that black thing he listens through is witchcraft. And the voice of his stomach says again and again, not at all discouraged, that he is hungry and will faint again soon if food does not come.

At last Jabavu reaches the doctor, who listens to his chest, taps him, looks in his throat and eyes and armpits and groin, and peers at the secret parts of Jabavu's body in a way that makes anger mutter in him like thunder. He wishes to kill the white doctor for touching him and looking at him so. But there is also a growing patience in him, which is the first gift of the white man's city to the black man. It is patience against anger. And when the doctor has said that Jabavu is strong as an ox and fit for work, he may go. The doctor has said, too, that Jabavu has an enlarged spleen, which means he has had malaria and will have it again, that he probably has bilharzia, and there is a suspicion of hookworm. But these are too common for comment, and what the doctor is looking for are diseases which may infect the white people if he works in their houses.

Then the doctor, as Jabavu is turning away, asks him why the blackness came into him so that he fell down, and Jabavu says simply that he is hungry. At this a policeman comes forward and asks why he is hungry. Jabavu says because he has had nothing to eat. At this the policeman says impatiently: 'Yes, yes, but have you no money?' – for if not, Jabavu will be sent to a camp where he will get a meal and shelter for that night. But Jabavu says Yes, he has a shilling. 'Then why do you not buy food?' 'Because I must keep the shilling to buy what I need.' 'And do you not need food?'

People are laughing because a man who has a shilling in his pocket allows himself to fall down to the ground with hunger, but Jabavu remains silent.

'And now you must leave here and buy yourself some food and eat it. Have you a place to sleep tonight?'

'Yes,' says Jabavu, who is afraid of this question.

The policeman then gives Jabavu a pass that allows him to seek work for a fortnight. Jabavu has put back his clothes, and now he takes from the pocket the roll of papers that includes his situpa, in order to put the new pass with them. And as he fumbles with them a piece of paper flutters to the floor. The policeman quickly bends down, picks it up and looks at it. On it is written: Mr. Mizi, No. 33 Tree Road, Native Township. The policeman looks with suspicion at Jabavu. 'So Mr. Mizi is a friend of yours?'

'No,' says Jabavu.

'Then why have you a piece of paper with his name on it?'

Jabavu's tongue is locked. After another question he mutters: 'I do not know.'

'So you do not know why you have that piece of paper? You know nothing of Mr. Mizi?' The policeman continues to make such sarcastic questions, and Jabavu lowers his eyes and waits patiently for him to stop. The policeman takes out a little book, makes a long note about Jabavu, tells him that it would be wise for him to go to the camp for people newly come to town. Jabavu again refuses, repeating that he has friends with whom to sleep. The policeman says Yes, he can see what his friends are – a remark which Jabavu does not understand – and so at last he is free to leave.

Jabavu walks away from the Pass Office, very happy because of this new pass which allows him to stay in the city.

He does not suspect that the first policeman who took his name will hand it in to the office whose business it is, saying that Jabavu is probably a thief, and that the policeman in the Pass Office will give his name and number as a man who is a friend of the dangerous agitator Mr. Mizi. Yes, Jabavu is already well-known in this city after half a day, and yet as he walks out into the street he feels as lost and lonely as an ox that has strayed from the herd. He stands at a corner watching the crowds of Africans streaming along the roads to the Native Township, on foot and on bicycle, talking, laughing, singing. Jabavu thinks he will go and find Mr. Mizi. And so he joins the crowds, walking very slowly because of the many new things there are to see. He stares at everything, particularly at the girls, who seem to him unbelievably beautiful in their smart dresses, and after a time he feels as if one of them is looking at him. But there are so many of them that he cannot keep any particular one in his mind. And in fact many are gazing at him, because he is very handsome in his fine yellow shirt and new trousers. Some even call out to him, but he cannot believe it is meant for him, and looks away.

After some time, he becomes certain that there is one girl who has walked past him, then come back, and is now walking past him again. He is certain because of her dress. It is bright yellow with big red flowers on it. He stares around him and can see no other dress like it, so it must be the same girl. For the third time she saunters by, close on the pavement, and he sees she has smart green shoes on her feet and wears a crocheted cap of pink wool, and she carries a handbag like a white woman. He is shy, looking at his smart girl, yet she is giving him glances he cannot mistake. He asks himself, distrustfully: Should I talk to her? Yet everyone says how immodest are these women of the towns, I should wait until I understand how to behave with her. Shall I smile, so that she will come to me? But the smile will not come to his face. Does she like me? The hunger rises in Jabavu and his eyes go dark. But she will want money and I have only one shilling.

The girl is now walking beside him at the distance of a stretched arm. She asks softly: 'Do you like me, handsome, yes?' It is in English, and he replies: 'Yes, very much I like.'

'Then why do you frown and look so cross?'

'I do not,' says Jabavu.

'Where do you live?' – and now she is so close he can feel her dress touching him.

'I do not know,' he says, abashed.

At this she laughs and laughs, rolling her eyes about: 'You are a funny, clever man, yes that's true!' And she laughs some more, in a loud, hard way that surprises him, for it does not sound like laughter.

'Where can I find a place to sleep, for I do not wish to go to the camp run by the Native Commissioner,' he asks politely, breaking into the laughter, and she stops and looks at him in real surprise.

'You are from the country?' she asks, after a long time, looking at his clothes.

'I came today from my village, I have got a pass for looking for work, I am very hungry and I know nothing,' he says, his voice falling into a humble tone, which annoys him, for he wishes to act the big man with this girl, and now he is speaking like a child. Anger at himself makes a small, feeble movement and then lies quiet: he is too hungry and lost. As for her, she has moved away to the edge of the pavement, and there walks in silence, frowning. Then she says: 'Did you learn to speak English at a mission?'

'No,' says Jabavu, 'in my kraal.'

Again she is silent. She does not believe him. 'And where did you get that fine smart shirt and the white-man trousers just like new?'

Jabavu hesitates, then with a swagger says: 'I took them this morning from a garden as I went past.'

And now again the girl laughs, rolls her eyes, and says: 'Heh, heh, what a clever boy, he comes straight from the kraal and steals so clever!' At once she stops laughing, for she has said this to gain time; she has not believed him. She walks on, thinking. She is a member of a gang who look out for such raw country boys, steal from them, make use of them as is necessary for their work. But she spoke to him because she liked him – it was a holiday from her work. But now what should she do? For it seems that Jabavu is a member of another gang, or perhaps works by himself, and if so, her own gang should know about it,

Another glance at him shows her that he walks along with a serious face, apparently indifferent to her – she goes up to him swiftly, eyes flashing, teeth showing: 'You lie! You tell me big lie, that's the truth!'

Jabavu shrinks away – hau! but what women these are! 'I do not lie,' he says, angrily. 'It is as I have said.' And he begins to walk away from her, thinking: I was a fool to speak to her, I do not understand the ways of these girls.

And she, watching him, notices his feet, which are bare, and they have certainly never worn shoes – he is telling the truth. And in this case – she makes up her mind in a flash. A raw boy who can come to town, steal so cleverly without being caught, this is talent that can be turned to good use. She goes after him, says politely: 'Tell me how you did the stealing, it was very cunning.'

And Jabavu's vanity spurs him to tell the story exactly as it happened, while she listens thoughtfully. 'You should not be wearing those clothes now,' she says at last. 'For the white missus will have told the police, and they will be watching the boys new to town in case they have the clothes.'

Jabavu asks in surprise: 'How can they find one pair of trousers and one shirt in a city full of shirts and trousers?'

She laughs and says: 'You know nothing, there are as many police watching us as flies around porridge; you come with me, I will take those clothes and give you others, as good as those, but different.' Jabavu thanks her politely but edges away. He has understood she is a thief. And he does not think of himself as a thief – he has stolen today, but he hardly gives it that name. Rather he feels as if he has helped himself to crumbs from the rich man's table. After a pause he inquires: 'Do you know Mr. Mizi, of 33 Tree Road?'

For the second time she is surprised into silence; then distrust fills her, and she thinks: This man either knows nothing at all or he is very cunning. She says, sarcastically, in the same tone that the policeman in the Pass Office used: 'You have fine friends. And how should I know a great man like Mr. Mizi?'

But Jabavu tells her of the encounter at night in the bush, of Mr. and Mrs. Samu and the other, of what they said, and how they admired him for learning to read and write by himself, and gave him Mr. Mizi's name.

At last this girl believes him, and understands, and she thinks: 'Certainly I must not let him slip away. He will be of great help in our work.' And there is another thought, even more powerful: Heh! but he is handsome. . . .

Jabavu asks, politely: 'And do you like these people, Mr. Samu and Mrs. Samu and Mr. Mizi?'

She laughs scornfully and with disappointment, for she wishes him only to think of her. 'You mad? You think I am mad too? Those people stupid. They call themselves leaders of the African people, they talk and talk, they write letters to the Government: Please Sir, Please. Give us food, give us houses, let us not carry passes all the time. And the Government throws them a shilling after years of asking and they say, Thank you, sir. They are fools.' And then she sidles up to him, lays her hand inside his elbow, and says: 'Besides, they are skellums – did you not see that? You come with me, I help you.'

Jabavu feels the warm hand inside his bare arm, and she swings her hips and makes her eyes soft. 'You like me, handsome?' And Jabavu says: 'Yes, very much,' and so they walk down the road to the Native Township and she talks of the fine things there are to do, of the films and the dances and the drinking. She is careful not to talk of the stealing or of the gang, in case he should be frightened. And there is another reason: there is a man who leads the gang who frightens her. She thinks: If this new clever man likes me, I will make him marry me, I will leave the gang and work with him alone.

Because her words are one thing and what she is thinking another, there is something in her manner that confuses Jabavu, and he does not trust her; besides, that dizziness is coming back in waves, and there are moments when he does not hear what she says.

'What is the matter?' she asks at last, when he stops and closes his eyes.

'I have told you that I am hungry,' he says out of the darkness around him.

'But you must be patient,' she says lightly, for it is such a long time since she has been hungry she has forgotten how

it feels. She becomes irritated when he walks slowly, and
even thinks: This man is no good, he's not strong for a
girl like me – and then she notices that Jabavu is staring at a
bicycle with a basket on the back, and as he is reaching out
his arm for the bread in the basket, she strikes down his
arm.

'You crazy?' she asks in a high, scared voice, glancing
around. For there are people all around them. 'I am hungry,'
he says again, staring at the loaves of bread. She quickly
takes some money from a place in front of her dress, gives
it to the vendor and hands a loaf of bread to Jabavu. He
begins to eat as he stands, so hungrily that people turn to
stare and laugh, and she gazes at him with shocked, big eyes
and says: 'You are a pig, not a smart boy for me.' And she
walks away ahead of him thinking: This is nothing but a
raw kraal boy, I am crazy to like him. But Jabavu does not
care at all. He eats the bread and feels the strength coming
back to him, and the thoughts begin to move properly
through his mind. When he has finished the bread he looks
for the girl, but all he can see is a yellow dress far down the
road, and the skirt of the dress is swinging in a way that
reminds him of the mockery of her words: You are a pig.
. . . Jabavu walks fast to catch her; he comes up beside her
and says: 'Thank you, my friend, for the bread. I was very
hungry.' She says, without looking around. 'Pig, dog without manners.' He says: 'No, that is not true. When a man is
so hungry, one cannot talk of manners.' 'Kraal boy,' she
says, swinging her hips, but thinking: 'It does no harm to
show him I know more than he does.' And then says Jabavu,
full of bread and new strength: 'You are nothing but a bitch
woman. There are many smart girls in this city, and as pretty
as you.' And with this he marches off ahead of her and is
looking around for another pretty girl when she runs up to
him.

'Where are you going?' she asks, smiling. 'Did I not say
I would help you?'

'You shall not call me kraal boy,' says Jabavu magnificently, and with real strength, since he truly does not care
for her more than the others he sees about him, and so she
gives him a quick, astonished look and is silent.

Now that Jabavu's stomach is filled he is looking around

him with interest again, and so he asks questions continually and she answers him pleasantly. 'What are these big houses with smoke coming out?' 'They are factories.' 'What is this place full of little bits of garden with crosses and stone shaped like children with wings?' 'It is the cemetery for the white people.' So, having walked a long way, they turn off the main road into the Native Township, and the first thing Jabavu notices is that while in the city of the white people the soil lies hidden under grass and gardens or asphalt, here it billows up in thick red clouds, gives the sun a dulled and sullen face, and makes the trees look as if a swarm of locusts had passed, so still and heavy with dust are they. Also, there are now such swarms of Africans all around him that he has to make himself strong, like a rock in the middle of a swift river. And still he asks questions, and is told that this big, empty place is for playing football, and this for wrestling, and then they come to the buildings. Now these are like the house of the Greek, small, ugly, bare. But there are very many, and close together. The girl strolls along calling out greetings in her high, shrill voice, and Jabavu notices that sometimes she is called Betty, sometimes Nada, sometimes Eliza. He asks: 'Why do you have so many names?' and she laughs and says: 'How do you know I am not many girls?' And now, and for the first time, he laughs as she does, high and hard, doubling up his body, for it seems to him a very good joke. Then he straightens and says: 'I shall call you Nada,' and she says quickly: 'My village name for a village boy!' At once he says: 'No, I like Betty,' and she presses her thigh against his and says: 'My good friends call me Betty.'

He says he wishes to see all this town now, before it grows dark, and she says it will not take long. 'The white man's town is very big and it takes many days to see it. But our town is small, though we are ten, twenty, a hundred times as many.' Then she adds: 'That is what they call justice,' and looks to see the effect of the word. But Jabavu remembers that when Mr. Samu used it it sounded different, and he frowns, and seeing his frown she leads him forward, talking of something else. For if he does not understand her, she understands that what the men of light – for this is how they are called – have said to Jabavu marked his mind deeply, and she thinks: If I am not careful he will go to Mr. Mizi and I will lose him and the gang will be very angry.

When they pass Mr. Mizi's house, number 33 Tree Road, she makes some rude jokes about him, but Jabavu is silent, and Betty thinks: Perhaps I should let him go to Mr. Mizi? For if he goes later, it may be dangerous. Yet she cannot bear to let him go, already her heart is soft and heavy for Jabavu. She leads him through the streets very kindly and politely, answering all his questions, though their foolishness often makes her impatient. She explains that the better houses, which have two rooms and a kitchen, are for the rich Africans, and the big, strangely-shaped houses are called Nissen huts, where twenty single men sleep, and these old shacks are called the Old Bricks, and they are for those who earn only a little, and this building here is the Hall, for meetings and dances. Then they reach a big open space which is filled with people. It is the market, and policemen are everywhere, walking with whips in their hands. Jabavu is thinking that one small loaf of bread, although it was white and fine to eat, was not much for a stomach as long empty as his, and he is looking at the various foodstuffs when Betty says: 'Wait, we shall eat better than this, later.' And Jabavu looks at the people who buy some groundnuts or a few cooked maize-cobs for their supper, and already feels superior to them because of what Betty says.

Soon she pulls him away, for she has lived so long here that she cannot find interest, as he does, in watching the people; and now they walk away from the centre and she says: 'Now we are going to Poland.' Her face is ready for laughter, Jabavu sees it is a joke and asks: 'And what is the joke in Poland?'

She says, quickly, before her laughter gets too strong: 'In the war of the white people that has just finished, there was a country called Poland, and there was a terrible fight, with many bombs, and so now we call where we are going Poland because of the fights and the trouble there.' She lets her laughter loose, but stops when she sees Jabavu stern and silent. He is thinking: I do not want fighting and trouble. Then she says in a little, foolish voice, like a child: 'And so now we are going to Johannesburg,' and he, not wanting to appear afraid, asks: 'What is the joke in this?' She says:

'This place is also called Johannesburg because there are fights and trouble in the township of Johannesburg.' And now she bends double with laughing, and Jabavu laughs from politeness. Then, seeing it is only politeness, she says, wishing to impress him, and with a big, important sigh: 'Ah, yes, these white people, they tell us: See how we have saved you from the wicked fighting of the tribes; we have brought you peace – and yet see how they make wars and kill so many people one cannot understand the numbers when they are written in the newspaper.' This she has heard Mr. Mizi say at a meeting; and when she notices that Jabavu is impressed, she goes on proudly: 'Yes, and that is what they call civilization!' At this Jabavu asks: 'I do not understand, what is civilization?' And she says, like a teacher: 'It is how the white men live, with houses and bioscope and cowboys and food and bicycles.' 'Then I like civilization,' says Jabavu, from the pulse of his deepest hunger, and Betty laughs amiably and says: 'Heh, but you are one big fool my friend, I like you.'

They are now in an evil-looking place where there are many tall brick shelters crowded together in rows, and shacks made of petrol tins beaten flat, or of sacks and boxes, and there is a foul smell. 'This is Poland Johannesburg,' says Betty, walking carefully in her nice shoes through the filth and ordure. And the staring and horrified eyes of Jabavu see a man lying huddled in the grass. 'Has he nowhere to sleep?' he asks, stupidly, but she pulls at his arm and says: 'Fool, leave him, he is sick with the drink.' For now he is on her territory, and afraid, she uses a more casual tone with him, she is his superior. Jabavu follows her, but his eyes cannot leave that man who looks as if he were dead. And his heart, as he follows Betty, is heavy and anxious. He does not like this place, he is scared.

But when they turn into a small house that stands a little by itself, he is reassured. The room they stand in is of bare red brick, with a bench around the walls and some chairs at one end. The floor is of red cement, and there are streamers of coloured paper festooned from nails in the rafters. There are two doors, and one of these opens and a woman appears. She is very fat, with a broad, shiny black face and small, quick eyes. She wears a white cloth bound round her head, and her dress is of clean, pink cotton. She holds a nice clean little boy by one hand. She looks in inquiry at Betty, who says: 'I am bringing Jabavu, my friend, to sleep here to-night.' The woman nods and gazes at Jabavu, who smiles at her. For he likes her, and thinks: 'This is a nice woman of the old kind, decent and respectable, and that is a nice little boy.'

He goes into a room off the big one with Betty, and it is as well he does not say what he is thinking, for it is probable that she would have given him up as a fool beyond teaching, for while it is true that this woman, Mrs. Kambusi, is kind in her way, and respectable in her way, it is also true that her cleverness has enabled her to run the most profitable she-been in the city for many years, and only once has she been taken to the courts, and that in the capacity of a witness. She has four children, by different fathers, and the three elder children have been sent by this wise and clever woman far away to Roman school where they will grow up educated with no knowledge of this place where the money comes for their schooling. And the little boy will be going next year also, before he is old enough to understand what Mrs. Kambusi does. Later she intends that the children will go to England and become doctors and lawyers. For she is very very rich.

The room where he stands makes Jabavu feel cramped and restless. It is so small that there is room for one narrow bed – a bed on legs, with a space around it for walking. Some dresses hang on a nail on the wall from wooden sticks. Betty sits on the bed and looks provocatively at Jabavu. But remains still, rolling his eyes at the low ceiling and the narrow walls, while he thinks: My fathers! But how can I live in boxes like a chicken!

Seeing his absence of mind, she says softly: 'Perhaps you would like to eat now?' and his eyes return to her and he says: 'Thanks, I am still very hungry.'

'I will tell Mrs. Kambusi,' she says, in a soft, meek voice that he does not altogether like, and goes out. After a little while she calls him to follow her, so he leaves the tiny room, crosses the big one, and goes through the second doorway into a room which makes him stare in admiration. It has a table with a real cloth on it, and many chairs around the table, and a big stove after the fashion of the white man. Never has Jabavu sat on a chair, but he does so now, and thinks: Soon, I too, will have such chairs for the comfort of my body.

Mrs. Kambusi is busy at the stove, and wonderful smells come from the pots on it. Betty puts knives and forks on the table, and Jabavu wonders how he will dare to use them without appearing ignorant. The little boy sits opposite and gazes with big, solemn eyes, and Jabavu feels inferior even to this child, who understands chairs and forks and knives.

When the food is ready, they eat. Jabavu makes his thick fingers handle the difficult knife and fork as he sees the others do, and his discomfort is soon forgotten in his delight at this delicious new food. There is fish again, which comes all the way from the big lakes in Nyasaland, and there are vegetables in a thick and savoury liquid, and there are sweet, soft cakes with pink sugar on them. Jabavu eats and eats until his stomach is heavy and comfortable, and then he sees that Mrs. Kambusi is watching him. 'You have been very hungry,' she observes pleasantly, speaking in his own tongue. It seems to Jabavu that he has not heard it for many months, instead of only three days, and he says gratefully: 'Ah, my friend, you are of my people.'

'I was,' says Mrs. Kambusi, with a smile that has a certain quality, and again discomfort fills him. There is a hardness in her, and yet the hardness is not meant as cruelty against him. Her eyes are quick and shrewd, like black sparks, and she says: 'Now I will give you a little lesson, listen. In the villages we may enter and greet our brothers, and take hospitality from them by right of blood and kinship. This is not the case here, and every man is a stranger until he has proved himself a friend. And every woman, too,' she adds, glancing at Betty.

'This I have heard, my mother,' says Jabavu, gratefully.

'What have I been telling you? I am not your mother.'

'And yet,' says Jabavu, 'I come to the city and who sets food before me but a woman from my own people?'

And changing to English she says, quietly: 'You will pay for your food, also, you come here as Betty's friend and not as my friend.'

Jabavu's spirits are chilled by this coldness, and because he has no money for the food. Then he sees again the clever eyes of this woman, and knows this is meant as kindness.

Speaking in their mutual tongue she continues: 'And now listen to me. This girl here, whose name I will not say so that she does not know we are speaking of her, has told me your story. She has told me of your meeting with the men of light in the bush at night, and how they took a liking to you and gave you the name of their friend here – I will not say the name, for the people who are friends of the girl who sits here trying to understand what we say do not like the men of light. You will understand why not when you have been in the city a little longer. But what I wish to tell you is this. It is probable that like most boys who come newly to the city you have many fine ideas about the life, and what you will do. Yet it is a hard life, much harder than you now know. My life has been hard, and still is, though I have done very well because I use my head. And if I were given the chance to begin again, knowing what I know now, I would not lightly throw away that piece of paper with the name written on it. It means a great deal to enter that house as a friend, to be the friend of that man – remember it.'

Jabavu listens, his eyes lowered. It seems that there are two different voices speaking inside him. One says: This is a woman of great experience, do as she says, she means you well. Another says: So! Here is another busybody giving you advice; an old woman who has forgotten the excitements of being young, who wishes you to be as quiet and sleepy as herself.

She continues, leaning forward, her eyes fixed on his: 'Now listen. When I heard you had fallen in with the men of light before you even entered the city, I asked myself what kind of good luck it was that you carry with you! And then I remembered that from their hands you had fallen into those which we now see lying on the table, twitching crossly because what we say is not understood. Your luck is very mixed my friend. And yet it is very powerful, for many thousands of our people enter this city and know nothing of either the men of light or the men of darkness – for whom this very bad girl sitting here works – save what they hear through other mouths. But since it has fallen out that you have a choice to make, I wish to tell you, speaking now as one of your own people, and as your mother, that you are a fool if you do not leave this girl and go immediately to the house whose number you know.'

She ceases speaking, rises, and says: 'And now we shall have some tea.' She pours out cups of very strong, sweet tea, and for the first time Jabavu tastes it, and it seems very good to him. He drinks it, keeping his eyes lowered for fear of seeing the eyes of Betty. For he can feel that she is angry. Also, he does not want Mrs. Kambusi to see what he is thinking, which is that he does not want to leave Betty – later, perhaps, not at once. For now that his body is fed and rested his desire is reaching out for the girl. When they both rise he still keeps his eyes lowered, and so watches how Betty puts money on the table for the meal. But what money! It is four shillings each, and wonder fills him at these women who handle such sums so casually. And then a quick glance at Mrs. Kambusi shows him that she watches him with a heavy ironical look, as if she understands quite well everything in his mind. 'Thank you for what you have told me,' he says, since he does not want to lose her favour; and she replied; 'It will be time to thank me when you have profited by it,' and without looking his way again, reaches for a book, lifts her child on her knee, and so sits teaching the child from the book as the young people go out, saying good night.

'What did she say to you?' asks Betty, as soon as the door is closed.

'She gave me good advice about the city,' says Jabavu, and then says, wishing to be told about her: 'She is a kind and clever woman.' But Betty laughs scornfully: 'She is the biggest skellum in the city.' 'And how is that?' he asks, startled; but she flaunts her hips a little and says: 'You will see.' Jabavu does not believe her. They reach her room, and now Jabavu pushes her on to the bed and puts his arm around her so that his hand is on her breast.

'And how much?' she asks, with contempt that is meant to goad him.

Jabavu sees how her eyes are heavy, and says simply: 'You know from my own mouth that I have no money.'

She lies loosely in his arm and says laughing, to tease him: 'I want five shillings, perhaps fifteen.'

Jabavu says, scornfully: 'And perhaps fifteen pounds.'

'For you no money,' she says, sighing; and Jabavu takes her for his own pleasure, allowing hers to look after itself, until he has had enough and lies sprawled across the bed, half-naked, and thinks: This is my first day in the city, and what have I not done? Truly Mrs. Kambusi is right when she says I have powerful luck with me. I have even had one of these smart town girls, and without paying. The words turn into a song.

> Jabavu is stronger than the city.
> He has a yellow shirt and new trousers,
> He has eaten food like a lion,
> He has filled a woman of the town with his strength.
> Jabavu is stronger than the city.
> He is stronger than a lion.
> He is stronger than the women of the town.

This song moves sleepily through his mind and dies in sleep, and he wakes to find the girl sitting on the foot of the bed, looking impatiently at him and saying: 'You sleep like a chicken with the setting of the sun.' He says, lazily: 'I am tired with the journey from my kraal.'

'But I am not tired,' she says lightly, and adds: 'I shall dance tonight, if not with you, with someone else.' But Jabavu says nothing, only yawns and thinks: This girl is only a woman like any other. Now I have had her I do not care. There are many in the city.

And so after a while she says, in that sweet, humble voice: 'I was teasing you only. Now get up lazy boy. Do you not want to see the dancing?' She adds, cunningly: 'And to see also how the clever Mrs. Kambusi runs a shebeen.'

But by now Mrs. Kambusi and what she has said seem unimportant to Jabavu. He yawns, gets off the bed, puts on his trousers and then combs his hair. She watches him with bitterness and admiration. 'Kraal boy,' she says, in a soft voice, 'you have been in the city half a day, and already you behave as if you were tired of it.' This pleases him, as it was meant to do, and so he fondles her breasts a little, and then her buttocks, until she slaps him with pleasure and laughs, and so they go together into the other room. And now it is full of people sitting around the walls on the benches, while there are some men with things to make music sitting on the chairs at the end. Through the open door is the dark night, and continually more people enter.

'So this is a shebeen?' says Jabavu, doubtfully, for it looks very respectable, and she replies: 'You will see what it is.' The music begins. The band is a saxophone, a guitar, a petrol tin for a drum, a trumpet, and two tins to bang together. Jabavu does not know this music. And to begin with the people do not dance. They sit with tin mugs in their hands, and allow their limbs to move. While their heads and shoulders begin to nod and jerk as the music enters them.

Then the other door opens and Mrs. Kambusi comes in. She looks the same, clean and nice in her pink dress. She carries a very big jug in her hand, and moves around from mug to extended mug, pouring in liquor from the jug and holding out her free hand for the money. A little boy follows her. It is not her own child, who is asleep in the room next door and forbidden ever to see what happens in this room. No, this is a child whom Mrs. Kambusi hires from a poor family, and his work is to run out into the darkness where there is a drum of skokian buried, to bring supplies as needed, so that if the police should come it will not be found in the house, and also to take the money and put it in a safe place under the walls.

Skokian is a wicked and dangerous drink, and it is illegal. It is made quickly, in one day, and may contain many different substances. On this night it has mealie-meal, sugar, tobacco, methylated spirits, boot polish and yeast. Some skokian queens use magic, such as the limb of a dead person, but Mrs. Kambusi does not believe in magic. She makes plenty of money without it.

When she reaches Jabavu she asks in a low voice in their language: 'And so you wish to drink?'

'Yes, my mother,' he says, humbly, 'I wish to taste it.'

She says: 'Never have I drunk it, though I make it every day. But I will give you some.' She pours him out half a cup instead of filling it, and Jabavu says, in the voice of his surly, hungry, angry youth: 'I will have it full.' And she stops in the act of turning away and gives him a glare of bitter contempt. 'You are a fool,' she says. 'Clever people make this poison for fools to drink. And you are one of the fools.'

But she pours out more skokian until it slops over, smiling so that no one may know how angry she is, and moves on up the line of seated men and women, making jokes and laughing, while the little boy behind her holds out a tray full of sweets and nuts and fish and cakes with the sugar on top.

Betty asks, jealously: 'What did she say to you?'

Jabavu says: 'She gives me the drink for nothing because we come from the same district.' And it is true she has forgotten to take money from Jabavu.

'She likes you,' says Betty, and he is pleased to see she is jealous. Well, he thinks, these clever town women are as simple as the village girls! And with this thought he gives a certain smile across the room to Mrs. Kambusi, but he sees how Mrs. Kambusi only looks contemptuous, and so Betty laughs at him. Jabavu leaps to his feet to hid his shame and begins to dance. He has always been a great dancer.

He dances invitingly around the girl, throwing out his legs, until she laughs and rises and joins him, and in a moment the room is full of people who wriggle and stamp and shout, and the air fills with dust and the roof shakes and even the walls seem to tremble. Soon Jabavu is thirsty and dives towards his mug on the bench. He takes a big mouthful – and it is as if fire entered him. He coughs and chokes while Betty laughs. 'Kraal boy,' she says, but in a soft, admiring voice. And Jabavu, taunted, lifts the mug and drains it, and it sinks through him, lighting his limbs and belly and brain with madness. And now Jabavu really dances, first like a bull, standing over the girl with his head lowered and shoulders hunched forward, sniffing at her breasts while she shakes them at him, and then like a cock, on the tips of his toes with his arms held out, lifting his knees and scraping his heels, and all the time the girl wriggles and shakes in front of him, her hips writhing, her breasts shaking, the sweat trickling down her. And soon Jabavu grabs her, swings her through the dancers into the other room, and there he flings her on the bed. Afterwards they return and continue to dance.

Later Mrs. Kambusi comes round with the big white jug, and when he holds out his mug, she refills it saying, with a bright, hard smile: 'That's right, my clever friend, drink,

drink as much as you can.' This time she holds out her hand for money, and Betty puts money into it. He swallows it all in a gulp, so that he staggers with the power of it, and the room swings around him. Then he dances in the packed mass of sweating, leaping people, he dances like a devil and there is the light of madness on his face. Later, but he does not know how long afterwards, there is Mrs. Kambusi's voice calling 'Police!' Betty grabs him and pulls him to the bench, and they sit, and through a haze of drink and sickness he sees that everyone has drained his mug empty and that the child is quickly refilling with lemonade. Then, at a signal from Mrs. Kambusi, three couples rise and dance, but in a different way. When two black policemen enter the room there is no skokian, the dancing is quiet, and the men of the band are playing a tune that has no fire in it.

Mrs. Kambusi, as calm as if she were grinding meal in her village, is smiling at the policemen. They go round looking at the mugs, but they know they will not find skokian for they have raided this place often. It is almost as if old friends enter it. But when they have finished the search for the skokian they begin to look for people who have no passes; and it is at this point that two men duck quickly under their arms and out of the door, while Mrs. Kambusi smiles and shrugs as if to say: Well, is it my fault they have no passes?

When the policemen reach Jabavu he shows them the pass for seeking work and his situpa, and they ask, When did he come to town, and he says: 'This morning,' and they look at each other. Then one asks: 'Where did you get those smart clothes?' Jabavu's eyes roll, his feet tense, he is about to spring towards the door in flight when Mrs. Kambusi comes forward and says that she gave them the smart clothes. The policemen shrug, and one says to Jabavu: 'You have done well for one day in town.' It is said with unpleasantness, and Jabavu feels Betty's hand on his arm saying to him: Be quiet, do not speak.

He remains silent, and when the policemen go they take with them four men and one woman who have not had the right passes. Mrs. Kambusi follows them outside the door and slips a pound into the hand of each; they exchange formalities with good humour, and Mrs. Kambusi returns, smiling.

For Mrs. Kambusi has run this shebeen so long and so profitably, not only because she is clever at arranging that the skokian and the large sums of money are never found in the house, but also because of the money she pays the police. And she makes it easy for them to leave her alone. As far as such places can be called orderly, hers is orderly. If the police are searching for a criminal they go first to the other skokian queens; and often Mrs. Kambusi sends them a message: You are looking for so and so who was fighting last night? Well, you will find him in such a place. This arrangement is helpful for everybody, except perhaps the people who drink the skokian, but it is not Mrs. Kambusi's fault that there are so many fools.

After a few minutes quiet, for the sake of caution, Mrs. Kambusi nods at the band, and the music changes its rhythm and the dancing goes on. But now Jabavu is no longer conscious of what he is doing. Other people see him dancing and shouting and drinking, but he remembers nothing after the police left. When he wakes he is lying on the bed, and it is midday, because the slant and colour of the light says it is. Jabavu moves his head and lets it fall back with a groan that is torn out of him. Never has he felt as he does now. Inside his head there is something heavy and loose which rolls as he moves it, and each movement sends waves of terrible sickness through him. It is as if his very flesh were dissolving, yet struggling not to dissolve, and pain moves through him like knives, and where it moves his limbs hang heavy and powerless. And so he lies, suffering and wishing himself dead, and sometimes darkness comes into his eyes then goes in a dazzle of light, and after a long time he feels there is a heavy weight on his arm and remembers that there is also a girl. And she, too, lies and suffers and groans, and so they remain for a long time. It is late afternoon when they sit up and look at each other. The light still flickers inside their eyes, and so it is not at once that they can see properly. Jabavu thinks: This woman is very ugly. And she thinks the same of him, and staggers off the bed and towards the window where she leans, swaying.

'Do you often drink this stuff,' asks Jabavu in wonder.

'You get used to it,' she says, sullenly.

'But how often?'

Instead of replying directly, she says: 'What are we to do? There is one hall for all of us, and there are many thousands of us. Into the hall only perhaps three or four hundred may go. And there they sell bad beer, made by white men, who cannot make our beer. And the police watch us like children. What do they expect?'

These bitter words do not affect Jabavu at all because they are not what she feels to be true, but are what she had heard people say in speeches. Besides, he is lost in wonder that she often drinks this poison and survives. He leans his head in his hands and rocks back and forth gently, groaning. Then the rocking makes him sick and so he keeps still. Again the time goes past, and the dark begins to settle outside.

'Let us walk a little,' she says, 'it will relieve the sickness.'

Jabavu staggers off the bed and out into the other room, and she follows. Mrs. Kambusi, hearing them, puts her head through her door and inquiries, in a sweet, polite, contemptuous voice: 'Well, my fine friend, and how do you like skokian?' Jabavu lowers his eyes and says: 'My mother, I shall never taste this bad drink again.' She looks at him, as if to say: 'We shall see!' and then asks: 'Do you wish to eat?' and Jabavu shudders and says, through a wave of sickness: 'My mother, I shall never eat again!' But the girl says: 'You know nothing. Yes, we shall eat. It will help the sickness.'

Mrs. Kambusi nods and goes back inside her door; the two go outside to walk, moving like sick hens through the shanties of tin and sacking, and then out to the area of bedraggled and dirty grass.

'It is a bad drink,' she says indifferently, 'but if you do not drink it every day it does no harm. I have lived here now for four years and I drink perhaps two or three times in a month. I like the white man's drink, but it is against the law to buy it, for they say it may teach us bad ways, and so we have to pay much money to the Coloured people who buy it for us.

And now they feel their legs will not go any further, and they stand, while the evening wind sweeps into their faces, coming from far over the bush and the kopjes which can be seen many miles away, massed dark against the young stars. The wind is fresh, the sickness lies quiet in them and so they go back, walking slowly but more strongly. In one of the doorways of the brick sheds a man lies motionless, and now Jabavu does not need to ask what is wrong with him. Yet he halts, in an impulse to help him, for there is blood on his clothes. The girl gives him a quick, anxious look, and says: 'Are you crazy? Leave him,' and she pulls him away. Jabavu follows her, looking back at the hurt man, and he says: 'In this city it is true that we are all strangers!' His voice is low and troubled, and Betty says quickly, for she knows he is ashamed: 'And is it my fault? If we are seen near that man, people may think we hurt him . . .' And then, since Jabavu still looks sullen and unhappy, she says in a changed voice, full of sadness: 'Ah, my mother! Sometimes I ask myself what it is I do here, and how my life is running away with fools and skellums. I was educated in a mission with the Roman sisters, and now what is it I am doing? She glances at Jabavu to see how he takes her sadness, but he is not affected by it. His smile makes anger rise in her and she shouts: 'Yes, it is because men are such liars and cheats, every one. Five times has a man promised to marry me so that I may live properly in a house such as they rent to married people. Five times has this man gone away, and after I have bought him clothes and food and spent much money on him.' Jabavu walks quietly along, frowning, and she continues, viciously: 'Yes, and you too – kraal boy, will you marry me? You have slept with me not once, but six seven times, and in one night, and you have spent not one penny of money, though I see you have a shilling in your pocket, for I looked while you slept, and I have given you food and drink and helped you.' She has come close to him, eyes narrow and black with hate, and now Jabavu's mouth falls open with surprise, for she has opened her handbag and taken out a knife, and she moves the knife cunningly so that a pale gleam from the sky shows on it. Hau! thinks Jabavu, I have lain all night beside a woman who searches my pockets and carries a knife in her handbag. But he remains silent, while she comes so close her shoulders are against his chest and he feels the point of the knife pressing to his stomach. 'You will marry me or I kill you,' she says, and Jabavu's legs go weak. Then the courage comes to him with his contempt for her and he takes her wrist and twists it so that the knife falls to the ground. 'You are a bad girl,' he says, 'I not marry a bad girl with a knife and ugly tongue.'

And now she begins to cry while she kneels and scuffles after the knife in the dust. She rises, putting the knife carefully in her bag, and she says: 'This is a bad town and the life here is bad and difficult.' Jabavu does not soften, for inside him is a voice saying the same thing, and he does not want to believe it, since his hunger for the good things of the town is as strong as ever.

For the second time he sits at Mrs. Kambusi's table and eats. There are potatoes fried with fat and salt, and then boiled mealies with salt and oil, and then more of the little cakes with pink sugar that he likes so much, and finally cups of the hot, sweet tea. Afterwards he says: 'What you say is true – the sickness is gone.'

'And now you are ready to drink skokian again?' asks Mrs. Kambusi, politely. Jabavu glances quickly at her, for the quality of her politeness has changed. It seems to him that her eyes are very frightening, for now they are saying, in that cool, quietly bitter look: Well, my friend, you may kill yourself with skokian, you may spend your strength on this girl until you have none left, and I do not care. You may even learn sense and become one of the men of light – I do not care about that either. I simply do not care. I have seen too much. She rests her bulky body against the back of her chair, stirs her tea round and round with a fine, shiny spoon, and smiles with her cool, shrewd eyes until Jabavu rises and says: 'Let us go.' Betty also rises, pays eight shillings as she did the night before and, having said good night, they go out.

'Not only have I paid much money for your food,' says Betty, bitterly, 'but you sleep in my room, and your nice Mrs. Kambusi, who you call your mother, charges me a fine rent for it, I can tell you.'

'And what do you do in your room?' asks Jabavu, laughing, and Betty hits him. He holds her wrists, but with one hand, and puts his other on her breasts, and she says: 'I do not like you,' and he lets her go, laughing, and she says: 'That I can see.' He goes into her room and lies on her bed as if this were his right, and she comes meekly after him and lies beside him. He is thinking, and besides even his bones are tired and aching, but she wishes to make love and begins to tease him with her hand, but he pushes it away and says: 'I wish only to sleep.' At this she rises angrily from beside him and says: 'You are a man? No, you are only a kraal boy.' This he cannot bear, so he gets up, throws her down and makes love to her until she no longer moves or speaks; and then he says, with swaggering contempt: 'Now you shut up.' But in spite of his pride in his knowledge of the nature of women it is a bad time for Jabavu, and sleep will not come. There is a fight going on inside him. He thinks of the advice Mrs. Kambusi has given him, then, when it seems difficult to follow, he tells himself she is nothing but a skellum and a skokian queen. He thinks of Mr. and Mrs. Samu and their friend, and how they liked him and thought him clever, and just as he decides to go to them he groans with the thought of the hardness of their life. He thinks of this girl, and how she is a bad girl, without modesty or even beauty, except what the smart clothes give her, and then the pride rises in him and a song forms itself: I am Jabavu, I have the strength of a bull, I can quieten a noisy woman with my strength, I can . . .

And then he remembers he has one shilling only and that he must earn some more. For Jabavu still thinks that he will do proper work for his money, he does not think of thieving. And so, though only half an hour before he made the girl sleep, he now shakes her, and she wakes reluctantly, crinkling the skin around her eyes against the glare from the unshaded yellow bulb that hangs from the roof. 'I want to know what work is paid best in this city?' he demands.

At first her face is foolish, then when she understands she laughs derisively, and says: 'You still do not know what work pays the best?' She closes her eyes and turns away from him. He shakes her again and now she is angry. 'Ah, be still, kraal boy, I will show you in the morning.'

'Which work is the most money?' he insists. And now she turns back, leans on her elbow and looks at him. Her face is bitter. It is not the truthful bitterness that can be seen on Mrs. Kambusi's face, but rather the self-pity of a woman. After a while she says: 'Well, my big fool, you can work in the white people's houses, and if you behave well and work many years you may earn two or three pounds a month.' She laughs, because of the smallness of the sum. But Jabavu thinks it is a great deal. For a moment he remembers that the food he has eaten with Mrs. Kambusi has cost four shillings, but he thinks: She is a skellum after all, and probably cheats me. His confusion is really because he cannot believe that he, Jabavu, will not have what he wants simply by putting out his hand and taking it. He has dreamed so long and so passionately about this town, and the essence of a dream is that it must come disguised, smiling brightly, its dark side hidden where is written: This is what you must pay . . .

'And in the factories?' asks Jabavu.

'Perhaps one pound a month and your food.'

'Then tomorrow I shall go to the houses of the white men, three pounds is better than one.'

'Fool, you have to work months or years to earn three pounds.'

But Jabavu, having settled his own mind, falls asleep at once, and now she lies awake, thinking she is a fool to take up with a man from the kraals who knows nothing about the city; then she is sad, with an old sadness, because it is in her nature to love the indifference of men, and it is by no means the first time she has lain beside a sleeping man, thinking how he will leave her. Then she is frightened, because soon she must tell her gang about Jabavu, and there is the one man, who calls himself Jerry, clever enough to know that her interest in Jabavu is a good deal more than professional.

Finally, seeing no way out of her troubles, she drifts into the bitterness which is not her own, but learned from what others say; and she repeats that the white men are wicked and make the black live like pigs, and there is no justice, and it is not her fault she is a bad girl – and many things of this sort, until her mind loses interest in them and she falls asleep at last. She wakes in the morning to see Jabavu combing his hair, looking very handsome in the yellow shirt. She thinks, maliciously: The police will be looking for that shirt, and he will get into trouble. But it appears her desire to hurt him is not as strong as she thinks, for she pulls a suitcase from under the bed, takes out a pink shirt, throws it at him and says: 'Wear this, otherwise you will be caught.'

Jabavu thanks her, but as if he expects such attention, then says: 'Now you will show me where to go to find good work.'

She says: 'I will not come with you. I must earn money for myself today. I have spent so much on you I have none left.'

'I did not asked you to spend money on me,' says Jabavu, cruelly, and she flashes out her knife again, threatening him with it. But he says: 'Stop being a stupid woman. I am not afraid of your knife.' So she begins to cry. And now Jabavu's manhood, which has been fed with pride so much that he feels there is nothing he cannot do, tells him that he should comfort her, so he puts his arm around her and says: 'Do not cry' and 'You are a nice girl, though foolish,' and also, 'I love you.' And she weeps and says: 'I know about men, you will never come back to me,' and he smiles and says: 'Perhaps I will, perhaps not.' And saying this, he rises and goes out, and the last thing she sees of him that morning are his white teeth flashing in a gay smile. And so for a while she weeps, then she grows angry, then she goes in search of Jerry and the gang, thinking all the time of that impudent smile and how she may speak to them so that they make Jabavu one of the gang.

Jabavu goes from the place which is called Poland and Johannesburg, walks through the Native Township, along the busy road to the white man's city, and so to where the fine houses are. And here he saunters along, choosing which house he likes best. For his success since he came to the city had given him such a swelled head he imagines the first he enters will open its door saying: Ah, here is Jabavu, I have been waiting for you! When he has made up his mind, he walks in through the gate and stands looking around, and an old white woman who is cutting at some flowers with a shiny pair of scissors says, in a sharp voice: 'What do you want?' He says: 'I want work.' She says: 'Go to the back of the house. What cheek!' He stands insolently in front of her, till she shouts: 'Did you hear? Get to the back; since

when do you come to the front of a house asking for work?'
And so he walks out of the garden, cursing her to himself,
listening to how she grumbles and mutters about spoilt
kaffirs, and goes to the back of the house, where a servant
tells him that here there is no work for him. Jabavu is
angry. He strolls into the sanitary lane, letting his anger
make words of hatred: White bitch, filthy woman, white
people all pigs. Then he goes to the back part of another
house. There is a big garden here, with vegetables, a cat
sitting fat and happy on a green lawn, and a baby in a basket
under a tree. But there is no one to be seen. He waits, he
walks about, he looks through the windows carefully, the
baby coos in its basket, waving its legs and arms, and then
Jabavu sees there are a row of shoes on the back verandah
waiting to be cleaned. He cannot help looking at the shoes.
He measures them with his eyes against his feet. He glances
around – still no one in sight. He snatches up the biggest
pair of shoes and goes into the sanitary lane. He cannot believe it is so easy, his flesh is prickling with fear of hearing
angry voices or feet running after him. But nothing happens,
so he sits down and puts on the shoes. Since he has never
worn any, he does not know whether his discomfort is because they are too small or because his feet are not used to
them. He walks on them and his legs make small, mincing
steps of pain, but he is very proud. Now he is dressed, even
his feet, like a white man.

He goes into the back of another house, and this time the
woman there asks him what work he knows. He says 'Everything.' She asks him: 'Are you cook or houseboy?' And
now he is silent. She asks: 'What money did you earn before?' And when he is still silent she asks to see his situpa.
As soon as she looks at it, she says angrily: 'Why do you tell
me lies? You are a raw boy.' And so he goes out into the
sanitary lane, angry and sore, but thinking of what he has
learned, and when he goes to the next house and a woman
asks what he knows, he puts on a humble look and says in
a cringing voice that he has not worked in a white house
before, but that he will learn quickly. He is thinking: I look
so fine in my clothes, this woman will like a smart man like
me. But she says she does not want a boy without experience. And now, as Jabavu walks away, his heart is cold and

unhappy and he feels that no one in the whole world wants him. He whistles jauntily, making his fine new shoes stamp, and says he will surely find a good job with much money soon, but in the next house the woman says she will take him for rough work at twelve shillings a month. And Jabavu says he will not take twelve shillings. And she hands him back his situpa and says, pleasantly enough, that he will not get more than twelve shillings without experience. Then she goes back into the house. This happens several times until in the afternoon Jabavu goes to a man chopping wood in a garden, who he has heard speaking his own language, and he asks for advice. The man is friendly and tells him that he will not earn more than twelve or thirteen shillings a month until he has learned the work, and then, after many months, a pound. He will be given mealie-meal every day to make his porridge with, and meat once or twice a week, and he will sleep in a small room like a box at the back of the house with the other servants. Now all this Jabavu knows, for he has heard it often from people passing through the village, but he has not known it for himself; he has always thought: For me it will be different.

He thanks the friendly man and wanders on through the sanitary lanes, careful not to stop or loiter, otherwise a policeman may notice him. He is wondering: What is this experience? I, Jabavu, am the strongest of the young men in the village. I can hoe a field in half the time it takes any other; I can dance longer than anyone without tiring; all the girls like me best and smile as I go past; I came to this city two days ago and already I have clothes, and I can treat one of the clever women of the town like a servant and she loves me. I am Jabavu! I am Jabavu, come to the white man's town. He dances a little, shuffling through the leaves in the sanitary lane, but then he sees dust filming his new shoes, and so he stops. The sun will soon be sinking; he has not eaten since last night, and he wonders whether he should return to Betty. But he thinks: There are other girls, and he goes slowly through the sanitary lanes looking over the hedges into the gardens, and where there is a nanny hanging up clothes or playing with children, he looks carefully at her. He tells himself that he wants just such another girl as Betty, yet he sees one with her look of open and insolent attraction, and though he hesitates, he moves on, until at last he sees a girl standing by a white baby in a small cart on wheels, and he stops. She has a pleasant, round face, and eyes that are careful of what they say. She wears a white dress and has a dark-red cloth bound round her head. He watches her for a time and then says, in English: 'Good morning.' She does not at once answer, but looks at him first. 'Can you help me?' he asks again. Then she says: 'What can I tell you.'

From the sound of her voice he thinks she may be from his district, and he speaks to her in his language, and she answers him, smiling, and they move close and speak over the hedge. They discover that her village is not more than an hour's walking from his, and because the old traditions of hospitality are stronger than the new fear in both of them, she asks him to her room, and he goes. There, while the baby sleeps in its carriage, they talk, and Jabavu, forgetting how he has learned to speak to Betty, treats this girl as respectfully as he would one in the village.

She tells him he may sleep here tonight, having first said that she is bound to a man in Johannesburg, whom she will marry, so that Jabavu may not mistake her intention. She leaves him for a time, to help her mistress put the baby to bed. Jabavu is careful not to show himself, but sits in a corner, for Alice has said that it is against the law for him to be there, and if the police should come he must try and run away, for her mistress is kind and does not deserve trouble from the police.

Jabavu sits quietly, looking at the little room, which is the same size as Betty's and has the same brick walls and floor and tin roof, and sees that three people sleep here, for their bedding is rolled into separate corners, and he tells himself he will not be a houseboy. Soon Alice returns with food. She has cooked mealie-meal porridge, not as well as his mother would do, for that needs time, and it must be done on the mistress's stove. But there is plenty of it, and there is some jam her mistress has given her. As they eat they speak of their villages and of the life here. Alice tells him she earns a pound a month and the mistress gives her clothes and plenty of mealie-meal. She speaks with great affection of this woman, and for a time Jabavu is tempted to change his mind and find just such another for himself. But a pound a month – no, not for Jabavu, who despises Alice for being satisfied with so little. Yet he looks kindly at her and thinks her very pretty. She has stuck a candle in its own grease on the door-sill, and it gives a nice light, and her cheeks and eyes and teeth glisten. Also she has a soft, modest voice, which pleases him after the way Betty uses hers. Jabavu warms to her and feels her answering warmth for him. Soon there is a silence and Jabavu tries to approach her, but with respect, not as he would handle Betty. She allows him, and sits within his arm and tells him of the man who promised her marriage and then went to Johannesburg to earn money for the lobola. At first he wrote and sent money, but now there has been silence for a year. He has another woman now, so travellers have told her. Yet she believes he will come back, for he was a good man. 'So Johannesburg is not all bad?' asks Jabavu, thinking of the many different things he has heard. 'It seems that many like it, for they go once and then go again and again,' she says, but with reluctance, for it is not a thought she enjoys. Jabavu comforts her; she weeps a little, then he takes her, but with gentleness. Afterwards he asks her what would happen if there was a baby. She says that there are many children in the city who do not know their fathers; and then she tells him things that make him dizzy with astonishment and admiration. So that is why the white women have one or two or three children or none at all? Alice tells him of the things a woman may use, and a man may use; she says that many of the more simple people do not know of them, or fear them as witchcraft, but the wise people protect themselves against children for whom there are no fathers or homes. Then she sighs and says how much she longs for children and a husband, but Jabavu interrupts her to ask how he may obtain these things she has spoken about, and she tells him it is best to ask a kind white person to buy them, if one knows such a white person, or one may buy them from the Coloured people who traffic in more things than liquor, or if one is brave enough to face a snubbing, one may go and ask in a white man's shop – there are some traders who will sell to the black people. But these things are expensive, she says, and need care in use, and . . . she continues to talk, and Jabavu learns another lesson for life in the big city, and he is grateful to her. Also he is grateful and warm to her because here is a girl who keeps her gentleness and her knowledge of what is right even in the city. In the morning he thanks her many times and says good-bye to her and to the other men who came in to sleep in the room late at night, after visiting, and while she thanks him also, for politeness' sake, her eyes tell him that if he wished he could take the place of the man in Johannesburg. But Jabavu has already learned to be afraid of the way every woman in the city longs only for a husband, and he adds that he wishes for the early return of her promised husband so that she may be happy. He leaves her, and before he has reached the end of the sanitary lane is thinking what he should do next, while she looks after him and thinks sadly of him for many days.

It is early in the morning, the sun is newly risen, and there are few people in the streets. Jabavu walks for a long time around the houses and gardens, learning how the city is planned, but he does not ask for work. When he has understood enough of the place to find his way without asking questions at every corner he goes to the part of the town where the shops are, and examines them. Never has he imagined such richness and variety. Half of what he sees he does not understand, and he wonders how these things are used, but in spite of his wonder he never stands still before a window; he makes his legs move on even when they would rather stop, in order that the police may not notice him. And then, when he has seen windows of food and of clothes, and many other strange articles, he goes to the place where the Indian shops are for natives to buy, and there he mixes with the crowds, listens to the gramophones playing music, and keeps his ears attentive so that he may learn from what people say, and so the afternoon slowly passes in learning and listening. When he grows hungry he watches until he sees a cart with fruit on it, he walks quickly past and takes half a dozen bananas with a skill that seems to have been born in his fingers, for he is astonished himself at their cunning. He walks down a side-street eating the bananas as if he had paid money for them, quite openly; and he is thinking what he should do next. Return to Betty? He does not like the thought. Go to Mr. Mizi, as Mrs. Kambusi says he should? But he shrinks from it – later, later, he thinks, when I have tasted all the excitements of the town. And in the meantime, he still owns one shilling, nothing else.

And so he begins to dream. It is strange that when he was in the village and made such dreams they were far less lofty and demanding than the one he makes now; yet, even in the ignorance of the village, he was ashamed of those small and childish dreams, while now, although he knows quite well what he is thinking is nonsense, the bright pictures moving through his mind grip him so fast he walks like a mad person, open-mouthed, his eyes glazed. He sees himself in one of the big streets where the big houses are. A white man stops him and says: I like you, I wish to help you. Come to my house. I have a fine room which I do not use. You may live in it, and you may eat at my table and drink tea when you like. I will give you money when you need it. I have many books; you may read them all and become educated ... I am doing this because I do not agree with the colour bar and wish to help your people. When you know everything that is in the books, then you will be a man of light, just the same as Mr. Mizi, whom I respect very much. Then I will give you enough money to buy a big house, and you may live in it and be a leader of the African people, like Mr. Samu and Mr. Mizi. . . .

This dream is so sweet and so strong that Jabavu at last stands under a tree, gazing at nothing, quite bewitched. Then he sees a policeman cycling slowly past and looking at him, and it does not mix well with the dream, and so he makes his feet walk on. The dream's sad and lovely colours are all around him still, and he thinks: The white people are so rich and powerful, they would not miss the money to give me a room and books to read. Then a voice says: But there are many others beside me, and Jabavu shakes himself crossly because of that voice: He cannot bear to think of others, his hunger for himself is so strong. Then he thinks: Perhaps if I go to the school in the Township and tell them how I learned to read and write by myself they will take me in ... But Jabavu is too old for school, and he knows it. Slowly, slowly, the foolish sweetness of the dreaming leaves him, and he walks soberly down to the road to the Township. He has no idea at all of what he will do when he gets there, but he thinks that something will happen to help him.

It is now early in the evening, about five, and it is a Saturday. There is an air of festivity and freedom, for yesterday was pay-day, and people are looking how best to spend their money. When he reaches the market he lingers there, tempted to spend his shilling on some proper food. But now it has become important to him, like a little piece of magic. It seems to him he has been in the city for a very long time, although it is only four days, and all that time the shilling has been in his pocket. He has the feeling that if he loses it he will lose his luck. Also there is another thought – it took his mother so long to save it. He wonders that in the kraal a shilling is such a lot of money, whereas here he could spend it on a few boiled mealies and a small cake. He is angry with himself because of this feeling of pity for his mother, and mutters: 'You big fool, Jabavu,' but the shilling stays in his pocket and he wanders on, thinking how he may find something to eat without asking Betty, until he reaches the Recreation Hall, which has people surging all round it.

It is too early for the Saturday dancing, and so he loiters through the crowd to see what is happening. Soon he sees Mr. Samu with some others at a side door, and he goes closer with the feeling: Ah, here is someone who will help me. Mr. Samu talks to a friend, in the way which Jabavu recognizes, as if that friend is not one person but many; and Mr. Samu's eyes move from one face near to him to another, and then on, always moving, as if it is with his eyes that he holds them, gathers them in, makes them one. And his eyes rest on Jabavu's face, and Jabavu smiles and steps forward – but Mr. Samu, still talking, is looking at someone else. Jabavu feels as if something cold hit his stomach. He thinks, and for the first time: Mr. Samu is angry because I ran away that morning; and at once he walks jauntily away, saying to himself: Well, I don't care about Mr. Samu, he's nothing but a big talker, these men of light, they are just fools, saying Please, Please to the Government! Yet he has not gone a hundred yards when his feet slow, he stops, and then his feet seem to turn him around so that he must go back to the Hall. Now the people are crowding in at the big door, Mr. Samu has gone inside, and Jabavu follows at the back of the crowd. By the time he has got inside the hall is full, and so he stands at the back against the wall.

On the platform are Mr. Samu, the other man who was with him in the bush, and a third man, who is almost at once introduced as Mr. Mizi. Jabavu's eyes, dazed with so many people all together, hardly see Mr. Mizi's face, but he understands this is a man of great strength and cleverness. He stands as straight and tall as he can so that Mr. Samu may see him, but Mr. Samu's eyes again move past without seeing, and Jabavu thinks: But who is Mr. Samu? Nothing besides Mr. Mizi. ... And then he looks how these men are dressed, and sees their clothes are dark and sometimes old sometimes even with patches on them. There is no one in this hall who has as bright and smart clothes as Jabavu himself, and so the small, unhappy child in Jabavu quietens, appeased, and he is able to stand quietly, listening.

Mr. Mizi is talking. His voice is powerful, and the people in the benches sit motionless, leaning forward, and their faces are full of longing, as if they are listening to a beautiful story. Yet what Mr. Mizi says is not at all beautiful. Jabavu cannot understand and asks a man near him what this meeting is. The man says that the men on the platform are the leaders for the League for the Advancement of the African People; that they are now discussing the laws which treat Africans differently from the white people ... they are very clever, he says; and can understand the laws as they are written, which it takes many years to do. Later the meeting will be told about the management of land in the reserves, and how the Government wishes to reduce the cattle owned by the African people, and about the pass laws, and also many other things. Jabavu is shown a piece of paper which numbers 1, 2, 3, 4, 5, and 6, and opposite these numbers are written words like Destocking of Cattle. He is told this piece of paper is an Agenda.

First Mr. Mizi speaks for a long time, then Mr. Samu, then Mr. Mizi again, and sometimes the people in the hall seem to growl with anger, sometimes they sigh and call out 'Shame!' and these feelings, which are like the feelings of one person, become Jabavu's also, and he, too, claps and sighs and calls out 'Shame, Shame!' Yet he hardly understands what is said. After a long time Mr. Mizi rises to speak on a subject which is called Minimum Wage, and now Jabavu understands every word. Mr. Mizi says that not long ago a member of the white man's Parliament asked for a law which would make one pound a month a minimum wage for African workers, but the other members of Parliament said 'No,' it would be too much. And now Mr. Mizi says he wishes every person to sign a petition to the members of the Parliament to reconsider this cruel decision. And when he says this, every man and woman in the hall roars out 'Yes, yes,' and they clap so long that Jabavu's hands grow tired. And now he is looking at those great and wise men on the platform, and with every nerve of his body longs to be like them. He sees himself standing on a platform while hundreds of people sigh and clap and cry 'Yes, yes!'

And suddenly, without knowing how it has happened, his hand is raised and he has called out, 'Please, I want to speak.' Everybody in the hall has turned to look, and they are surprised. There is complete silence in the hall. Then Mr. Samu stands up quickly and says, after a long look at Jabavu: 'Please, this is a young friend of mine, let him speak.' He smiles and nods at Jabavu, who is filled with immense pride, as if a great hawk carried him into the sky on its wings. He swaggers a little as he stands. Then he speaks of how he came from his kraal only four days ago, how he outwitted the recruiters who tried to cheat him, how he had no food and fainted with hunger and was handled like an ox by the white doctor, how he has searched for work ... The words flow to Jabavu's tongue as if someone very clever stood behind his shoulder and whispered them into his ear. Some things this clever person does not mention, such as how he stole clothes and shoes and food, and how he fell in with Betty and spent the night at the shebeen. But he tells how in the white woman's garden he has been rudely ordered to the back, 'which is the right place for niggers' – and this Jabavu tells with great bitterness – and how he has been offered twelve shillings a month and his food. And as Jabavu speaks the people in the hall murmur, 'Yes, yes.'

Jabavu is still full of words when Mr. Samu stands up,

interrupting him, saying: 'We are grateful to our young friend for what he has said. His experiences are typical for young men coming to town. We all know from our own lives that what he says is true, but it does no harm to hear it again.' And with this he quietly introduces the next subject, which is how terrible it is that Africans must carry so many passes, and the meeting goes on. Jabavu is upset, for he feels that it is not right the meeting should simply go on to something else after the ugly things he has told them. Also, he has seen that some of the people, in turning back to the platform, have smiled at each other, and that smile stung his pride. He glances at the man next to him, who says nothing. Then, since Jabavu continues to look and smile, as if wanting words, the man says pleasantly: 'You have a big mouth my friend.' At this, such rage fills Jabavu that his hand lifts by itself, and very nearly hits the man, who swiftly clasps Jabavu's wrist and murmurs: 'Quiet, you will make big trouble for yourself. We do not fight here.' Jabavu mutters in anguish: 'My name is Jabavu, not Big Mouth,' and the man says: 'I did not speak of your name, I do not know it. But in this place we do not fight, for the men of light have troubles enough without that.'

Jabavu struggles his way towards the door, for it is as if his ears were full of mocking laughter, and Big Mouth, Big Mouth, repeated often. Yet the people are standing packed in the door and he cannot go out, though he tries so that he disturbs them, and they ask him to be quiet. And while Jabavu stands there, angry and unhappy, a man says to him: 'My friend, what you said spoke to my heart. It is very true.' And Jabavu forgets his bitterness and at once is calm and full of pride; for he cannot know that this man spoke only so as to see his face clearly, for he comes to all such meetings pretending to be like the others in order to return later to the Government office which wishes to know who of the Africans are troublemakers and seditious. Before the meeting is over, Jabavu has told this friendly man his name and his village, and how much he admires the men of light, information which is very welcome.

When Mr. Samu declares the meeting closed, Jabavu slips out as quickly as he can and goes out to the other door where the speakers will come. Mr. Samu smiles and nods when he sees him, and shakes his hand, and introduces him to Mr. Mizi. None congratulate him on what he has said, but rather look at him like village elders who think: That child may grow up to be useful and clever if his parents are strict with him. Mr. Samu says: 'Well, well, my young friend, you haven't had good luck since you came to the city, but you make a mistake if you think yours is an exceptional case.' Then, seeing Jabavu's dismayed face, he says, kindly: 'But why did you run away so early, and why did you not go to Mr. Mizi, who is glad to help people who need help?' Jabavu hangs his head and says that he ran away so early because he wished to reach the city soon and did not want to disturb their sleep for nothing, and that he could not find Mr. Mizi's house.

Mr. Mizi says: 'Then come with us now, and you will find it.' Mr. Mizi is a big man, strong, heavy-shouldered. If Jabavu is like a young bull, clumsy with his own strength, then Mr. Mizi is like an old bull who is used to his power. His face is not one a young man may easily love, for there is no laughter in it, no easy warmth. He is stern and thoughtful and his eyes see everything. But if Jabavu does not love Mr. Mizi, he admires him, and at every moment he feels more like a small boy, and as this feeling of dependence, which is one he hates and makes him angry, grows in him, he does not know whether to run away or stay where he is. He stays, however, and walks with a group of others to Mr. Mizi's house.

It is a house similar to that of the Greek. Jabavu knows now that compared with the houses of the white men it is nothing, but the front room seems very fine to him. There is a big mirror on the wall, and a big table covered with soft green stuff that has thick, silky tassels dangling, and around this table, many chairs. Jabavu sits on the floor as a mark of respect, but Mrs. Mizi, who is welcoming her guests, says kindly: 'My friend, sit on this chair,' and pushes it forward for him. Mrs. Mizi is a tiny woman, with a merry face and eyes that dart everywhere looking for something to laugh at. It seems that there is so much laughter in Mrs. Mizi that there is no room for it in Mr. Mizi, while Mr. Mizi thinks so much he has taken all thought from Mrs. Mizi. Seeing Mrs. Mizi alone it is hard to believe she should have a big stern, clever husband; while seeing Mr. Mizi, one would not think of his wife as small and laughing. Yet together they fit each other, as if they make one person.

Jabavu is so full of awe at being here that he knocks over the chair and feels he would like to die of shame, but Mrs. Mizi laughs at him with such good nature that he begins to laugh too, and only stops when he sees that this gathering of friends is not only for friendship, but also for serious talking.

Seated around the table are Mr. Samu and Mrs. Samu and the brother, and Mr. Mizi and Mrs. Mizi and a young boy who is the Mizi's son. Mrs. Mizi sets tea on the table, in nice white cups, and plenty of the little cakes with pink sugar. The young boy drinks one cup of tea quickly, and then says he wishes to study and goes next door with a cake in his hand, while Mrs. Mizi rolls up her eyes and complains that he will study himself to death. Mr. Mizi, however, tells her not to be a foolish woman, and so she sits down, smiling, to listen.

Mr. Mizi and Mr. Samu talk. It appears that they talk to each other, yet sometimes they glance at Jabavu, for what they are saying is not just what comes into their heads but is chosen to teach Jabavu what it is good for him to know.

Jabavu does not at once understand this, and when he does that familiar storm of resentment clouds his hearing; one voice says: I, Jabavu, treated like a small child; while the other says: These are good people, listen. So it is only in fragments that their words enter his mind, and there they form a strange and twisted idea that would surprise these wise and clever men if they could see it. But perhaps it is a weakness of such men, who spend their lives studying and thinking and saying things such as: The movement of history, or the development of society, that they forget the childhood of their own minds, when such phrases have a strange and even terrible sound.

So there sits Jabavu at the table, eating the cakes which Mrs. Mizi presses on him, and his face is first sullen and unwilling, then bright and eager, and sometimes his eyes are lowered to hide what he thinks, and then they flash up, saying: Yes, yes, that is true!

Mr. Mizi is saying how hard it is for the African when he first comes to the town knowing nothing save that he must leave everything he has learned in the Kraal behind him. He says that such a young man must be forgiven if out of confusion he drifts into the wrong company.

And here Jabavu instinctively lifts his arms to cross them over his bright new shirt, and Mrs. Mizi smiles at him and refills his cup.

Then Mr. Samu says that such a young man has the choice of a short life, with money and a good time, before prison or drink or sickness overtake him, or he may work for the good of his people and ... but here Mrs. Mizi lets out a yell of laughter and says: 'Yes, yes, but that may be a short life too, and prison, just as much.'

Mr. Mizi smiles patiently and says that his wife likes a good joke, and there is a difference between prison for silly things like stealing, and prison for a good cause. Then he goes on to say that a young man of intelligence will soon understand that the company of the matsotsis leads only to trouble, and will devote himself to study. Further, he will soon understand that it is foolish to work as a cook or houseboy or office-boy, for such people are never more than one or two or three together, but he will go into a factory, or even to the mines, because ... But for the space of perhaps ten minutes Jabavu understands not one word, since Mr. Mizi is using such phrases as the development of industry, the working class, and historical mission. When what Mr. Mizi says becomes again easy to follow, it is that Jabavu must become such a worker that everyone trusts him, and at night he will study on his own or with others, for a man who wishes to lead others must not only be better than they, but also know more ... and here Mrs. Mizi giggles and says that Mr. Mizi has a swelled head, and he is only a leader because he can talk louder than anyone else. At which Mr. Mizi smiles fondly, and says a woman should respect her husband.

Jabavu, breaking into this flirtation between Mr. and Mrs. Mizi asks, suddenly: 'Tell me, please, how much money will I earn in a factory?' And there is the hunger in his voice so that Mr. Mizi frowns a little, and Mrs. Mizi makes a little grimace and a shake of the head.

Mr. Mizi says: 'Not much money. Perhaps a pound a month. But . . .'

And here Mrs. Mizi laughs irrepressibly and says: 'When I was a girl at the Roman school, I heard nothing but God, and how I must be good, and sin is evil, and how wicked to want to be happy in this life, and how I must think only of heaven. Then I met Mr. Mizi and he told me there is no God, and I thought: Ah, now I shall have a fine, handsome man for a husband, and no Church and plenty of fun and dancing and good times. But what I find is that even though there is no God, still I have to be good and not think of dancing or a good time, but only of the time when there is a heaven on earth – sometimes I think these clever men are just as bad as the preachers.' And at this she shakes with laughter so much she puts her hand over her mouth, and she makes big eyes at her husband over her hand, and he sighs and says, patiently: 'There is a certain amount of truth in what you say. There was once a time in the development of society when religion was progressive and held all the goodness of mankind, but now that goodness and hope belongs to the movements of the people everywhere in the world.'

These words make no sense to Jabavu and he looks at Mrs. Mizi for help, like a small child at its mother. And it is true that she knows more of what is passing through his mind than either of the two clever men or even Mrs. Samu, who has none of the child left in her.

Mrs. Mizi sees Jabavu's eyes, demanding love from her, and protection from the harshness of the men, and she nods and smiles at him, as if to say: Yes, I laugh, but you should listen, for they are right in what they say. And Jabavu drops his head and thinks: For the whole of my life I must work for one pound a month and study at nights and have no fine clothes or dancing . . . and he feels his old hunger raging in him, saying: Run, run quickly, before it is too late.

But the men of light see so clearly what should be Jabavu's proper path that to them it seems no more needs to be said, and they go on to discuss how a leader should arrange his life, just as if Jabavu were already a leader. They say that such a man must behave so that no one may say:

He is a bad man. He must be sober and law-abiding, he must be careful never to infringe even the slightest of the pass-laws, nor forget to have a light on his bicycle or be out after the curfew, for – and here they smile as if it were the best of jokes – they get plenty of attention from the police as things are. If they are entrusted with money they must be able to account for every penny – 'As if,' says Mrs. Mizi, giggling, 'it were money from heaven which God will ask them to account for.' And they must each have one wife only, and be faithful to her – but here Mrs. Mizi says, playfully, that even without these considerations, Mr. Mizi would have one woman only, and so he needn't blame that on the evils of the time.

At this, everyone laughs a great deal, even Mr. Mizi; but they see Jabavu does not laugh at all, but sits silent, face puckered with difficult thought. And then Mr. Samu tells the following story, for the proper education of Jabavu, while the voices bicker and argue inside him so loudly he can hardly hear Mr. Samu's voice above them.

'Mr. Mizi,' says Mr. Samu, 'is an example to all who wish to lead the African people to a better life. He was once a messenger at the Office of the Native Commissioner, and even an interpreter, and so was respected and earned a good salary. Yet, because he was forbidden as employee of the Government, to talk at meetings or even be a member of the League, he saved his money, which took him many years, until he had enough to buy a little store in the Township, and so he left his employment and became independent. Yet now he must struggle to make a living, for it would be a terrible thing for the League if a leader should be accused of charging high prices or cheating, and this means that the other stores always make more money than the store of Mr. and Mrs. Mizi, and so . . .'

Very late, Jabavu is asked if he will sleep there for that night, and in the morning work will be found for him in a factory. Jabavu thanks Mr. Mizi, then Mr. Samu, but in a low and troubled voice. He is taken to the kitchen, where the son is still sitting over his books. There is a bed in the kitchen for this son, and a mattress is put on the floor for Jabavu. Mrs. Mizi says to her son: 'Now that is enough studying, go to bed,' and he rises unwillingly from his books and leaves the kitchen to wash before sleeping. And Jabavu stands awkwardly beside the mattress and watches Mrs. Mizi arrange the bedclothes of the son more comfortably; and he feels a strong desire to tell her everything, how he longs to devote himself to becoming a man of light, while at the same time he dreads it; but he does not, for he is ashamed. Then Mrs. Mizi straightens herself up and looks kindly at him. She comes to him and puts her hand on his arm, saying: 'Now my son, I tell you a little secret. Mr. Mizi and Mr. Samu are not so alarming as they sound.' Here she giggles, while she keeps giving him concerned glances, and pushes his arm once or twice as if to say: Laugh a little, then things will seem easier! But Jabavu cannot laugh. Instead, his hand goes into his pocket and he brings out the shilling, and before he knows what he is doing he has pushed it into her hand. 'Now what is this?' she asks, astonished. 'It is a shilling. For the work.' And now he longs above all that she should take the shilling and understand what he is saying. And at once she does. She stands there, looking at the shilling in her palm, then at Jabavu, and then she nods and smiles. 'That is well, my son,' she says, in a soft voice. 'That is very well. I shall give it to Mr. Mizi and tell him you have given your last shilling to the work he does.' And she again puts her two hands on his arms and presses them warmly, then bids him good night and goes out.

Almost at once the son comes back and, having shut the door so that his mother will not see and scold him, goes back to the books. Jabavu lies on his mattress, and his heart is warm and big with love for Mrs. Mizi and her kindness, also his good intentions for the future. And then, lying warm and idle there, he sees how the son's eyes are thick and red with studying, how he is serious and stern, just like his father, and yet he is the same age as Jabavu, and a cold dismay enters Jabavu, in spite of his desire to live like a good man, and he cannot help thinking: And must I also be like this, working all day and then at night as well, and all this for other people? It is in the misery of this thought that he falls asleep and dreams, and although he does not know what it is he dreams, he struggles and calls out, so loudly that Mrs. Mizi, who has crept to the door to make sure her son has been sensible and gone to bed, hears him and clicks her tongue in compassion. Poor boy, she thinks, poor boy.... And so goes again to her bed, praying, as is her habit before sleep, but secretly, for Mr. Mizi would be angry if he knew. She prays, as she has been taught in the Mission School of the Romans, for the soul of Jabavu, who needs help in his struggle against the temptations of the shebeens and matsotsis, and she prays for her son, of whom she is rather afraid, since he is so serious all the time and has always known exactly what he intends to become.

She prays so long, sitting in her bed, that Mr. Mizi wakes and says: 'Eh, now, my wife, and what is this you are doing?' And she says meekly: 'But nothing at all.' And he says gruffly: 'And now sleep; that is better for our work than praying.' And she says: 'Surely times are so bad for our people that praying can do no harm, at least.' And he says: 'You are nothing but a child – sleep.' And so she lies down, and husband and wife go to sleep in great contentment with each other and with Jabavu. Mr. Mizi is already planning how he will first test Jabavu for loyalty, and then train him, and then teach him how to speak at meetings, and then ...

Jabavu wakes from a bad dream when a cold, grey glimmer is already coming through the small window. The son is lying across his bed, asleep, still fully dressed, he has been too tired to remove his clothes.

He rises, light as a wild-cat, and goes to the table where the books lie tumbled, and looks at them. The words on them are so long and difficult he does not know what they mean. There he stands, silently, stiffly, in the small, cold kitchen, his hands clenched, his eyes rolling this way and that, first towards the clever and serious young man, who is worn out with his studying, and then towards the window, where the morning light is coming. For a very long time does Jabavu stand there, suffering with the violence of his feelings. Ah, he does not know what to do. First he takes a step towards the window, then he moves towards his mattress as if to lie down, and all the time his hunger roars and burns in him like a fire. He hears voices saying: Jabavu, Jabavu – but he does not know whether they commend a rich man with smart clothes or a man of light with knowledge and a strong, persuasive voice.

And then the storm dies in him and he is empty, all feeling gone. He tiptoes to the window, slips the catch up, and
is over the sill and out. There is a small bush beneath, and
he crouches behind it, looking around him. Houses and
trees seem to rise from shadows of night into morning,
for the sky is clear and grey, flushed pink in long streaks,
and yet there are street lamps glimmering pale above dim
roads. And along these narrow roads move an army of
people going to work, although Jabavu had imagined
everything would still be deserted. If he had known, he
would never have risked running away; but now he must
somehow get from the bush to the road without being seen.
There he crouches, shivering with cold, watching the people
go past, listening to the thudding of their feet, and then it
seems to him as if one of them is looking at him. It is a young
man, slim, with a narrow, alert head, and eyes which look
everywhere. He is one of the matsotsis, for his clothes say
so. His trousers are narrow at the bottom, his shoulders are
sharp, he wears a scarf of bright red. Over this scarf, it
seems, his eyes peer at the bush where Jabavu is. Yet it is
impossible, for Jabavu has never seen him before. He
straightens himself, pretends he has been urinating into the
bush, and walks calmly out into the road. And at once the
young man moves over and walks beside him. Jabavu is
afraid and he does not know why, and he says nothing,
keeping his eyes fixed in front of him.

'And how is the clever Mr. Mizi?' inquires the strange
young man at last, and Jabavu says: 'I do not know who
you are.'

At this the young man laughs and says: 'My name is
Jerry, so now you know me.' Jabavu's steps quicken, and
Jerry's feet move faster also.

'And what will clever Mr. Mizi say when he knows you
climbed out of his window?' asks Jerry, in his light, unpleasant voice, and he begins to whistle softly, with a smile
on his face, as if he finds his own whistling very nice.

'I did not,' says Jabavu, and his voice quivers with
fear.

'Well, well. Yet last night I saw you go into the house with
Mr. Mizi and Mr. Samu, and this morning you climb out
of the window, how is that?' asks Jerry, in the same light

voice, and Jabavu stops in the middle of the road and asks: 'Why do you watch me?'

'I watch you for Betty,' says Jerry, gaily, and continues to whistle. Jabavu slowly goes on, and he is wishing with all his heart he is back on Mrs. Mizi's mattress in the kitchen. He can see that this is very bad for him, but he does not yet know why. And so he thinks: Why am I afraid? What can this Jerry do? I must not be like a small child. And he says: 'I do not know you, I do not want to see Betty, so now go away from me.'

Jerry says, making his voice ugly and threatening: 'Betty will kill you. She told me to tell you she will come with her knife and kill you.'

And Jabavu suddenly laughs, saying truthfully: 'I am not afraid of Betty's knife. She talks too much of it.'

Jerry is quiet for a few breaths, he is looking at Jabavu in a new way. Then he, too, laughs and says: 'Quite right, my friend. She is silly girl.'

'She is very silly girl,' agrees Jabavu, heartily, and both laugh and move closer together as they walk.

'What will you do next?' asks Jerry, softly, and Jabavu answers: 'I do not know.' He stops again, thinking: If I return quickly I can climb back through the window before anyone wakes, and no one will know I climbed out. But Jerry seems to know what he is thinking, for he says: 'It is a good joke you climb out of Mr. Mizi's window like a thief,' and Jabavu says quickly: 'I am not a thief.' Jerry laughs and says: 'You are a big thief, Betty told me. You are very clever she says. You steal quickly so that no one knows.' He laughs a little and says: 'And what will Mr. Mizi say if I tell him how you steal?'

Jabavu asks, foolishly: 'And will you tell him?' Again Jerry laughs, but does not answer, and Jabavu walks on silently. It takes some time for the truth to come into his head, and even then it is hard to believe. Then Jerry asks, still light and gay: 'And what did Mr. Mizi say when you told him you had been at the shebeen and about Betty?'

'I told him nothing,' says Jabavu, sullenly, then he understands at last why Jerry is doing this, and he says eagerly: 'I told him nothing at all, nothing, and that is the truth.'

Jerry only walks on, smiling unpleasantly. Then Jabavu

says: 'And why are you afraid of Mr. Mizi. . . .' But he cannot finish for Jerry has whipped round and glares at him: 'Who has told you I am afraid? I am not afraid of that . . . skellum.' And he calls Mr. Mizi names Jabavu has never heard in his life.

'Then I do not understand you,' says Jabavu, in his simplicity, and Jerry says: 'It is true you understand nothing. Mr. Mizi is a dangerous man. Because the police do not like him for what he does, he is very quick to tell the police if he knows of a theft or a fight. And he is making big trouble. Last month he held a meeting in the Hall, and he spoke about crime. He said it was the duty of every African to prevent skokian drinking and fighting and stealing, and to help the police close the shebeens and clean up Poland Johannesburg.' Jerry speaks with great contempt, and Jabavu thinks suddenly: Mr. Mizi does not like enjoying himself so he stops other people doing it. But he is half-ashamed of this thought; first he says to himself: Yes, it would be good if Poland Johannesburg were cleaned up, then he says, hungrily: But I like dancing very much. . . .

'And so,' Jerry goes on calmly, 'we do not like Mr. Mizi.'

Jabavu wishes to say that he likes Mr. Mizi very much, and yet he cannot. Something stops him. He listens while Jerry talks on and on about Mr. Mizi, calling him those names that are new to Jabavu, and he can think of nothing to say. And then Jerry changes his voice, and asks, threateningly: 'What did you steal from Mr Mizi?'

'I steal from Mr. Mizi?' says Jabavu, amazed. 'But why should I steal there?' Jerry grabs his arm, stops him, and says: 'That is rich man, he has a store, he has a good house. And you tell me you stole nothing? Then you are a fool, and I do not believe you.' Jabavu stands helpless because of his surprise while he feels Jerry's quick fingers moving as light as wind through his pockets. Then Jerry stands away from him, in complete astonishment, and unable to believe what his own fingers have told him, goes through every pocket again. For there is nothing there but a comb, a mouth-organ and a piece of soap. 'Where have you hidden it?' asks Jerry, and Jabavu stares at him. For this is the beginning of that inability to understand each other which will one day, and not so long distant, lead to bad trouble. Jerry simply cannot believe that Jabavu let an opportunity for stealing go past; while Jabavu could no more steal from the Mizi's or the Samu's than he could from his parents or his brother. Then Jerry decides to put on a show of belief, and says: 'Well, I have been told they are rich. They have all the money from the League in their house.' Jabavu is silent. Jerry says: 'And did you not see where it is hidden?' Jabavu makes an unwilling movement of his shoulders and looks about for escape. They have reached a cross-roads, and Jabavu stops. He is so simple that he thinks of turning to the right, on the road that leads to the city, with the idea that he may return to Alice and ask her help. But one look at Jerry's face tells him it is not possible, and so he walks beside him on the other road that leads towards Poland Johannesburg. 'Let us go and see Betty,' says Jerry. 'She is a silly girl, but she's nice too.' He looks at Jabavu to make him laugh, and Jabavu laughs in just the way he wants; and in a few moments the two young men are saying of Betty that she is like this and like that, her body is so, her breasts so, and anyone looking at the two young men as they walk along, laughing, would think they are good friends, happy to be together.

And it is true that there is a part of Jabavu that is excited at the idea he will soon be in the shebeens and with Betty, although he comforts himself that soon he will run away from Jerry and go back to the Mizi's and he even believes it.

He expects they will go to Betty's room in Mrs. Kambusi's house, but they go past it and down a slope towards a small river, and up the other side, and there is an old shack of a building which looks as if it were disused. There are trees and bushes all around it, and they go quickly through these, and to the back of the place, and through a window which looks as if it were locked, but opens under the pressure of Jerry's knife, which he slides up against the latch. And inside Jabavu sees not only Betty, but half a dozen others, young men and a girl; and as he stands in fear, wondering what will happen, and looking crookedly at Betty, Jerry says in a cheerful voice: 'And this is the friend Betty told you about,' and winks, but so Jabavu does not see. And they greet him, and he sits down beside them. It is an empty room which was once a store, but now has some boxes for chairs and a big packing-case in the middle where there are candles stuck in their grease, and packs of cards, and bottles of various kinds of drink. No one is drinking, but they offer Jabavu food, and he eats. Betty is quiet and polite, and yet when he looks at her eyes he knows she likes him as much as before, and this makes him uneasy, and he is altogether uncomfortable and full of fear because he does not know what they want with him. Yet as time passes he loses his fear. They seem full of laughter, and without violence. Betty's knife does not leave her handbag, and all that happens is that she comes to sit near him and says, with rolling eyes: 'Are you pleased to see me again?' and Jabavu says that he is, and it is true.

Later they go to the Township and see the film show, and Jabavu is lifted clean out of his fear into a state so delirious that he does not notice how the others look at each other and smile. For it is a film of cowboys and Indians and there is much shooting and yelling and riding about on horses, and Jabavu imagines himself shooting and yelling and prancing about on a horse as he sees it on the screen. He wishes to ask how the pictures are made, but he does not want to show his ignorance to the others who take it all for granted. Afterwards it is midday and they go back, but in ones and twos, secretly to the disused store, and play cards. And by now Jabavu has forgotten that part of himself that wishes to become like Mr. Mizi and be Mrs. Mizi's son. It seems natural that he should play cards and sometimes put his hand on Betty's breasts, and drink. They are drinking kaffir beer, properly made, which means it is illegal, since no African is allowed to make it in the Township for sale. And when evening comes Jabavu is drunk, but not unpleasantly so, and his scruples about being here seem unimportant and even childish, and he whispers to Betty that he wishes to come to her room. Betty glances at Jerry, and for a moment rage fills Jabavu, for he thinks that perhaps Jerry, too, sleeps with Betty when he wishes – yet this morning he knew it, for Jerry said so, and then he did not mind, he and Jerry were calling her names and a whore. Now it is all different and he does not like to remember it. But Betty says meekly, Yes, he may come, and he goes out with her, but not before Jerry has told him to meet him next morning so that they may work together. At the word 'work' everyone laughs, and Jabavu too. Then he goes with Betty to her room, and is careful to slip in through the big room filled with dancers at a time when Mrs. Kambusi is not in it, for he is ashamed to see her, and Betty humours him in everything he does and takes him to her bed as if she has been thinking of nothing else ever since he left. Which is nearly true but not quite; she has been made to think by Jerry, and very disagreeably indeed, of her disloyalty and folly in becoming involved with Jabavu. When she first told him he was much angrier than she had expected, although she knew he would be angry. He beat her and threatened her and questioned her so long and brutally that she lost her head, which is never very strong at any time, and told all sorts of lies so conflicting that even now Jerry does not know what is the truth.

First she said she did not know Jabavu knew Mr. Mizi, then she said she thought it would be useful to have someone in the gang who could tell them at any time what Mr. Mizi's plans were – but at this Jerry slapped her and she began to cry. Then she lost her head and said she intended to marry Jabavu and they would have a gang of their own – but it was not long before she was very sorry indeed she had said that. For Jerry took out his knife, which unlike hers was meant for use and not show, and in a few moments she was writhing with inarticulate terror. So Jerry left her, with clear and certain orders which even her foolish head could not mistake.

But Jabavu, on this evening, is thinking only that he is jealous of Jerry, and will not support that another man sleeps with Betty. And he talks so long of it that she tells him, sulkily, that he has learned nothing yet, for surely he can see by looking at Jerry that he is not interested in women at all? This subtlety of the towns is so strange to Jabavu that it is some time before he understands it, and when he does he is filled with contempt for Jerry, and from this contempt makes a resolution that it is folly to be afraid of him, and will go to the Mizi's.

In the morning Betty wakes him early and tells him he must go and meet Jerry in such and such a place; and Jabavu says he does not wish to go, but will return to the men of light. And at this Betty springs up and leans towards him with frightened eyes and says: 'Have you not understood that Jerry will kill you?' And Jabavu says: 'I will have reached the Mizi's house before he can kill me,' and she says: 'Do not be like a child. Jerry will not allow it.' And Jabavu says: 'I do not understand this feeling about Mr. Mizi – he does not like the police either.' And she says: 'Perhaps it is because once Jerry himself stole money from Mr. Samu that belonged to the League and ...' But Jabavu laughs at this and embraces her into compliance, and whispers to her that he will go to the Mizi's and change his life and become honest, and then he will marry her. He does not mean to do this, but Betty loves him, and between her fear of Jerry and love for Jabavu, she can only cry, lying on the bed, her face hidden. Jabavu leans over her and says that he longs only for that night so that he may see her again, a thing that he heard a cowboy say on the pictures which they all visited together, and then he kisses her long and hard, exactly as he saw a kiss done between that cowboy and the lovely girl, and with this he goes out, thinking he will go quickly to Mr. Mizi's house. But almost at once he sees Jerry waiting for him behind one of the tall brick huts.

Jabavu greets Jerry as if he were not at all surprised to see him there, which does not deceive Jerry in the least, and the two young men go towards the market, which is already open for buying, although it is so early, because the sellers sleep on their places at night, and they buy some cold boiled mealies and eat them walking along the road to the city. They walk in company with many others, some on bicycles. It is now about seven in the morning. The house-boys and cooks and nannies have gone to work a good hour since, these are the workers for the factories, and Jabavu sees their ragged clothes, and how poor they are, and how much less clever than Jerry, and cannot help feeling pleased he is not one of them. So resentful is he against Mr. Mizi for wanting him to go into a factory, he begins to make fun of the men of light again and Jerry laughs and applauds, and every now and again says a little bit more to spur Jabavu on.

So begins the most bewildering, frightening and yet exciting day Jabavu has ever known. Everything that happens shocks him, makes him tremble, and yet – how can he not admire Jerry, who is so cool, so quick, so fearless? He feels like a child beside him, and this happens before they have even begun their 'work'.

For Jerry takes him first to the back room of an Indian trader. This is a shop for Africans to buy in, and they may enter it easily with all the others who move in and out and loiter on the pavement. They stand for a while in the shop, listening to a gramophone playing jazz music, and then the Indian himself looks at them in a certain way, and the two young men slip unnoticed into a side room and through that into the back room. It is heaped with every kind of thing: second-hand clothes, new clothes, watches and clocks, shoes – but there is no end to them. Jerry tells Jabavu to take off his clothes. They both do so, and put on ordinary clothes, so that they may look like everyone else; khaki shorts, and Jabavu's have a patch at the back, and rather soiled white shirts. No tie, and only canvas sandals for their feet. Jabavu's feet are very happy to be released from the thick leather shoes, yet Jabavu mourns to part with them, even for a time.

Then Jerry takes a big basket, which has a few fresh vegetables in it, and they leave the back room, but this time through the door into the street. Jabavu asks who the Indian is, but Jerry says, curtly, that he is an Indian who helps them in their work, which tells Jabavu nothing. They walk up through the area of kaffir shops and Indian stores, and Jabavu looks marvelling at Jerry, who seems to be quite different, like a rather simple country boy, with a fresh and open face. Only his eyes are still the same, quick, cunning, narrow. They come to a street of white people's houses, and Jerry and Jabavu go to a back door and call out that they have vegetables for sale. A voice shouts at them to go away. Jerry glances quickly around: there is a table on the back verandah with a pretty cloth on it, and he whisks it off, rolls it so fast that Jabavu can scarcely see his fingers move, and it vanishes under the vegetables. The two walk slowly away, just like respectable vegetable sellers. And in the next house, the white woman buys a cabbage, and while she is fetching money from inside, Jerry takes, through an open window, a clock and an ashtray, and these are hidden under the vegetables. In the next house there is nothing to be stolen, for the woman is sitting on her back verandah knitting where she may see everything, but in the next there is another cloth.

Then there is a moment which makes Jabavu feel very bad, though to Jerry it is a matter for great laughter: a policeman asks them what they carry in the basket, but Jerry tells him a long, sad story, very confused, about how they are for the first time in the city and cannot find their way, and so the policeman is very kind and helps them with good advice.

When Jerry has finished laughing at the policeman, he says: 'And now we will do something hard, everything we have done so far has been work for children.' Jabavu says he does not want to get into trouble, but Jerry says he will kill Jabavu if he does not do as he is told. And this troubles Jabavu for he never knows, when Jerry laughs and speaks in such a way, whether he means it or not. One minute he thinks: Jerry is making a joke; the next he is trembling. Yet there are moments, when they make jokes together, when he feels Jerry likes him – altogether, he is more confused about Jerry than about anyone he has known. One may say: Betty is like this or that, Mr. Mizi is like this, but about Jerry there is something difficult, shadowy, and even in the moments when Jabavu cannot help liking him.

They go into a shop for white people. It is a small shop, very crowded. There is a white man serving behind the counter, and he is busy all the time. There are several women waiting to buy. One of them has a baby in a carriage and she has put her handbag at the foot of this carriage. Jerry glances at the bag and then at Jabavu, who knows quite well what is meant. His heart goes cold, but Jerry's eyes are so frightening that he knows he must take it.

The woman is talking to a friend and swinging the carriage a little way forwards, a little back, while the baby sleeps. Jabavu feels a cold wetness running down his back, his knees are soft. But he waits for when the white man has turned to reach something down from a shelf and the woman is laughing with her friend, and he nips the bag quickly out and walks through the door with it. There Jerry takes it and slips it under the vegetables. 'Do not run,' says Jerry, quietly. His eyes are darting everywhere, though his face is calm. They walk quickly around a corner and go into another shop. In this shop they steal nothing, but buy six-pence worth of salt. Afterwards Jerry says to Jabavu, and with real admiration. 'You are very good at this work. Betty told the truth. I have seen no one before who is so good so soon after beginning.' And Jabavu cannot help feeling proud, for Jerry is not one who gives praise easily.

They leave that part of the town and do a little more stealing in another, collecting another clock, some spoons and forks, and then, but by chance, a second handbag which is left on a table in a kitchen.

And then they return to the Indian shop. There Jerry bargains with the Indian, who gives them two pounds for the various articles, and there is five pounds from the two handbags. Jerry gives Jabavu one-third of the money, but Jabavu is suddenly so angry that Jerry pretends to laugh, and says he was only joking, and gives Jabavu the half that is due to him. And then Jerry says: 'It is now two o'clock in the afternoon. In these few hours we have each earned three pounds. The Indian takes the risk of selling those things that were stolen and might be recognized. We are safe. And now – what do you think of this work?'

Jabavu says, after a pause that is a little too long, for Jerry gives him a quick, suspicious look: 'I think it is very fine.' Then he says timidly: 'Yet my pass for seeking work is only for fourteen days and some of those have gone.'

'I will show you what to do,' says Jerry, carelessly. 'It is easy. Living here is very easy for those who use their heads. Also, one must know when to spend money. Also, there are other things. It is useful to have a woman who makes a friend of a policeman. With us, there are two such women. Each has a policeman. If there should be trouble, those two policemen would help us. Women are very important in this work.'

Jabavu thinks about this, and then says quickly: 'And is Betty one of the women?'

Jerry, who has been waiting for this, says calmly: 'Yes,

Betty is very good for the police.' And then he says: 'Do not be a big fool. With us, there is no jealousy. I do not allow it. I would not have women in the gang, since they are foolish with the work, except they are useful for the police. And I tell you now, I will have no trouble over the policeman. If Betty says to you: Tonight there is my policeman coming, then you say nothing. Otherwise ...' And Jerry slips the half of his knife a little way from his pocket so that Jabavu may see it. Yet he remains smiling and friendly, as if it is all a joke. And Jabavu walks on in silence. For the first time he understands clearly that he is now one of the gang, that Jerry is his leader, that Betty is his woman. And this state of affairs will continue – but for how long? Is there no way of escaping? He asks, timidly: 'How long has there been this gang?'

Jerry does not reply at once. He does not trust Jabavu yet. But since that morning he has changed his mind about him, for he had planned to make Jabavu steal and then see that he got into trouble with the police in such a way that would implicate no one else, thus removing him as a danger. Yet he is so impressed with Jabavu's quickness and cleverness at the 'work' that he wishes to keep him. He thinks: After another week of our good life, when he has stolen several times and perhaps been in a fight or two, he will be too frightened to go near Mr. Mizi. He will be one of us, and in perfect safety for us all. He says: 'I have been leader of this gang for two years. There are seven in the gang, two women, five men. The men do the stealing, as we have this morning. The women are friends of the police, they make a friend of anyone who might be dangerous. Also, they pick up kraal boys who come to the town and steal from them. We do not allow the women to go into the streets or shops for stealing, because they are no good. Also, we do not tell the women the business of the gang, because they talk and because they do foolish things.' Here there is a pause, and Jabavu knows that Jerry is thinking that he himself is just such a foolish thing that Betty did. But he is flattered because Jerry tells him things the women are not told. He asks: 'And I would like to know other matters: supposing one of us gets caught, what would happen then?' And Jerry replies: 'In the two years I have been leader not one has been caught. We are very careful. But if you are caught, then you will not speak of the others, otherwise something will happen you won't like.' Again he slips up the haft of his knife, and again he is smiling as if it is all a joke. When Jabavu asks another question, he says: 'That is enough for today. You will learn the business of the gang in good time.'

And Jabavu, thinking about what he has been told, understands that in fact he knows very little and that Jerry does not trust him. With this, his longing for Mr. Mizi returns, and he curses himself bitterly for running away. And he thinks sadly of Mr. Mizi all the way along the road, and hardly notices where they are going.

They have turned off to a row of houses where the Coloured people live. The house they enter is full of people, children everywhere, and they go through to the back and enter a small, dirty room that is dark and smells bad. A Coloured man is lying on a bed in a corner, and Jabavu can hear the breath wheezing through his chest before he is even inside the door. He rises, and in the dimness of the room Jabavu sees a stooping man, yellow with sickness beyond his natural colour, his eyes peering through the whitish gum that is stuck around the lashes, his mouth open as the breath heaves in and out. And as soon as he sees Jerry he slaps Jerry on the shoulder, and Jerry slaps him, but too hard for the sickness, for he reels back, coughing and spluttering, gripping his arms across his painful chest, but he laughs as soon as he has breath. And Jabavu wonders at this terrible laughter which comes so often with these people, for what is funny about what is happening now? Surely it is ugly and fearful that this man is so sick and the room is dirty and evil, with the dirty, ragged children running and screaming along the passages outside? Jabavu is stunned with the horror of the place, but Jerry laughs some more and calls the Coloured man some rude and cheerful names, and the man calls Jerry bad names and laughs. Then they look at Jabavu and Jerry says: 'Here is another cookboy for you,' and at this they both rock with laughter until the man begins coughing again, and at last is exhausted and leans against the wall, his eyes shut, while his chest heaves. Then he gasps out, smiling painfully:

'How much?' and Jerry begins to bargain, as Jabavu has heard him with the Indian. The Coloured man, through coughing and wheezing, sticks to his point, that he wants two pounds for pretending to employ Jabavu, and that every month; but Jerry says ten shillings, and at last they agree on one pound, which Jabavu can see was understood from the first – so why these long minutes of bargaining through the ugly, hurtful coughing and smell of sickness? Then the Coloured man gives Jabavu a note saying he wishes to employ him as a cook, and writes his name in Jabavu's situpa. And then, peering close, showing his broken, dirty teeth, he wheezes out: 'So you will be a good cook, hee, hee, hee. . . .' And at this they go out, both young men, shutting the door behind them, and down the dim passage through the children, and so out into the fresh and lovely sunshine, which has the power of making that ugly, broken house seem quite pleasant among its bushes of hibiscus and frangipani. 'That man will die soon,' says Jabavu, in a small, dispirited voice; but all he hears from Jerry is: 'Well, he will last the month at least, and there are others who will do you this favour for a pound.'

And Jabavu's heart is so heavy with fear of the sickness and the ugliness that he thinks: I will go now, I cannot stay with these people. When Jerry tells him he must go to the Pass Office to have his employment registered, he thinks: And now I shall take this chance to run to Mr. Mizi. But Jerry has no intention of letting Jabavu have any such chance. He strolls with him to the Pass Office, on the way buying a bottle of white man's whisky from another Coloured man who does this illegal trade, and while Jabavu stands in the queue of waiting people at the Pass Office, Jerry waits cheerfully, the bottle under his coat, and even chats with the policeman.

When at last Jabavu has had his situpa examined and the business is over, he comes back to Jerry thinking: Hau, but this Jerry is brave. He fears nothing, not even talking to a policeman while he has a bottle of whisky under his coat.

They walk together back to the Native Township, and Jerry says, laughing: 'And now you have a job and are a very good boy.' Jabavu laughs too, as loudly as he can. Then Jerry says: 'And so your great friend Mr. Mizi can be

pleased with you. You are a worker and very respectable.'
They both laugh again, and Jerry gives Jabavu a quick look
from his cold, narrow eyes, for he is above all not a fool,
and Jabavu's laughter is rather as if he wishes to cry. He is
thinking how best to handle Jabavu when chance helps him,
for Mrs. Samu crosses their path, in her white dress and
white cap, on her way to the hospital where she is on duty.
She first looks at Jabavu as if she does not know him at all;
then she gives him a small, cold smile, which is the most her
goodness of heart can do, and is more the goodness of Mrs.
Mizi's heart, who has been saying: 'Poor boy, he cannot
be blamed, only pitied,' and things of that sort. Mrs. Samu
has much less heart than Mrs. Mizi, but much more head,
and it is hard to know which is most useful; but in this case
she is thinking: Surely there are better things to worry
about than a little skellum of a matsotsis? And she goes on
to the hospital, thinking about a woman who has given birth
to a baby who has an infection of the eyes.

But Jabavu's eyes are filled with tears and he longs to run
after Mrs. Samu and beg for her protection. Yet how can a
woman protect him against Jerry?

Jerry begins to talk about Mrs. Samu, and in a clever
way. He laughs and says what hypocrites! They talk about
goodness and crime, and yet Mrs. Samu is Mr. Samu's
second wife, and Mr. Samu treated his first wife so badly she
died of it, and now Mrs. Samu is nothing but a bitch who
is always ready, why she even made advances to Jerry himself at a dance; he could have had her by pushing her over.
... Then Jerry goes on to Mr. Mizi and says he is a fool for
trusting Mrs. Mizi, whose eyes invite everybody, and there
is not a soul in the township who does not know she sleeps
with Mrs. Samu's brother. All these men of light are the
same, their women are light, and they are like a herd of
baboons, no better ... and Jerry continued to speak thus,
laughing about them, until Jabavu, remembering the coldness of Mrs. Samu's smile, half-heartedly agrees, and then
he makes a rude joke about Mrs. Samu's uniform, which
is very tight across her buttocks, and suddenly the two
young men are roaring with laughter and saying women
are this and that. And so they return to the others, who are
not in the empty store now, for it does not do to be in one

place too often, but in one of the other shebeens, which is much worse than Mrs. Kambusi's. There they spend the evening, and Jabavu again drinks skokian, but with discretion, for he fears what he will feel next day. And as he drinks he notices that Jerry also drinks no more than a mouthful, but pretends to be drunk, and is watching how Jabavu drinks. Jerry is pleased because Jabavu is sensible, yet he does not altogether like it, for it is necessary for him to think that he is the only one stronger than the others. And for the first time it comes into his head that perhaps Jabavu is a little too strong, too clever, and may be a challenge to himself some day. But all these thoughts he hides behind his narrow, cold eyes, and only watches, and late that night he speaks to Jabavu as an equal, saying how they must now see that these fools get to bed without harm. Jabavu takes Betty and two of the young men to Betty's rooms, where they fall like logs across the floor, snoring off the skokian, and Jerry takes one girl and the other men to a place he knows, an old hut of straw on the edge of the veld.

In the morning Jerry and Jabavu wake clear-headed, leaving the others to sleep off their sickness, and they go together to the town, where they steal very well and cleverly, another clock and two pairs of shoes and a baby's pillow from under its head, and also, and most important, some trinkets which Jerry says are gold. When these things are taken by the Indian, he offers much money for them. Jerry says as they walk back to the Township: 'And on the second day we each make five pounds . . .' and looks hard at Jabavu so that he may not miss what he means. And Jabavu today is easier about Mr. Mizi, for he admired himself for not drinking the skokian, and for working with Jerry so cleverly that there is no difference between them.

That night they all go to the deserted store where they drink whisky, which is better than the skokian, for it does not make them sick. They play cards and eat well; and all the time Jerry watches Jabavu, and with very mixed thoughts. He sees that he does as he pleases with Betty, although never before has Betty been so humble and anxious with a man. He sees how he is careful what he drinks – and never has he seen a boy raw from the kraals learning sense so quickly with the drink. He sees how the others already, after two days, speak to Jabavu with almost the respect they have for him. And he does not like this at all. Nothing of what he is thinking does he show, and Jabavu feels more and more that Jerry is a friend. And next day they go again to the white streets and steal, and afterwards drink whisky and play cards. The next day also, and so a week passes. All that time Jerry is soft-speaking, polite, smiling; his cold, watchful eyes hooded in discretion and cunning, and Jabavu is speaking freely of what he feels. He has told of his love for Mrs. Mizi, his admiration for Mr. Mizi. He has spoken with the free confidence of a little child, and Jerry has listened, leading him on with a soft, sly word or a smile, until by the end of that week there is a strange way of speaking indeed. Jerry will say: 'And about the Mizi's . . .' And Jabavu will say: 'Ah, they are clever, they are brave.' And Jerry will say, in a soft, polite voice: 'You think that is so?' And Jabavu will say: 'Ah, my friend, those are men who think only of others.' And Jerry will say: 'You think so?' But in that soft, deadly, polite voice. And then he will talk a little, as if he does not care at all, about the Mizi's or the Samu's, how once they did this or that, and how they are cunning, and then state suddenly and with violence: 'Ah, what a skellum!' or 'Now that is a bitch.' And Jabavu will laugh and agree. It is as if there are two Jabavu's, and one of them is brought into being by the clever tongue of Jerry. But Jabavu himself is hardly aware of it. For it may seem strange that a man can spend his time stealing and drinking and making love to a woman of the town and yet think of himself as something quite different – a man who will become a man of light, yet this is how things are with Jabavu. So confused is he, so bound up in the cycle of stealing, and then good food and drink, then more stealing, then Betty at night, that he is like a young, powerful, half-broken ox, being led to work by a string around his horns which the man hardly allows him to feel. Yet there are moments when he feels it.

There is a day when Jerry asks casually, as if he does not mind at all: 'And so you will leave us and join the men of light?' And Jabavu says, with the simplicity of a child: 'Yes, that is what I wish to do.' And Jerry allows himself to laugh, and for the first time. And fear goes through Jabavu like a knife, so that he thinks: I am a fool to speak thus to Jerry. And yet in a moment Jerry is making jokes again and saying, 'Those skellums,' as if he is amused at the folly of the men of light, and Jabavu laughs with him. For above all Jerry is cunning in the use of laughter with Jabavu. He leads Jabavu gently onwards, with jokes, until he becomes serious, and in one moment, and says: 'And so you will leave us when you are tired of us and go to Mr. Mizi?' And the seriousness makes Jabavu's tongue stick in his mouth, so that he says nothing. He is like the ox who has been led so softly to the edge of the field, and now there is a pressure around the base of his horns and he thinks: But surely this man cannot mean to make a fool of me? And because he does not wish to understand he stands motionless, his four feet stubborn on the earth, blinking his foolish eyes, and the man watches him, thinking: In a moment there will be the fighting, when this stupid ox bellows and roars and leaps into the air, not knowing it is all useless since I am so much more clever than he is.

Jerry, however, does not think of Jabavu quite as the man thinks of the ox. For while he is in every way more cunning and more experienced than Jabavu, yet there is something in Jabavu he cannot handle. There are moments when he wonders: Perhaps it would be better if I let this fool go to Mr. Mizi, why not? I shall threaten to kill him if he speaks of us and our work. ... Yet it is impossible, precisely because of this other Jabavu which is brought into being by the jokes. Once with the Mizi's, will not Jabavu have times when he longs for the richness and excitement of the stealing and the shebeens and the women? And at those moments will he not feel the need to call the matsotsis bad names, and perhaps even tell the police? Of course he will. And what will he not be able to tell the police? The names of all the gang, and the Coloured men who help them, and the Indian who helps them. ... Jerry wishes bitterly that he had put a knife into Jabavu long ago, when he first heard of him from Betty. Now he cannot, because Betty loves Jabavu, and therefore is dangerous. Ah, how Jerry wishes he had never allowed women into the work; how he wishes he could kill them both. ... Yet he never kills, unless it is really necessary and certainly not two killings at once. But his hatred for Jabavu, and more particularly Betty, grows and deepens, until it is hard for him to shut it down and appear smiling and cool and friendly.

But he does so, and gently he leads Jabavu along the path of dangerous laughter. The jokes they make are frightening, and when Jabavu is frightened by them, he has to say: 'Well, but it is a joke only.' For they speak of things which would have made him tremble only a few weeks before. First he learns to laugh at the richness of Mr. Mizi, and how this clever skellum hides money in his house and so cheats all the people who trust him. Jabavu does not believe it, but he laughs, and even goes on with the joke, saying: 'What fools they are,' or 'It is more profitable to run a League for the Advancement of the African People than to run a shebeen. And when Jerry speaks of how Mrs. Mizi sleeps with everyone or how Mrs. Samu is in the movement only because of the young men whom she may meet, Jabavu says Mrs. Samu reminds him of the advertisement in the white man's papers: Drink this and you will sleep well at night. Yet all the time Jabavu does not believe any of these things, and he sincerely admires the men of light, and wishes only to be with them.

Later Jerry tightens the leash and says: 'One day the men of light will be killed because they are such skellums,' and he makes a joke about such a killing. It takes a few days before Jabavu is ready to laugh, but at last it seems unimportant and a joke only, and he laughs. And then Jerry speaks of Betty and says how once he killed a woman who had become dangerous, and he laughs and says a stupid woman is as bad as a dangerous one, and it would be a good idea to kill Betty. Many days pass before Jabavu laughs, and this is because the idea of Betty being dead makes his heart leap with joy. For Betty has become a burden on his nights so that he dreads them. All night she will wake him, saying: 'And now marry me and we will run away to another town,' or 'Let us kill Jerry, and you may be leader of this gang,' or 'Do you love me? Do you love me? Do you love me?' – and Jabavu thinks of the women of the old kind who do not talk of love day and night; women with dignity; but at last he laughs. The two young men laugh together, reeling across the road, sometimes, as they speak of Betty, and of women and how they are this and that, until things have changed so that Jabavu laughs easily when Jerry speaks of killing Betty, or any other member of the gang, and they speak with contempt of the others, how they are fools and not clever in the work, and the only two with any sense are Jerry and Jabavu.

Yet underneath the friendship both are very frightened, and both know that something must happen soon, and they watch each other, sideways, and hate each other, and Jabavu thinks all the time of how he may run to Mr. Mizi, while Jerry dreams at night of the police and prison, and often of killing, Jabavu mostly, but Betty too, for his dislike of Betty is becoming like a fever. Sometimes, when he sees how Betty rubs her body against Jabavu, or kisses him, like the cinema, and in front of the others, and how she never takes her eyes away from Jabavu, his hand goes secretly to the knife and fingers it, itching with the need to kill.

The gang itself is confused, for it is as if they have two leaders. Betty stays always beside Jabavu, and her deference towards him influences the others. Also, Jerry has owed his leadership to the fact that he is always clear-headed, never drunk, stronger than anyone else. But now he is not stronger than Jabavu. It is as if some fast-working yeast of dissolution were in the gang, and Jerry names this yeast Mr. Mizi.

There comes a day when he decides to get rid of Jabavu finally one way or the other, although he is so clever with the stealing.

First he speaks persuasively of the mines in Johannesburg, saying how good the life is there, and how much money for people like themselves. But Jabavu listens indifferently, saying: 'Yes,' and 'Is that so?' For why should a man make the dangerous and difficult journey South to the richness of the City of Gold when life is rich where he is? So Jerry drops that plan and tries another. It is a dangerous one, and he knows it. He wishes to make a last attempt to weaken Jabavu by skokian. And for six nights he leads them to the shebeens, although usually he discourages his gang from drinking the bad stuff because it muffles their will and their thinking. On the first night things are as usual, the rest drink, but Jerry and Jabavu do not. On the second it is the same. On the third, Jerry challenges

Jabavu to a contest and Jabavu first refuses, then consents. For he has reached a state of mind which he by no means understands – it is as if he is ceasing to care what happens. So Jabavu and Jerry drink, and it is Jerry who succumbs first. He wakes on the fourth afternoon to find his gang playing cards, while Jabavu sits against a wall, staring at nothing, already recovered. And now Jerry is filled with hatred against Jabavu such as he has never known before. For Jabavu's sake he has drunk himself stupid, so that he has lain for hours weak and out of his mind, even while his gang play cards and probably laugh at him. It is as if Jabavu is now the leader and not himself. As for Jabavu, his unhappiness has reached a point where something very strange is happening to him. It is as if very slowly he, the real Jabavu, is moving away from the thief and the skellum who drinks and steals, and watches with calm interest, not caring. He thinks there is no hope for him now. Never can he return to Mr. Mizi; never can he be a man of light. There is no future. And so he stares at himself, and waits, while a dark grey cloud of misery settles on him.

Jerry comes to him, concealing what he is thinking, and sits by him and congratulates him on having a stronger head. He flatters Jabavu, and then makes jokes at the expense of the others which they cannot hear. Jabavu assents without interest. Then he begins calling Betty names, and then all women names, for it is in these moments, when they are hating women, that they are most nearly good friends. Jabavu joins in the game, indifferently at first, and then with more will. And soon they are laughing together, and Jerry congratulates himself on his cunning. Betty does not like this, and comes to them, and is pushed aside by both, and returns to the others, filled with bitterness, calling them names. And Jerry says how Betty is a dangerous woman, and then tells how once before he killed a girl in the gang who fell in love with a policeman she was supposed to be keeping sweet and friendly. He tells Jabavu this partly to frighten him, partly to see how he will react now at the thought of Betty being killed. And into Jabavu's mind again flickers the thought how pleasant if Betty were no longer there, always boring him with her demands and her complaints, but he pushes it away. And when Jerry sees him frown he swiftly changes the joke into that other about how funny it would be to rob Mr. Mizi, Jabavu sits silent, and for the first time he begins to understand about laughter and jokes, how it is that people laugh most at what they fear, and how a joke is sometimes more like a plan for what will some day be the truth. And he thinks: Perhaps all this time Jerry really is planning to kill, and even to rob Mr. Mizi? And the thought of his own foolishness is so terrible that the misery, which has lifted in the moment of comradeship with Jerry, returns, and he leans silent against the wall, and nothing matters. But this is better for Jerry than he knows, for when he suggests they go to the shebeens, Jabavu rises at once. On that fourth night Jabavu drinks skokian and for the first time willingly, and with pleasure, since he came to the Township and drank it at Mrs. Kambusi's. Jerry does not drink, but watches, and he feels an immense relief. Now, he thinks, Jabavu will take to skokian like the others, and that will make him weak like the others, and Jerry will lead him like the rest.

On the fifth day Jabavu sleeps till late, and wakes as it grows dark, and finds that the others are already talking about going to the shebeen. But the sickness in him rises at the thought and he says he will not go to the shebeen, but will stay while the others go. And with this he turns his face to the wall, and although Jerry jokes with him and cajoles and jokes, he does not move. But Jerry cannot tell the others that he wishes them to go to the shebeen only for the sake of Jabavu, and so he has to go with them, cursing and bitter, for Jabavu remains in the disused store. So the next day is the sixth, and by now the gang are sodden and sick and stupid with the skokian, and Jerry can hardly control them. And Jabavu is bored and calm and sits in his place against the wall, looking at his thoughts, which must be so sad and dark, for his face is heavy with them. Jerry thinks: It was in such a mood that he agreed to drink the night before last, and woos Jabavu to drink again, and Jabavu goes. That is the sixth night. Jabavu gets drunk as before, with the others, while Jerry does not. And on the seventh day Jerry thinks: Now this will be the last. If Jabavu does not come willingly to the shebeen tonight, I will give up this plan and try another.

On that seventh day Jerry is truly desperate, though it does not show on his face. There he sits against the wall, while his hands deal out the cards and gather them in, and his eyes watch those cards as if nothing else interested them. Yet from time to time they glance quickly at Jabavu, who is sitting, without moving, opposite him. The others are still not conscious, but are lying on the floor, groaning and complaining in thick voices.

Betty is lying close by Jerry, in a loose, disgusting heap, and he looks at her and hates her. He is full of hate. He is thinking that two months ago he was running the most profitable gang in the Township, there was no danger, the police were controlled sufficiently, there seemed no reason why it should not all go on for a long time. Yet all at once Betty takes a liking to this Jabavu, and now it is at an end, the gang restless, Jabavu dreaming of Mr. Mizi, and nothing is clear or certain.

It is Betty's fault – he hates her. It is Jabavu's fault – ah, how he hates Jabavu! It is Mr. Mizi's fault – if he could he would kill Mr. Mizi, for truly he hates Mr. Mizi more than anyone in the world. But to kill Mr. Mizi would be foolish – for that matter, to kill anyone is foolish, unless there is need for it. He must not kill needlessly. But his mind is filled with thoughts of killing, and he keeps looking at Betty, rolling drunkenly by him, and wishing he could kill her for starting all this trouble, and as the cards go flick! flick! flick! each sharp, small noise seems to him like the sound of a knife.

Then all at once Jerry takes a tight hold of himself and says: I am crazy. What is this? Never in all my life have I done a thing without thought or cause, and now I sit here without a plan, waiting for something to happen – this man Jabavu has surely made me mad!

He looks across at Jabavu and asks, pleasantly: 'Will you come to the shebeen tonight for some fun, hey?'

But Jabavu says: 'No, I shall not go. That is four times I have drunk the skokian and now what I say is true. I shall never drink it again.'

Jerry shrugs, and lets his eyes drop. So! he thinks. Well, that has failed. Yet it succeeded in the past. But if it has failed, then I must now think and decide what to do – there must be a way, there is always a way. But what? Then he thinks: Well, and why do I sit here? Before there was just such a matter, when things got too difficult, but that was in another town, and I left that town and came here. It is easy. I can go south to another city. There are always fools, and always work for people like myself. And then, just as this plan is becoming welcome in his mind, he is stung by a foolish vanity: And so I should leave this city, where I have contacts, and know sufficient police, and have an organization, simply because of this fool Jabavu? I shall not.

And so he sits, dealing the cards, while these thoughts go through his mind, and his face shows nothing, and his anger and fear and spiteful vanity seethe inside him. Something will happen, he thinks. Something. Wait.

He waits, and soon it grows dark. Through the dirty windowpanes comes a flare of reddish light from the sunset which makes blotches and pools of dark red on the floor. Jerry look at it. Blood, he thinks, and an immense longing fills him. Without thinking, he slides up his knife a little, lovingly fingering the haft of it. He sees that Jabavu is looking at him, and suddenly Jabavu shudders. An immense satisfaction fills Jerry. Ah, how he loves that shudder. He slides up the knife a little further and says: 'You have not yet learned to be afraid of this as you should.' Jabavu looks at the knife, then at Jerry, then drops his eyes. 'I am afraid,' says Jabavu, simply, and Jerry lets the knife slide back. For a moment the thought slides into him: This is nothing but madness. Then it goes again.

Jerry's own feet are now lying in a pool of reddish light from the window, and he quickly moves them back, rises, takes candles from the top of the wall where they lie hidden, sticks them in their grease on the packing-cases, and lights them. The reddish light has gone. Now the room is lit by the warm yellow glow of candles, showing packing-cases, bottles stacked in corners, the huddled bodies of the drunken, and sheets of spider web across the rafters. It is the familiar scene of companionship in drink and gambling, and the violent longing to kill sinks inside Jerry. Again he thinks: I must make a plan, not wait for something to happen. And then, one after another, the bodies move, groaning, and sit up, holding their heads. Then they begin to laugh weakly. When Betty heaves herself up from the floor she sees she is some way from Jabavu, and she crawls to him and falls across his knees, but he quietly pushes her aside. And this sight, for some reason, fills Jerry with irritation. But he suppresses it and thinks: I must make these stupid fools sensible, and wait until they have come out of the skokian, and then I shall make a plan.

He fills a large tin with fresh tea from the kettle that boils on the fire he has made on the floor, and gives mugs of it to everyone, including Jabavu, who simply sets it down without touching it. This annoys Jerry, but he says nothing. The others drink, and it helps their sickness, and they sit up, still holding their heads.

'I want to go to the shebeen,' says Betty, rocking sideways, back and forth, 'I want to go to the shebeen.' And the others, taking up her voice without thought, say: 'Yes, yes, the shebeen.' Jerry whips round, glaring at them. Then he holds down his irritation. And as easily as the desire came into them, it goes. They forget about the shebeen, and drink their tea. Jerry makes more, even stronger, and refills their mugs. They drink. Jabavu watches this scene as if it were a long way from him. He remarks, in a quiet voice: 'Tea is not strong enough to silence the anger of the skokian. I know. The times I have drunk it, it was as if my body wanted to fall to pieces. Yet they have drunk it each night for a week.' Jerry stands near Jabavu, and his face is twitching. Into him has come again that violent need to kill; and yet again he stops it. He thinks: Better if I leave all these fools now. ... But this sensible thought is drowned by a flood of rising vanity. He thinks: *I* can make them do what I want. Always they do as I say.

He says calmly: 'Better if you each take a piece of bread and eat it.' In a low voice to Jabavu he says: 'Shut up. If you speak again I will kill you.' Jabavu makes that indifferent movement of his shoulders and continues to watch. There is a blank look in the darkness of his eyes that frightens Jerry.

Betty staggers to her feet and walks, knees rocking, to the wall where a mirror is hanging on a nail. But before she gets there she says: 'I want to go to the shebeen.' Again the others repeat the words, and they rise, planting their feet firmly so as not to fall down.

Jerry shouts: 'Shut up. You will not go to the shebeen tonight.'

Betty laughs, in a high, weak way, and says: 'Yes, the shebeen. Yes, yes, I want that badly, to go to the shebeen. . . .' The words having started to make themselves, they are likely to continue, and Jerry takes her by her shoulders and shakes her. 'Shut up,' he says. 'Did you hear what I said?'

And Betty laughs, and sways, and puts her arms around him and says: 'Nice Jerry, handsome Jerry, oh, please Jerry . . .' She is speaking in a voice like a child trying to get its way. Jerry, who has stood rigid under her touch, eyes fixed and black with anger, shakes her again and flings her off. She goes staggering backwards till she reaches the other wall, and there she sprawls, laughing and laughing, till she straightens again and goes staggering forward towards Jerry, and the others see what she is doing, and it seems very funny to them and they go with her, so that in a moment Jerry is surrounded by them, and they put their arms around his neck and pat his shoulders, and all say, in high, childish voices, laughing as if laughter in them is a kind of a spring, bubbling up and up and forcing its way out of their lips: 'Nice Jerry, yes, handsome, please clever Jerry.'

And Jerry snaps out: 'Shut up. Get back. I'll kill you all . . .'

His voice surprises them into silence for one moment. It is high, jerky, crazy. And his face twitches and his lips quiver. They stand there around him, looking at him, then at each other, blinking their eyes so that the cloud of skokian may clear, then all move back and sit down, save Betty, who stands in front of him. Her mouth is stretched in such a way across her face that it might be either laughter or the sound of weeping that will come from it, but it is laughter again, and with a high, cackling sound, just like a hen, she rocks forward, and for the third time her arms go around Jerry and she begins pressing her body against his. Jerry stands quite still. The others watching, see nothing but that Betty is hugging and squeezing him, with her body and her arms, while she laughs and laughs.

Then she stops laughing and her hands loosen and then fall and swing by her side. Jerry holds her with his hand across her back. They set up a yell of laughter because it seems to them very funny. Betty is making some sort of funny joke, and so they must laugh.

But Jerry, in a flush of anger and hatred such as he has never known before, has slipped his knife into Betty, and the movement gave him such joy as he has not felt in all his life. And so he stands, holding Betty, while for a moment he does not think at all. And then the madness of anger and joy vanishes and he thinks: I am truly mad. To kill a person, and for nothing, and in anger. . . . He stands holding her, trying to make a plan quickly, and then he sees how Jabavu, just beside him on the floor, is looking up, blinking his eyes in slow wonder, and at once the plan comes to him. He allows himself to stagger a little, as if Betty's weight is too much, then he falls sideways, with Betty, across Jabavu, and there he makes a scuffling movement and rolls away.

Jabavu, feeling a warm wetness come from Betty, thinks: He has killed her and now he will say I killed her. He stands up slowly, and Jerry shouts: 'Jabavu has killed her, look, he has killed Betty because he was jealous.'

Jabavu does not speak. The thought in his mind is one that shocks him. It is an immense relief that Betty is dead. He had not known how tired he was of this woman, how she weighed on him, knowing that he would never be able to shake her off. And now she lies dead in front of him.

'I did not kill her,' he says. 'I did not.'

The others are standing and staring, like so many chickens. Jerry is shouting: 'That skellum – he has killed Betty.'

Then Jabavu says: 'But I did not.'

Their eyes go first to Jerry, and they believe him, then they go to Jabavu, and they believe him.

Jerry stops saying it. He understands they are too stupid to hold any thought in their heads longer than a moment.

He seats himself on a packing-case and looks at Betty, while he thinks fast and hard.

Jabavu, after a long, long silence while he looks at Betty, seats himself on another. A feeling of despair is growing so

strong in him that his limbs will hardly move. He thinks:
And now there is nothing left. Jerry will say I killed her;
there is no one who will believe me. And – but here is
that terrible thought – I was pleased he killed her. Pleased.
I am pleased now. And from here his mind goes darkly
into the knowledge: It is just. It is punishment. And he sits
there, passive, while his hands dangle loosely and his eyes
go blank.

Slowly the others seat themselves on the floor, huddling
together for comfort in this killing they do no understand.
All they know is that Betty is dead, and their goggling,
empty eyes are fixed on Jerry, waiting for him to do something.

And Jerry, after sorting out his various plans, lets his
tense body ease, and tries to put quietness and confidence
into his eyes. First he must get rid of the body. Then it will
be time to think of the next thing.

He turns to Jabavu and says, in a light, friendly voice:
'Help me put this stupid girl outside into the grass.'

Jabavu does not move. Jerry repeats the words, and still
Jabavu is motionless. Jerry gets up, stands in front of him,
and orders him. Jabavu slowly lifts his eyes and then shakes
his head.

And now Jerry comes close to Jabavu, his back to the
others, and in his hand he holds his knife, and this knife
he presses very lightly against Jabavu. 'Do you think I'm
afraid to kill you too?' he asks, so low only Jabavu can hear.
The others cannot see the knife, only that Jerry and Jabavu
are thinking how to dispose of Betty. They begin to cry a
little, whimpering.

Jabavu shakes his head again. Then he looks down, feeling the pressure of the knife. Its point is at his flesh, he can
feel a slight cold stinging. And into his mind comes the angry
thought: He is cutting my smart coat. His eyes narrow, and
he says furiously: 'You are cutting my coat.'

He's mad, thinks Jerry, but it is the moment of weakness
that he knows and understands. And now, using every scrap
of his will, he narrows his eyes, stares down into Jabavu's
empty eyes, and says: 'Come now, and do as I say.'

And Jabavu slowly rises and, at a sign from Jerry, lifts
Betty's feet. Jerry takes the shoulders. They carry her to the

door, and then Jerry says, shouting loudly so that it will be strong enough to get inside the fog of drink: 'Put out the candles.' No one moves. Then Jerry shouts again, and the young man who sleeps at night with Jerry gets up and slowly pinches out the candles. The room is now all darkness and there is a whimper of fear, but Jerry says: 'You will not light the candles. Otherwise the police will get you. I am coming back.' The whimper stops. They can hear hard, frightened breathing, but no one moves. And now they move from the blackness of the room to the blackness of the night. Jerry puts down the body and locks the door, and then goes to the window and wedges it with stones. Then he comes back and lifts the shoulders of the body. It is very heavy and it rolls between their gripping hands. Jerry says not a word, and Jabavu is also silent. They carry her a long way, through grass and bushes, never on the path, and throw her at last into a deep ditch just behind one of the shebeens. She will not be found until morning, and then it will be the people who have been drinking in the shebeen who will be suspected, not Jerry or Jabavu. Then they run very quickly back to the disused store, and as they enter they hear the others wailing and keening in their terror of the darkness and their muddled understanding. A window-pane has been smashed where someone tried to get out, but the wedged stones held the frame. They are crowded in a bunch against the wall, with no sense or courage in them. Jerry lights the candles and says: 'Shut up!' He shouts it again, and they are quiet. 'Sit down!' he shouts, and they sit. He also sits against the wall, takes up his cards, and pretends to play.

Jabavu is looking down at his coat. It is soaked with blood. Also, as he pulls the cloth over his chest, there is a small cut, where the point of the knife pressed. He is asking himself why he is so stupid as to mind about a coat. What does a coat matter? Yet, even at that moment, Jerry nods at a hook on the wall, where there hang several coats and jackets, and Jabavu goes to the hook, takes down a fine blue jacket, and then looks again at Jerry. And now their eyes stare hard across the space between them. Jabavu's eyes drop. Jerry says: 'Take off your shirt and your vest.' Jabavu does so. Jerry says: 'Put on the vest and shirt you will find among the others in that packing-case.' Jabavu goes, as if he has no will, to the packing-case, finds a vest and a shirt that will fit him, puts them on, and puts on the blue jacket. Now Jerry quickly rises, strips off his own jacket and shirt, which have blood on them, wipes his knife carefully on them, and then gives the bundle to Jabavu.

'Take my things out with yours and bury them in the ground,' he says. Again the two pairs of eyes stare at each other, and Jabavu's eyes drop. He takes all the bloodied things and goes out. He makes his way in the darkness to a place where the bushes grow close, and then he digs, using a sharp stick. He buries the clothes, and then goes back to the store. And as he enters he knows that Jerry has been talking, talking, talking to the others, explaining how he, Jabavu, killed Betty. And he can see from the way their frightened eyes look at him that they believe it.

But it is as if that in burying the soiled and cut clothes he also buried his weakness towards Jerry. He says, quietly: 'I did not kill Betty,' and with this he goes to the wall and seats himself, and gives himself up to whatever may happen. For he does not care. Most deeply he does not care. And Jerry, seeing this deep lassitude, misunderstands it entirely. He thinks: Now I can do what I like with this one. Perhaps it was a good thing I killed that stupid woman. For at last Jabavu will do as I tell him.

But he ignores Jabavu, whom he thinks is safe, and goes to the others and tries to calm them. They are weeping and crying out, and sometimes they call out for skokian as a remedy for the fear of this terrible night. But Jerry speaks firmly to them, and makes more strong tea, and gives each a piece of bread and makes them eat it, and finally tells them to sleep. But they cannot. They huddle in a group, talking about the police, and how they will all be blamed for the murder, until at last Jerry makes them drink some tea in which he has put some stuff he bought from an Indian, which is to make people sleep. Soon every one is lying again on the floor, but this time in a sleep which will heal them and drive away the sickness of the long skokian drinking.

For all the long hours of the night they lie, groaning sometimes, sometimes calling out, making thick, frightened words. And Jerry sits and plays cards and watches Jabavu, who does not move.

Jerry is now full of confidence. He makes plans, examines them, alters them; all the night his mind is busy, and all the fear and weakness has gone. He decides that killing Betty was the only clever thing he has ever done without planning it.

The night struggles on in the flick of the playing cards and groans from the sleepers. The light comes grey through the dirty window, then rose and gold as the sun rises, then strengthens to a steady, warm yellow. And when the day is truly there, Jerry kicks the sleepers awake, but so that when they sit up they will not know they have been kicked.

They sit up, to see Jerry playing cards and Jabavu slumped against the wall, staring. And into each mind comes a wild, confused memory of murder and fighting, and they look at each other and see that the memory shows in every face. Then they look towards Jerry for an explanation. But Jerry is looking at Jabavu. And they remember that Jabavu has killed Betty, and their faces turn greyish and their breath comes with difficulty. Yet they are no longer stupid with skokian, only weak and tired and frightened. Jerry has no fear at all that he may not be able to handle them. When they are properly awake and he can see the knowledge in their faces, he begins to talk. He explains, in a quiet and offhand way, what happened last night, saying that Jabavu has killed Betty, and Jabavu says nothing at all.

It is only the silence of Jabavu that upsets Jerry, for he has not expected it. But he is so confident that he takes no notice. He explains that according to the rules of the gang, if suspicion should fall on them, Jabavu must give himself up to the police, saying nothing of the others. But if the trouble should pass, they must all keep silence and continue as if nothing had happened. Jerry speaks so lightly that they are reassured, and one slips out to buy some bread and some milk for tea, and they eat and drink together, even laughing when Jerry makes a joke. The laughter is not very deep, but it helps them. And all this time Jabavu sits against the wall, apart, saying nothing.

Jerry has now made all his plans. They are very simple. If the police show signs that day of finding out who killed Betty, he will quickly slip away, go to people he knows who will help him, and travel South, with papers that have a different name, leaving all the trouble behind him. But he has very little money left, after the week of drinking. Perhaps five shillings. His friends may give him a little more. Jerry does not like to think of going all the way to Johannesburg with so little. He wants some more. If the police do not know on whom to put the blame, Jerry will stay here, in this store, with Jabavu and the others, until the evening. And then – but now the plan is so audacious that Jerry laughs inside himself, longing to tell the others, because it is such a good joke. Jerry plans nothing else than to go to Mr. Mizi's house, take the money that will be there, and with it run away to the South. He believes that there is money in the house, and a great deal. When he robbed Mr. Samu, five years ago, and in another town, he took nineteen pounds. Mr. Samu had the money in a big tin that had once held tobacco, and it was in the grass roof of a hut. Jerry believes that he has only to go to Mr. Mizi's house to find enough money to take him in luxury and safety, with plenty of funds for bribery, to Johnnesburg. And he will take Jabavu with him. Jabavu is now safe, sullen, and too afraid to tell Mr. Mizi. Also, he must know where the money is.

It is all very simple. As soon as Jabavu has given the money to Jerry, Jerry will tell him to go back to the others and wait for his return. They will wait. It will be some days before they understand he has tricked them, and by then he will be in Johnnesburg.

Towards midday, Jerry brings out the last bottle of whisky and gives everyone a little of it. Jabavu refuses, with a small shake of the head. Jerry ignores him. So much the better.

But he takes care that all the group are sitting playing cards, drinking a little whisky, and that they have plenty to eat. He wishes them to like him and trust him before explaining his plan, which might frighten them in their condition of being softened by the drinking and the murder.

In the middle of the afternoon he slips out again and mingles with the people in the market, where he hears much talk of the killing. The police have questioned a lot of people, but no one has been arrested. This will be a case like so many others – yet another of the matsotsis killed in a brawl, and no one cares much about that. The newspapers will print a paragraph; perhaps a preacher will make a sermon. Mr. Mizi might make another speech about the corruption of the African people through poverty. At this last idea Jerry laughs to himself and returns to the others in a very good humour indeed.

He tells them that everything will be safe, and then speaks of Mr. Mizi, half as part of his plan, but partly because of the pleasure it gives him. He gives a fine imitation of Mr. Mizi making a speech about corruption and degradation. Jabavu does not stir through this, or even lift his eyes. Then Jerry makes a lot of jokes about Mrs. Mizi and Mrs. Samu and how they are immoral, and everyone laughs except Jabavu.

And everyone, including Jerry, misunderstands this silence of Jabavu. They think that he is afraid, and above all afraid of them because they know he has killed Betty, for by now they all believe it; they even believe they saw it.

They do not understand that what is happening in Jabavu is something very old. His mind is darkening in despair, in acceptance of what destiny has willed for him, and turning towards death. This feeling of destiny, of fate, is very strong in the life of the tribe, where guilt and the responsibility for evil is decided by the old ways of magic. Perhaps, if these young people had not lived so long in the white man's city they might understand what they see now in Jabavu. Even Jerry does not, although there are moments when this long silence annoys him. He would like to see Jabavu a little more afraid, and respectful.

Late in the afternoon Jerry takes his last five shillings, gives it to the girl who worked with Betty, and who is more troubled than the rest, and tells her that because of her cleverness she is the one chosen to go again to the market and buy food. She is pleased, and returns in half an hour with bread and cold boiled mealies, saying that people are no longer speaking of the murder. Jerry urges them all to eat. It is very important that they must be full and comfortable, and when they are, he speaks of his plan. 'And now I must tell you a good joke,' he says, laughing already.

'Tonight we shall rob from the house of Mr. Mizi; he is very rich. And Jabavu will do the stealing with me.'

For a second there is uncertainty. Then they look at each other, see Jabavu's heavy eyes, lifted painfully towards them, and then they roll on the floor with laughing and do not stop for a long time. But Jerry is looking at Jabavu. He decides to taunt him a little: 'You kraal nigger,' he says. 'You're scared.'

Jabavu sighs, but does not move, and panic moves through Jerry. Why does Jabavu not cry out, protest, show fear?

He decides to wait for a show of strength until the moment itself. As the others cease laughing and look at him for the next good joke, he makes a grimace towards Jabavu, inviting their complicity, and they grin and look at each other. He lights the candles, and makes them come together in a small, lit space around a packing-case, with Jabavu outside in the shadow, and there they all play cards, with much noise and laughter, and Jerry coaxes their excitement into the cards so that their attention is not on Jabavu. And all the time he is thinking of every detail of the plan, and his mind is set hard on his purpose.

At midnight, with a wink at the others, he gets up and goes to Jabavu. He is sweating with the effort of his will. 'It is time,' he says, lightly, and fixes his eyes on Jabavu. Jabavu does not lift his eyes, or move. Jerry kneels, very swiftly, and exactly as he did the night before, keeping his back to the others, he presses the tip of his knife lightly against Jabavu's chest. He stares hard, hard at Jabavu, and he whispers: 'I am cutting the coat.' He narrows his eyes, forcing their pressure at Jabavu, and says again: 'I am cutting the coat, soon the knife will go into you.' Jabavu lifts his eyes. 'Get up,' says Jerry, and Jabavu rises like a drugged man. Jerry is a little dizzy with the relief of that victory, but resting his hand against the wall he turns and says to the others: 'And now listen to what I shall tell you. We two go now to Mr. Mizi's house. Blow the candles out and wait in darkness – no, you may keep one candle, but set it on the floor so that no sign of light may show. I know that there is a great sum of money hidden in Mr. Mizi's house. This we shall bring back. If there is trouble, I shall go quickly to one of our friends. There I shall stay perhaps one day, perhaps two. Jabavu will return here. If I am not here by tomorrow morning, then you may leave here one by one, not together. Do not work together for a few days, and do not go near the shebeens, and I forbid you to touch skokian again until I say. I shall tell you when it is safe for us to meet again. But all this is if there is trouble, and there is no need for it. Jabavu and I will be back in three-quarters of an hour with the money. Then we shall share it out between us. It will mean there is no need to work for a week, and by that time the police will have forgotten the murder.'

For the first time Jabavu speaks. 'Mr. Mizi is not rich and he has no money in his house.' Jerry frowns, and then swiftly draws Jabavu after him into the darkness. The candles flicker out in the room behind. There is dark everywhere, the trees are swinging in a fast, cool wind, mounds of thick cloud move across the sky, showing damp, weak stars between. It is a good night for stealing.

Jerry thinks: 'Why does he say that? It is strange.' But what is strange is that in all these weeks Jerry had believed Jabavu is lying about the money, and Jabavu has never understood that Jerry truly thinks there is money.

'Come,' says Jerry, quietly. 'It will be over soon. And now, as we go, think of what you saw in the Mizi's house, and where the money will be hidden.'

Suddenly across Jabavu's mind flickers a picture, then another. He sees how on that evening Mr. Mizi went to the corner of the room, lifted a piece of plank from the flooring, and leaned down into the dark hole underneath to bring up books. That is where he keeps books which the police might take away from him. But following this picture comes another, which he has not seen at all, but which his mind creates. He sees Mr. Mizi reaching up a large tin filled with rolls of paper money. Yes, Jerry is very clever, for the old hunger in Jabavu raises its head and almost speaks. Then the pictures vanish from his mind, and the hunger with them. He plods along beside Jerry, thinking only: We are going to Mr. Mizi. Somehow I will speak to him when we get there. He will help me. Jerry says, in a loud voice: 'Don't stamp so loud, you fool.' Jabavu does not change the way he walks. Jerry glances all around him through the dark, thinking nervously: Surely Jabavu is not mad? Or perhaps he has some drug I know nothing of? For his behaviour is very strange. Then he comforts himself: See how the killing of Betty turned out well, although it was not meant. See how this night is so good for stealing, although I did not choose it. My luck is very strong. Everything will be all right. ... And so he does not again tell Jabavu about walking quietly, for the wind is swishing the branches back and forth and raising swirls of dust and leaves around their feet. It is very dark. The lights are out in the houses, for now they are walking in the respectable part of the city where people rise early for work and so must sleep early. Then Jabavu stumbles over a stone and there is a big noise, and Jerry whips out his knife and nudges Jabavu with his elbow until he turns and looks. 'I'll stick this into you if you call out or run away,' he says, softly, but Jabavu says nothing. He is thinking that Jerry is very strange indeed. Why does he go to Mr. Mizi for money? Why does he take him, Jabavu? Perhaps the killing of Betty hurt his mind and he has gone crazy? And then Jabavu thinks: Yet it is not so strange. He makes jokes about killing Betty and then he killed her, and he made jokes about stealing from Mr. Mizi and now we are doing that too. ... And so Jabavu plods on, through the noise of the wind and the blackness that is full of dust and moving leaves, and his head is empty and he does not feel. Only he is very heavy in his limbs, for he is tired with so little sleep, and then the nights of dancing and the skokian, and above all, he is tired from the despair, which tells him all the time: There is nothing for you, you will die, Jabavu. You will die. Words of a song form themselves, a sad, slow song, as for someone who has died. 'Eh, but see Jabavu, there he goes the big thief. The knife has spoken, and it says: See the murderer, Jabavu, he who creeps through the dark to rob his friend. See Jabavu, whose hands are red with blood. Eh, Jabavu, but now we are coming for you. We are coming Jabavu, there is no escape from us....

Under the street lights, but at great distances, since there are few lamps in the Native Townships, shed small patches of yellow glimmer. Jabavu blunders straight into such a patch of light. 'Be careful, fool' says Jerry, in a violent, frightened voice. He drags Jabavu aside, and then stops. He is thinking: Perhaps this man is mad? How, otherwise, could he behave like this? How can I take a mad fool on a dangerous job like this? Perhaps I had better not go to the house. ... Then he looks at Jabavu, who is standing quiet and patient beside him, and he thinks: No, it is simply that he is so afraid of me. So he goes on walking, gripping Jebavu by the wrist.

Then Jabavu laughs out loud and says: 'I can see the Mizis' house, and there is a light in the window.'

'Shut up,' says Jerry, and Jabavu goes on: 'The men of light study at night. There are things you know nothing of.'

Jerry slams his hand over Jabavu's mouth, and Jabavu bites the hand. Jerry jerks it away and for a moment stands trembling with the desire to slip his knife sweetly home between Jabavu's ribs. But he keeps himself tight and controlled. He stands there, quietly shaking his bitten hand, looking at the light in the Mizis' house. Now he can almost see the money, and the desire for it grows strong in him. He cannot bear to stop now, to turn back, to change the plan. It is so easy simply to go forward, the money will be his inside five minutes, then he will give Jabavu the slip and in another fifteen minutes he will be in the house of that friend who will shelter him safely till morning. It is all so easy, so easy. And to go back difficult and, above all, shameful. So he shuts his teeth close and promises himself: You wait, my fine kraal nigger. In a moment I'll have got the money, and you might be caught. And even if you're not, what will you do without me? You'll go back to the gang, and without me they're like a lot of chickens, and you'll be in trouble with the police inside a week. The thought gives him great pleasure, so strongly he nearly laughs, and in good humour he takes Jabavu's wrist and pulls him forward.

They walk until they are ten paces from the window, just beyond where the light falls dimly, showing the ground, rough and broken, and the bush under the window standing dense and black. The damp and windy dark is loud in their ears. They can see how Mr. Mizi's son lies sprawled on his bed, still dressed. He has fallen asleep with a book in his hand.

Jerry thinks rapidly, then he says: 'You will climb quickly

in at the window. Do not try to be clever. I can throw a knife as well as I can use it close, so ...' He wriggles it lightly against the cloth of Jabavu's coat and with what exultation feels Jabavu move away! It is strange that Jabavu has no fear for himself, but it hurts him even now to imagine his jacket cut and spoilt. He has moved away instinctively, almost with irritation, as if a fly were pestering him, yet he moved, and he hears Jerry's voice, now strong and confident: 'You will keep away from the door into the other room. You will stand against the wall, with your back to it, and reach out your arm sideways and switch the light off. You needn't think you can be clever, for I shall keep my torch on you, so ...' And he switches on the tiny torch he has in the palm of his hand, that sends a single, strong beam of light, as narrow as a pencil. He switches it off and grips his teeth tight, against the desire to curse, because the blood where Jebavu bit him is making the torch slippery. 'Then I shall come into the room and tie that fool on the bed quickly, and then you will show me the money.'

Jabavu is silent, and then he says: 'But this money. I have told you there is no money. Why do you really come to this house?'

Jerry grips his arm and says: 'It's time to stop joking.'

Jabavu says: 'Sometimes I said that there was money, but it was when we were making jokes. Surely you understood. ...' He stops, thinking about the nature of those jokes. Then he thinks: It does not matter, for when I am inside I shall call the Mizi's.

Jerry says: 'And how could there not be money? Where does he keep the money for the League? Did you not see the place where such people keep what is forbidden? When I took money from Mr. Samu it was in such a place. ...' But Jabavu has pulled his arm free and is walking forward through the light to the window, making no effort to quieten his steps. Jerry hisses after him: 'Quiet, quiet, you fool.'

Then Jabavu pushes his heavy shoulder against the window so that it slides up with a bang, and he climbs in. Behind him Jerry is dancing and swearing with rage. For a second he wavers with the thought of running away. Then it is as if he sees a big tin full of money, and he flings himself across the lit space after Jabavu and climbs in the window.

The two young men have climbed in at a window filled with light, and made a great deal of noise. The boy on the bed stirs, but Jerry has leaned over him, tangled his eyes in a cloth and stuffed into his mouth a handkerchief into which is kneaded some wet dough, while in the same movement he has knelt on his legs. He ties him with some thick string and in a moment the boy cannot move or see or cry out. But when Jabavu sees Mr. Mizi's son lying tied up on the bed, something inside him moves and speaks, the heavy load of fatalistic indifference lifts, and he raises his voice and shouts: 'Mr. Mizi, Mrs. Mizi!' It is the voice of a terrified child, for his terror of Jerry has returned. Jerry whips round, cursing, and lifts his arm with the knife in it. Jabavu jumps forward and grabs his wrist. The two stand swaying together under the light, their arms straining for the knife, when there is a noise in the room behind. Jerry springs aside, very quickly, so that Jabavu staggers, and then he jumps away and out of the window. As the door opens Jabavu is staggering back against the door with the knife in his hand.

It is Mr. Mizi and Mrs. Mizi, and when they see him Mr. Mizi leaps forward and grips his arms to his body with his own, and Jabavu says: 'No, no, I am your friend.'

Mr. Mizi speaks over his shoulder to Mrs. Mizi: 'Leave that boy. Give me some cloth to tie this one with.' For Mrs. Mizi is moaning with fear over her son, who is lying helpless and half suffocated under the cloth. And Jabavu stands limp under Mr. Mizi's hands and says: 'I am not a thief, I called you, but believe me, Mr. Mizi, I wanted to warn you.' Mr. Mizi is too angry to listen. He grips Jabavu's wrists and watches Mrs. Mizi let her son loose.

Then Mrs. Mizi turns to Jabavu and says, half crying: 'We helped you, you came to our house, and now you steal from us.'

'No, no, Mrs. Mizi, it is not so, I will tell you.'

'You will tell the police,' says Mr. Mizi roughly. And Jabavu, looking at the hard, angry face of Mr. Mizi, feels that he has been betrayed. Somewhere inside him that well of despair slowly begins to fill again.

The boy who is now sitting on the bed holding his jaw, which has been wrenched with the big lump of dough, says: 'Why did you do it? Have we harmed you?'

Jabavu says: 'It was not I, it was the other. '

But the son had had cloth wound over his eyes before he even opened them, and has seen nothing.

Then Mr. Mizi looks at the knife lying on the ground and says: 'You are a murderer as well as a thief.' There is blood on the floor. Jabavu says: 'No, the blood must be from Jerrys' hands, which I bit.' Already his voice is sullen.

Mrs. Mizi says, with contempt: 'You think we are fools. Twice you have run away. Once from Mr. and Mrs. Samu when they helped you in the bush. Then from us, when we helped you. All these weeks you have been with the matsotsis, and now you come here with a knife and expect us to say nothing when you tie our son and fill his mouth with uncooked bread?'

Jabavu goes quite limp in Mr. Mizi's grip. He says, simply: 'You do not believe me.' Despair goes through his veins like a dark poison. For the second time that despair takes the people with him by surprise. Mr. Mizi let go his grip and Mrs. Mizi, who is crying bitterly, says: 'And a knife Jabavu, a knife!'

Mr. Mizi picks up the knife, sees there is no blood on it, looks at the blood on the floor, and says: 'One thing is true. The blood does not come from a knife wound.' But Jabavu's eyes are on the floor, and his face is heavy and indifferent.

Then the police come, all at once, some climbing through the window, some from the front of the house. The police put handcuff's on Jabavu and take a statement from Mr. Mizi. Mrs. Mizi is still crying and fluttering around her son.

Only once does Jabavu speak. He says: 'I am not a thief. I came here to tell you. I wish to live honestly.'

And at this the policemen laugh and say that Jabavu, after only a few weeks in the Township is known as one of the cleverest thieves and a member of the worst gang. And now, because of him, they will all be caught and put into prison.

Jabavu hears this with indifference. He looks at Mrs.

Mizi, and it is with the bitter look of a child whose mother has betrayed him. Then he looks at Mr. Mizi, and it is the same look. They look in a puzzled way at Jabavu. But Mr. Mizi is thinking: All my life I try to live in such a way to keep out of sight of the police, and now this little fool is going to make me waste time in the courts and get a name for being in trouble.

Jabavu is taken to the police van, and is driven to the prison. There he lies that night, and sleeps with the dark, dreamless sleep of a man who has gone beyond hope. The Mizi's have betrayed him. There is nothing left.

In the morning he expects to be taken to the court, but he is transferred to another cell in the prison. He thinks this must be very serious indeed, for it is a cell to himself, a small brick room with a stone floor and a window high up with bars.

A day passes, then another. The warders speak to him and he does not answer. Then a policeman comes to ask him questions, and Jabavu does not say a word. The policeman is first patient, then impatient, and finally threatening. He says the police know everything and Jabavu will gain nothing by keeping quiet. But Jabavu is silent because he does not care. He wishes only the policeman would go away, which at last he does.

They bring him food and water, but he does not eat or drink unless he is told to do so, and then he eats or drinks automatically, but is likely to forget, and sit immobile, with a piece of bread or the mug in his hand. And he sleeps and sleeps as if his soul is drugging itself so that he may slip easily into death. He does not think of death, but it is there with him, in his cell, like a big, black shadow.

And so a week passes, though Jabavu does not know it.

On the eighth day the door opens and a white preacher comes in. Jabavu is asleep, but the warder kicks him till he wakes, then gives him a shake so that he stands up, and finally he sits when the preacher tells him to sit. He does not look at the preacher.

This man is a Mr. Tennent from the Church of England, who visits the prisoners once a week. He is a tall man, lean, grey, stooping. He moves slowly, speaks slowly, and gives an impression of distrusting even the words he chooses to use.

He is deeply doubting man, as are so many of his persuasion. Perhaps, if he were from another church, that which the Africans call the Romans, he would enter this cell in a different way. Sin is this, a soul is that, there would be definite things to say, and his words would have the ring of a faith which does not change with changing life.

But Mr. Tennent's church allows him much latitude in belief. Also, he has been working with the poorer Africans of this city for many years, and he sees Jabavu rather as Mr. Mizi sees him. First, there is an economic process, and caught in it like a leaf in a whirlpool, there is Jabavu. He believes that to call a child like Jabavu sinful is lack of charity. On the other hand, a man who believes in God, if not the devil, must put the blame on something or someone – and what or who should it be? He does not know. His view of Jabavu robs him of comfort, even for himself.

This man, who comes to the prison every week, hates this work from the bottom of his heart because he does not trust himself. He enters Jabavu's cell taking himself to task for lack of sympathy, and at the first glance towards Jabavu he hardens himself. He has often seen such prisoners weeping like children and calling on their mothers, a sign which is deeply distasteful to him because he is English and despises such shows of emotion. He has seen them stubborn and indifferent and bitter. This is bad, but better than the weeping. He has also, and very often, seen them as Jabavu is, silent, motionless, their eyes lacking sight. It is a condition he dislikes more than any other, because it is foreign to his own being. He has seen prisoners condemned to death as Jabavu is today; they are dead long before the noose goes round their neck. But Jabavu is not going to be hung, his offence is comparatively light, and so this despair is altogether irrational, and Mr. Tennent knows by experience that he is not equipped to deal with it.

He seats himself on an uncomfortable chair that the warder has brought in, and wonders why he finds it hard to speak of God. Jabavu is not a Christian, as can be seen from his papers, but should that prevent a man of God from speaking of Him? After a long silence he says: 'I can see that you are very unhappy. I should like to help you.'

The words are flat and thin and weak, and Jabavu does not move.

'You are in great trouble. But if you spoke of it, it might ease you.'

Not a sound from Jabavu, and his eyes do not move.

For the hundredth time Mr. Tennent thinks that it would be better if he resigned from this work and let one of his colleagues do it who do not think of better housing and bigger wages rather than of God. But he continues in his mild, patient voice: 'Perhaps things are better than you think. You seem to be too unhappy for the trouble you are in. There will be only light charges against you. Housebreaking and being without proper employment, and that is not so serious.'

Jabavu remains motionless.

'There has been such a long delay in the case because of the number of people involved in it. Your accomplice, the man they call Jerry, has been denounced by his gang as the person who incited you to rob the Mizis' house.'

At the name Mizi, Jabavu stirs slightly, then remains still.

'Jerry will be charged with organizing the robbery, for carrying a knife, and for being in the city without proper employment. The police suspect he has been involved in many other things, but nothing can be proved. He will get a fairly heavy sentence – that is to say, he will if he is caught. They think he is on his way to Johannesburg. When they catch him he will be put in prison. They have also caught a Coloured man who has been giving Africans, you among them, false employment. But this man is very ill in hospital and is not expected to live. As regards the other members of the gang, the police will charge them with being without proper employment, but that is all. There has been such a cloud of lies and charges and counter-charges that it has been a very difficult case for the police. But you must remember it is your first offence, and you are very young, and things will not go badly for you.'

Silence from Jabavu. Then Mr. Tennent thinks: Why should I comfort this boy as if he were innocent? The police tell me they know him to have been involved with all kinds of wickedness, even if they cannot prove it. He changes his voice and says, sternly: 'I am not saying the fact that you were known to be a member of a gang will not influence your sentence. You will have to pay the penalty for breaking the law. It is thought you may get a year in prison. . . .'

He stops, for he can see that if he said ten years it would be the same to Jabavu. He remains silent for some time, thinking, for he has a choice to make which is not easy. That morning Mr. Mizi came to his house and asked him if he intended to visit the prison. When he said Yes, Mr. Mizi asked him if he would take a letter to Jabavu. Now, it is against the rules to take letters to prisoners. Mr. Tennent has never broken the law. Also, he dislikes Mr. Mizi, because he dislikes all politics and politicians. He thinks Mr. Mizi is nothing but a loud-voiced, phrase-making demagogue out for power and self-glory. Yet he cannot disapprove of Mr. Mizi entirely, who asks nothing for his people but what he, Mr. Tennent, sincerely believes to be just. At first he refused to take the letter, then he stiffly said Yes, he would try. . . . The letter is in his pocket now.

At last he takes the letter from his pocket and says: 'I have a letter for you.' Jabavu still does not move.

'You have friends waiting to help you,' he says, loudly, trying to make his words pierce Jabavu's apathy. Jabavu lifts his eyes. After a long pause he says: 'What friends?'

It gives Mr. Tennent a shock to hear his voice, after such a silence. 'It is from Mr. Mizi,' he says, stiffly.

Jabavu snatches it, scrambles up and stands under the light that falls from the small, high window. He tears off the envelope, and it falls to the floor. Mr. Tennent picks it up and says: 'I am not really supposed to give you letters,' and understands that his voice sounds angry. And this is unjust, for it is his own responsibility that he agreed. He does not like injustice, and he controls his voice and says: 'Read it quickly and then give it back to me. That is what Mr. Mizi asked.'

Jabavu is staring at the letter. It begins: 'My son . . .' And at this the tears begin to roll down his cheeks. And Mr. Tennent is embarrassed and put out, and he thinks: 'Now we are going to have one of these unpleasant displays, I suppose.' Then he chides himself again for lacking Christian charity, and turns his back so as not to be offended by

Jabavu's tears. Also it is necessary to watch the door in case the warder should come in too soon.

Jabavu reads:

I wish to tell you that I believe you told the truth when you said you came unwillingly to my house, and that you wished to warn us. What I do not understand is what you expected us to do then. For certain members of the gang have come to me saying that you told them you expected me to find you employment and look after you. They came to me thinking I would then defend them to the police. This I shall not do. I have no time for criminals. If I do not understand this case, neither does anyone else. For a whole week the police have been interviewing these people and their accomplices, and very little can be proved, except that the brain was the man Jerry, and that he used some kind of pressure on you. They appear to be afraid of him, and also of you, for it seems to me there are things you might tell the police if you wished.

And now you must try to understand what I am going to say. I am writing only because Mrs. Mizi persuaded me to write. I tell you honestly I have no sympathy with you. . . .

And here Jabavu lets the paper fall, and the coldness begins to creep around his heart. But Mr. Tennent, tense and nervous at the door, says: 'Quickly, Jabavu. Read it quickly.'

And so Jabavu continues to read, and slowly the coldness dissolves, leaving behind it a feeling he does not understand, but it is not a bad feeling.

Mrs. Mizi tells me I think too much from the head and too little from the heart. She says you are nothing but a child. This may be so, but you do not behave like a child, and so I shall speak to you as a man and expect you to act like one. Mrs. Mizi wishes me to go to the Court and say we know you, and that you were led astray by evil companions, and that you are good at heart. Mrs. Mizi uses words like good and evil with ease, and perhaps it is because of her mission education, but as for me, I distrust, them and I shall leave them to the Reverend Mr. Tennent, who I hope will bring you this letter.

I know only this, that you are very intelligent and gifted and that you could make good use of your gifts if you wanted. I know also that until now you have acted as if the world owes you a good time for nothing. But we are living in a very difficult time, when there is much suffering, and I can see no reason why you should be different from everyone else. Now, I shall have to come to Court as a witness, because it was my house that was broken into. But I shall not say I knew you before, save casually, as I know hundreds of people – and this is true, Jabavu. . . .

Once again the paper drops, and a feeling of resentment surges through Jabavu. For harder than any other will be this lesson for Jabavu, that he is one of many others and not something special and apart from them.

He hears Mr. Tennent's urgent voice: 'Go on, Jabavu, you can think about it afterwards.' And he continues:

Our opponents take every opportunity to blacken us and our movement, and they would be delighted if I said I was a friend of a man whom everyone knows is a criminal even if they cannot prove it. So far, and with great effort, I have kept a very good character with the police as an ordinary citizen. They know I do not thieve or lie or cheat. I am what they call respectable. I do not propose to change this for your sake. Also, in my capacity as leader of our people, I have a bad character, so if I spoke for you, it would have a double meaning for the police. Already they have been asking questions which make it clear that they think you are one of us, have been working with us, and I have denied it absolutely. Also, it is true that you have not.

And now my son, like my wife, Mrs. Mizi, you will think I am a hard man, but you must remember I speak for hundreds of people, who trust me, and I cannot harm them for the sake of one very foolish boy. When you are in Court I will speak sternly, and I will not look at you. Also, I shall leave Mrs. Mizi at home, for I fear her goodness of heart. You will be in prison for perhaps a year, and your sentence will be shortened if you behave well. It will be a hard time for you. You will be with other

criminals who may tempt you to return to the life, you
will do very hard work, and you will have bad food. But
if there are opportunities for study, take them. Do not
attract attention to yourself in any way. Do not speak of
me. When you come out of prison come to see me, but
secretly, and I will help you, not because of what you are,
but because your respect for me was a respect for what I
stand for, which is bigger than either of us. While you are
in prison, think of the hundreds and thousands of our
people who are in prison in Africa, voluntarily, for the
sake of freedom and justice, in that way you will not be
alone, for in a difficult and roundabout way I believe you
to be one of them.

I greet you on behalf of myself and Mrs. Mizi and our
son, and Mr. Samu and Mrs. Samu, and others who are
waiting to trust you. But this time, Jabavu, you must trust
us. We greet you...

Jabavu lets the paper drop and stands staring. The word
that has meant most to him of all the many words written
hastily on that paper is *We*. We, says Jabavu, We, Us. Peace
flows into him.

For in the tribe and the kraal, the life of his fathers was
built on the word *we*. Yet it was never for him. And between then and now has been a harsh and ugly time when
there was only the word I, I, I – as cruel and sharp as a knife.
The word *we* has been offered to him again, accepting all
his goodness and his badness, demanding everything he can
offer. *We*, thinks Jabavu, We ... And for the first time that
hunger in him, which has raged like a beast all his life, wells
up, unrefused, and streams gently into the word *We*.

There are steps outside clattering on the stone.

Mr. Tennent says: 'Give me the letter.' Jabavu hands it
to him and it slides quickly into Mr. Tennent's pocket. 'I
will give it back to Mr. Mizi and say you have read it.'

'Tell him I have read it with all my understanding, and
that I thank him and will do what he says and he may trust
me. Tell him I am no longer a child, but a man, and that his
judgement is just, and it is right I should be punished.'

Mr. Tennent looks in surprise at Jabavu and thinks, bitterly, that he, the man of God, is a failure; that an intem-

perate and godless agitator may talk of justice, and of good and evil, and reach Jabavu where he is afraid to use these terms. But he says, with scrupulous kindness: 'I shall visit you in prison, Jabavu. But do not tell the warder or the police I brought you that letter.'

Jabavu thanks him and says: 'You are kind, sir.'

Mr. Tennent smiles his dry, doubting smile, and goes out, and the warder locks the door.

Jabavu seats himself on the floor, his legs stretched out. He no longer sees the grey walls of the cell, he does not even think of the Court or of the prison afterwards.

*We*, says Jabavu over and over again, *We*. And it is as if in his empty hands are the warm hands of brothers.

# Other Panthers For Your Enjoyment

## Highly-Praised Modern Novels